What the critics are saying...

Five Angels "Yet again Lorie O'Clare writes a gut-wrenching story that stays with you long after you read it." ~ *Fallen Angel Reviews*

Five Stars "The passion and energy of Darius and Tara propel the story along at lightening speed as they pull the reader deeper into Ms. O'Clare's world." ~ *eCataRomance*

Five Cups "Ms. O'Clare creates a world of vivid characters that jump off the pages of her book." ~ *Coffee Time Romance*

"Ms O'Clare has written a wonderful futuristic story what will, this reviewer hopes, continue for many more books." ~ *Love Romances*

Five Unicorns "A very thought provoking tale that deals with real issues women and worlds have had to deal with as we've evolved through time." ~ *Enchanted In Romance*

Five Stars "Lorie O'Clare will have readers' emotions in turmoil throughout TARA THE GREAT - everything from pure rage to tears and back again." ~ *Romance Junkies*

Lorie O'Clare

NUWORLD
Tara the Great

Cerridwen Press

A Cerridwen Press Publication

www.cerridwenpress.com

Tara the Great

ISBN #1419954857
ALL RIGHTS RESERVED.
Tara the Great Copyright © 2005 Lorie O'Clare
Edited by Briana St. James
Cover art by Syneca

Electronic book Publication July 2005

Trade Paperback Publication August 2006

With the exception of quotes used in reviews, this book may not be reproduced or used in whole or in part by any means existing without written permission from the publisher, Ellora's Cave Publishing Inc., 1056 Home Avenue, Akron, OH 44310-3502.

This book is a work of fiction and any resemblance to persons, living or dead, or places, events or locales is purely coincidental. The characters are productions of the authors' imagination and used fictitiously.

Cerridwen Press is an imprint of Ellora's Cave Publishing, Inc.®

Also by Lorie O'Clare

Nuworld 1: The Saga Begins
Nuworld 3: All for One
Nuworld 4: Do or Die
Nuworld 5: The Illegitimate Claim
Nuworld 6: Thicker than Water

If you are interested in a spicier read (and are over 18), check out the author's erotic romances at Ellora's Cave Publishing (www.ellorascave.com).

Cariboo Lunewulf 1: Taming Heather
Cariboo Lunewulf 2: Pursuit
Cariboo Lunewulf 3: Challenged

Dead World

Elements Unbound

Fallen Gods 1: Tainted Purity
Fallen Gods 2: Jaded Prey
Fallen Gods 3: Lotus Blooming
Fallen Gods 4: Embracing Temptation

Issue of Trust
Lunewulf 1: Pack Law
Lunewulf 2: In Her Blood
Lunewulf 3: In Her Dreams
Lunewulf 4: In Her Nature
Lunewulf 5: In Her Soul
Lunewulf 6: Full Moon Rising

Sex Slaves 1: Sex Traders
Sex Slaves 2: Waiting For Yesterday
Sex Slaves 3: Waiting For Dawn
Shara's Challenge
Taking it All
Things That Go Bump in the Night IV *(Anthology)*
Torrid Love 1: The First Time
Torrid Love 2: Caught!
Torrid Love 3: After Dusk

About the Author

All my life, I've wondered at how people fall into the routines of life. The paths we travel seemed to be well-trodden by society. We go to school, fall in love, find a line of work (and hope and pray it is one we like), have children and do our best to mold them into good people who will travel the same path. This is the path so commonly referred to as the "real world".

The characters in my books are destined to stray down a different path other than the one society suggests. Each story leads the reader into a world altered slightly from the one they know. For me, this is what good fiction is about, an opportunity to escape from the daily grind and wander down someone else's path.

Lorie O'Clare lives in Kansas with her three sons.

Lorie welcomes comments from readers. You can find her website and email address on her author bio page at www.cerridwenpress.com

NUWORLD
TARA THE GREAT
ഊ

Chapter One

What a meeting. It was all Tara could do to keep her eyes open while she drove her motorcycle home. Her position as future ruler of all Runner clans could be taxing to her impressive stores of energy. She had just endured a tiring session with the clan leaders, fulfilling one of her responsibilities to meet with them once every cycle. They usually conferred through a Runner transmission on their landlink network, but since several of the clans were in the area, Tara suggested they meet on the Blood Circle Clan site outside Bryton.

Thus had begun a frustrating afternoon as she reviewed the same material with the Gothman and Runners more times than she cared to think about. Neither warrior race understood why she was willing to negotiate trade rights for oil with their adversaries, the Neurians, even though the natural resource was needed desperately.

Not that Tara held a warm place in her heart for the Neurians. Not long ago their leader had held her captive as part of a conspiracy woven by one of her own Runners. Six cycles of her life had been stolen, as she lay drugged in a Neurian shed.

Tara shook off her troubled thoughts. This was business. Runners and Gothman needed to establish trade rights with the Neurians.

She'd known from the outset that Runner leaders, as well as Gothman, would be hesitant to start negotiations with the southern race. Patha, her papa and the greatest leader the Runners had ever known, always said starting something new took patience. The resistance she'd encountered would test that patience to the maximum. Her associates' arguments danced in her head.

"After what they've done to you?"

"We should be declaring war."

"How can you possibly believe they can be trusted?"

Tara struggled to push aside the troubling thoughts as she drove her motorcycle into the backyard of the large house she shared with her Gothman claim, Lord Darius. He had grown up in this house, and their babies had been born in it. Although Tara's nomadic Runner blood would always be with her, she felt this was her home now, too.

"Mama! Mama!"

"Hi, babies!" Tara climbed off her bike, smiling at her twins.

"I'm not a baby. I'm a big boy." Two-winters-old Andru frowned.

"That's right. You sure are." Tara knelt and grabbed her son.

"Me, Mama. Hold me, Mama!" Little Ana ran from the other side of the yard.

Tara grabbed the little girl, and pulled her into her arms, as well. "Where's Syra?" She planted a kiss on each cheek and glanced around the yard. Their blond curls tickled her face as she walked through the yard looking for her niece, who only had sixteen winters, but usually proved to be a good nanny to the twins. At the moment, the teenager appeared to be missing in action. "Don't tell me you two are playing outside by yourselves?"

The two children watched their mama with large gray eyes as Tara carried them into the house.

"Is Syra in here?" Tara plopped the twins on the kitchen floor, then straightened as she addressed Hilda.

Darius' mama turned and straightened her long gray dress over her stout figure.

"She went out with the twins a short bit ago." Hilda squatted, slipping a cookie to each child. "I daresay she hasn't had that much time to disappear, no."

"Will you watch them for a minute?"

Hilda nodded, shooing the children into the living area where they would have more room to play.

Tara returned to the yard. Nothing seemed out of place as she walked across the lawn. "Syra?" As she neared the tool shed in the corner of the yard, a noise triggered her attention and she quickly pulled open the shed's door.

"What are you doing in there?" Tara asked, as she took in Syra's appearance.

Syra's black Runner outfit looked disheveled, and the teenager pulled at her black shirt to straighten it. Her headscarf wasn't secured well and twisted, so the girl had to tug it in order to see what she was doing. "Nothing." Syra offered a sheepish gaze with her green eyes peering through her headscarf, which still didn't quite cover her head as it should.

Tara grabbed her niece's shoulder and pulled her the rest of the way out of the shed.

Syra groaned, but remained quiet.

A very uncharacteristic trait for the girl, Tara thought. She barely had her niece into the sunshine when she noticed another figure standing in the shadows of the shed. "What the hell?" Tara focused on the figure and realized it was Torgo, Darius' younger brother, who was watching her warily. When Tara noticed him, his eyes shifted to his feet.

Fury raced through Tara when she realized Torgo had her niece in the shed when the girl should have been watching the twins. She balled her hands into fists and took a step toward the boy, who flinched and looked at her with the eyes of a trapped animal.

"No," Syra pleaded, grabbing Tara's arm.

"You're supposed to be watching my children." Tara stood in the entrance of the shed, not budging as she glared at her niece, then at her young brother-in-law.

"I, uh, was… I mean, I just left for a second." Syra yanked her headscarf from her head, unable to straighten it without removing it. A guilty blush crept across the pretty girl's cheeks. "Don't tell Papa, Tara, please."

"Get the children and head to the nursery. I'll be up to talk to you in a minute." Tara worked to maintain her anger as she watched Syra give Torgo a pathetic glance, then run across the yard toward the house. Tara now turned her hard glare on Torgo.

"Tara, we weren't doing anything. We weren't." He cleared his throat. "Well, not much anyway."

"Don't you ever take her away from my children again. Understand?"

The boy nodded.

"It will be a humiliation you won't forget soon if word gets out you were taken down by a woman."

"That's for sure," Darius spoke from behind Tara.

She turned, not willing to show that she hadn't heard him approach.

"What's going on here?" he asked.

Torgo glanced at Tara. "It won't happen again." He pushed past both of them and ran to the house.

Tara turned and Darius stood in front of her, waiting for an explanation.

She pointed to the shed. "Your brother and my niece were in there."

Darius smiled and his gray eyes showed their amusement.

"She was supposed to be watching the children."

"Are the children all right?"

"Yes."

"Bryton men are simply irresistible." Darius pushed Tara into the shed.

Tara pushed back. "They're too young."

"And how old were you?"

She pushed harder and walked past him.

The tall, well-built leader of Gothman kept pace alongside her on their way to the house. "I'll talk to him, I will."

"I can only imagine what that conversation would be like."

Darius grabbed Tara from behind and slipped his hand under her shirt to fondle a breast.

Tara wrapped her fingers around his hand, but his grip on her simply tightened. Tara fought her body's immediate reaction. She looked up into dark gray eyes that appeared to focus on her mouth. "Darius, Syra and Torgo need to learn responsibility," she said, then failed to stifle a groan when he bit her neck.

Darius chuckled. "Fine, my lady. Go beat the crap out of your niece."

Tara didn't escape the yard before Darius slapped her on the rear.

Syra sat cross-legged on the living room floor, stacking blocks with the twins. She appeared appropriately chastised as Tara worked to remain calm and explain that a responsibility as simple as watching children would help train Syra to be a better warrior.

"And I doubt you want the future of a Gothman claim if that boy gets you pregnant," Tara added. That caught the girl's attention, who looked up at her with beautiful green eyes.

"It won't happen," Syra whispered.

Tara prayed the teenager had enough sense to see that it wouldn't. She entered her bedroom to find Darius sitting at their landlink.

He glanced over as she sat next to him, on the corner of the desk. "How was your Runner meeting this afternoon?"

"Fine." Tara smiled as she studied her claim's face. "The Blood Circle Clan is returning. They should be arriving tomorrow."

Tara's clan had been gone for the last six cycles. Patha, her papa, had left at the beginning of the new winter, with snow still on the ground, and she hadn't heard from him or any of her other family members in the clan since. Tara knew they had traveled toward the mountain range, which lay to the east of them. No clan had climbed the mountains before, and Tara had worried about them, so she had been elated when Patha had contacted her announcing the return of her people. Her family was coming home.

* * * * *

Darius noticed the excitement and anticipation in Tara's eyes. He knew Tara would have traveled with her clan if it weren't for him. The fact that she stayed by his side proved the extent of her love. Tara's nomadic blood would always exist, but Darius knew he had tamed her a bit. He doubted any other man ever could keep a hold on this beautiful woman sitting next to him.

"What are your plans for their return?" Darius asked.

"Hilda's in charge of the *settling in* of the clan. It's hard to believe your mama, who once cringed at the mention of a Runner, is now working the poor Gothman women in town to death in preparation of the Runner ceremony." Tara giggled.

Darius watched her pale blue eyes grow bright.

"I had to give her all the details about the festivity. There will be a banquet tomorrow night in Bryton so the Gothman and Runners can celebrate together."

Darius nodded. He stared at the pictures of his children and Tara hanging on the wall above the desk. He'd hung them there, himself, over a winter ago, after Tara had disappeared for six cycles, imprisoned by the Neurians. The only time he'd ever hung anything on a wall.

His thoughts shifted to that time without her, and how he had been crazy in the head with longing. It now seemed so far in the past.

"We also talked about the Neurians." Tara met his glance quickly and added, "We need their oil."

"I won't deal with Gowsky. I won't, Tara." He still boiled inside when he thought about the man who had held Tara hostage for all those cycles, unconscious, lying in his barn. Dorn Gowsky, the leader of the Neurian council, had claimed no one had touched Tara, but Darius knew no man could keep Tara captive for so long and not enjoy her.

"Their economy is bad. We could have the upper hand in the negotiations. I believe it's worth an initial contact," urged Tara.

"Who'll make this contact with them?"

"That hasn't been decided yet."

When Tara wouldn't look at him, Darius knew she was lying. And he knew who would be going.

Chapter Two

Syra helped secure the twins in sidecars attached to Tara and Darius' motorcycles.

Tara noticed the teenager's bike sparkled and imagined that Syra wished to impress her papa, Balbo. The older woman also surmised that Syra worried she might discuss the scene in the shed with Balbo. The girl had a wild side to her. Tara could see that. She doubted talking to Balbo would do anything other than make the man worry. Tara remembered the power she had felt when the teenage boys in Tara's clan had fallen at her feet with desire. More than once, she had disappeared with a boy and fooled around. Syra did the same with Torgo.

The small procession departed for the Blood Circle Clan, where Tara's clan had permanent rights to land just north of Bryton. Darius and Tara rode in front, a blond curly haired child riding alongside each of them. Syra followed, while two guards, one Gothman and one Runner, brought up the rear. Each guard displayed symbols on the rear of their bike, representing two nations who had fought many bloody winters against each other, and now rode next to each other in peace.

Tara's clan had grown in size over the past few winters. Hilda, Darius' mama, often teased that the Gothman had taught Runners the joy of breeding. Small children ran through tall grass in the plush valley that would be home to the clan through the remainder of the winter.

Tara clicked the mouthpiece attached to a thin wire that secured her communication device around her ear. "Patha? We're here." Tara listened to Patha's response, then smiled at Darius. "He's ready for us."

Members of the Blood Circle Clan spread in clusters across the open field outside Bryton. Runners, all clad in black, worked to assemble tents, line trailers in rows where they would be grounded for the next few cycles, and, in general, turned the nomadic clan into a settled community in preparation for the new winter. Older children hauled branches, while those younger eagerly followed with bundles of sticks, so fires could be started throughout the clan. Those fires would provide light once darkness arrived, and would also be the focal point around which Runners would enjoy social time after work ended. And as tradition merited, the *settling in* celebration would allow Runners to relax and party after their clan turned itself into a small town.

Runners ceased activity to salute the procession as Tara and Darius entered the clan site.

"Long live Tara."

"Hail to Tara and Lord Darius."

"Behold, Tara the Great!"

Her clan members remembered Tara fighting successfully in the Test of Wills, a contest in which Tara had won and claimed the right to lead the clans once Patha stepped down. Tara had defeated every other warrior in the contest, an unheard-of feat in Runner history. The Test of Wills had made Tara a legend in her own time.

She smiled and waved at familiar faces as they drove across the field, while more and more Runners stopped their activities to welcome the small party.

"Tara-girl!" Reena embraced her daughter before she had a chance to climb off her bike.

"This is quite a reception," Tara whispered to Reena as she watched ten or twelve Runner guards contain the crowd.

"Ah, the stories around the campfire have made you larger than life, they have. I daresay the story has grown with each telling to the point that I do believe you killed a hundred giants with the swing of your hand, you did." Reena smiled, running her bony fingers through Tara's golden brown hair. "And look at you, the most beautiful lady in the land, yes. You have everything, you do. A mama couldn't be more proud."

"And we hear about it all the time." Patha approached the women, arms extended to hug his daughter.

Tara noticed how old he looked. His bear hugs used to take all the wind from her lungs. Now, his shaking limbs merely patted her back as he embraced her.

Patha turned to shake Darius' hand.

Tara saw an exchange of looks, making her wonder if they hadn't formed a tighter bond than she'd realized.

"I'm ready whenever you are," Patha said.

Tara turned quickly. "Ready? Where are we going?"

"Back to the house." Darius' expression was unreadable.

"I'd like to walk around and say hello to the clan." She pointed toward the trailers parked around them. "Patha, you always used to do that whenever we settled in."

"I know, child, I did." He patted his daughter on the back. "But I'm an old man now, and you'll have plenty of time for public relations tonight at this party you're throwing." He reached for both Tara and Darius, turning them toward their bikes. "Come. Tell me of the goings-on."

"Well, hello, dear sis."

The voice came from behind Tara and she turned.

Syra looked wide-eyed at her aunt as if she'd never seen her before. Andru took the opportunity to escape Syra's grasp and run to his papa.

Tasha laughed. "I didn't startle you, did I, Syra?"

"Uh, no." Syra stiffened with a look of indifference.

"Go get the children loaded up." Tara frowned, wondering why Syra would react to Tasha as if startled to see her. "I'll be there in a second." Tara turned to Tasha. "Welcome back."

Tasha's smile was hesitant.

A hand on Tara's shoulder stopped her from asking her sister about her trip to the mountains.

"Let's go," Patha said.

"How nice to have your children taken care of for you." Tasha's familiar tone of displeasure didn't faze Tara.

Tara intentionally ignored the comment. "I'm lucky to have everything I have." She added a quick, silent prayer: *Thank you, Crator. It's you I owe for all of it.*

"I didn't say I was impressed by what you've got," Tasha snapped. "I just commented on how you get treated."

"Tasha, watch your tongue." Patha's baritone was almost a growl as he glared at his daughter.

"See what I mean?" She held her hand out to Patha as an example.

"Tasha," Tara spoke quietly to her sister's rising voice. "If you have a problem with me, I'd be more than willing to talk to you about it. But not here." Tara indicated all the people could overhear them. "And not now." Tara turned to leave with Patha.

"At least it's reassuring to see how far a bastard half-breed can make it in this world," Tasha spat under her breath.

Tara glanced at Reena, her Gothman mama, then over at Patha, her Runner papa.

"With all the bastards Gothman breeds, maybe others will follow in your path." Tasha chuckled, ignoring Darius as he turned his attention on her.

Tara lunged at Tasha.

Darius moved even faster and grabbed Tara around the waist.

Tasha glared at her family, her eyes fuming with hatred.

Darius pulled Tara toward the bike, even though she dug her heels into the ground and pushed at the steel grip his arms had around her.

"How dare you!" Anger ran through her like the venom from a snakebite while Tara watched Tasha stand by Patha's trailer, keeping her distance from the group of clan members who still lingered. Tasha's eyes were bloodshot, making them look red through the openings in her headscarf.

"I wish Gowsky would have killed you!" Tasha moved closer to Tara as Darius continued pulling her away. "Tell us, dear sister, what did you do to talk him out of it? And Kuro...did you weaken his defenses too, before you killed him?"

Tara's jaw dropped at the implication that she had acted inappropriately while held captive in the Neurian nation. And her sister had to know that Tara hadn't killed Kuro. After surviving the Test of Wills, Kuro had been killed by Darius after the Gothman leader had heard his confession. Kuro had admitted to being responsible for Tara being held captive by the Neurians. All this was common knowledge.

Tasha had spoken with intentional cruelty, and her hatred could only spawn trouble.

The woman must learn to respect Tara's position and not throw disrespectful comments in public.

"That's enough!" Patha's hands went to his hips.

Tara ripped herself from Darius' grasp and leaped toward her sister, only to have him grab her arm and yank her back into his embrace.

"You have no idea what I've been through, you little bitch!" Tara snarled as Darius literally carried her toward the bikes. "I'll get you for this!"

Tasha looked briefly at the family she despised, tossed her head, turned on her heels, and walked away.

Tara could sense the feelings of the different family members, but she couldn't read her claim's reaction to the emotional scene they'd just endured. His face was sober, expressionless. As soon as they pulled into the yard, one of his personal assistants approached him. All she could hear was something about a landlink program not working, then they were lost in quiet conversation.

She remained by the shed for a few minutes, grabbing a rag and absently wiping down her bike. She worked to mollify her rage. *Bastard half-breed* indeed! The words cut deeply. She viewed her heritage as an advantage that had been augmented when the Lord of Gothman had claimed her. Tasha had made it all sound so despicable.

"Evil has arrived, child."

The voice caused Tara to jump.

It was an old, cracked, rough voice. A familiar voice.

Tara couldn't believe her ears. "I thought you were dead. I buried you."

The words almost stuck in her throat as she stared at the old lady before her. Quite short and hunched over, she looked up at Tara with glassy brown eyes. Her silver hair, thick and coarse, wrapped around the top of her head in a braid. A long, tan dress made from animal skin, hung askew as she leaned on a twisted stick.

She reached for Tara's hand and touched her. "Focus, child, you must stop this."

Her touch sent a warm, skin-crawling sensation through Tara, forcing a shiver. "What are you saying?"

"It's been done and cannot be reversed. You have to address it." The old lady removed her hand. "Now!"

Tara glanced over toward Darius. He didn't seem to be aware of the old lady's presence, which surprised Tara. He stood with his back to her, talking to his assistant, and didn't turn his attention toward Tara as the woman spoke.

"What am I suppose to address?" She glanced back, but the elderly sage was gone. A large dog caught Tara's eye as it ran across the field, disappearing behind distant rocks.

Evil has come. That didn't help much. The only evil she could think of at the moment was her sister...her half-sister.

Tara remained still, rag in hand, staring off into the distance. She still felt a tingling sensation where the old lady had touched her hand.

Suddenly, Tara realized the rage had left her. Her head was clear, her thoughts orderly.

Tara jumped back on her bike and quickly drove toward the Blood Circle Clan site. She didn't look back to see if Darius followed, although she knew he would. Instead, Tara sent a silent prayer to Crator that she could act before her claim stopped her.

Chapter Three

The Blood Circle Clan buzzed with activity, and Tara used caution as she steered her bike through the densely packed parked trailers and motorcycles. She looked for Tasha, which wasn't an easy task since she had no idea what kind of trailer her half-sister might have or what kind of bike she rode.

Tara moved through the camp, greeting people the way she'd originally planned. Her comm beeped.

"Tara?" Darius' baritone almost growled.

"Yes?"

"What are you doing?"

"I'm greeting my clan members."

"Your papa told you to do that tonight, he did."

"Darius, I've got to do this." She cut communication at that point, not wishing to hear any lectures on obedience. Spotting Balbo walking alongside several trailers, Tara pulled up next to him.

"Tara, now this is a welcome sight." Balbo opened his arms.

Tara jumped off her bike to run into them. Her older stepbrother had always been there for her as she grew up. She longed to unload on him the insults Tasha had spoken. As a child, he'd often comforted her after she and her sister fought. Tara knew Tasha felt jealous. After all, Tasha's mama had taken Tara and helped raise her. And it was Tara's presence preventing Tasha from being heir. But Tara wasn't a child anymore, and her half-brother didn't need the burden of her problems, so Tara held her tongue.

Besides, Balbo had always been a jovial man. Probably because he was not in line to rule the clans, and thus didn't concern himself with affairs of leadership. Tara never wanted to change that trait in him. She could handle Tasha by herself.

"It's so good to see you." She smiled and let go of Balbo. "I think someone else might be anxious to see you as well, not that she'd admit it."

"Has she behaved herself?" Balbo seemed prepared to hear the worse.

"She's been a great help." Tara avoided the answer she knew Balbo dreaded hearing. Over Balbo's shoulder, a familiar figure approached. Tara stiffened, her heart picking up pace while adrenaline rushed through her. Apparently noticing a change in expression, Balbo turned to see what had caught her attention.

The figure disappeared between two trailers, and Tara looked back at Balbo.

"What was it?"

"Nothing. I'll talk with you soon." She gave him a quick hug and started walking toward the spot where she'd just seen her sister.

As Tara walked between the two trailers, the sun disappeared behind one of them. Cool air from the shade ran a chill through her. Children played at the other end of the trailers. A sight pleasant enough, but for some reason an ominous sensation trickled through her.

Tara remembered the excitement of settling in and having an area she could call her own for a while. She reached down to help steady a toddler that had taken off too fast. Several feet away, an infant sat on the ground holding steadfast to the long hair of an older child who wailed profusely in protest. Tara gently released the child's hair from the infant's grasp. The child cried miserably and ran in the apparent direction of her mama.

"Well now, is this fun?" Tara smiled and reached down to scoop up the infant. The child reached for Tara's necklace, a teardrop-shaped ruby with a silver circle around it. The symbol of the Blood Circle Clan. A gift from Darius. "No, no," she said gently and held the child's hand.

The baby boy looked up into her face, and Tara froze. He had blond curls and the darkest gray eyes, identical to her own children. She stared at the child in disbelief. He looked like Andru had at that age.

Two hands roughly ripped away the infant from her. "What are you doing?"

"I was..." Tara started, surprised, realizing the child had distracted her to the point of not recognizing the voice. She stood up straight and the amiability left her as she stared at her sister.

Tasha held the child too close to her chest and cuddled him, smiling wickedly.

Tara was dumbfounded.

The little boy looked at Tasha, then at Tara. His chubby hand reached for Tara.

Tasha pulled it back, snuggling it with her own hand. "This is your Aunt Tara," she whispered to the baby although loud enough for Tara to hear. "You two have a lot in common." Again the wicked smile.

Remembered words stormed through Tara's head: *at least it's reassuring to know how far a bastard half-breed can make it in this world.* An illegitimate child conceived of two different races. She looked in horror at the child.

"I don't believe I've ever seen you speechless before," Tasha spoke with a venomous tongue. "Tigo is your nephew." Her gaze appeared triumphant as she added, "I'm sure you can tell by looking, he's also your children's half-brother. Many thanks to that darling claim of yours." A challenging, toothy grin crossed Tasha's face.

Tara and Tasha stood in an open area. Several mamas watched as the two sisters spoke. As Tasha uttered the bold words, one of the women, appearing to fear for Tigo's life, ran up to Tasha and grabbed the toddler.

Simultaneously, Tara swung out and struck her sister across the face with enough drive to knock Tasha backwards. Although Tasha didn't possess her sister's warrior skills, she'd held her own in a battle or two. Not to mention the uncountable times she'd fought off an aggressor who had caught wind of her risqué reputation. She could take a blow or two and even reciprocate.

Tasha stood several feet away from Tara and leered at her. "The truth hurts, doesn't it, big sis?"

"You're lying," Tara said, unconvincingly.

"You know I'm not." Tasha laughed and rubbed her stinging cheek. "After your claim took me, I almost died giving birth to that child. But I finally have one up on you."

"You'll die for this." Tara leapt through the air, striking her sister to the ground and falling on top of her.

Accustomed to this kind of aggression, Tasha managed to free herself and jumped to her feet. Tripping several times, she reached her bike, parked nearby. Within seconds, the bike roared to life. "It's all your fault, you know. You're the one who left him!" Tasha laughed loudly as she accelerated away.

* * * * *

Tara jumped to her feet and raced back to her bike. Curious onlookers began to increase in numbers, but in her rage she didn't notice.

Balbo stood among the women and children watching as the heir to the Runner clan zigzagged through the trailers. He pulled a comm out of his pocket and fastened it to his ear. "Lord Darius." He instructed the landlink as to the destination of his call. "Uh, sir, this is Balbo."

"What can I do for you?"

"We've got a problem here."

"Why are you telling me?"

"Sir, uh…it's Tara…and um…Tasha."

A brief silence followed, and Balbo thought he heard muffled curses.

"Where are they?"

"They just left the trailers, heading north."

The communication went dead. Balbo pulled the comm from his ear and stuffed it in his pocket. He looked at the point where his two sisters had disappeared from sight, then turned and walked away from the concerned group of women. He considered going after the two women, but knew Darius could handle the situation. The two women had fought before, and although from the stories around the fire, it seemed this dispute wouldn't be solved with a few punches, Balbo knew nothing he could do would change what had been done. He decided to visit his daughter.

* * * * *

Tara gained speed on her sister as the two came upon open prairie north of the clan site.

"You have no right to parade that child around as if he were some trophy," Tara screamed at her sister.

Tasha turned back to see Tara gaining on her. "You have no idea the horrors Darius put me through when he got me pregnant," she screamed through the wind and increased her speed. "He raped me, Tara. Haven't you heard? That damn Gothman of yours took me, just because he thought you were dead, and he raped me again and again."

Tara's fury soared to the point of drowning all rational thinking. She accelerated, then lunged her bike toward Tasha.

In return, Tasha jerked her bike to the right causing it to slide on the rocks hidden by the prairie grass. She slowed down drastically to prevent her bike from falling.

Tara decreased as well and lunged again. "If there is any truth in your words, I'm sure it was you who threw yourself at him," Tara screamed. With all her force, Tara pushed herself off her bike and flew through the air toward Tasha. She grabbed her sister, yanking her from the bike.

The screams of the two women violated the peaceful countryside as they rolled across the rocky terrain. Their Runner clothing withstood the abuse and prevented major lacerations. The protruding rocks, however, bruised and bashed their bodies. Tara's exposed face received several excruciating scrapes and cuts.

The wind knocked out of them, moments passed before either rose to her feet. Tara wiped dirt and blood from her face and stood up slowly, not completely coherent. Everything about her was spinning. She struggled to focus and approach her sister. A severe cut on her forehead caused blood to continually drip into her left eye. If it hadn't been for the rage she felt, the pain would have overwhelmed her. With what energy she had, she kicked Tasha in the side of the head.

Tasha fell back and wailed, grabbing her face.

Tara staggered, then stood over her sister.

Tasha remained on her knees as she straightened her headscarf. "I'll not die today," Tasha spit blood as she spoke. "You can't reverse what's happened. No one can."

"Maybe I can't change the past, but I can prevent this from continuing," Tara's voice sounded garbled from the blood.

Tasha stood and slowly pulled a dagger from a pocket in the leg of her pants. She aimed the sharp point toward her sister. "You have no idea what happened," Tasha hissed. "Darius beat, tortured and raped me. He left me, almost dead, in the middle of the wilderness. I could hardly birth Tigo because of it."

Tara's heart hardened. She gritted her teeth at the thought of her sister engaging in any type of act with Darius. "The only regret I have is that he didn't kill you." Blood filled her mouth as she spoke.

The pair heard the sounds of approaching motorcycles and a jeep.

Tasha turned and braced herself.

As her sister's head turned, Tara jumped at her like a cat attacking its prey. She kicked the hand holding the knife.

Tasha maintained a solid grip on its handle though, and fought to bring it hard into Tara's back. The two of them fell to the uneven ground.

Patha, Darius, and two Runner guards in a jeep pulled up next to the sisters.

Tasha jumped up and stepped back, stumbling as she moved. "I'm not the one to attack," she screamed. "I've already been beaten once. Attack him!" She pointed her finger at Darius.

Patha got off his bike and approached the bloody sight of his two daughters cautiously. "You two have had enough."

Tara didn't respond to his words. She charged at her sister, headfirst, and threw her to the ground.

Tasha scooted away, crablike. She took the knife and thrust it at Tara.

The knife dug deep into her arm and Tara screamed. She leaned over and spewed bloody spit at her sister's face.

Instantly, the two guards were on the women, separating them.

"Let go of me this instant," Tara breathed and the guard released her.

Tasha fell several times as the other guard slowly helped her to her feet.

Tara's eyes overflowed with hatred and she glared at the guard, causing him to back up several feet. Then she turned her hatred toward her sister. "If you and that...that child aren't out of here by nightfall, I'll have you killed. You're banned from the Blood Circle Clan. If you're seen among these people again, you'll be shot on sight." The intensity of her voice increased with each word.

The small group remained quiet, and other than the animosity boiling within each of them for various reasons, the prairie was peaceful and serene.

Tara held her injured arm, her entire shirtsleeve soaked dark red. Her bruised and bloody face was swelling quickly. She staggered backward toward her bike.

Darius quickly dismounted his bike and moved to assist her.

"Don't touch me!" The red glow of rage from her eyes caused him to stop.

"Tara, you're hurt." He raised his hand for her to take, but the calm control in his voice pissed her off further.

"Damn straight I'm hurt." She spit blood at him as well. "Get her out of here!" she yelled and the guards jumped to obey. "If anyone does anything to prevent her from leaving this nation," she turned her enraged gaze first to Darius, then to Patha, "I'll personally see to their execution." Blood dribbled from her mouth, the salty-copper taste lingering, further fueling her anger.

Tara reached her bike and fell onto it. One of the guards helped Tasha into the jeep while several others lifted her bike to the trailer behind it. The men then turned hesitantly, as if waiting to see if there were further orders.

"You're dead to your clan, Tasha. Don't ever try to return." Tara smeared blood on her bike as she struggled to straighten herself. "Get her out of here!"

The guards slowly drove the jeep away from the morbid scene.

Tara started her bike and awkwardly turned it, almost tipping over. With a useless arm, she struggled to keep it upright and cringed.

"Tara," Darius almost pleaded. "You can't drive, no."

"Leave me alone." She managed to make the bike move. She drove north, away from the clan site.

* * * * *

Patha put his hand on Darius' arm. "We knew this would happen," he said quietly.

"I won't let her take off by herself, I won't." Darius stared at the old man.

"I know." Patha watched as Tara slowly disappeared in the tall prairie grass. "Stay with her then. She'll probably pass out from lack of blood soon. Don't let her know you're following her, though. She'll push herself too hard." Patha walked toward his bike and shook his head slowly. "The birth of that bastard of yours is going to continue to cause problems, I fear."

Chapter Four

Tall blades of prairie grass felt like knives as they slapped against Tara's legs. She maneuvered the bike with her good arm and held the other one close to her body. Tears, blood, and sweat blurred her vision. Her pride felt more bruised and tattered than her flesh and clothes.

Ever since her return from the Neurians, Tara had believed Darius dedicated to their claim. Although the man came from a society of men who used women without thought to their feelings, Darius had shown Tara he could move beyond that mindset and view her as an equal. Or at least, she thought he had. In a matter of hours, everything she had believed about Darius had been shambled.

He had been unfaithful. He had impregnated another woman, and that woman just happened to be Tara's half-sister.

Nothing got past Darius; he knew his bastard child existed. Tara felt more tears burn her eyes when she tried, but could not understand why Darius had allowed this atrocity to happen.

The prairie grass finally dispersed and tall evergreens appeared. The bike sputtered with deceleration as she moved through them. The sound of running water distracted her. Squinting to focus, she noticed a waterfall through the trees.

Her left eye had swelled shut, and a ringing in her ears had grown past annoying. As Tara drove through the overgrown wooded area, a pointed branch dug at her leg, the pain wrenching through her. She howled and the bike swerved as she lost control. Unable to regain balance, she jumped free of the heavy machine. Every muscle in her body screamed as she tumbled across the uneven terrain. The mossy ground eased her landing, but not her pain.

Tara lay next to her bike for a long time. Everything around her seemed dark as she tried unsuccessfully to focus through her one good eye. She wasn't sure if it was still daylight or not. The pounding in her head matched the beat of her heart. With every thud, new agony seared around the open wound on her forehead. Her arm had blown up like a balloon. When she tried to raise her hand to wipe her eye, she realized it would no longer move.

The dirt and moss in her mouth mixed with the not quite coagulated blood, forming a thick, nasty-tasting paste. The ground grew cold and offered little comfort as she gagged. Her face ached and pulling her lips together in order to spit proved to be quite a challenge. It hurt to pucker. The spittle dribbled down her chin, but she ignored it and spit again.

Tara tried to push herself to a sitting position, and failed, her good arm slipping under her weight. She cursed out loud. She had defeated warriors twice her size in the Test of Wills. Her clan members knew her as a skilled fighter, yet one round with her tramp half-sister, and she couldn't get off the ground.

She spat again, feeling a small accomplishment at the success of the feat, and forced herself to try moving again. Several attempts later, Tara pulled herself up and stumbled forward, surveying her surroundings.

A waterfall dumped its cold mountain spring water into a small pond. The water invited her with its gurgling noises and splashing sounds. Tara rubbed her eye with her sleeve until she could focus. She could see clearly to the bottom of the pond, which wasn't that deep. The air felt damp and she imagined it soothing her cuts as she stood next to the pond, breathing the crisp air. The tangy scent of moss, mixed with a more pungent smell from the trees around her, provided a delightful bouquet. It was a tranquil spot.

The first step was to clean the wound on her arm and determine its severity. There would be no easy way to remove her shirt with the arm in its useless state, and the rest of her bruised and sore. She tried pulling it over her head, but the intensity of pain in her arm raced through her body and overwhelmed her. She pulled at her shirtsleeve, and fresh blood began to ooze as she broke what little healing existed. Tara grew frustrated when she couldn't see the severity of the laceration in her forearm. The amount of blood made her think the knife had cut fairly deep, and she knew if she didn't tend it quickly, infection would set in.

First order of business: remove the sleeve. None of the jagged rocks Tara found to help her sharpen the end of a stick worked. One hand just couldn't complete the task. Frustrated, Tara threw the wood into the water. The only option left was to clean her arm with the shirt still on.

The water was cold, very cold. It revived all her sensations, thereby focusing her brain. She felt every cut and scrape with new vitality.

Tara screamed.

Letting loose her rage enabled it to subside just enough for her to realize the severity of her injuries. Every muscle in her body cramped, and she began shaking uncontrollably. Everything around her blurred, and she couldn't stop shaking.

This was all Tasha's fault.

The slut probably sought out Darius as soon as she knew Tara had left.

And it hadn't been Tara's fault that she had been gone six cycles. The Neurians had held her hostage; she hadn't been able to return sooner. Darius hadn't sought another claim in her absence, and he had made no attempt to declare her dead.

Tara felt the ground move under her. She staggered before regaining balance, beginning to fear she might pass out. Her mind churned in turmoil as she continued to jump from thoughts of Tasha to Darius, wondering how this terrible turn of events could have been allowed to play out.

Someone would pay for the birth of this bastard. She would see to it personally.

* * * * *

Darius had no difficulty following Tara as she zigzagged through the trees. He parked at the top of a small cliff and watched as his claim lost control of her bike.

Don't help her yet. Wait until she's ready to pass out.

Tara was injured more from a spat with her sister than he had ever seen her after any fight. He wanted to rip apart Tasha for throwing that child in Tara's face.

As far as he could tell, Tasha had placed herself in worse standing than she had ever before experienced by confronting her sister. And now he would have to calm Tara's wrath and find a way to convince her that this child meant nothing to him.

He held his emotions in check as he watched her struggle to move toward the water. He clearly saw she wouldn't be able to remove her shirt after watching her try and fail. When she screamed, he got off his bike and reached for a small bag he had tied to his seat before he followed her.

Darius could think of very few warriors who would have the stamina to continue as Tara had, considering the amount of blood she'd lost. He wondered if he would have been able to endure the cuts and lacerations and continue to move. The woman was incredible!

As he watched her half-sit, half-lie by the clear water, he realized how hurt she'd obviously been after discovering Tasha had his child. Darius had known the babe would damage Tara's pride, but now he sensed his claim had been hurt by the knowledge of this bastard more than he'd anticipated.

It wasn't his fault, damn it.

During the six cycles of Tara's absence, he hadn't been able to think clearly. That had been the main reason he had left Gothman, so he could clear his head and try to move on without Tara. And on that night Tasha found him outside Gothman land, he had been convinced Tara was dead.

He'd been drunk, and Tasha had a reputation as a slut.

Raping her had seemed so trivial. He never dreamed Tasha would conceive. So the bitch had the kid. He could have easily resolved the problem by eliminating both Tasha and the child. And possibly he should have done that sooner, but he hadn't thought their existence would hurt Tara like it had.

He pushed aside these thoughts and focused on what needed to be done now.

Darius didn't hesitate as he began walking toward Tara. The cold water must have sent her into a state of shock because she didn't appear to be aware of his presence. No warriors ever kept their back to someone approaching from behind. He squatted behind her and gently placed his hands on her shoulders.

Tara didn't meet his gaze when he looked at her. Her expression turned dark when she realized he was there, and she reached for her injured arm. "I told you to leave me alone."

"I know." He ignored the glare she gave him and slowly took her injured arm in his grip. "This is going to hurt."

He cut her sleeve with a small pair of scissors he'd removed from the bag.

Tara gritted her teeth and refused to allow her pain to show.

Darius slid the material down her arm and dropped it on the ground. Blood began trickling down her arm again.

Tara had closed her eyes during the process, but opened them when she felt air hit her wound. She clenched her teeth in apparent determination not to break apart when she saw the severity of her wound. Her arm had been sliced wide open.

Darius took a white cloth from the bag and covered the injury. He held her arm tightly with his hand to stop the bleeding.

* * * * *

Tears welled in Tara's eyes from the agony, but she kept her face blank. She blinked a few times and looked up into Darius' face, unable to speak.

He wiped the tear from her cheek and smiled. "If you weren't such a damn good warrior, the pain could overtake you and you'd pass out, you would. Then it wouldn't hurt as bad." He rubbed her swollen cheek with his rough thumb, his voice remaining quiet and calm. "I'm going to put a salve on it."

He removed the white cloth. The underside of the cloth now showed bright red, and the zigzagged tear in Tara's arm looked clean, yet deep.

Tara worked to stay focused, telling herself that if she were at the clan site, Dr. Digo could repair the wound with little effort. She would be fine. But out here, with Darius' large hands attempting to place skin together to close the wound, the damage appeared a lot worse.

Darius applied a salve that Tara recognized as a Gothman medicine. She wondered how Darius had come by the salve, but couldn't keep her thoughts focused long enough to determine an answer.

The ointment stung and Tara winced. "I'll do it." She tried to grab the jar of salve from him, but Darius pulled it back and she fell into him. Her arm hit his shirt and covered him with blood. Tara reached for the ground with her good hand, but grabbed air. Although she only leaned against Darius for a moment before he steadied her, the pain almost made her pass out.

"I don't want your help." She choked on phlegm and broke into a cough. Clearing her throat, Tara struggled to breathe. With every deep breath, she felt knives sear into her rib cage. Something was seriously wrong. Panic rushed over her when she couldn't catch her breath.

* * * * *

Darius watched Tara place fingers delicately along her ribs while she tried to stabilize her breathing. He frowned and took her hand, then placed his own fingers along her rib cage, feeling gently.

Tara yelped when he touched her, then scooted so her back was to him.

Darius realized there was more damage than just her sliced arm. "We need to wrap you. Those ribs are broken." He crawled around to face her. "Your shirt needs to come off."

"You're not going to touch me," she hissed, but her voice was weakening.

She waved her good hand, as if dismissing him, and he noticed she had begun shaking.

"You are not going to die today, my lady, no. Either you let me take care of you, or I'll knock you out and take care of you while you're unconscious, yes."

Tara remained frozen with her good arm blocking him. She glared with eyes that were blurred and glassy.

Darius reached into the bag and pulled out a small syringe. He removed the plastic cover from the end, revealing a long, thin needle.

"No," Tara choked and tried to scoot away.

Darius ignored her feeble attempt to flee, grabbed her good arm, and injected the serum into her vein.

As her surroundings went black, she heard Darius' voice speak to her soothingly.

"I love you, I do. Don't worry…you'll be fine. I'll see to it, I will."

* * * * *

Tara wasn't sure how long she slept. Distorted figures and echoes of voices trailed through her thoughts. She blinked and closed her eyes, trying to capture the fleeing thoughts and make sense of them. Her sister's sneering face appeared in her mind's eye, and Tara frowned and wanted to punch her. Then the fight refocused and Tara imagined beating her sister all over again. She attempted a fist, then felt momentary confusion when her hand didn't immediately cooperate.

A sudden vision of a baby boy took over her thoughts, and Tara experienced a foul taste in her mouth. She tried licking her lips and realized her tongue felt like sandpaper, and her lips seemed too thick. A lump grew in her gut as the baby looked up at her, reached for her. Tara tried to mouth the word, *no*. Her mouth still wouldn't cooperate, but tears formed in her eyes. The lump in her gut threatened to explode as she saw that child's face—a face looking so like her own son's face. But this child wasn't her son.

How could she endure the pain of this child's existence?

She opened her eyes and took in her surroundings. Tears fogged her vision, and she tried moving her hands again. One hand finally budged, but a weight blocked her from moving it to her face.

She lay on a thick wool blanket and another one covered her. Darius' leather jacket draped over the top of the blanket providing extra warmth. Tara slid her hand from under the blankets, and touched her face. With as much delicacy as she could muster, she ran her fingers along the sore on her forehead, then licked her lips and felt them with her fingers.

The image of the child still lingered in her thoughts, and she couldn't determine if the pain from the knowledge of him was worse than the pain of her physical injuries.

Darius had another child. Her sister's child. A bastard.

The man sat several feet away, tending a fire. The brightness from the flames splashed around the campsite. A small wild turkey rotated on a stick over the flames.

Tara sat up slowly and groaned as her head fought the gravity.

"You'll feel queasy for a while until the drug wears off." He didn't look up. "Then you'll just feel the pain, you will. I'd say at least three ribs might be broken."

"Why did you come here when I told you not to?"

"My lady, in case you've forgotten, you're *heir* to the Runner clans, you are. Your papa's still alive, yes. You do not lead yet, and therefore have no rank. Also, you chased your sister out of Blood Circle land, which is the only land Runners have jurisdiction in. You're in Gothman territory, you are. Again, you've no jurisdiction. I'm Lord of Gothman."

She clenched her teeth. The man couldn't possibly think she had no say in the matters of his bastard. Rank had nothing to do with this.

Her head ached the more she thought about it, and she took slow breaths to ease the pain. "Why are we still here?" She pulled the leather coat around her shoulder to block the mountain chill.

"It wouldn't be a good idea to move you on a bike right now, I'd say." He poured hot tea into a large mug and brought it over to her.

Tara wondered when he would have thought to pack all these provisions on his bike, but couldn't rouse herself to worry about it. She looked at the cup but made no move to accept it.

"I didn't want to hurt you."

"A little late for thoughts like that," she snapped.

He sighed, took her hand, and put the warm cup in it. "I thought you were dead when your sister—"

"I don't want to hear this." Tara shut her eyes and shook her head.

"I want you to hear this, I do." He lifted her face and forced her to meet his eyes. She felt groggy and had little resistance to fight him. "What I did to your sister…not even she deserved, she didn't. I'm actually amazed she lived through it." He took a deep breath and glanced into her eyes, rubbing her cheekbone with his thumb. "I'd left Gothman, I had. I couldn't accept the fact you were dead and was so angry with myself for letting you get away, I couldn't focus on anything else, no. Patha suggested I travel so I could pull myself together. He said it always worked for him, he did."

She didn't look away from him when he paused.

He glanced at her, then looked up toward the stars. "I'll deny ever saying this, but I tell you now, I wasn't fit to rule, I wasn't. I don't like being out of control of a situation, and it outraged me that you had slipped through my fingers, it did. I couldn't think straight and everyone annoyed me. I refused to allow anyone to say you were dead, I did. And, I despised the Neurians." He faced her now and let his gaze penetrate her. "More than once, I wanted to travel down there with an army larger than a city, and kill those Neurians one by one for taking you from me."

Tara fought the urge to reassure him he had no way of knowing she was still alive. She buried the thoughts. She wasn't ready to release her outrage.

"That particular night," he continued, "I'd driven since before sunrise and had just set up camp, I had. I was numbing all thoughts, so to speak. I wanted to pass out and not be able to dream. The more whiskey I drank, the angrier I got. It wasn't working. Instead of going numb, the whiskey fueled my outrage, yes. That's when she showed up."

"Darius," she interrupted, not wanting to hear how he'd slept with her sister. "Nothing you can say—"

He interrupted by gently placing his hand on her mouth. "Tara, you must know I've remained loyal to you, I have."

"My sister has your child." Tara struggled to say the words and instinctively took a gulp of the tea. She immediately felt a sickening sweetness sink down her throat and saturate her stomach, as it likewise floated to her head. The fumes from the scent of the tea floated around her.

She looked up at Darius and struggled to focus on his face. "Opium," she said after a long minute.

Darius smiled gently and ran his fingers through her hair. "There's no reason for you to feel all this pain, I'm thinking."

"Or try to go anywhere," she added and forced herself to remain sober. "Darius, that child is in line as heir to the Gothman nation. He's a threat to Andru and Ana."

"I'm aware of that." His tone turned fierce. Tara had hit a nerve. He ran his fingers through his hair as if now the conversation was unpleasant for him.

Tara relished his discomfort. She continued to fight the opium high, struggling to keep her thoughts in order. She didn't want to miss out on this opportunity to catch him with his defenses down. The man thought he could justify his actions and she did not see them as justifiable. His actions were unforgivable and she wanted him to realize that.

"As soon as I found out she was pregnant, I sent several men to bring her to me. Whether the child was mine or not, I would force her into an abortion. She disappeared from the clan before I could capture her. She reappeared with Kuro less than a cycle before the Test of Wills. When the Blood Circle Clan left, she went with them. Patha and I remained in contact until they lost transmission in the mountains. He informed me she was having problems from some still-damaged internal organs. I thought she'd die, I did."

"Why didn't you kill her when you had the chance?"

He looked at her quickly and his face turned to stone. "I thought it would hurt her more to let her live." His tone was ice.

Tara's head was swimming. The opium had full effect over her, and she discovered she couldn't organize her thoughts into words.

Darius scooted forward and put his arm around her.

She wasn't able to protest, but every inch of her body wanted his hands off her.

Gently, he moved her into a lying position, wrapping the blankets around her, and once again draping his leather jacket over the blankets. "Get some sleep, my lady, yes."

She tried to protest, but the blankets imprisoned her and the opium took over.

* * * * *

Darius watched the flames dance in the fire, trying to escape from themselves. He'd told Tara the truth. That particular night over a winter ago had been a night to forget. Yet for Tara's sake he had conjured the memory and shared it with her. She had to know that he wouldn't have done that for just anyone.

Tasha had made a terrible mistake.

Darius could tell Tara recognized that truth. Tasha never should have approached a Gothman drinking alone; the woman was no more than a stupid bitch. Any Gothman would have been in his right for treating her like the whore she was known to be.

As for that bastard, Darius wouldn't have Tasha claiming him as the papa. Darius would see to it. And now that he had shared the details of that ridiculous rendezvous he had with Tara's sister, his conscience was clear. When Tara mended and her head was clear, he would tell her his decision on the matter. Then it would be Tara's job to get over it.

He sighed deeply, thinking about what he'd just told her. There was no attraction to Tasha. She was beautiful, like her sister, but ruined and ugly inside. The woman was a whore and had nothing to offer. Tara had everything.

He glanced over at her sleeping body. Even with her swollen face, she was beautiful. He'd seen worse and her wounds would heal.

She'd put up quite a fight with Tasha. Darius knew if he and Patha had been minutes later, Tara would have killed her sister. Tasha's life had been spared a second time.

Tasha had to be seriously injured, though. Maybe she would die yet.

No, her papa would see to it that she lived. Patha loved both his daughters.

Tasha had run to her clan for protection from Darius after Kuro died, and Patha had given it to her. When Darius had sent his men to bring Tasha to him, Patha had intervened, sending them on their way.

Patha seldom interfered with Darius' wishes. Darius hadn't pressed the issue after that. He'd had no desire to cross Patha. The man was old, but he had earned Darius' respect. He was an obstacle Darius had yet to figure out how to overcome.

But Patha wouldn't live forever. If Tasha were still alive when Patha died, Darius would see to her death.

But what about that fight? Surely, that was a sign of how much Tara must love him. Otherwise his claim wouldn't insist he remain faithful to her, wouldn't be bothered by the thought of him with another woman. Wouldn't have been so outraged with the news that Tasha had borne Darius' bastard child.

Tara was angry and hurt, he understood. But she had fought for his honor. For their honor.

He sighed, wishing he and Patha had prevented her from learning the truth. Tara wasn't prepared for news like that. They'd tried to get her off the clan site as quickly as possible.

But Tasha had intentionally sought out Tara. She couldn't wait to tell her sister about her son.

If Tara had been Gothman…no, if Tara had been *any other woman*…none of this would be an issue, Darius rationalized. Most women—especially Gothman women—understood that a man needed to prey on women, that he needed to fulfill sexual urges that women simply didn't have.

Darius guessed any woman might feel threatened with knowledge of a bastard. Some Gothman preferred their bastard children to the children from their claim. But Darius didn't feel that way. He loved the twins as much as he loved Tara. No other child would take away that love. Tara should know that.

What a stubborn woman she was. She challenged him and he liked it. In fact, he loved it. He loved her. He loved to conquer, and he would spend the rest of his life trying to conquer Tara.

But there was the child. And a baby boy at that. Tara's concerns were valid, and he'd lain awake many nights since he'd found out Tasha had birthed a boy. If anything happened to Andru, Tasha's baby would be next in line to rule his kingdom since, by Gothman law, Ana could not rule. She was female. Also, the mother of the child had no bearing. Only the order in which the man sired his children mattered. That was the law.

Oh yes, he could change the law, but now wasn't the time. His people weren't ready for such a fundamental part of their culture to be changed. Maybe later, in five or ten winters, he'd consider it. But...not now.

Maybe he'd have the boy taken from Tasha. Now there was a thought. He knew his papa had taken similar action with his own bastards.

Darius could give the boy to some Gothman woman to raise; someone who didn't know the child's heritage. Someone who would raise him as her own, thinking he was an orphan. That might be his best bet, then he could keep an eye on the boy, watch how he grew, and make any necessary decisions later. Just for insurance, he could ban the caretaker from the claim as Lord Jovis had with Reena.

Darius thought about this for a while. He'd have to be careful. Patha could not know. And, by all means, he'd have to convince Tara that the child was dead.

And Tasha?

Darius reached for a stick to poke the dwindling fire. Patha would protect her as long as she remained in the Blood Circle Clan. Darius would have to see to it that she somehow left that clan.

* * * * *

Voices. Where were they coming from? Tara's thoughts were muddled and she felt disoriented. The hard surface underneath her was damp, sending chills rushing through her, and something poked at her side. At the same time she was too warm, yet her face was cold. None of it made sense. Where was she? What had happened? She fought to focus her thoughts and dug through her memory.

Slowly, visual flashes appeared before her eyelids. Again and again, the face of a baby. Not her baby, but it looked like her baby. It was all wrong, an awful nightmare. That baby couldn't really exist. How could they allow it to happen?

The dog-woman entered her thoughts. "A child conceived from evil," the old voice whispered.

What can I do?

"The supplies you'll need are in the trailer."

Another voice, coming somewhere to the side of her, interrupted her vision.

Tara searched her thoughts for the dog-woman. Where was she? Who said that? Consciousness crept through her. The voices became more audible.

"We'll do just fine, we will."

"When will you leave?"

"Right away."

Tara struggled to open her eyes. Who was leaving? What was happening? The voices were familiar. She fought to regain control of her mind.

"You know, you can't keep her that way forever."

"She'd be in a lot of pain without it."

"Ahh, and she'd be raking you over the coals, too." Patha chuckled. "Might as well let her get it out of her system."

Tara blinked. She focused on the two men standing by the fire. The bright flames had burned down to smoldering logs. Patha held a portable light in his hand, which lent a surreal atmosphere to the campsite. Fog surrounded her thoughts, but she tried hard to understand the words they were saying.

"She does have quite the temper on her, doesn't she? I'll bring her around after we get going, I will."

Where were they going? Tara blinked again and noticed several others approaching the campsite.

Torgo and two Gothman guards entered the circle of light. Torgo looked down toward her and noticed she was staring at him.

Tara met his eyes and saw the look of a boy who was almost a man. She winked at him.

He quickly looked toward his brother. "The bikes are loaded, they are, my lord." Torgo stood tall and at attention in front of his brother.

"You're the man of the house in my absence, you are." Darius patted his brother's shoulder. "You're barely a man, though. All decisions shall be cleared through Patha, yes."

"Yes, my lord." Torgo's face was stone just like his brother. "Everything's ready, it is."

"Remember to chart your course in the computer as you go. I've entered the route my sources have suggested. There are clothes for the two of you in the trailer that should help you assimilate into their culture. I want a daily report." Patha nodded toward Tara. "From both of you."

Tara had successfully pulled herself into a sitting position before anyone noticed she'd moved.

"Ah, you've joined the living." Patha smiled at his daughter. "Very well then, we'll meet you up at the trailer. Come on, boy." Patha grabbed hold of Torgo's arm, appearing to need it more for support than anything else, and started walking up the slight incline.

Tara pulled off the covers and slowly rose to her feet. Her head was spinning still.

Darius was at her side in a second.

"Don't touch me." She watched him warily as she tested her balance. "Where are we going?"

"North. Can you walk?"

Tara didn't answer, but instead started moving slowly in the direction of Patha and Torgo. Her arm ached with a dull throb, but other than that, she felt no pain.

Darius left the two guards to clean up the camp and followed Tara.

She stopped when she reached an open area among the trees. A small group of motorcycles were parked next to a mobile home, prepared for travel. What the hell was going on here?

Chapter Five

Patha insisted Dr. Digo examine Tara. She'd managed to walk unassisted to the open meadow and up to the area that was readied for a trip; Tara and Darius' bikes were secured to a flatbed trailer behind the mobile home.

Darius' personal assistant walked out the door as Tara and Dr. Digo entered. The doctor offered his hand.

Tara held his strong fingers tightly as she climbed the two stairs into the living room. She didn't smile as she shut the door on Darius and Patha, leaving them standing outside the trailer.

Turning slowly, she looked at Dr. Digo. "I need something to get this opium out of my system. He gave it to me in a tea."

"Opium, huh?" The doctor chuckled to himself. "Even the great Lord Darius is scared of your temper. How long ago were you drugged?"

"I don't know. It was still light out."

"Unless he's drugged you while you slept, you're probably just groggy from waking up. Let's take a look." The doctor determined her ribs weren't broken but bruised. He removed the bandage from her arm and scrutinized the amateur stitches Darius had applied.

Tara had no memory of Darius giving her stitches, and concluded he must have done it while she was unconscious.

"You'll have a scar, but I see no infection," Dr. Digo said as he applied a salve to the cut above her eye. She squirmed from his touch when the antiseptic's sharp sting hit her. "Hold still, girl. We don't want those infected. You're way too beautiful to have ugly scars left on your face. If you'd had on your headscarf, these wouldn't be here."

"No lectures, Doc. Please." She groaned, but held still as he massaged the gritty green salve over the wounds.

He wiped off the excess with a cloth. "There now...I'm satisfied. You'll live."

"Doctor?" Tara watched as Dr. Digo washed his hands at the sink. "Tasha, is she...?"

"She'll live. You two have had your fights before, but not like this. I've always been able to patch up both of you so you can do it again, and I didn't fail this time."

"I don't care that she's alive." Her tone caused the doctor to turn and give her his attention. "Has she left the clan yet?"

"Tara, she's in no condition to travel."

"So you told Patha you wanted her to stay?"

"That wasn't discussed, but she's still in my care. Tara, it was all she could do to birth—"

"I don't want to hear it." She felt drugged, sluggish, either from opium or having just awakened from a long sleep. And she was frustrated that Patha had overruled her orders to ban Tasha. She descended from the trailer and glared at the patient expression on her papa's face.

"You and Darius will leave here in a few minutes. You're headed north toward the mountain range. The land is uncharted, and I expect you to chart it. We have reason to believe the cave people live in these mountains, as well as the range of mountains to the west. You'll confirm if it's true."

"I think it would be best if you found someone else to go." Tara's tone was cold.

"You two are best for this mission," Patha said simply.

"I won't go anywhere with him." Tara's glare was as icy as her tone. "He'd probably keep me drugged the entire time."

"The Warrior Blood Pact is in effect. How the two of you handle each other is not my affair."

Tara's mouth fell. She knew damn well the Warrior Blood Pact was in effect. She and Darius had performed the ritual during the Runner wedding ceremony, shortly after the Test of Wills.

The night of the ceremony, Patha had approached and asked them to partake in the ancient pact. Tara reflected on how honored she had been to mix her blood with Darius' during the ritual. A small ornate knife had been used so they could prick their fingers and allow their blood to be combined in a small vial. Both had sworn to lead their nations. They also swore their allegiance to each other as leaders. The pact stated if either died at the hand of the other, the other would no longer rule. They'd signed the pact with their blood. The document was Patha's insurance policy that they wouldn't kill each other.

Tara fought to keep her emotions in check. "I'm aware of the Warrior Blood Pact. It has been honored. Darius is not dead, but I will not stand by his side."

Patha turned and walked toward his bike. "Good luck," he said to no one in particular.

"Patha!" Tara ignored the look of disapproval Darius gave her, and Patha as well, when he turned slowly to face her. "If I see Tasha again, she will die!"

She didn't stand down as Patha walked toward his daughter until he was inches from her face. "You will obey me without question. You are not the leader of the Runners, yet. Do not give orders. Is that clear?"

Tara looked at her papa's eyes for one brief second, then turned and stormed back into the trailer. She headed for the bedroom and slammed the door behind her. Fury numbed pain as she kicked the dresser until it was in front of the door. The piece of furniture would not prevent Darius from entering, but she believed it made her point clear. She wanted nothing to do with him.

She would have loved to throw herself onto the bed and cry, but the action would hurt too much. Pain from moving the dresser consumed her. Tired as she was, she sat down at the computer and sent a long transmission to her mama.

There would be no complaints to Reena about a bastard half-breed child being allowed to live. Reena had given birth to such a child, and that child had been named heir to all the Runner clans. But Reena had been a caring and compassionate mother. She had given Tara the opportunity to be raised in the best of worlds.

Tasha didn't possess that level of compassion. Any child raised by that bitch would be backstabbing and deceitful, just like Tasha.

Tara would see to it that history did not repeat itself.

Darius moved around in the front half of the trailer and before long she heard him approach the door. "I need the map from the computer to meet our destination, I do."

"I found Gothman from Southland without a landlink. Find the mountains yourself."

He grunted and walked away from the door. Tara looked up the map and studied it. She read the briefs Patha sent to them concerning their mission. Disjointed thoughts jumped around in her head, and she fought blurring vision. Her work would have to wait until later, and she gratefully crawled onto the bed.

Tara was asleep before she could form another thought.

She swore she awoke a moment later, but the opium no longer infiltrated her system. Her side ached and pain shot down her arm. A loud pounding caused Tara to jump. She sat up in the bed and untangled her legs from twisted blankets. The sun shone through the east window. She saw mountains and realized Darius had obviously driven through the night.

Tara jumped when the dresser made a screeching sound as it began to move across the bedroom floor.

"It's time to get up, yes." He entered the room and walked over to the closet, then began tossing several items of clothing at Tara. "Put these on." Darius grabbed clothes for himself, as well, then began to undress in front of her, his back turned.

Tara watched muscles move in Darius' back, and cursed herself for being aroused by the incredible man, now naked at the end of the bed. She moistened her lips with her tongue and studied his firm rear end, his legs corded with muscles and covered with downy blond hair. She wondered if she possessed the inner strength to keep this man completely to herself throughout their winters, and she knew beyond a doubt that she wouldn't be able to live with him if he didn't remain loyal to her.

Her heart constricted as she thought of his betrayal, and the lump moved to her throat. She forced the thoughts from her head with a deep cleansing breath that she exhaled silently.

Tara eyed the clothes he'd thrown to her, identical to his own—a bright green pantsuit and a long brown cloak with a hood. Changing outfits would be a trick for her, but she wouldn't admit she needed help. Grabbing the clothes, she walked into the living area, the only other room in the trailer. Changing in here would be no easier, but at least Darius wouldn't witness the difficulty she would endure in getting the task done.

She still wore her Runner shirt with one sleeve gone. She found she could pull it above her breasts, but when she stretched to bring the shirt over her head, pain raked through her midsection. Tara had experienced bruised ribs before, and knew the agony would be with her for a while before subsiding. Well, she didn't have a while to wait. She clenched her teeth and pulled the shirt from her body with a single movement, then stood still until the room quit spinning from the extreme pain resulting from the simple act.

She shook out the new shirt with her uninjured arm and pulled it over her head. Sliding her injured arm through the sleeve hole took some effort, and Tara cursed her inability to move with ease. Putting on the bright colored pants proved to be just as challenging as donning the rest of the clothes. She didn't like being slowed, for any reason. And the fact that her injuries were from her half-sister infuriated her even more.

Darius finished dressing and entered the living room, the long cape swooshing around his legs. He watched Tara for a second as she struggled with her cape. "How do you feel?" he asked as he took her cape without permission and placed it around her shoulders.

"Okay," she lied.

"There's more opium."

Tara wasn't sure if he was offering it to help with her pain, or warning her to shape up or he'd knock her out again.

* * * * *

Darius had printed destination plans from the landlink in the bedroom while Tara dressed, and studied them as he spread out one after another on the counter. Then he started driving. After an hour, they arrived at the base of the northern mountain range.

He had never seen mountains before. In awe, he stopped the trailer when they first came into view. He didn't have time to be moved by their glory, and told himself as much as he took that opportunity to familiarize himself with their orders. They were to park the trailer in a large cave covered with vines.

Darius continued driving with orders in hand, until the mountains loomed over and around them.

His beautiful claim slept again. He stroked her hair, then kissed her cheek before leaving her in the trailer to investigate their surroundings. Less than a half-hour walking around the base of the mountain passed before he discovered a cave that matched the description on the printout.

He returned to the trailer, and though Tara was now awake, drove toward the cave without speaking to her. Then they set out on foot.

"Why are we on this mission?" Tara asked as she walked behind Darius. "I mean, why didn't you send a team of explorers out here?"

"Patha thought it would be a good idea if you and I made up the team, he did." He continued walking as he spoke and made no attempt to look at her.

* * * * *

The two continued in silence. They climbed more than they walked as one boulder after another blocked their path. Tara felt a headache growing, and the ache in her side turned to pain as she persisted in their trek up the mountain. More than once, she reached to stabilize herself with both arms, only to feel the stinging retaliation in her slowly mending arm.

Several days hadn't proved to be enough time to recuperate before endeavoring such a hike, yet Tara refused to complain and continued to follow Darius.

* * * * *

After an hour or so had passed, Darius stopped and leaned against a rock larger than he was. He had paid attention to Tara's breathing behind him, and noted how it became more and more labored. The hike wasn't overly intense, but he could feel the air thin as they increased altitude, and knew Tara's bruised ribs would aggravate her as she took deeper breaths. More than once, he had heard her grab something behind him, and imagined how she winced in pain trying to use her injured arm. Although he could have continued, he decided to stop to allow her breathing to ease.

The woman should be home in her bed, with servants seeing to her needs. But Darius knew Tara would never submit to behaving as a lady should. More than once, he cursed her determination to behave as a man.

* * * * *

Tara found a smaller rock and sat. Every inch of her body pulsated with pain, and she was more than content to take a break. She pulled her flat landlink out of her inside pocket and began typing.

"I'm not showing any signs of people," she commented after a minute.

Breathing was hard, which made speaking difficult. Every deep breath she took, turned into more of a gasp, which she blamed on the thin air. Her ribs screamed in protest as her lungs worked overtime.

"There's iron in the rocks, there is. Cave people don't live aboveground. They live in the mountain, yes."

"What else do you know about this mission?"

"I daresay Patha heard some disturbing news when he was among the cave people. He has a source that transmitted information giving us an entry location. We're close to that spot now, we are."

Tara forced herself to remember everything she had been told since the clan returned from the eastern mountain range. She needed to focus on their mission, not on the pain from her injuries. Staying focused seemed to subdue the pain. "I never had time to read Patha's briefing from the clan's visit with the cave people. But if the clan visited the eastern mountain range, why are we entering the northern mountain range?"

"While the clan spent time with the cave people living in the eastern mountain range, Patha received transmissions from another group in these mountains." Darius didn't look up from his landlink.

"Did he hear disturbing news?" Tara stared at the top of Darius' head.

"We believe they've invented a type of weapon, yes."

"What type of weapon?"

"We're not positive. So far, information is hearsay. We've heard it's some type of gas that can kill entire cities at once, it is." Darius met her gaze. "What we need to determine is why they would want to create such a weapon, if it does, in fact, exist."

Tara began reconfiguring her small handheld landlink. "What do you know about this entry location?"

"There's a hidden panel of sorts. We'll have to look for it, we will." He stood and moved toward her. "Tara," he said softly, and his hands touched her shoulders.

"We've got work to do." She shot him an icy glare, then looked away from his dark gray eyes quickly. They only made her think of her children…and that other child. Her hands began shaking as she reconfigured her landlink so she could search through the iron in the rock.

Darius stood over her; his closeness rattled her nerves. But dwelling on Darius only brought her pain, which fogged her thinking, and she wouldn't allow that. She couldn't allow that. The man would not break her heart again. So she said nothing about his close proximity and ran the scanning programs loaded on her landlink. If there was trouble among these cave people, she would do her best to determine the problem, then report back to Patha.

"It's hollow behind that rock over there," she said, breaking the weighted silence.

Darius moved the rather large rock himself. It must have been hollow, because it shifted with ease.

A long hallway, filled with shadows, appeared before them. It was wide enough that several people could walk side-by-side, and tall enough that even Darius didn't need to duck when he entered. Tara could smell the dirt around them when she entered, and touched the tunnel wall to confirm that packed dirt had been painted with some kind of sealant, more than likely to keep roots at bay.

Tara entered while Darius moved the rock, concealing the entry way once again, and leaving them in the dark. Using the beam he'd brought, Darius flashed light along the walls and floor while they walked.

Their footsteps echoed in the passageway as they walked in the damp darkness toward a light ahead. After several minutes, they reached the end of the tunnel and the light source.

Tara stood stunned at the sight before her.

They looked out into a cavern large enough to hold a city. In fact, it *was* a city. An underground city.

Roads lined with buildings several stories high, trees and bushes, all created the scene in front of them. Tara looked at the busy street, then beyond it, at the different-sized buildings with outside stairwells and many windows.

The size of the cavern impressed Tara even more than the thriving city within it. She couldn't see to the other end, but she could tell that buildings ran along several roads, at least.

The height of the cave overwhelmed her. Crystallized rock made up the roof of the community, and even buildings several stories tall did not come close to touching it.

Tall white lamps lit the streets and appeared to be the source of light. Although everything was illuminated, the light couldn't compete with sunlight. The community appeared to be in a permanent stage of twilight. Moss replaced grass and the trees were spongy, looking more like large mushrooms.

Then there were the people, so many of them that Tara and Darius weren't even noticed in the teeming throng. Tara observed that everyone walked as if late to an appointment. There were no greetings of familiarity as people passed each other. Instead, most focused on the ground and amazingly didn't run into each other. The town seemed to be set in high speed.

All of this Tara took in within a matter of minutes. She had entered enough new societies to look for the ways of the people so she could assimilate. Glancing at Darius, she noticed he observed the people around him as well. She wondered how he reacted to this new community, having never been out of Gothman. The man, as always, wore a neutral expression, until he looked down and noticed her watching him. His gray eyes warmed, and she looked back toward the crowd.

"Come on," he whispered into her ear. He guided her through the crowd so her injured arm was next to his body. "Over here."

They moved along a path of flat, rock-shaped clay, and Darius quickly matched the hurried pace of the townspeople, keeping a firm hold on Tara as he maneuvered them down the street. They crossed an intersection, and Tara noticed tables set along the edges of the path. People huddled around the tables, and bartering filled the air.

Darius slowed and Tara watched the activity in the market area. Men, women, and children walked from table to table, intent on their purchases. Owners of merchandise called out their specials, making the street a noisy, chaotic scene.

Darius escorted her to a table in the middle of the commotion. "I would like yellow silk, like the sun, can you do that?" He faced a man who stood behind a booth, which was piled high with folded material.

"It will cost you."

"I have gold."

The man looked at Darius and Tara for a minute, then almost whispered, "Come back at half break, and I'll show you the silk I have."

Darius nodded, and he and Tara returned to the crowded path. They walked slowly through the market place, looking at the different booths. While they recognized bags of rooted vegetables and fish from the surface, most of the food products were unfamiliar.

Clay bowls and pots painted with bright colors adorned one booth. Another had ready-made clothing for men, women, and children. All were dyed with bright colors and in a variety of fashions. Tara noticed that under the brown capes, all the cave people wore colorful clothing.

A loud siren sounded and Tara looked around quickly.

"Half break." Darius' breath was hot against her ear.

The man at the booth looked up when they returned and said, "I can show you that silk now."

He led the two along the street and entered one of the buildings. Inside, they climbed stairs to the third floor and walked silently down a dimly lit hallway.

After hiking up the mountain and now the stairs, Tara's injuries throbbed, threatening to consume her focus. She managed to keep pace with the others, not wanting to draw attention to her injuries and cause unwarranted questions from this man they followed.

He placed his palm against a flat disc on one of the doors. After a minute, it beeped and the door slid silently into the wall.

Tara studied the flat disc for a second as she walked past it, seeing only a round dark glass plate secured on the wall. Possibly, these people maintained security by using handprints to verify identity. That might make it hard to travel without one of the denizens, she reasoned. The thought of having to rely on someone else when a ready escape might be needed didn't sit well with her.

Tara followed the two men into the room, and realized it appeared to be more like personal housing. Simple, plain furniture was adorned by the bright colors of a blanket tossed over a couch along the wall. Pictures hung on one of the walls, and Tara recognized the man with them in several of the poses. The door slid silently behind the three of them, and Tara wondered if the man's hand offered the only means of opening it again. She suddenly felt trapped.

"Pee-coo?" a woman's voice spoke from an adjoining room of the small apartment.

"Pee-coo-mee, come here. We have company."

A young woman with pale skin and sandy hair came around the corner and stood before them. She was petite, almost frail, and wore a loose-fitting, bright pink dress that modestly displayed her attractive body.

"This is my mate, Pee-coo-mee. She handles all the books. I'm no good with numbers. I sell the material. Oh my, where are my manners? Let me take your robes and please join us for half break."

Darius pulled off his robe and handed it to Pee-coo. Tara followed his lead.

"Oh my," Pee-coo said again when Tara took off her cloak. He smiled, showing several black holes where teeth once had been, and his pasty skin turned pink around his cheeks and ears. He scratched sandy hair of identical texture as his wife's and cocked his head as he stared at Tara. Then after glancing at Darius, he turned and looked at his mate.

"What my mate means to say." Pee-coo-mee walked over and slid her arm through his, discreetly elbowing him. "We were expecting two men."

She smiled quickly at Tara. "You're most welcome. What we have studied of Gothman...I mean, we were under the impression that Gothman women, well, that they stayed home."

"I'm not Gothman." Tara returned the smile.

"Oh my." Pee-coo suddenly looked very nervous and wrapped his arm around Pee-coo-mee.

"Now I've forgotten my manners." Darius sounded so pleasant that Tara looked up at him quickly. He affected a gentle smile that she was sure she'd never seen before. "I am Soray, and this is Kara. She's a Runner."

"Are you mated?" Pee-coo asked politely.

Darius looked down at Tara affectionately but she avoided his glance. "Yes, we are." And he gallantly wrapped his arms around Tara's shoulders.

"Now this might work out nicer than we anticipated." Pee-coo smiled at Pee-coo-mee. "We always like working with mates. Everything is so much more thought through. Don't you agree?"

Darius smiled his agreement and one of his hands lowered and squeezed Tara's hip. She kept her face expressionless but let her gaze shoot him a look of warning.

"This is fine," Pee-coo-mee smiled. "Now please, come join us for half break."

They sat down at a small table in an adjoining room and were treated to a mushroom salad. Pee-coo and his mate dug into the salad eagerly and nodded for Darius and Tara to join them.

Tara had a lifetime of experiences at trying foods from different cultures. She took a large bite of the salad, and although she found it repulsive, she nodded that she liked it and continued to eat.

Darius, however, did not have this advantage.

He nibbled at several bites and had just managed to eat half the helping on his plate when Tara leaned forward and scooped a large amount of the salad out of the serving bowl and dumped it on his plate.

His look of dismay made her smile sweetly in retaliation.

"Now then…" Pee-coo leaned back in his chair and patted his belly. "Half break is almost over. I need to get back to my booth. Pee-coo-mee will show you where your apartment is, and we'll be able to discuss our arrangement at end day."

"Why don't you take Soray with you to the booth?" Pee-coo-mee nudged Pee-coo until he got out of his chair.

"Oh my, they do try and own you, don't they?" Pee-coo chuckled at his sexist joke.

Darius smiled that incredibly friendly smile again and stared at Tara. "They do at that, yes."

She saw right through the smile and let him know what she thought of his patronizing smile with a very private, vindictive gaze.

The two men walked out of the apartment, and Tara found herself staring at the foreign woman.

The walls closed in around her. All Tara could think of was the many walls past the ones in that room, and that they were underground. Her heart pounded quickly, while every slow, deep breath she took to stay calm made her acutely aware of her injuries. Once again, she felt trapped.

Chapter Six

Pee-coo-mee smiled without parting her lips as she slowly cleared the table.

Tara knew the routine. She'd spent several winters now in a society where women were servants. Obviously, the cave people were a lot like Gothman. Wouldn't Darius be happy with this piece of knowledge?

Less than a minute passed before Tara found her theory was wrong.

Pee-coo-mee stacked the dishes into a compartment built into the wall and pushed a button next to it. A door closed over the dishes and a humming noise began. Pee-coo-mee turned and stared at Tara. "In our society, your mate would take the name Kara and you would become Kara-mee." Pee-coo-mee gestured for Tara to follow her into a small room at the back of the apartment. She sat down at a shiny-surfaced stone desk and pulled a lever on the side of it. A flat monitor rose from the surface. "Unfortunately, men don't often think clearly. If my mate introduces your mate as Soray, then you'll have to be Soray-mee."

Tara nodded, somewhat confused, and watched Pee-coo-mee press several spots on the desk. The monitor flashed and a picture appeared. It was a picture of Tara.

Pee-coo-mee looked up at Tara with a triumphant smile, and Tara froze.

"I was very proud of myself when I successfully tapped into your transmissions. Of course, I didn't tell Pee-coo who the two of you were. He has his instructions and too much information can cause him to fumble with his work. Is your man that way?"

"I've never thought about it before," Tara mumbled, dumbfounded by what she was hearing.

"Well now, we are different, aren't we?" Pee-coo-mee pointed to a chair alongside the wall. "Pull that over here. Let's get down to business, shall we?"

Tara settled by her and studied the landlink built into the stone desk. It didn't seem practical to house the equipment within stone. But the landlink looked nice lodged into the highly polished rock. Cave people obviously enjoyed some amenities.

Tara examined the screen bearing the statistics on her. There were one or two minor mistakes. She wondered who compiled the information.

Pee-coo-mee pushed a few more buttons, and the screen changed. Now there was a bio on the history of a weapon called UGA9. "This is the weapon that has triggered your mate's interest. When we received word that your races had concerns about it, I compiled this information to share with you. The UGA9, underground gas annihilation, is something a faction on the west side has created. It is in the preliminary stages, but ideally it will emit gas from the ground that will wipe out humans in a predetermined range within a matter of hours. Fortunately, it has not been tested."

Tara was horrified. So it did exist. She wouldn't let this woman know she was in the dark as to their mission, and she hoped her silence wouldn't reveal her ignorance. Now all she needed to know was why. Why would the cave people want such a weapon? Were they plotting a war? And why was this couple willing to share this information with her? She kept her questions to herself and listened.

"Now then, we've a faction of our own here on the north side. We encouraged our mates to participate in the theft of this weapon as well as the contact of your people." Pee-coo-mee looked at Tara, then patted her leg with her fragile, pasty-white hand. "You can imagine how taken back I was when I saw you had come with your mate. As I said, I expected two men. We planned on sending this disc home with one of them so they could examine it and hopefully put it in your hands. Obviously, we are more comfortable talking with females. It's so hard to picture a nation where men are in charge."

Tara stifled a giggle. "The best nation, I think, is when men and women are equal."

"Equal? Really? Is that the way Runners are?" Pee-coo-mee ran her pale fingers through her hair, shaking her head slowly. "Oh my, that is very different. Well now, that is something to think about, but not right now, I'll think about that later. Right now, we must go see Tar-lo-mee. She's the leader of our faction and also has her mate working as governor of our fair city. Korth is one of the largest cities of the north side."

Pee-coo-mee got up from the landlink and hurried into the living area. She grabbed her cape and handed Tara's to her. She paused for a moment and studied Tara's face. When Tara realized the woman was staring, it dawned on her that her wounds must look quite alarming.

Tara put her hands to her face. "I fell while we were climbing the mountain," she said, thinking it sounded like a lie a woman would create to cover the fact that her husband had beaten her.

Pee-coo-mee's smile didn't reveal her thoughts. "Does it hurt? It looks like it does. I have some medicine we can put on it."

"I think I'm okay for now." Tara smiled politely, just as Darius had. "But thank you."

They left the apartment and departed from the building the same way they'd entered. The streets were still crowded and Tara couldn't help but wonder why there were so many people wandering around. They all seemed in a hurry to get where they were going. Pee-coo-mee included. Although Tara stood head and shoulders over the petite woman, she stayed alert in order not to lose her in the crowd of people. After a few minutes of pushing and shoving, Tara realized they were headed toward the table where Pee-coo and Darius were.

"And how is business today, my mate?" Pee-coo-mee walked around the table and looked at the transaction sheet.

Suddenly, a large explosion shook the ground. Several booths at the end of their row flew up toward the rocks. People screamed and began running in every direction. Tara dove for the ground and scrambled around the booth to get a protected view. She found Pee-coo on the ground next to her with his hands over his head.

"I knew we couldn't pull this off, I just knew it," he wailed.

"Everything will be okay." Pee-coo-mee rubbed his back. "Let me think."

"We can't stay here." Darius moved in over Tara with his laser pulled.

"Do you know who's firing?" Tara asked Pee-coo-mee.

"Not yet, but I'll find out." Pee-coo-mee peeked above the table at the mass confusion on the street. "Come on, let's go."

They took off running down the street, the opposite direction from which they'd come. Another explosion blasted behind them, and the crowd ran faster. Tara looked around her and realized she'd lost Pee-coo and Pee-coo-mee. She slowed and dodged into a door well to see if she could figure out who was attacking and why.

People everywhere were shouting at each other, climbing the outer stairs of the buildings, slamming doors behind them. She was still trying to determine the source of the explosions, when another blast went off right in front of her.

It hit one man, sending body parts flying everywhere. Blood splattered Tara. Several other people were thrown brutally from the force. Screams filled the air and the few remaining people in the area ran for cover in a panic. The vibrations from the detonation caused rocks to fall from nearby walls, and dust filled the air.

In the confusion, Tara moved out of the door well and dove behind several barrels by the road. From one of the buildings across the street, someone opened fire, shooting at something down the street. Several more locations opened fire, then the whistle of a small bomb flew past her and exploded at the end of the street by the market. Tara realized a civil war of some kind was possibly underway.

Pee-coo-mee had given no indication that there was unrest among her people. Or had she? She'd made reference to a faction developing among her people in response to an already existing faction from the west side.

"Tara!" Darius crawled alongside her, then ducked as another explosion went off directly in front of them. "Let's get out of here."

"I'm open for suggestions." She coughed from the rising dust and debris.

"Come on, this way." He grabbed her uninjured arm and quickly led her in the direction of the tunnel where they had entered this underground community.

The street was far less occupied at this point. Looters had descended on the deserted market place. Crashing and banging could be heard as they ravished the forgotten merchandise. Something was burning nearby and the tainted smell in the air made it hard to breathe.

Tara kept her face down and focused on the ground as she allowed Darius to guide her. Suddenly she came to a dead halt causing Darius to lose his grip on her hand. He turned quickly to look at her.

"Look." She pointed to the ground. Someone had drawn a circle with a tear shape drawn in the middle. The symbol of the Blood Circle Clan.

Tara looked up, first at Darius' face, then at the buildings surrounding them. There was no one in sight. She absently fingered the necklace Darius had given her a long time ago, knowing it matched the symbol on the ground. The circle was drawn outside a closed door. Tara took her foot and quickly wiped the evidence away.

"Come on," she said, reaching for the handle.

The heavy stone door opened slowly into a dark room. Once inside, the two closed the door. Tara reached inside her cloak and fumbled through the pockets of her clothing until she found the small beam she'd brought with her from the trailer. Pulling it out, she flipped the switch and a dull bluish light illuminated the room.

In the corner, surrounded by many candles, stood the dog-woman.

* * * * *

Darius had seen her in dreams after Tara had disappeared in the southern continent. The dreams had stopped after he'd raped Tasha. He'd never seen her in person and was stunned. The old woman looked up and smiled, but her eyes didn't appear to see them.

She seemed smaller and more fragile than in his dreams. He had seen her as a vibrant old woman, with a calm demeanor that soothed him when he had experienced her presence. But now, as he faced her for the first time, Darius felt nothing calming about this person. She appeared disconnected with them somehow, and he admitted a small amount of disappointment that she wasn't the spirit of peace and reassurance that his dreams had conjured.

"Come children, beg forgiveness from Crator." She opened her arms to them and bowed her head.

"Beg forgiveness for what?" Darius stood tall and his voice sounded cool.

"For your greed, child." The old woman didn't look up.

Tara stepped closer to the old woman. Something was odd. The candles surrounding her didn't appear to let off any light. "Why were we greedy?" She watched the old woman warily.

"Child, you have come here to steal a weapon. Crator knows that."

Tara studied the old woman. Her head was lowered and she appeared to be looking down at something. Tara saw nothing but the ground. The old woman wore the same clothes she had on the day she died. Her hands appeared to be doing something but there was nothing in them.

"No one is here to steal a weapon," Darius barked. "Gothman doesn't need a coward's weapon!"

The old woman didn't speak. In fact, she didn't move. Tara looked closely at her, then placed her hand on Darius' arm, instinctively trying to make him read her thoughts. Something was wrong here. The old woman still hadn't moved.

"Come, kneel and tell Crator your sins." The dog-woman spoke without focusing on either of them, but kept her gaze on some unknown object on the ground.

"What have we done wrong?" Tara asked.

"You know what you've done wrong," the old woman said.

Tara realized the woman's mouth hadn't moved. She knelt and Darius stood firmly behind her. Surreptitiously, she picked up some small pebbles and tossed them at the dog-woman. The pebbles brushed against the dog-woman, and sparks appeared as the small rocks disappeared into nothingness.

Tara jumped back quickly and pulled her laser.

"Why did you do that?" The dog-woman lifted her head and looked at Tara with her unseeing eyes. Her mouth moved this time, but it didn't match the words that came out. "Crator didn't like that."

"Crator knows why we're really here." Tara pointed the laser at the dog-woman.

"You need to come tell Crator why you're here. He wants to hear you confess."

"Crator has nothing to do with this," Tara said and shot the dog-woman. The laser hit her in the chest. She didn't move. The laser went through her, filling the room with sparks, and hit the wall behind her. The old woman remained positioned as she had before.

Tara backed up; her beam now attached to the top of her laser. She scanned the entire room with the laser. Darius pulled his weapon as well.

"That's not the dog-woman," she whispered to him. "Something is very wrong here."

At that moment, light flooded the room. The dog-woman and all her candles disappeared. Another door banged open.

Tara and Darius didn't hesitate. Firing their lasers simultaneously, they blanketed the entrance with fire. Anyone on the other side would not be able to see them until they stepped into the line of fire.

Darius set his laser to automatic fire and pulled an Eliminator from underneath his robe.

Tara was shocked that he'd brought it. At this particular moment, however, she was also elated. He manipulated the Eliminator until he held it comfortably in one hand. Tara reached over to take his laser from him, which he willingly gave up. She covered him, holding both lasers at the door, firing at will.

Darius leapt to the center of the floor, landing on his belly. He aimed the Eliminator straight into the open doorway and fired.

A huge explosion followed. Screams and echoed cries filled the small room. Tara moved over Darius, to cover him if necessary. The two of them looked down a long hallway as the ball of fire from the Eliminator rolled toward an unknown destination. They strained to see through the falling rock, raised dust, and smoke, but couldn't determine how many people were in the passage, though they realized many bodies were falling, appearing as shadows through the thick haze of smoke. Some fell into the room.

An entire army had been sent to capture them, using the guise of the dog-woman as a trap.

"Let's go!" Darius grabbed Tara and bolted toward the door leading to the street.

Their chances for escape were minimal. Both of them knew that. They ran down the street, this time in the direction of the entrance into the large cavern, with the city of Korth on fire around them.

One glance over their shoulders told them a large number of soldiers chased them. More soldiers appeared in front, forcing them to a stop.

They were surrounded.

Men and women in dark brown uniforms, stood attentive with long black pistols pointed at the two foreigners.

"I shouldn't be so surprised by this demonstration of your abilities," a tall robed man spoke as he moved through the soldiers to stand within ten feet of Darius and Tara. "Your reputations precede you."

An equally tall woman came up from behind the man. Her pale skin looked like death as the hood of her cape hung around her face. She walked into the circle of guards and stood before Darius and Tara.

"I'll admit it's an honor to have captured you. For a second, it appeared we wouldn't be able to do it." The woman smiled a toothy smile as if she had just pleasantly introduced herself. "Get them out of here," she said, still smiling.

Chapter Seven

A half-dozen guards surrounded Darius and Tara and took their weapons, before forcing them back the way they'd come.

Tara looked around as their small procession marched down the street. Piles of rubble stood where buildings once had been. The air smelled of burnt rubber, possibly electrical fires, and smoke from the explosions. The stench clogged her senses.

Tara studied the piles of rock and small fires that so recently had been a functioning city. The citizens of Korth seemed to have disappeared, or at least watched in hiding. The streets were barren except for the horde of soldiers escorting their captives.

A hallway similar to the one Tara and Darius had left in rubble appeared at the end of the street. Tara wondered how many of these lit hallways disappeared into the rocks. Two guards led them into it while the remaining troops marched behind them. Tara could only assume the man and woman in charge brought up the rear.

Her sore arm had been nudged repeatedly by the guard's pistols. Her ribs had been poked one too many times as well. The pain made her irritable, and she began resenting her captors for the way they treated her. Whoever these people were, they treated her like a criminal, and although she and Darius had arrived here incognito, they had committed no crime she knew of.

Finally, the end of the hallway appeared. Two immense white doors opened. They walked into a large room, also white from the tile on the floor to the smooth stone walls. The ceiling soared at least twelve feet above them and consisted of white panels, hiding the fact they were in a cave.

Attached to the ceiling panels, large yellow bulbs filled the room with bright, artificial sunlight. Tara could feel their warmth.

Each of the four walls had a white-framed door in its middle. The double doors swung closed behind them, and she stared at the three closed doors in front of them.

Several guards searched Tara and Darius one more time for any hidden weapons, and Tara felt a wave of relief when the laser inserted in her right boot was overlooked. To be held captive without knowing her charges, or who her captors were was one thing, but to be rendered unarmed would have been more than Tara could have handled at the moment. Her body ached, she felt like a common criminal, and she needed what little security her one hidden weapon provided her.

Tara watched as a door opened. The four guards forced them through the doorway and down a long flight of stairs to another large room, similar to the one they'd left. Tara began to feel disoriented as they traveled through this mazelike underground structure. Even though her body distracted her with aches and pains, she struggled to focus on every turn and hallway; so, hopefully, they could get out of there, if escape became an option.

"In there," one of the guards mumbled, and pointed as a door to their right slid open.

Darius led the way, with Tara behind him. She turned when the door slid closed behind her and realized the guards had not followed. The two of them were alone in the room.

"Now where are we?" Darius grumbled as he turned in front of Tara and glanced at their surroundings.

It was a small room. Dark green carpet stretched from wall to wall; flowery paper spanned from ceiling to floor. Large pictures hung on the walls.

Each picture was a skyline view of strange cities. Names underneath each picture identified them. Chicago, San Francisco, Tokyo, Sydney, and Buenos Aires.

Tara wondered where these cities were. The pictures appeared very old, and the blue of the sky in each shot was all wrong.

"Well, here you are." The tall woman who had instigated their capture on the street entered the room from a metal door on the other side. "Let's go in here where we'll be more comfortable."

She led them into a large office. A man sat behind a desk at the end of the room violently typing away at a computer. He focused on his work, and Tara couldn't see his face.

"Please, sit down." He waved his hand toward several leather chairs facing the desk, not bothering to look away from his monitor. "I'll be with you in just a second."

"Where are we?" Darius asked without sitting. "And why have you brought us here?"

"Who else would we bring here?" The woman smiled as she plopped into one of the chairs. She seemed more attractive without her long robe and hood. A gray pantsuit fit nicely over her thin frame. Her eyes were as pale as her skin however, which made her gaze appear haunted.

The man's features were similar. His hair was white with blond streaks running through it, offering little highlights to a complexion otherwise void of color. But when he looked up from his work, his eyes compelled Tara, drawing her to stare into them. They were the lightest blue she had ever seen. Almost clear, as if she could look straight through to his thoughts.

"I apologize for having you wait." The man's clear eyes probed Tara. He glanced at Darius, then looked quickly down at his hands. "As to where you are," he waved his thin arm across the room, "we call this place New Luna."

"You are the colonists from the moon?" Tara asked.

The man looked impressed and gave the woman a triumphant smile. "You're right."

"Why are you here?" Darius asked.

"This is our home," the woman answered, appearing to be surprised by the question.

The man silenced her with a look, then focused on Darius and Tara. "Let's begin again." He smiled, got up and walked over to a shelf in the wall. He lifted an ornate glass bottle filled with blue liquid from the shelf, and set it on his desk. He then grabbed four small glasses and turned to face Tara and Darius. "I am Brev, and this is my wife, Polva. I am an advisor for Luna. We've been sent here to meet you."

"You've a strange way of meeting people." Tara didn't look away when Brev met her gaze and appeared to study her for a minute.

His expression didn't waver, but when he turned his attention to the glasses, Tara noticed his hands shake. She watched him steal a quick glance toward his wife, then focus on pouring the drinks. A nervous tension seemed to fill the room as Polva watched her husband prepare the drinks.

Darius' hands rested gently on Tara's shoulders. His fingers tightened ever so slightly. He'd noticed it too. Brev and Polva were afraid of them.

"I apologize for any inconvenience." The look of authority had returned to his face. He passed out the small glasses of blue liquid. "It was necessary in order to meet with you. Everyone will suspect the cave people captured you."

Darius flinched at the word *captured*. "Why do you want to meet with us?"

"We know through your marriage…oh, you call it a claim…you two rule the largest group of people on this planet. It made sense to contact you first." Brev ran his hand through his hair, then shot a glance at Polva.

Darius' hands tightened again on Tara's shoulders. Just slightly, enough for Tara to know he was getting ready to do something.

"Now that you have your captives," Darius stated, "what do you plan to do?"

Brev flinched at the growl in Darius' tone. "Sir, you're not our captives."

"Good," Darius said quickly, not allowing Brev to continue. "My claim is injured, she is. Return our weapons to us. You may contact us in Gothman, yes." He indicated with his hands that Tara should stand, and she did.

Brev also stood, quickly. He reached his hands out, and they were shaking. "Please, we would be honored if you would stay with us, just tonight, as our guests. We will personally escort you to your trailer tomorrow."

"The escort will not be necessary, no." Darius' tone was low and quiet, the authoritative voice he used to command. "We'll stay, but only tonight. You'll return our weapons and allow us to contact our people, in order to prevent an attack."

Brev scooted around the desk, past both of them, and hurried toward the door. His wife looked as if she would follow, but kept her chair. He opened the door where two guards were positioned outside. "Please escort our guests to the south wing."

Tara and Darius were led to a large, comfortable room. No sooner were they alone than a light began to beep on a desk in the middle of the room. The light was on a small square black box with a receiver on it. Tara picked up the receiver and the light disappeared. She brought it up to her face as she sank into a chair.

"Hello?" A voice spoke from the small oval-shaped device in her hand.

"Yes," she responded.

The voice explained to her how to turn on the landlink, then walked her through setting up a transmission with a Gothman link. "I can't believe they did it," Tara muttered under her breath.

"Of course they did it." Darius grinned. "Move over, I'll do this, I will."

Tara hardened. "I'm not yours to command."

Darius spun her around in the chair, reached under her arms, and lifted her up, squeezing her sore ribs. She flinched but maintained composure. Her eyes met his and he stared at her intently.

His mouth was inches from hers as he whispered, "Maybe not, but you are mine." He brushed his lips against hers and lifted her higher. She closed her eyes as pain racked her body. He walked over to the incredibly large bed and tossed her down on it. She bounced against the softness and instantly he was on top of her. Again he whispered, "You know as well as I do that they are scared of us. They aren't telling us everything. And they view us as a superior power because we're together, they do."

"Which shows how much they really know about us." Tara mocked him. "I wonder if they know how many other women you are *together* with."

"You put any personal vendetta you have against me out of your head right now. These people have a reason for contacting us, and we're going to find out what it is, we are. Don't let yourself be distracted." Darius then softened his whisper and added, "You know they're watching and listening to everything we say and do, they are." He took his hand that had been resting on her neck and moved it slowly down her body. "We have to be convincing. If they feel our unity is in danger, they may not have an interest in us, no. At this point, we don't know if that would jeopardize us or not." As he spoke, he ran his hands gently over her breasts and down to her crotch, where he stopped and squeezed.

"You're hurting me. Get up." She ignored his hand.

Darius rolled onto his side and propped himself on his elbow. Tara exerted a lot of effort trying to sit up. He finally placed his hand gently on her back and helped her sit. She returned to the landlink.

* * * * *

Darius lay back on the bed, exasperated, then slowly got up and moved toward her. His thoughts leaned toward wrapping his hands around her thin neck and teaching her some respect in a discreet manner. His thoughts stopped however, as he focused on the landlink's screen.

She'd managed to link with a Runner transmission and quickly flipped from screen to screen, moving so fast anyone monitoring would have a hard time figuring out how she got to where she was. When the screen stopped flashing, a program began immediately.

First they saw a maze of hallways.

"We went down this way." He pointed to the screen. "And through those doors."

"To here." She pointed the clicker to give them information on their specific location.

A floor plan appeared on the screen and Darius quickly identified it as the room they were in. Several red spots blinked within the schematics of the room. They'd found the screen providing locations for microphones in their room. There was one above the entrance to the room, one above the table they both hovered over, and one in an adjoining bathroom.

Tara deleted the program, hopefully preventing anyone from copying it by sending a bug through the save portion of the menu. She then pulled her small laser from her shoe and shot above the door. She stood up and both of them backed up as she shot at the ceiling above the landlink.

* * * * *

Darius bent over and pulled up his pant leg, then slid a small laser out from his boot. Without speaking, he moved into the bathroom.

Tara saw white chips fall from the ceiling as he shot the laser. She quickly ran a variation of the program and verified the room they were in was now secure.

"Well done, my lady," Darius said, as he returned from the bathroom. He ran his hand through her hair, then cupped her chin with his hand. "We need a layout of this place, we do. Go back to that screen."

"We don't have to convince anybody now. Keep your hands off of me."

He grabbed the back of her hair and pulled tightly, forcing her head back. His expression turned hard with scorn. Then just as quickly as he'd acted, he loosened his grip on her hair and his face softened. He let out a slow sigh and stared into her eyes.

"Keep yourself focused on this mission," he said the words almost as if he were commanding his own thoughts as well as hers. "We need a layout and we don't have much time, I'm thinking. I don't imagine they're going to tolerate our disabling their room, my lady. They'll be here soon if they've got any warrior blood in them, yes." He let go of her and moved to the door, listening.

Tara backed out of the Runner transmission without making contact with her people. Now she was in uncharted territory. She couldn't move as fast. The Lunian landlink system ran differently than anything she'd ever seen before. She accessed their files easily enough, but the names on the files appeared to be coded, and she started playing guessing games.

She jumped when the light on the receiver began blinking and beeping again. Tara reached for it, but Darius grabbed it before she could. "If you wish to speak to us, you will do so in person," he said into the receiver before returning it to the cradle. "I don't know how much time that bought you, Tara, but move quickly, yes."

It didn't buy her enough time. Within seconds, the door slid open and Brev appeared with several guards. Darius stood at the entrance and held the laser tight in his hand but pointed at the floor. Brev glanced at the small burn hole in the ceiling above the landlink.

"As promised, here are your weapons." Brev's face looked strained.

Tara guessed he followed orders under protest.

Brev stood unmoving, with his hands clasped behind his back, and watched the guards turn over the confiscated weapons. His lips were pinched in a flat line, and his light-colored eyes followed the movement as his guards handed over lasers and the Eliminator to Darius.

The man did not look pleased. "I've also arranged for some food for you," Brev added as he continued to stand at the entrance of the room.

One of the guards placed a tray on the edge of the bed. The only other table in the room had the landlink on it, and Tara was still sitting there.

"After you eat, we would like to have you join us in our conference room. Would you be willing to do that?"

There was a note of sarcasm in Brev's voice — an implication that they might be too busy destroying the room to attend a meeting. At least, that was what Tara guessed were his thoughts.

"We'll be there, yes." Darius either ignored the sarcasm or didn't notice it. He bowed his head slightly in acknowledgment of the invitation.

Brev opened his mouth as if to speak, but then closed it. He looked from Darius to Tara, smiled slightly and bowed his head. "Good. I'll send an escort for you in an hour." He backed out of the room, along with his guards, and was gone.

A guard arrived at their room exactly one hour later. He led them down the long hallway, turned left to follow an adjacent hallway, then through two sliding doors into a large room.

"Welcome," Polva greeted them as they walked in the door. "Please, join us at the table. My husband will be here shortly."

Tara accepted a chair across the table from Polva and studied the woman, who chewed the corner of her finger and cast wide, pale eyes on Darius. Tara thought she saw a mixture of fear and curiosity in this foreign woman's expression, and watched as Polva shifted in her seat and glanced at the door. Polva might know her husband's work since she was here on this mission with Brev, and had been involved in Tara and Darius' capture. She also looked as jumpy as a rabbit, which might make her not think as clearly, and slip information that Brev felt Tara and Darius shouldn't know. *This might be the best time to probe for some answers.*

"How long have you been on Nuworld?" Tara began.

Polva jumped at the sound of the words. "I'm sorry?"

"Did you just arrive here?"

"Uh, yes, but we're from here. Earth is our home." Polva emphasized the word earth.

"Earth is dead," Darius said. "Your home no longer exists. This planet is called Nuworld now."

Polva stiffened and opened her mouth to respond, then seemed to stop herself and remained silent. Tara wondered what it was Polva felt reluctant to say.

"That is exactly why we have sought you out," Brev said as he entered the room.

All three turned to look at him. Tara caught his face in time to see a cold stare directed to his wife. It faded quickly and he smiled politely at Tara and Darius.

It dawned on Tara that she judged a warrior's ability, sight unseen, by the appearance of his or her body. This man was pale with little muscle tone. Therefore, her initial impression had been that he was no threat. But as Brev stood there before them, she felt a wave of caution pass through her that she couldn't identify.

While Brev couldn't harm them in physical combat, a threat of some sort definitely existed.

Chapter Eight

Brev took his place at the head of the table and picked up a flat control device. He pushed several buttons and a white, opaque screen lowered from the ceiling at the end of the room. "It is my great honor to moderate this meeting," Brev began, looking at no one. "In one moment we will be joined by Mr. Toulon, our President and a great leader."

Bright lights flashed from the white screen and all heads turned toward it. Colors began to appear. The image of a man from the chest up came into focus.

"Communication may begin," a voice from an unknown source said.

"Greetings, Tara of the Blood Circle Clan and Lord Darius of Gothman. It is a pleasure to be meeting with you at last. I am Dav Toulon, President of New America." The man speaking to them sat behind a large dark, square desk. His hands were folded confidently on top of it. A small smile didn't fade as he spoke.

Tara studied the man. He was balding and somewhat heavyset. His skin showed the paleness of his people and his eyes were the familiar washed-out blue. He spoke his words as if he'd memorized them. The reception on the screen went out of focus for a minute then fine-tuned once again as he continued.

"We are the people of Earth. We're descendants of a colony that settled here hundreds of years ago as space travel with NASA progressed. When Earth became uninhabitable, our forefathers believed they were stranded. Several generations ago, we discovered humans had not become extinct on our planet, but instead had migrated underground. We began to watch the planet as life slowly returned to the surface. We now feel our return to Earth is possible and have decided to make contact with you prior to doing so."

He paused at this point and Tara assumed he was waiting for a comment of some kind from either one of them. She didn't look at Darius or anyone else in the room but instead watched the man's face. Something about his small smile made Tara uneasy. His speech seemed too well-rehearsed. His voice inflection never changed from the pleasant tone of a friend. But his body remained rigid, not relaxed, and his hands, with fingers interlocked, never moved a muscle or twitched. Tara watched the man as he stared blankly, not giving any indication that he was excited about the possibility of moving his people to a new home.

"What do you want from us?" Darius finally asked.

"At this point, I don't believe we need anything from you. Our transit should be an uneventful, peaceful movement. I don't predict any problems. We've planned this thoroughly." Mr. Toulon sounded like he was discussing a family picnic in the country.

Tara started to ask where they planned to live on Nuworld, but a loud explosion in the hallway caused all parties to jump to their feet. The screen went blank.

Brev quickly picked up one of the transmitters and shouted instructions to whoever was on the other end. Another explosion sounded, this one more muffled, as if not as close.

"We've got to get out of here." Polva ran to Brev's side and grabbed his arm.

Darius moved to the door, his laser drawn.

"Move away from the door," Brev stopped talking on his transmitter and pointed a long black gun toward Darius.

Darius didn't change his position but moved his gaze toward Brev.

Tara pulled her laser and pointed it at Brev. "I suggest you put that thing away."

Brev turned to look at Tara, and his gun moved with his gaze, so that it now pointed at Tara. She watched the weapon shake in his grip, allowing her to see how nervous he was.

Darius stepped in behind Brev when the man turned to face Tara and slipped Brev's weapon from his hand with little effort.

"I just didn't want you to get hurt," Brev spoke quietly, his pale eyes jumping nervously from Darius to Tara.

Another booming sound came from far behind the walls. This sound however, was different from the others. It started out quiet and muffled, but grew louder and louder as it appeared to move through the walls, coming closer. Tara turned to the wall, alarmed, her body braced, desperately trying to figure out how to fight…a sound.

* * * * *

Darius also focused on the direction of the explosive-like noise. He grabbed Tara's arm and pulled her across the room so quickly her feet almost left the ground. "We've got to get out of here!"

He pushed the button on the side of the door, as he'd seen the others do. The door slid to the side and he yanked Tara out of the room, almost throwing her up against the wall in the hallway.

He looked up and down the hallway with all instincts in high gear. No weapon known to Gothman could travel through walls. But it was safe to guess, as it passed by them, it would take out the ceiling and the walls, suffocating them underground as they were buried alive. The only thing they could do was to run as far from the sound as they could. He wrapped one arm around Tara's waist and flew down the hallway on long, muscular legs, literally carrying Tara at his side.

The hallway wall behind them blew out and rock flew everywhere. He dove to the ground, pulling Tara underneath him. Debris stung his back as they ducked from the explosion. Electronic crackling and popping noises sounded above them.

Tara lay flat on the ground, breathing heavily, and he imagined feeling the pain of her preexisting injuries. He left her lying there and stood, brushing debris from his clothes. Tara moved at his feet, but he didn't turn to assist her. Instead, he scanned the area that a second ago had been a hallway behind them. "I hope that wasn't the only way out of here."

Coughing from the other side of the rubble silenced him. Tara moved behind him and also stood silently looking at the pile.

"This is all your fault," a muffled voice spoke from beyond the rubble. "If you'd been content with the cave people, we wouldn't have this problem."

"You don't know that." The voice was Polva's. "You have no idea who is attacking."

"We shouldn't have attacked the cave people's town to get them," replied Brev. "After feeding them with all those false rumors about an eastern faction. These people are stupid. They were like a time bomb waiting to go off."

"Which is why I didn't want them," Polva's voice rose in pitch. "Now how are we going to get out of here and find those two?"

"I've radioed for help. Don't worry. If they've been killed, I'll get you two more."

"I don't want two more. I want them. Someone else can have two more. You promised me a child. They are the best there is among these primitive beasts. I want my child, then I want my home," Polva whined worse than a spoiled child.

Tara looked horrified when Darius glanced her way. She didn't return his gaze but instead stared at the pile of rubble, her eyes wide open, not blinking.

"Come on." Darius moved away from the debris.

Flat panels providing light flickered on and off as Tara and Darius moved in the only direction they could go. Once the walls had been a sterilized white. Now, they appeared light brown as dirt and small rocks appeared here and there from cracks in the seams of the walls. They stopped at each intersection and quickly decided which way to continue. There had to be a way back to the large cave that had once been the city of Korth.

They hit their third intersection and began hearing voices. Shouts. Yelling and confusion. A lot of people were somewhere very close.

"Where are they?" Tara asked.

"This way." Darius pointed to the hallway on their left.

Parts of the white walls were completely gone. Packed dirt and roots from plants looked like guts hanging out of a wounded animal. They stepped over rocks and paneling.

"Wouldn't roots indicate we're close to the surface?" Tara wondered out loud as they moved cautiously down the hallway. The lights flickered then went out, forcing them to use the light behind them to see what lay ahead. The hallway ended within a few more feet and double doors stood in front of them.

"I can see between the doors," Darius whispered, as he put his face to the wood.

* * * * *

Tara pushed herself around him and looked through the crack at a large, cave-like room. Torches and small fires scattered throughout the space. Shadows dancing along the rough walls made it difficult to determine how many people were actually in there. Voices behind them caused them to turn away from the doors and look back in the direction they had just been.

"We're trapped." Tara hated that sensation more than anything.

"Wait." He pushed her up against the half-smooth, half-rough wall. "They won't be able to see us. We didn't see the doors until we were on top of them. We're in the dark back here."

"So who exactly did you contact?" It was a female voice.

"Well, I spoke to two of them when you had me handling the communication. They'd heard rumors. We'd heard rumors. You said they could help us." It was Pee-coo. The other voice must be Pee-coo-mee.

"I know, I know. But you shouldn't have called them. Now we really have problems."

"I didn't know what else to do. They were gone and I was scared."

The two were walking toward Darius and Tara. Darius walked out into the center of the hallway.

Pee-coo-mee stopped suddenly and grabbed Pee-coo. She pulled her gun and pointed it straight at Darius.

"Who are you?" she asked, squinting to identify the tall figure.

"Who did you contact?" Darius stepped into the light, blocking Tara, who stood behind him.

Pee-coo gasped and Pee-coo-mee's mouth fell. She still held the gun toward him. "I, uh, well I, um, contacted the Runner," Pee-coo stammered. "Patha."

"Oh, great." Tara leaned back against the wall.

"I need your landlink so that I can contact him," Darius ordered. "How long ago did you talk to him?"

"Right after we lost…" Pee-coo hesitated and looked at Pee-coo-mee. "I mean after we couldn't find you."

"We need a landlink," Tara said to Pee-coo-mee.

"Of course." Pee-coo-mee lowered her gun and moved past Darius and Tara. "Follow me. Keep your hoods low and don't talk to anyone."

She reached for the doors that led into the large underground area. "I sure am glad to see you, by the way." She smiled at Tara, then pushed open the doors slowly.

The noise of the room, if that's what the large cave-like structure could be called, engulfed them. People were everywhere. Some were sitting around small fires. Others stood, huddled into groups, talking in animated voices. A few hurried along in various directions with hands full of blankets or other supplies. No one paid any attention to them, and the four worked their way through the people, avoiding piles of clothing heaped here and there, or a mama with several children cuddled up on her.

"I've made a spot for us over here." Pee-coo-mee pointed to an area along the wall at the far end of the room. She'd taken several of the cloths that Pee-coo sold at his booth and draped them over sticks to make two walls. They walked to the other side of them and found a small semi-secluded spot with a couple of blankets on the ground. Pee-coo-mee reached underneath her cloak and handed a flat computer panel to Tara before sitting.

Tara held the landlink with her good hand, but when she tried to twist her body and adjust her long cape with her other hand, she stopped quickly as pain racked her body.

Darius grabbed the landlink and held her cape out so she could sit.

"I don't know how long we're safe here. The eastern faction could attack again at any time," Pee-coo-mee said as she observed Darius' chivalrous actions.

"It's not the eastern faction," he said, sitting on the other side of Tara. Darius handed her the landlink.

"What?" Pee-coo-mee looked from Darius to Tara.

"Members of a colony from the moon are here." Tara studied the landlink. "Did you know that?"

"From where?" Pee-coo-mee looked startled.

"The moon," Darius continued. "They've fed you false information about an eastern faction and the UGA-9 bomb."

"Can you prove this?" Pee-coo-mee wrinkled her brow. "I've intercepted the eastern faction's transmissions myself."

Tara was busy typing on the computer. "Patha's quite relieved we're okay."

"Has he sent troops?"

"Scouts." Tara stared at the small monitor on the flat disc. "He says they'll meet us at the rendezvous point." She looked up at Darius who was studying the screen. "Where's that?"

"Tell him we'll be there soon."

Tara met his eyes for a moment then typed the response.

Pee-coo-mee made a slight guttural sound in her throat. Tara realized this man, who was so in control of the situation, bothered Pee-coo-mee. And he *was* in control. He and Patha had a plan, and she hadn't known anything about it. She looked at him again and his glance lowered to her body.

"How do you feel?"

"I'm okay."

"Right."

"Pee-coo-mee?" A woman called from the other side of the makeshift walls. "Are you back here?"

Pee-coo-mee was on her feet in an instant with Pee-coo at her side, moving toward the owner of the calling voice.

"Darius, we need to get out of here." Tara leaned to watch Pee-coo-mee and Pee-coo talking to an older lady and her mate. "Those moon people, or whatever they call themselves, want our children. I was scared to tell Patha that. I don't know how secure the cave people's transmission is."

"Not very, I'm sure," he grumbled. "I don't think they want our children that we already have, I don't. I think they want us to make a child for them."

Tara looked up at him quickly. "Somehow we need to get word to Patha. I want all the information on these people we can find—their weaknesses, their strengths, and most of all, where they plan on living."

He took the flat landlink out of Tara's lap and poked at the keys with his thick fingers, then stared at it for a moment. He typed some more, then set it down. "Come on, we're leaving now, we are." He stood and reached to help up Tara.

Pee-coo-mee turned and approached them. "Have you made a plan?" she asked Tara.

"We've seen enough." Darius seemed somewhat annoyed at Pee-coo-mee's inability to acknowledge his authority. "Time for us to leave."

"Please." Pee-coo-mee looked at Darius this time. Under her hood, her pale face showed sincerity as she spoke, "I'm sorry I doubted your knowledge of the people who are attacking us. It was an initial shock."

She stopped for a minute as if she expected Darius to say something. As if she expected him to act the way a man should according to her culture — asking guidance and offering any information he might have on the issue at hand.

Darius did none of these things. He stared at her. His face was stone, completely unreadable.

Pee-coo-mee stared back. "Well then." She sighed. "Allow us to show you a quick way to the surface."

"Good." Darius' voice sounded a little deeper than normal.

Tara was sure he was flaunting his masculinity. Then to make matters worse, he guided Tara through the cave as if she were a delicate flower. Tara wanted Pee-coo-mee to see that men could be intelligent and capable just like women, but Darius' gallant dominance wasn't helping a bit. She shot him a dirty look in an attempt to get him to behave, but to no avail.

Minutes later, they reached the surface. Only moonlight lit their way, and Pee-coo-mee and Pee-coo were willing to accompany them as far as their trailer.

"I fear a very disturbing war is about to begin," Pee-coo-mee spoke after they'd walked some distance along the side of the mountain. "We have new information about those who attacked us. A handful of our people were taken hostage in a cavern we don't use often. I guess that's where these moon people had set up camp. It's amazing we didn't notice them sooner, really it is."

"You weren't looking for them," Tara offered.

"What's your new information?" Darius seemed to tire quickly of the trivial chitchat.

"I'm getting ready to tell you." Pee-coo-mee snapped, and a scowl could be seen beneath the shadows on her face from under the hood. "Well now, the hostages we retrieved don't remember a lot about their captivity. They were all found strapped in beds and hooked up to machines. Our doctors have turned in their reports about them."

"What did the reports show?" Tara felt impending doom consume her.

"Nothing at first. So our governor asked our doctors to do a more thorough examination. That's the report we just got back. It appears that each female hostage was impregnated. Some of the women had the pregnancy aborted, and some of the women we recovered are still pregnant. They used the male hostages to impregnate the female hostages." Pee-coo-mee wrinkled her nose. "Can you believe such a thing?"

Darius led the small procession through the trees and now raised his hand indicating they should stop. He put his finger to his lips, then pointed through the trees ahead of them. A handful of dark figures wearing long flowing capes moved around the trailer. They'd successfully pulled it out of the cave where Darius had parked it. Several more figures emerged from the cave pushing Darius and Tara's bikes.

"How many do you count?" Darius whispered.

"Ten or eleven." Tara scanned the area wondering what transportation these people had used to get here or if they, too, had walked. "We can't use the Eliminator, it would take out our bikes and the trailer as well."

"We can't let them take our only means of transportation out of here."

"Agreed." She pointed to bushes alongside the men. "I'll work my way over there. Then we open fire on them. All we need to do is get our bikes."

Darius looked ready to disagree. He turned Tara's face toward him, grabbing firmly onto her chin.

Tara knew he could see the determination in her expression. And there was no time to lose by arguing.

"Be careful now," he growled and then, before she had the chance to pull away, he lowered his face to hers and gently kissed her on the lips.

Tara blinked as the heat from his fingers scorched her cheekbone and chin. As his lips brushed over hers, the denied love she felt for Darius swam through her system like a euphoric drug. Tara meant to pull away from him, reminding her she couldn't feel affection for this man. But she didn't pull away, and she knew in her heart that she didn't *want* to pull away.

Darius ended their kiss and straightened, his expression blocked by shadows. Tara said nothing, not trusting the emotions running through her.

Within seconds, she reached her destination.

The robed intruders were leaning over the two bikes, either studying them or trying to figure out how to start them, or both. Regardless, they hadn't noticed Tara and now she was several yards away from them.

Okay. I'm relying on you, Darius. She knew no matter how angry she was with him, he wouldn't let her down in battle. And this was more than battle. The survival of Nuworld could well rest on their ability to reach Patha before the Lunians made their next move.

Tara drew her laser, aimed it at the robed figures, and fired. Immediately, laser fire came from Darius' direction. Gunfire exploded through the air, as well. It took Tara a second to realize it was Pee-coo-mee and Pee-coo firing alongside Darius.

They took the would-be thieves by complete surprise. Tara successfully eliminated the two men hovering over her bike. She rushed to her motorcycle and got on it before the remaining robed figures had an opportunity to react.

But they did react in the next second. Those standing by the trailer pulled long, flat, black weapons identical to the guns the Lunians used and opened fire on Darius.

Tara drove the bike back into the bushes, using them as a shield and struggled to breathe as pain reminded her she wasn't in fit condition. Doing her best to ignore her body's warning signals, she threw off the robe and immediately regretted the fact that she wore the bright green outfit underneath. An easy target in the darkness. She hugged her bike and drove around bushes and trees until she reached Darius.

"Head down the side of the mountain," Darius said as she pulled up behind him. He'd positioned himself behind a large rock and was returning fire at the robed figures who protected themselves by hiding behind the trailer. "There's a group of rocks that thrust fifteen feet into the air, maybe a mile or two south of here, there is. It looks like a hand sticking out of the ground. That's the rendezvous point. Get going. I'll meet you there, I will."

"I'm not going to leave here without you," She spoke quickly, too quickly. Tara realized the affection she tried to suppress came through in her words.

Darius noticed it, too. A small grin—a triumphant grin— appeared on his face and his dark gray eyes danced wickedly.

"You can't handle this by yourself," she added and frowned stubbornly.

He was undaunted and his triumphant grin didn't fade.

Gunfire shot through the air at that moment and a loud scream followed. Pee-coo fell backward just in front of Darius, ripping through the bushes as his body hit the ground.

"No," Pee-coo-mee screamed and threw herself at Pee-coo, trying to catch him.

Another blast of bullets filled the air, and Pee-coo-mee fell to the ground next to Pee-coo, both dead.

Darius remained hunched behind the rock. Tara was behind him on her bike. He held his hand flat out behind him, indicating she should stay still and not make a sound. He did the same.

The robed figures did not move either and the evening became deathly still. Darius' bike stood out in the open and the lights in the trailer were off. Both Tara and Darius could see slight movement by the trailer. Darius pulled the Eliminator out from under his robe.

"You can't use that," she hissed. "It'll take out the entire camp. You'll lose your bike."

"I'm going to show these people who they're messing with, I am." He leaned his chin down above the Eliminator, focusing on his target. "Besides, I'm sure they've called for reinforcements. This may be our only chance to get out of here, yes."

"Darius, we're too close. You'll have to fire on the run if we're going to get down this mountain once that trailer explodes." She damned him for his willfulness.

"Scoot back." He grabbed her handlebar with one hand, but kept the Eliminator focused on its target.

Tara looked at him, ready to protest that it was her bike and she would drive it.

He stole a quick glance at her. "Now." His growl meant business. "You won't argue this time, no."

She narrowed her eyes at him, but complied.

He swung his long leg over her bike with ease, and Tara found herself wrapping her arms around his firm, muscular body. Instantly, Darius shot out from behind the large rock that had served as their shield. Before their aggressors had an opportunity to react, he fired.

The hit was direct and the explosion large. The trailer blew up into the air and parts of it slammed against the ground in all directions. Metal siding and interior boards that had made up the walls slammed against surrounding trees and hurled into the air. Fireballs screamed, landing in scattered patterns amidst the wooded side of the mountain.

Darius tore down the side of the mountain, avoiding the falling metal and burning debris raining around them. A large rectangular shape in flames—possibly the trailer door—landed in the top of a large evergreen. Within moments, the tree gave in and fell to the ground. Darius slammed on the brakes to avoid being crushed and allowed the bike to slide sideways before regaining control.

A large ravine provided the next obstacle. Accelerating with a vengeance, he managed to clear the abyss, although barely. Tara did not need to be told to hang on for dear life as she buried her head deep into his back, making her body one with his.

Darius lowered his body, allowing acceleration to reach its maximum force so they could outrun the falling debris from the trailer. They were well down the mountain and cruising over the high plateau before Darius slowed down. He brought the bike to a stop, and the two of them looked back at the burning mountainside.

Tara realized she'd tightened her brow with such fury that as she relaxed, she felt blood pulse through her veins in her forehead, aggravating her injuries. Instinctively, she put her hand to her face to check for bleeding. There was none. Her arm also throbbed as she loosened her grip on Darius. Suddenly she felt quite weak.

Darius turned his head to study her face. "I bet that hurts." He smiled and rubbed her leg.

"I don't have any new injuries." She glared at him coolly and picked up his hand with hers and placed it on his own leg.

His grin widened which annoyed her. His gaze drifted then, his lips flattening into a thin line of concentration.

Darius pointed with his thumb toward the mountain. "We've got company."

Chapter Nine

"What is it now?" Patha had entered the small communications room across the hall from the master bedroom and nursery, and stood behind Torgo, who sat hunched over the computer screen.

The young lad studied the contents of one monitor while talking into his comm. He ran his hands through his hair, causing curls to fall haphazardly. Then turning off his comm, he typed furiously into the computer. It was then that he looked up at Patha, realizing he'd just been asked a question.

"Sir, we've lost their signal, we have." Torgo straightened in his chair.

"What do you mean, we've lost their signal?"

"I have an open transmission with their computer," Torgo began to explain, pointing to the monitor. "I guess I should say I had an open transmission. About fifteen minutes ago, it disappeared, it did."

"It disappeared?" Patha crossed his arms and looked stern. "How does something just disappear?"

Torgo wondered what he had done wrong. "Sir, it's almost as if their computer is no longer there, I'd say."

Patha studied the screen. "Do we have any lock on the trailer?"

Torgo clicked through several screens, then plucked at the keys. "We did, but it too seems to have disappeared, it has."

"What about Tara or Darius, do we have any kind of lock on them?"

Again, Torgo worked the computer. When the appropriate screen came up he pulled back his hands. Then they froze in midair.

He couldn't utter the words. He didn't have to.

His worse nightmare was something happening to his brother. The last thing he ever wanted was to be Lord of Gothman. His papa and his brother were ruthless leaders. They had the ability to quit loving someone if they felt that person would endanger Gothman or their rule. A quality Torgo didn't possess and, in fact, found abhorrent.

The computer showed Tara's transmission, but the transmission for Darius had been terminated.

"Where did you put the monitoring devices?"

"I put them on their, uh," Torgo hesitated, trying to remember. His mind wasn't clear. Nothing could happen to his brother. His brother was undefeatable. He'd proven that over and over again. "There is one under each of the seats on their bikes, there is."

"Why not their clothes?"

"They were going to change clothes, they were," The boy spoke quickly, heat rising to his face. "I didn't bring enough tracking devices with me when you said we had to prepare for their departure."

"Contact the scouts and determine if they've arrived at the rendezvous point."

Torgo breathed deeply as he fought to bury the panic creeping through him at the thought of his brother being dead. *Darius wasn't dead.* Torgo breathed out slowly. Something had happened, and Darius probably would be angry with him for not being more thorough with his work. He mentally lashed himself for not performing better.

"I've given you an order," Patha barked. "If you can't do the job, I'll replace you."

Torgo jumped and began clicking on the appropriate screen. "The scouts haven't reached their destination." Torgo turned and looked up at Patha. His face was full of fear. "Patha, I'm—"

"Save it," Patha said.

He began pacing in the small room, and Torgo watched him. Patha was silent for a few moments, and Torgo racked his brain, trying to think of something constructive to say to the old man. He couldn't, so he remained silent.

"I want Gothman and the Blood Circle Clan put on alert." Patha broke the silence, but continued to pace.

Torgo watched him, assuming there was more.

"Gear up the armies and have them ready." Again, Patha paced. Then he pointed his finger at Torgo. "Something is very wrong here. I don't feel that Darius is dead. But why would his bike get destroyed? Something is definitely wrong."

Patha finally stopped pacing and turned Torgo around in his chair, so he faced the computer once again, and the older man gripped the back of the chair. "Tell those scouts to get to the rendezvous point as quickly as possible. Then let's send an army of about fifty out there, as well. Just in case."

Patha waved a hand at the two other computers on the table next to Torgo. They were turned off. "Bring some assistants in here, too. I want open communication with everyone effective immediately. Where's Syra?" Patha acted as if he'd noticed for the first time that she wasn't in her customary position right next to Torgo.

"She left to get something to eat. She'll be back any minute, she will."

"Okay. Keep me posted." Finally, Patha left the room.

Torgo exhaled. He stared at the door for a minute, then turned his head back to the computer. His mind drifted to Syra. He had no idea where that girl was at the moment. She'd probably gotten herself something to eat while she'd been gone. It wasn't completely a lie. But he knew she hadn't left for that reason.

Torgo thought about the conversation he and Syra had right before she stormed out of the computer room. The girl had left in a rage. Usually when he worked alone with Syra on the computers, he really enjoyed their time together. But today she had made him so angry, he had wanted to shake sense into her.

They had started talking about the Runner pregnancy prevention drug. Torgo didn't want a drug coming between their lovemaking. Why couldn't she see that? He'd tried to explain that the drug made their sex seem cheap. No, he didn't want a baby. Well, not yet. That wasn't what he'd meant at all.

She'd challenged him. Ways existed to prevent becoming pregnant. Gothman ways. Herbs. Tonics. This Runner medicine prevented her body from making what would be part of a baby if he added his seed. He just thought it was wrong. And Syra didn't understand.

They were from two different races. Two different cultures. He worried sometimes this unchangeable fact might be their ultimate downfall. He suspected she wouldn't be back anytime soon. Although he admitted to himself, he had hoped she'd be back by now.

Torgo contacted two other Runners to report to his computer room. Of course, he tried to contact Syra. When she didn't answer, he tried again. Same thing…no response. So he told her that Patha had ordered a military alert and she needed to come back, then clicked off his comm. He could only hope she would listen. Hardheaded girl.

Patha returned less than an hour later dressed in full Runner garb, well armed with lasers clipped to his belt on either hip. "Have all military units remain in full contact, and I want all clan members and townspeople to report in. Program the computer to confirm as they do. All Gothman and Runners must identify themselves with their login numbers. We've had several people reported missing today. The computer can tell us who they are." Patha paused. "I don't want panic to set in."

Patha's eyes swept over the two Runners sitting at the other computers. "Syra hasn't come back?"

"No, sir." Torgo tried not to show concern. "She'll be back soon."

Patha eyed Torgo, then wrapped his comm around his ear before flipping it on. "Syra."

Torgo watched intently as Patha stood with a blank gaze waiting for a response.

There wasn't one.

Patha didn't look at Torgo. "Balbo."

This time there was a quick response.

"Do you know where your daughter is?"

Brief silence.

"No, she isn't here."

Another pause.

"Find her. She's not reporting in." Patha shut off his comm. "I want everyone to have a comm device on them at all times so the computer can track them. Tell me as soon as it's done." With that, he left the room.

Torgo began the program that would start the count. "I need you to notify all unit leaders and inform them of Patha's instructions," he said to the Runner next to him.

"Sure thing." The young man who nodded was just a few winters older than Torgo.

"Why wouldn't Syra answer her comm?" the other Runner mused.

Torgo glared at him, and the Runner returned his attention to his monitor. But Torgo couldn't focus on his work.

Syra should have answered when Patha contacted her. She was bullheaded, but she respected authority.

Something was definitely wrong.

* * * * *

Darius and Tara looked back toward the burning mountain and watched as multitudes of black objects descended the mountainside and headed toward them. In the darkness, the objects didn't really look like bikes, but they weren't jeeps, either. Neither of them felt the need to sit there and watch these people move closer. The exodus didn't appear to be a rescue party.

Darius took off so quickly Tara grabbed him, holding on tightly. She almost screamed from pain as her body slammed back, but her arms remained wrapped around her claim's torso.

He covered her hands with one of his and held on to her.

She would have pushed away his hand, but she didn't dare move the position of her own for fear of losing her balance. His grasp remained steady, ensuring her safety, whether she cared to admit it or not.

They drove at high speed across the flat, high land in the darkness. Occasionally, Darius would turn and look behind them, but Tara didn't move her head. She kept it down, her chin almost resting on his shoulder blade. Her body was a wave of solid pain.

"Excellent," Darius muttered, and slowed the bike drastically as Tara focused her eyes in the dark. They'd come to a large formation protruding from the ground. Several large rocks, taller than any man, stood straight and proud, surrounded by the prairie grass. The rocks resembled four fingers, possibly the fingers of a god, sticking up through the ground.

On either side of the rock formation were Gothman warriors. Tara counted ten. The Gothman pulled their weapons as the two approached on Tara's motorcycle.

"Pay heed to the Lord of Gothman," Darius yelled into the darkness, causing a stir among the warriors.

One of the men slowly pulled his bike forward and greeted them. "To be sure, my lord." He stopped his bike next to the pair.

"Right good to see you, my lord, it is," another gruff voice broke through the darkness.

"I'd say the same, but I do wish there were more of you, I do." Darius accelerated until he could stop Tara's bike among the group of men. "I need a comm."

"Yes, my lord." The soldier handed him his own communications device. "A small army has been dispatched as well, it has. I'm told they should be here within the hour, yes."

Darius nodded and attached the comm to his ear. He'd parked the bike and slid off leaving Tara sitting there. As he spoke into the mouthpiece, he pointed to the night lens the soldier had on a string around his neck. The soldier handed it to him as Darius began to speak. "Patha," he paused and returned to Tara's side.

She'd gotten off her bike and moved stiffly. She hoped it looked as if she'd become stiff from sitting so long and not from the pain brought on from the rough terrain they'd traveled over.

"Of course I'm alive, old man. You worry like a woman, you do." Darius' laugh was a rich baritone, and the group of men around them chuckled along with him. "She's fine too…or that's what she'd have you think, it is."

Tara watched his face while he listened to Patha.

Darius' smile faded and the hardened warrior consumed him. He put the lens up to his eyes and searched the dark horizon. "How many are missing?"

"Missing?" Tara frowned.

"There are eight Gothman and one Runner missing, there are," he whispered.

"What? How long? What do they mean, missing?"

Darius held up his hand to silence her and she stood in front of him, disgruntled.

"I'll contact you when they get here." He switched off the comm and lifted the lens to his eyes once again.

"What is going on, Darius?" Tara asked.

"There's no one out there, no." Darius lowered the lens, then searched the darkness without it, as if not trusting the Runner device specifically designed to see across distances in the night.

"What did Patha say?" Tara watched him study the terrain.

"The Lunians have contacted Patha."

"They have?"

"Yes. They apologized for our treatment and informed him it wasn't their intention to attack us at the trailer. They thought we were cave people, they did. Patha said they told him they were searching our trailer in hopes of finding us there. They told Patha we must have thought they were preparing an ambush, and so we destroyed our own trailer for nothing."

"Well, there's a small part of the truth in all that. They weren't looking for us to protect us. You know that as well as I do."

"I know. They lied to Patha, they did. What we need to figure out is why."

"Who spoke to Patha?"

"Brev."

"Brev made the comment that he knew Runners and Gothman were the most powerful of Nuworld. So he doesn't want us as an enemy." Tara was puzzled by their behavior. Why would they bother contacting Patha at all? "They don't realize we overheard them talking. But you said there's Gothman and a Runner missing?"

"Yes, and I'm willing to guess these moon people have already reached Gothman and have kidnapped them, they have."

"Who's the Runner?"

"Syra."

"Oh, no!" Tara's hand went to her mouth. "Darius, you know why they've been kidnapped!"

"I can guess as well as you can, yes." Darius had that hardened look of a frustrated lord. "They'll impregnate the women for some demented thievery they have going on, they will."

"Are the Gothman all women?"

"No, they took four men and four women, all young, under the age of twenty winters."

"We've got to go back and get them."

"Fifty men are on their way. I anticipate they'll be here in less than an hour. I'll set up an outpost here. But I question whether they've taken their hostages back to the mountain, I do. All were reported missing this afternoon at the earliest. If they were headed this way, I would have seen them, I would. I want to find out where these people are setting up camp. The mountain was temporary for them, it was. Or maybe, they thought the mountain would be a good home but for some reason decided the cave people didn't suit their needs. Apparently, they feel we'd suit their needs better, yes. They learned of Gothman superiority after they might have arrived here, yes."

"So we send scouts out in all directions surrounding Gothman."

"Agreed."

It wasn't often Darius and Tara were able to discuss military strategy calmly without disagreements. He reached for her hand and wrapped his fingers around hers before bringing her hand up to his mouth and gently brushing his lips across her skin.

She despised the way her gut instantly responded to his hot breath on her skin. She also despised the way he could look into her eyes, as he was doing right now and see how her body reacted to his touch.

Fire danced in his eyes. A look of victory.

She didn't want him to feel that. She forced herself to picture that little baby she'd held briefly. That little baby that looked like her children, but was a bigger threat than the enemy they would be facing shortly.

She pulled her hand away from him. "Contact your scouts and get them moving," she ordered and turned to start cleaning her bike.

Chapter Ten

༄

Darius rolled over and pulled his blanket around his shoulder. It had grown cold through the night, and he felt chilled upon waking. As he stretched and moved his arms under the blankets, he realized he was alone in the small tent he and Tara had slept in the night before. Or rather, part of the night, at least for him. The night had been half over before he'd been informed a tent had been set up for them and that Tara had already retired for the evening.

After the troops had arrived the day before, he'd worked well into the late hours preparing them for battle. Small armies had been dispersed to find the Lunian camp.

Although he and Tara agreed on this strategy, it had been the only thing they'd agreed on. She'd wanted to go home. He knew their best leadership position was among the troops. She'd called him antiquated and told him his Gothman ways would be the downfall of him yet. He knew she'd been talking about more than his leadership methods.

Darius had disregarded her comments and had continued instructing the troops, all but forgetting Tara's anger until much later in the evening. He approached her as she cleaned her bike, watching her. He felt the first sign of remorse at the destruction of his own. Her only comment was that it was a little too late to have feelings like that.

When he realized her intentions were to drive back to Gothman to be with the children, he prohibited it. She turned on him with a rage he'd grown rather accustomed to seeing. Her timing was inappropriate however, and he made that quite clear. He was Lord. She could not address him in such a fashion, especially in front of troops.

That was when she marched off.

He wasn't sure he'd be allowed into the tent. When he crawled in, she was so soundly asleep, he'd been able to lie down next to her without disturbing her. Now, he looked around and noticed immediately that his comm was missing. He'd set it inside his left boot next to his side of the bedding before he had gone to sleep. Nothing else was gone.

Dressing quickly, he crawled out of the mini-tent and stretched in the morning air. The morning sun was barely visible on the horizon, providing a dim light across the open plateau. The heavy dew made him glad he'd brought his boots inside the tent the night before.

Before him, his small army spread across the wet grass. Each man slept in a resting bag next to his bike. A typical battle scene, one he'd seen many times.

Now where was that woman?

"My lord." Two guards on duty quickly straightened to full attention as they acknowledged Darius' presence. "All is calm, it is."

"Good." Darius couldn't ask them if there'd been any communication with Patha, or they would know he didn't have his comm. And he wouldn't ask if they'd seen Tara. She was his woman—his claim.

A man not capable of controlling his woman was marked a fool. For a Gothman Lord to suggest he didn't know the exact whereabouts of his claim would be the standing joke for many a cycle. The expression on the two men's faces revealed nothing, except possibly fear for being caught slouching on the job. They didn't know he was looking for Tara, and he damn sure wasn't going to allow his Runner claim to brand him a fool.

Relieved, he saw her bike parked where it had been the night before. At least she hadn't left in the middle of the night, defying his orders. That would have been just like her. The woman ignored his orders way too often, and there were days when he itched to flog her for disobedience.

He and Tara would make a great team if she just accepted his word.

Darius ran his fingers through the tangled curls on his head, squinted and scanned the quiet camp. He didn't want to fight with Tara, in fact, that was the last thing he wanted to do with her.

He wandered out into the field he and Tara had driven through the night before. The sun provided little light as it slowly rose to announce a new day. Then he saw her.

She sat on the ground, leaning against the smallest rock in the formation that had been their rendezvous point. As he approached, he saw her cheeks stained from tears. She stared straight ahead, not seeming to notice him. That, in itself, was odd. Her warrior training should alert her to anyone's approach, no matter how lost in thought she was. And he wasn't trying to sneak up on her.

Tara's chin rested on her knees, and she stared wide-eyed at the field in front of her. She'd wrapped her arms around her legs, and he noticed her hands were clenched in fists.

Darius wondered that she didn't grimace in pain from the way she held her body. He grew concerned as he drew within feet of her and she still didn't stir.

"Tara?" He quietly squatted next to her. "What is it, my lady?"

No response. Was she so mad at him? Her fury usually didn't last long.

The communication device lay next to her, and he picked it up.

She still didn't move to acknowledge him.

He then noticed a lone tear glide down her cheek and reached to stop its path.

No response. Her eyes remained wide, staring straight ahead.

He looked in the direction she stared and saw nothing but flowing prairie grass and distant mountains, barely visible on the horizon. *She* saw something though.

Suddenly, she cowered, just slightly, then more tears came.

He wiped them away, too.

He'd never seen her like this before, but suddenly he was sure of what was happening. Crator. The dog-woman. She was having a vision.

But why was she so upset? What was she seeing?

"Tara," he gently touched her clenched fist. "Can you hear me?"

She was icy cold and didn't stir, yet the tears flowed.

Darius scooted closer and put an arm around her while continuing to hold her clenched hand. He wished he could see what she saw.

What frustration! He didn't like being in the dark about anything. And he despised not being in control. He'd only seen the dog-woman in dreams, and those had stopped after Tara returned. Why did she come to Tara?

Tara's sobbing grew louder.

"Why are you doing this to her?" Darius looked around him. "She doesn't deserve these tears, no."

Nothing.

Tara continued to stare and cry.

"Stop this, I say!" He yelled to the empty field. He held her closer, tighter. "Please," he calmed his voice, feeling her pain. "Please," he begged. "I know I've questioned your existence, I have. But you know my thoughts and I do believe in you. I'm just not good at accepting the fact that there's someone out there with more control. I'm willing to try, I am."

Still she sobbed bitterly.

"Please. Torture me. Tara's done nothing wrong, she hasn't. Don't do this to her, don't."

Her eyes stared widely at an unknown source and she whimpered as her tears fell.

He continued to hold her, letting her cry like a child. He watched their surroundings protectively, waiting for whatever might happen next.

* * * * *

Tara awakened suddenly in their tent and realized morning had come. She wasn't surprised to see Darius sleeping next to her. He hadn't moved as she slowly pulled back the covers. His long body rose and fell slowly, and his breathing was deep. She'd stared at him for a moment and had a sudden desire to crawl into his arms and cuddle up to his broad, perfectly sculptured chest.

His blond curls half-covered a face deeply tanned from the sun. Oh, how she'd wanted to wrap those curls around her fingers and roll him onto his back. Her bruised ribs and torn arm hadn't allowed that pleasure though. Not to mention the fact that she was supposed to be angry with him. Furious was more like it.

She hadn't felt fury at that moment, though. She'd wanted him, desperately.

Yes, she remembered they'd fought the night before. He always pushed the fact that he was the lord and outranked her. His arrogance infuriated her. She was nothing until her papa died, and that was something she didn't want. The last thing she could imagine was Patha being gone from her life forever. But until then, she had no rank other than the claimed one of the Lord of Gothman. Which meant nothing.

Tara would have helped organize the camp after they had arrived; she knew military strategies as well as he did. She knew some of them better than he did. But Darius hadn't permitted her to give one little order. Not one. So she'd ignored him and cleaned her bike, a ridiculous thing to do in the dark.

However when the two of them were alone in their tent sleeping together, then she could give orders. Tara could tell him to roll over and please her, and he would obey. That thought had brought a smile to her lips. But no, she had to punish him.

As she had awakened, she hadn't even dwelt on his crimes. Not right then. She'd felt in good humor, full of desires she knew he could satisfy.

But then her thoughts had grudgingly drifted away from the sleeping man. She needed to contact Patha, and she knew he would be awake by now. She would check in with him and see if the scouts had detected any sign of the Lunians.

She'd leaned across Darius in order to grab his boot, suspecting his comm would be inside it. He always put valuable items in his boots when he retired at a campsite.

Her body had scorched with desire as she felt his firm muscular body underneath her.

No, get those thoughts out of your head. He's done you wrong and there's only one way to teach the man manners. Ugh! Why did it have to be such torture for her, too?

She took his comm, put on her boots, and slipped outside. Cold air wrapped around her, making her shiver. Her muscles tightened, the dull throb of pain from her injuries slowing her movements. Everything was damp with dew, and a dark shroud made the multiple sleeping bodies around the camp appear like dark mounds. She closed the tent securely and walked silently through the sleeping camp.

"No, we haven't found anything unusual yet," Patha said after she'd contacted him with Darius' comm.

"Do they know what they're looking for?"

"What do you mean?"

"Patha, these people live on the moon. I don't think they're accustomed to living out in the open. Certainly, they didn't live out in the open on the moon. There are no trees or grass there, it's all just…white." Tara had explained her thinking. "When they came here, the first place they went was underground, and they've probably set up camp there. The terrain to the north is rocky. It's sandier to the south. I'd guess they are to the west or east."

"Good logic, Tara-girl." Patha's tone had been tense. "You should have told me this last night."

"I wasn't permitted to have any say last night."

Patha sighed with exasperation. "My patience tires with this, Tara-girl. Accept him as your commanding officer and share any ideas that might be constructive. That's how a good warrior behaves." His words had been sharp and their accuracy stung. "I shouldn't have to tell you this. You know it already. You won't be a successful leader if you can't separate your ill will toward him with the need to lead a race. I have higher hopes for you than the way you're acting." Silence prevailed as he let his words hit home.

He had been right and she'd been negligent in her duties. Tara had focused all her energy in making sure Darius suffered for how he had wronged her, and she had accomplished nothing. He didn't see the error of his ways.

"I'll let you know if I have any more ideas." She'd reached to shut off her comm.

"Tara, I want you to talk to Torgo."

"Why?"

"He needs a speech similar to the one you just got. And, I think it would be a good idea for you to give it to him."

"Because Syra's missing?"

"Yes."

"Shouldn't Darius do that?"

"I want you to do it."

"Okay. I'll contact him now." Tara had switched off the comm and had decided to walk out to the edge of the campsite to talk to the boy privately. She'd always treated him gently. The other soldiers didn't need to overhear her conversation with him. It wouldn't help his reputation. He was already a shadow of his brother. She would give him the respect of a warrior, allowing him to receive his reprimand in private.

The strange rock formation had been visible across the field. She'd walked toward it and leaned against its jagged edge, putting it between her and the camp. A strange smell had suddenly tickled her nose. No, not strange, appealing. Her mouth began to water.

It was the smell of coffee.

Strong.

Hot.

She'd inhaled deeply and turned her head.

The dog-woman had been squatting on the ground at the other end of the rock formation. A small fire burned in front of her and a grill lay over it, supported by rocks. She had pulled a metal pot off the grill, and poured its steaming contents into a large tin cup. "Good to start the day off refreshed and alert." She'd slowly walked the hot cup over to Tara, shuffling her old leather boots over the uneven ground in small steps.

Tara had accepted the hot brew and looked at the old lady's glassy brown eyes. "And why do I have the honor of this visit?" She'd joyfully sipped the hot coffee…what a coveted treat.

"You need help, the evil is strong."

"My faith is strong." Tara had smiled as she kept the cup to her face enjoying the heat on her skin. "I know you'll take care of me."

"Crator will take care of you."

"Yes, and I'll accept His help."

"He knows that." The dog-woman smiled then, and the wrinkles on her face intensified. "Oldworld was destroyed for its evil."

Tara hadn't responded, not knowing what to say. The existence of Oldworld had been mentioned in some of her studies, but it wasn't a subject she knew much about.

"They'll destroy you, if you don't fight." The dog woman's look was stern. "You must fight with no other thoughts but survival."

"Are they going to take my children?" Tara had known she was being mighty bold to ask such a question about the future.

"They will try." Then the old woman looked down. "Crator wants you to know more. It will help you defeat the evil."

"What does he want me to know?"

The dog-woman had disappeared and so had Tara's hot cup of coffee.

* * * * *

She wasn't in the field anymore.

Cold stale air settled in around her. The darkness increased, limiting her vision, pressing in around her like an old thick blanket.

No more wet grass smells, or hot coffee. Everything smelled foul, an unclean stench. She covered her nose.

As her eyes adjusted, she realized she wasn't alone.

She was in a large room and there were people everywhere. Women everywhere. They leaned against the walls and sat cross-legged on the floor. They were dirty and poorly clad. In fact, only blankets covered some of them. They all looked forlorn, or beaten, waiting for some inevitable doom.

A door at the other end of the room opened and a bright light filled the space. Tara squinted, as did the others. Several large silhouetted figures entered the room. As her eyes adjusted, Tara could see three tall, thin men with pale skin and clear eyes.

Where was she? Had the dog-woman somehow sent her to the Lunians? *Crator wanted her to see more.* Her stomach riveted into knots.

"Let's take this one." The man in the lead, wearing an oversized white jacket, poked a long thin stick at one of the girls leaning against the wall.

Her body jerked and she let out a pathetic yelp.

The man behind her, dressed in plain gray, making him appear as drab as his surroundings, grabbed her and literally threw her to the third man, who was also dressed in drab gray.

"This one looks good, too." Again, the assembly line procedure occurred.

The man in white walked through the crowded room toward Tara.

She looked down, realizing she still wore her Runner clothing and wondering why he didn't gawk at her. She definitely stood out from the others in the room, who were all shabbily attired, if dressed at all.

The man continued to stroll through the room. He used his stick to pull back blankets, revealing the naked girls underneath. At one point, he smiled and pushed his stick down between a girl's legs.

Her body jerked but she didn't fight him, didn't look up, didn't speak.

Tara concluded the stick let out some type of electrical current if the man pushed a long rectangular black button on the side of it.

He grabbed the girl and pushed her toward the door, yanking her blanket from her, forcing her to walk naked. "The rest of you might get lucky next time." He laughed and headed out of the room.

"Hey." Tara pulled her laser.

The men didn't turn around. They didn't seem to hear her.

"You can't treat them like that." She stepped around the bodies as she followed them to the door, then into the hallway.

One of the men in gray shut the door behind them and locked it.

"Get them hosed down." The large man in white who had chosen the girls walked away, down the long hall.

"Come on, little bitches." One of the other men slapped the naked girl's behind.

"Don't talk to her like that." Tara reached for the man and was shocked to see her hand go right through his arm. A strange sensation washed through her, his indifference to his actions masking some perverted pleasure in what he did.

She wasn't really here! The dog-woman had her experiencing some torturous scene. But why? Where was she?

She followed as the men pushed the girls down the hallway. The next room they entered was perfectly square with high ceilings. The floor, walls, and ceiling were all painted gray, with several drains in the floor.

"Get out of your clothes," one of them yelled. "I don't know why they even bother giving bitches clothes," he added under his breath, opening a cabinet in the wall and pulling out a long hose with a narrow nozzle at its end.

"Got me," the other said and walked over to the wall where he began turning a large wheel.

Water poured from the hose, and a riveting blast was directed toward the girls.

"Get out of those clothes, bitch," the man wielding the hose barked and pounded the still-clothed girl with a powerful spray.

The powerful stream knocked her back a foot or two, but she managed to pull off the wet shirt.

"Okay, next cycle," he said to the man at the wall.

Foamy water now streamed out. It must have been fairly hot because the temperature in the room quickly rose.

The girls took the abuse submissively and spread their arms and legs when ordered.

Tara was repulsed by the treatment and wished there was something she could do to stop it.

The next cycle appeared to be cold water, and the room temperature lowered. The men soon appeared satisfied with their cleaning job, turned off the water, and left the three girls huddled, naked, in the middle of the room as they left and locked the door.

Minutes passed and it was unlocked again.

A different man entered the room and used the electrically charged stick to prod the girls out of the room and back down the hall.

Tara felt nauseous as she followed them to a doorway at the top of a set of stairs. They entered a comfortable-looking room with carpeting and pictures on the walls, similar to those she'd seen when Brev and Polva had captured her and Darius.

Her attention flew to Brev, who stood in the middle of the room. He had several other men with him and they were all dressed similarly—pullover smocks with loosely fitting slacks. Brev's outfit was striped gray and black, while the other men wore solid gray.

He looked over the three girls carefully. It wasn't a sexual look in his eyes. It was the look of a merchant, carefully scrutinizing a product prior to purchase.

"Is this the best you can do?" Brev seemed disgusted. "They don't look any better than the boys you brought up. Aren't any adults left?"

"No, sir, it's slim pickings down there." The older of the two men, who appeared to be the spokesman, shrugged. "Our stock's running pretty low. We turn them around so quickly anymore, they don't live that long."

Brev snorted and glanced quickly at the girls again. "She won't be happy with any of these."

"I could bring up others if you like."

"It doesn't sound like it will make any difference." Brev shrugged and waved his hands at the girls. "Take the one in the middle, I guess. But watch them and make sure there's a take."

With that, Brev walked out a door on the other side of the room, leaving the two men alone with the girls.

"I'll take the other two back down," The younger man, who had been quiet up until now, spoke.

"Okay." The older man grabbed the middle girl by her arm. "Come on, you. Hope you're in the taking mood. I don't have all day for this."

Tara followed the man and girl into an adjoining room where a tall thin boy, maybe eighteen at the most, stood awkwardly in the middle of the room. He, too, was naked, and the man threw the girl at him, stepped back, and closed the door.

Tara joined him as he walked into a small alcove with a tinted window where he could see the two inside the room.

The young girl had fallen against the boy but she backed up. With no emotion on her face, she lay on the concrete floor and spread her legs. The boy got down on his knees and climbed over her slowly.

His face was blank as well. If anything, he looked sad and tired. He covered her with his body and slowly began to move back and forth until he entered her. Only minutes passed before the boy stopped rocking and slowly lifted himself off the girl. He leaned back and sat on the hard floor.

The young girl pulled herself up into a sitting position, as well. They didn't speak or look at each other. Their expressions never changed. They stared at the floor almost appearing bored, and seemed to wait.

Tara had never seen a more abominable scene in her entire life. They made sex seem no more appealing then doing laundry. Her stomach repulsed. The man reached forward and grabbed a microphone attached to the wall.

"It's done, sir," he spoke simply, then flipped off the switch.

"I've seen enough," Tara said quietly, almost to herself. She looked up and walked out into the main room. "Did you hear me?" She called out to the empty room. "Crator? Old lady? I've seen enough."

Why am I here? I can't stop these people. They don't even know I'm here. She struggled with her thoughts as she looked around the room again. On an impulse, Tara walked quickly over to the door where Brev had exited and decided to find him. She reached for the doorknob, but found her hand went right through the door. Tara straightened, surprised only for a moment. Sucking in a deep breath, determined to make the best of this terrible dream, or whatever it was, she walked through the door with a determined stride.

Brev sat at a desk in a small office with a flat, rectangular walkie-talkie held to the side of his face. It was narrow and long enough that it went from his ear to his mouth. The instrument was similar to the communications device she'd used during her brief encounter with the Neurians.

Tara sat in the one chair by the wall. After walking through the door, Tara half expected to fall to the floor, but the chair held her. She stared at it, running her hands over the smooth armrests. Why could she feel this chair, yet walk through walls?

Brev didn't look up. Like the others, he didn't notice her.

"I don't think that would do much good, sir," Brev spoke into his mouthpiece.

Tara listened.

"Well sir, they're getting too young. We use the females so often, they only live for about five or ten years once they've been started." Brev picked up a pen and began doodling on a writing pad. "We need new breeding stock if we're going to solve this problem. The demand for babies is rising every year. I don't know about you, but I have a hard time telling my wife 'no' once she's set her mind to something." Brev forced a chuckle and a strained smile appeared on his face. "Yes, sir, we have a plan."

Tara leaned forward in her chair, studying every move of Brev's face.

"We would like to take an expedition down to the surface." He paused. "I know they're barbaric." Another pause. "I think they're our only chance for survival. We could colonize there, as our ancestors did here. The planet seems to be completely safe, and life is flourishing."

Tara touched Brev's desk with her fingers, and realizing her hand didn't go through the surface, she kicked her feet up and reclined them on Brev's desk. "I'll show you barbaric," she grumbled.

"That's a good point, sir." Brev frowned. "I know that too, sir."

"What do you know?" Tara mumbled.

"Well sir, if I may, I think we have that figured out." Brev now smiled, reached forward and doodled slowly. "We'll plead for their help. Show our respect for their positions and titles. That sort of thing. They won't even know what's happening."

"That's where you're wrong." Tara glared at the man.

"No, we can't do that. They're too militaristic. We've tested the incubators, and they seem to produce normal, healthy babies. These rulers won't even know their people are missing. We should be able to return them within hours of capture."

"What are you talking about?" Tara asked Brev, who obviously didn't answer. She then looked toward the ceiling and asked in a louder voice, "What is he talking about?"

"We'll be very careful, sir." Brev now leaned forward and tapped the desk with his fingers. "In the morning, sir. We're ready."

He put down the phone and leaned back in his chair, smiling.

"You're an evil man, Brev." Repulsion twisted in her gut, making her sick, while she stared at the monster sitting across from her.

The door opened and Polva walked into the office.

Tara had to jump out of the way to prevent the woman from sitting on her.

"Did you talk to Toulon?" she asked.

"Just hung up the phone with him." Brev grinned. "We leave in the morning."

"And my request?" She raised an eyebrow at him. "Did you mention my request?"

"Polva, I told you. I'll take care of that when we get down there."

"I won't have a child from any of those other barbarians."

"They're all barbarians, my sweet." He smiled and came around his desk.

Tara thought she would be sick if she saw these two being intimate together.

Brev just stood in front of Polva, though, without touching her.

She looked at him casually as if the thought of him touching her never entered her mind. "They have drive, though. We want our children to be leaders, don't we?" Polva continued without letting him answer. "Of course we do. And I don't want anyone else to have their children but us."

"From the records you've produced, that might be hard for us to pull off," Brev said. "He seems to like reproducing."

His words were like a blow to the face as Tara realized what Brev had just said.

"My point exactly. These people breed every time they connect." She made a repulsed face and intentionally shook her body. "And they like it. They will make outstanding breeding stock. Our people will grow, and once again rule Earth."

"They call it Nuworld now," Brev pointed out.

"A stupid name." Polva waved her hand.

Tara wanted to belt her.

"We'll rule Earth together, you and me," she continued, the cold gleam in her eye revealing the evil creature that she was. "And our children will rule after us. Toulon can have his moon. Earth is much bigger. All we have to do is get those people to attack each other, and they'll wipe each other out."

"So that's what you tried to do." Tara snorted. "Well, it didn't work, lady."

"I'll finish our packing, Brev. I'll see you back at home." With that, Polva turned and left the office, pulling the door closed behind her.

Simultaneous with the door closing, Tara's surroundings went black. She felt lightheaded, but before she had time to fight her new surroundings, she found herself back at the camp facing the dog-woman with the cup of coffee in her hand.

"There is more, child," the old lady spoke. "Are you ready?"

"What are you going to show me now?" She quickly took a drink of the still warm coffee.

Everything was dark again, and Tara felt the texture of the ground change under her feet. Her eyes adjusted and she realized she was in some kind of tunnel. She heard screams— loud, tortured screams from a woman. No. From a girl.

"We should sedate her." Tara recognized Brev's voice and moved forward through the darkness.

"It could harm the take." That was Polva's voice. She sounded unbelievably calm, considering the continued screaming.

Tara walked into a large, manmade cave. The walls had recently been dug out, considering the fresh smell of dirt. Electric lights stood on thin wooden poles, filling the room with unnatural light.

Tara gasped and her hands went to her mouth. In the middle of the cave was Syra. She had a chain secured around her neck and was completely naked. A young man, also naked and with a chain around his neck, held Syra's hands in one of his, while the other fondled her small breasts.

Syra fought him, but whenever she appeared to have the upper hand, one of the Lunians yanked her chain, causing her to lose her footing.

The man jumped on her again.

"No," Tara screamed and ran forward to stop the naked man. She ran right through him however and hit the dirt wall on the other side. She turned and saw Syra kick and scream as the young man forced her two hands to the ground and climbed on top of her.

"No, you can't do this." Syra struggled helplessly.

"Just following orders." The naked man grinned and spread her legs apart with his.

Tara tried to pick up a rock to throw at him, but her hand passed through it. Apparently, she wouldn't be allowed to touch objects in this dream as she had in Brev's office.

But this wasn't a dream. It was a nightmare.

Syra didn't have the strength to fight off the bigger man. The teenage girl just wasn't as strong. Her skills as a warrior weren't fine-tuned enough to allow her to think clearly. And the chain the Lunian continually pulled counteracted what skills she did have.

"Please stop," Syra cried, sounding like a child.

"You know none of the lads in Bryton will believe me when I tell 'em what I got to do with you, no," the naked man hissed loud enough for Tara to hear.

"You won't live to tell anyone," Syra yelled and kicked with her legs.

"I'll see to it that I will, m'lady." The chained Gothman pressed Syra's arms to the ground, forcing the girl's back against the hard floor.

Syra fought to keep her legs free and to kick at the man above her, while she shook her head back and forth. "No!" she screamed. "This is wrong. You can't do this."

Her screams turned to a plea as she lost the struggle to the man above her. Gothman had raped women for many winters, and the man atop Syra showed no signs of remorse.

Tears smeared Tara's cheeks as she stood completely helpless and watched her niece being raped.

The Lunians huddled at the other side of the room and whispered among themselves when the Gothman forced his entrance.

Syra's screams echoed off the walls.

Tara felt bile in her throat, as her vision blurred from her tears. "Crator!" She screamed His name, matching the velocity of Syra's howls. "Why would you do this to a child?"

Syra's screams turned to uncontrollable crying as the Gothman moved inside her. She continued to struggle, and managed to free one of her arms.

The Gothman raised his head, and Tara noted his closed eyes as he enjoyed the deep penetration.

Syra took advantage of the moment. She struck the man hard across the face, causing him to fall off her.

"You little tramp," the Gothman hissed.

The Lunians appeared awestruck as they whispered together, obviously discussing the interaction between the Runner and the Gothman.

"Don't you touch me," Syra screamed, although her voice now sounded raspy.

"Got to," the Gothman hissed and grabbed Syra.

She struggled in his arms, the chains hanging from both of their necks swaying and clanking against the cave floor. Tara again tried to stop the atrocious act by grabbing the Gothman's chain, but it rolled through her hand across the floor, then leapt from the ground when the Gothman strained to maintain his grip on Syra.

"Get your filthy paws off of me," Syra yelled and bit the man's forearm.

"Argh!" He backhanded her.

She sprawled across the cave floor.

Tara could see long red scrapes on her niece's bare backside.

"You'd do best to let me finish, Runner, or I daresay you won't live through the act."

Syra couldn't get to her feet before the Gothman once more climbed onto her and slammed his eager member deep inside.

Tara could see how Syra shook under the man, and how the girl's eyes squeezed closed as if she could will the nightmare away. The Gothman had his large hands pressed against Syra's wrists, and his hairy legs forced Syra's willowy legs to spread wide. His gyrations rocked Syra's body, and Tara could see how the floor had bruised the child.

Tara collapsed against the wall. "Crator, you can't allow this to happen!" She slid to a squatting position and shared Syra's pain.

When the act ended, two Lunian men dragged Syra toward a large metal cage with a solid bottom and top. Bars made up the four walls. One of the Lunians opened the barred door and the other one shoved Syra into it. They locked it with a key before dragging the man to another box.

"How long before we can transfer the fetus?" Brev asked.

Tara looked up in horror.

"I'm afraid this method could take a month or so," a tall man standing next to Brev, said way too calmly.

Syra screamed inside her cage. Tara cried with her.

Chapter Eleven

༄

Tara felt like she was waking from a nightmare. Her clothes were soaked and her face wet from tears. "Wait," she screamed into the nothingness. "Don't send me back yet. Give me some clue to fight this. You haven't told me anything I hadn't guessed." Except the part about Syra, she thought after she spoke. "Please I have to find out where they are!"

An incredible invisible force seemed to prevent her from standing. She fought with more muscle than she thought she had. Her body screamed in pain while she struggled to free herself from the force and run back to the dark tunnel that had led her to the underground cave. Nothing would stop her now. This had to be the way to the surface. There were no other tunnels leaving the cave.

Tara grinned with satisfaction when the short tunnel went directly uphill. Tara ran through several people standing outside the tunnel entrance. She stopped quickly and looked around.

A canopy covered the entrance to the tunnel. Surrounding the canopy were many tents with people walking among them. She scanned the horizon and looked at the sun. Then she collapsed to the ground.

* * * * *

"Tara!" Darius couldn't believe the strength she'd possessed to free herself from his arms. He'd feared for her safety when she began running like a crazy person across the field. Darius had to dive through the air after chasing her and knocked her to the ground.

She'd gone limp and he quickly moved off her, then cradled her in his arms. "Please, my lady, come back to me."

Tara blinked and looked up at him. She seemed confused and slowly worked herself to a sitting position on the ground next to him. "Crator showed me what's happening," she mumbled against his chest.

Tara made no attempt to fight Darius as he carried her through the quiet camp and back to their tent. He stooped and pushed the tent flap to the side with one arm, while keeping her limp frame pressed to his chest with his other arm.

She looked drained of color and exhausted as he placed her on their pile of blankets and secured the tent flap, allowing them privacy.

"You didn't enjoy what you saw, I'd say." He threw his large leather coat around her shoulders, taking care not to bump her injured arm.

"I saw Syra being raped. She was chained." Tara coughed and shivered as she used her good arm to secure Darius' coat around her. She chewed her lip and looked up at him with damp, blue eyes. "There was no way she could fight back. And I couldn't help her."

"My lady, that must have been awful for you." Darius brushed several strands of her sweat-soaked hair away from her face.

* * * * *

She met his eyes and realized rape was a part of his culture. She wouldn't censor her statement. Somehow she would make Darius see that forcing someone to do something against their will, anything, was wrong. He'd probably taken part in the act himself more than once. She shuddered at the thought and struggled to stay focused. "I know where they are. We have to leave right away." She worked to get to her feet.

"You need to see a doctor first, you do." Darius helped her stand. "I'll be told you haven't aggravated those injuries before I put you on active duty, yes." Darius brushed his fingers through her hair.

Tara looked at him, shocked. "There isn't time for that, Darius."

"I won't have you chasing after some dream, when you need help standing." Darius sounded firm, but kept his voice quiet.

Tara hated the fact that he felt he had final say over her actions. Nothing frustrated her more than continually reminding him they were equals in their relationship, especially when he didn't appear willing to even hear what needed to be done.

"I think we can prevent this," she spoke slowly. "I think part of what they showed me hasn't happened yet."

She turned toward the tent entrance, and he grabbed her arm. Tara spun on him, anger rising at his hesitation. "These people are going to impregnate our women, hold them for a month, then take the unborn child from them." She spit the words in his face as she moved very close, challenging him. "I'm going to stop this. You may come or you may stay."

She yanked her uninjured arm from his grasp and pulled open the tent flap. After storming out, she let the cloth door fall behind her.

Tara straddled her bike and started it simultaneously. Yanking the bike around, she began to take off when Darius grabbed the handlebar. His hand crushed hers and his gray eyes turned as dark as a thunderhead waiting to explode. His powerful jawline twitched as his teeth clenched together. The bike almost left the ground in an attempt to take off as the front tire spun. Tara released her grasp and the bike decelerated.

"Scoot back." His growl was low and controlled.

She stared at him.

"Now!"

Tara moved back on the bike and he climbed on in front of her. The bike then left the ground, in spite of the extra weight, as he accelerated with all the energy his temper provided. The Gothman warriors were slowly waking up and jumped to one side, appearing startled by their lord flying past them.

Darius began speaking, although Tara couldn't hear what he said.

She watched as he flipped off his comm, then back on, and spoke again. Darius probably issued instructions to his commander of the Gothman unit they'd just left, then contacted Patha about his insubordinate daughter.

When he'd turned off the comm, she hit him on the shoulder and pointed. "Go to the east."

He turned his head and yelled, "We're going home first."

"Darius!" She tightened her body around his, wishing she could shake sense into his thick head. "I have no clue how much time we have. Do as I say or get off this bike!"

"Enough, woman!" he yelled back. "*You* do as *I* say!"

"Darius, please." She softened her voice and leaned her chin on his shoulder so she could speak directly into his ear. "Send troops to the east. They have tents there and a canopy covers a dugout tunnel leading to an underground cave."

"You don't know that their camp is there yet, you say. We're looking for landlink activity in that direction."

"And in the meantime, they could seriously hurt Syra, not to mention the Gothman hostages they have."

They argued back and forth as Darius drove at high speed across the high lands north of Gothman.

It was not quite lunchtime when he pulled into the drive of his large house. Guards immediately took the bike to clean it as the two of them dismounted and entered the living room.

Patha called from the top of the stairs, informing them food would be brought to them. Tara realized she was famished.

After dismissing Torgo and the two other Runners from the landlink room, Tara explained every detail of her vision to Patha and Darius. They listened intently and sat silent for a moment after she'd finished.

Two young Gothman girls timidly entered with trays of food. She and Darius eagerly dug into the food while Patha clicked on different screens at the landlink in front of him.

Tara insisted the servants bring the twins to her. They immediately began climbing over her to better reach for cheese and apple slices. Tara divided her attention between them and the screens of info as Patha reviewed activity in the area.

More than once, Andru or Ana would grab her injured arm or lean against her injured rib cage. At first, she accepted the pain just to be close to them. But she couldn't pull Andru away from the tray of chocolate and fruit without grimacing.

Patha frowned at her, and she noticed he exchanged a look with Darius. Darius grabbed Andru from her and placed the child on his lap. Tara focused on the contents of the landlink screen to take her mind off the pain.

Patha's expression changed while he watched the monitor, his back straightening. He flipped screens and reached for his comm.

"What is it?" Tara looked at a screen identifying locations of Runners and Gothman through the personal landlinks on their bikes.

"Torgo is headed east outside Gothman," Patha spoke into his comm. "Did he tell anyone where he was going?"

"Oh no." Tara started pounding on the keys of the other landlink. "Torgo had this base unit set to audio." She looked at Darius. "He listened to our entire conversation."

Darius wrapped the comm link around his ear and adjusted the mouthpiece. "I want Torgo stopped and brought to me at once," he spoke sternly and was obviously upset as he firmly placed his son on the floor. The child began climbing up his papa's leg once again.

"Eavesdropping is a high crime, Darius." Patha also had a firm look on his face.

"And he'll pay for the crime he's committed." Darius picked up Andru and went to the window. "I'll not have this insubordination."

Tara watched him, wondering what he was thinking. Probably reflecting on Torgo. She knew Darius considered him weak and spoiled, and with some justification. Darius felt the guilt of not spending more time with his brother, training him to be a warrior. He had good reason to worry about the young man. Torgo could get killed or captured before he freed Syra.

"I don't suppose you spoke to him like I asked?" Patha asked Tara.

Darius turned to look at her.

"I didn't exactly have an opportunity to do that, Patha. After I spoke to you, I had that vision."

The two men seemed to accept this response, and Tara noticed Darius didn't ask what she was to speak to Torgo about. These two knew each other's thoughts, and she felt a bit left out. They made a dangerous team, and she wondered if she and Darius would ever have that bond. She also cringed at the thought that Torgo would receive the wrath of both of them once he was brought back.

"I'll talk to him as soon as he returns." And she would administer his punishment. Darius was in no frame of mind to be punishing a child.

"I'll deal with Torgo." There was a chill in Darius' voice as he spoke. "You're way too gentle with him, you are."

"Maybe Torgo wonders the same thing I am wondering," Tara threw out to the two men.

"What is that?" Patha narrowed his brow.

"What the Lunians will do to Syra when they discover she's on anti-conception medication," she spoke quietly after turning off the audio on the landlink. "How many times will they repeatedly rape her, and each time be unsuccessful in making her pregnant?"

"She's on what?" Darius and Patha spoke almost at the same time.

"She's just started the doses," Tara retorted. "She would have ended up pregnant, if she didn't take precautions."

Darius growled, showing his disapproval of the Runner drug.

* * * * *

Patha looked away, not willing to visualize what could possibly happen to the girl if such a situation did transpire. He also saw the anger Darius felt over such news and knew it would make Torgo's return even more unpleasant.

Darius would double the punishment if he thought his younger brother had encouraged anti-conception medication. He doubted that's what Tara intended to do by sharing this information with them. With a loud sigh he decided to change the subject. "I know this isn't the best time to mention it, but I've found in my winters of running a nation, when a crisis occurs it usually is accompanied by another."

A knock on the door interrupted the conversation, and Darius looked up. One of the young servant girls opened the door slowly.

"What now?" Darius asked wearily.

"I beg your pardon, M'lord," the girl's voice cracked and she lowered her head.

"What is it?"

"The doctor is here as you requested, M'lord."

"Send him up."

The young girl took an awkward step backward, then as if an afterthought reached for the doorknob and drew the door shut quickly.

Tara would have preferred Hilda to hire old women as servants, instead of teenage girls. She decided not to entertain the thought of Darius taking liberties with them. Instead, she focused on the doctor having been called at his request to examine her. But she wouldn't leave until she knew what Patha had to say. "What is our other crisis?" She looked at her papa.

"I received a message from Southland," he began, reaching for some papers. "I printed the message for you." He handed a page to each of them. "Apparently the Neurian government has discovered more oil south of its cities. They are interested in knowing if we would like to bid for purchasing rights."

"Bid for purchasing rights?" Darius read the contents of the message quickly. "It doesn't say who else they've contacted."

"Looks like Gowsky is learning a thing or two about ruling a nation," Tara said.

"Of course, he wouldn't let us know who else he's contacted," Patha added. "It gives him the upper hand. We might be persuaded to negotiate in order to keep other nations from getting the oil."

"Maybe he hasn't contacted other nations," Darius suggested. "Can we find out?"

"I'm working on it." Patha looked again at the landlink. "I've started a trace on the message to see if I can find any other paths for it."

"The Neurians are very advanced with their landlink technology. If they don't want us to detect a path, we won't be able to detect it." Tara looked at the landlink as it began beeping.

The message was from the head Gothman guard on duty. Torgo had been detained and would be arriving at the house within the half-hour. Tara's heart sank for the boy as she imagined him being brought to his own home like a hostage.

Darius caught the look on her face. He acknowledged the message, then stood and opened the door. "Come take these children, I say," he hollered into the empty hallway.

Tara could hear feet pattering up the staircase.

"Yes, m'lord." The same teenager who had announced the doctor curtsied in front of Darius.

"Mama." Ana reached her little arms toward her as the teenager carried the children from the room.

Tara felt a pang of regret that she couldn't give her children more time.

The landlink beeped again as Dr. Digo appeared in the hallway behind the servant girl. He glanced past Darius at Tara.

She could tell her claim's presence still made him nervous. She wished it didn't. Darius would only use that to his advantage. She raised a finger to the doctor, indicating he should wait a minute, then looked at Patha who was acknowledging the incoming message. "Who is it?"

"Darius, the team of scouts we sent out is contacting you." Patha stepped back to let Darius communicate with his men.

Darius sat at the landlink, pushing the keys on the pad as if he'd done it all his life. The muscles in his back moved through his shirt as he responded to the landlink-generated message.

Tara found herself undressing him with her eyes before she realized what she was doing. She blinked. "Well, what do they have to say?" She stood behind him to see the screen. And fought not to put her hands on his shoulders as she scanned his backside once more.

"They've been attacked," Darius said simply.

Tara moved closer.

"They're too far out of range for the comms to work, and so are sending messages through the landlink. They say they were able to chase off their aggressors, but they've lost several men."

"Lost them, how?" Tara asked. "Were they killed or taken hostage?"

Darius typed.

The answer appeared immediately.

"Taken hostage," he said and typed again.

Again, a quick response.

"They haven't seen any sign of a Lunian camp, though." Darius turned around.

Tara had to step aside to avoid his long legs.

"Patha, they are going to be out of communication range altogether if they go much farther." He looked up at Tara. "This campsite of yours must be farther away than we thought."

Tara focused on Patha. "Those troops need to keep going, but it's imperative we keep in contact."

"We shouldn't lose communication through the landlinks until they reach the mountains," Patha said. "What's their current location?"

Darius turned and typed the message. "They are within a half-day's travel of the mountains." He paused. "Wait. I've just been told these Lunians travel in some type of covered motorcycle that can hover above the ground and take off into the air."

Patha scratched his head. "I see."

"We need to boost communications and match their speed in travel." Tara remembered *obtaining* technology from other races in the past. She met Patha's eyes and saw he understood what she meant. If they could get their hands on one of those hovering bikes, they might be able to match the Lunian technology and their speed.

"Tell those scouts to continue in full pursuit, but not to go out of communication range without prior consent. Then dispatch several small armies to follow after them," Patha instructed.

Darius turned and typed, then adjusted the mouthpiece of his comm and issued the order for three armies to follow. Darius turned off his comm, then stood and reached for Tara. "If you'll excuse me, Patha, my claim has an appointment with her family doctor." He put his large hands around her narrow waist and held on firmly.

Tara tried to step to the side, but he seemed to enjoy having her right there in front of him. "Let go of me. I'm going." She struggled to pull away.

"I'm coming, too." Darius started walking her toward the door where the doctor stood waiting in the hallway. "Patha, would you mind assembling a team to figure out a way to boost communication power?"

Patha nodded and waved his hand to dismiss the two.

Darius released Tara when they were in the hallway, but followed silently as Tara led the way to their bedroom.

Chapter Twelve

Darius had gone from grouchy to annoyed.

Tara had refused to share a bed with him since they'd been back. She did have the good grace not to let anyone else know by entering the bedroom she shared with him upon retiring. Then she'd slip quickly into the nursery through the adjoining door.

She knew this act of hers got under his skin, because if he brooded openly the rest of the household would be wise to her act. She knew her days of doing this were numbered because she was healing nicely, and the looks he gave her let her know she'd submit to him soon, or else.

Tara annoyed Darius further when she'd approached Patha about obtaining one of the Lunian's flying vehicles; when he'd okayed the mission, she'd simply ordered the troops to leave. It was actually a surprise that she was able to give a command before Patha had a chance to share it with Darius.

"You don't send troops out without informing me first." His tone caused the children to look up curiously at their papa.

"I talked to Patha," she answered nonchalantly as she finished tying Andru and Ana's little boots.

"Papa," Ana called and reached her hands toward Darius. Her two-year-old chubby body stretched, and she went onto tiptoe.

"Papa talking," Andru scolded in his three-year-old tone, and wrapped his hands around his sister's waist, pulling her backwards until they both fell.

"I can talk too," Ana cried and struggled to be free of her brother's grasp.

Tara squatted to separate the bickering children. "That's enough, you two."

Darius pulled Tara from her position and spun her around to face him. "Our nations have a contract. I believe you and I signed it in blood, yes."

He held her tightly by the arms, high enough that her feet almost left the ground. She felt a strong urge to raise her legs quickly and rack him desperately with her knees. She refrained however and batted her eyelashes at him, then glared while her anger flared through her. "I'll make a point of notifying you in the future." Tara watched a nerve twitch along Darius' jaw. "Gothman wasn't infringed upon in any way by the order, but I can give you the details in a report if you like."

Darius stormed from the room without saying a word to the twins.

Tara heard him yell for Torgo as he stomped down the stairs.

* * * * *

Tara needed a break. She'd spent much of the night and the first part of the day working with a team to improve communications. Several simulations of programs to increase power had been tested and failed. A new program now ran through its simulation.

After spending time with the twins, having breakfast with them and dressing them for the day, Tara had decided to stretch her legs. She entered the yard where Darius was working with Torgo on the boy's fighting skills. The sight did nothing to relax her.

"I would've crushed you had this been true battle," Darius barked, and knocked Torgo across the yard with a fling of his arm.

Torgo picked himself up slowly and wiped sweat from his brow. He glared at his older brother, then lunged, only to be thrown again. He pulled himself onto all fours and breathed heavily.

"Get up," Darius ordered.

Tara thought back to how Darius had whipped Torgo with a vengeance when he'd been brought back from chasing after Syra. It took a good two weeks for him to recover. The second his lashes had scabbed, Darius insisted he start working on his fighting skills. They were up against an unknown enemy, he said, and Torgo spent too much time in front of landlinks.

She knew Darius believed Torgo too weak, and felt responsible to remedy that fact. Over the past several mornings, Darius had called Torgo to the backyard and had challenged him. If Torgo grumbled or refused, his brother started mocking and teasing him until Torgo grew angry enough to fight back.

Now the boy squatted on all fours, breathing heavily from exhaustion and humiliation. Tara's heart burned. She ignored Darius, who stood in the middle of the yard, legs spread, hands on his hips, and walked over to squat by Torgo.

"Don't let him get to you," she said softly. "Catch your breath and focus your mind. Ignore his insults and catcalls. They only distract you and he does it on purpose."

Torgo lifted his head and looked at her. "He's bigger and older than I am, he is. It's not a fair fight."

"You can take him. I've trained you, and you're not soft." Tara smiled at the boy, the almost-man. "Size doesn't matter. If your heart is true, you can defeat a giant."

"Come on, boy," Darius snarled. "Get away from her or I'll flog you again, I will."

"He's just trying to get under your skin, Torgo," Tara said again and threw Darius a scornful look. "If you're all upset, you'll never defeat him. Focus your thoughts and control the fight."

"He can't control this fight," Darius laughed. "He can't control much of anything, no. He's not a man yet."

* * * * *

Torgo glared at his brother. He stood, but kept his hands on his knees and bent over, trying to stop the fury Darius had just lit within him.

It was all a game to Darius, but Torgo wasn't taking it that way. He hadn't been exposed to many Gothman fighting rituals. He had been sheltered. But Tara had taught him a thing or two; it was time to see if he remembered them.

"Okay, Torgo," she said and started rubbing his back, which caused one of Darius' eyebrows to rise. "Remember those techniques we worked on a couple cycles ago?"

He looked at her. "Yeah, I think so."

"Better yet." Darius almost smiled. "I'll take on the both of you, I will. That might make it an even match, yes."

Tara looked at Torgo and whispered, "Now watch, this is where you tell your opponent what you really think of him." She turned and glared at him with her baby blues. "Even if you and your brother challenged me, it wouldn't be a fair fight. You're not even in my league." Tara paused wickedly. "My lord."

Torgo looked at Tara with astonishment. He'd heard her talk to his brother like that behind closed doors, but not in the open, where anyone could hear. She was brave...or stupid.

* * * * *

Darius also cocked an eyebrow. He saw a gleam in her eyes he hadn't seen in a while. She was having fun—sincerely enjoying a pastime of which she'd been deprived recently.

He watched Tara straighten and put her hands on her hips. Her breath quickened enough to make the rise and fall of her breasts a distraction, but one he enjoyed. He could think of another pastime she'd deprived herself of...as well as him.

He studied her face. She was getting wound up. Oh, that didn't bother him; he could defeat her in a fight and he knew it. He realized, though, she would tear him apart verbally if he didn't stop her soon. She had a few things to say, he could imagine, and the entire household didn't need to hear it.

"Show me that technique you two have worked on." He smiled enthusiastically at both of them. "We'll see if you're out of my league or not."

* * * * *

Tara noticed his blond curls dance around his head as a quick breeze raced through the yard. The white shirt he wore stretched over his broad chest and was just dirty and sweaty enough to make him look incredibly sexy. He smiled broadly when she looked up after he commented, a smile that allowed no woman to say "no" if he willed it.

Noting the fire in his eyes, she wondered how long poor Torgo would be able to remain in the fight. She also realized she could be in trouble. Because if she took out her frustrations in a good fight, she'd lose the edge from her anger at Darius. And then what would happen?

No, she wouldn't let her temper soar. A little sparring, for Torgo's sake, that's all she'd allow to happen.

She gave Darius a sideways glance before looking at Torgo. "He asked for it. This won't be as hard as you think. Just remember what I taught you."

Torgo looked nervous.

As she spoke to Torgo, Darius took his first shot. He moved quickly. A quick punch aimed directly at his younger brother's face.

Tara was just as quick. She returned the same maneuver, sending a direct punch toward the side of his head. Darius threw out his arm to block her punch as she shouted to Torgo, "What I taught you, now!"

Torgo jumped up, kicking his right leg out and slamming Darius hard in the chest. It was a full-impact blow. Torgo felt his foot connect with his older brother's well-developed chest. A physique Torgo was sure he would never possess. He pushed hard and was surprised to feel his brother's weight give way. Within the same fraction of a second, he released his foot and pulled it back. What shocked him most was that he actually landed on his feet.

"Not bad." Darius stepped back and smiled. "I'm impressed. Is that all you know?"

Torgo's ego fell. He hadn't even swayed his brother. Instead, Darius stood there, smiling at Torgo, saying, *good job*.

* * * * *

"Never hesitate," Tara instructed and threw another punch toward her claim's face. She followed through on the punch just long enough for Darius to raise his arm in defense, then she switched hands and slugged him hard in the rib cage.

He stepped back and lowered his arms. Tara pounded his face. Then she stepped back to allow him to regain composure. *Don't get too serious*, she told herself.

A quick glance at Darius told her she was now in trouble. He'd read her thoughts and her actions. She shouldn't have backed off. *Damn*.

Torgo surprised both of them at that moment.

He took advantage of his brother staring one second too long at Tara. He jumped forward and hit his brother in the stomach. It was an excellent punch, which was a good thing, because it was the only one he got. Darius turned on him and slammed a return punch that doubled Torgo over and had him gasping for breath.

Tara didn't bother to even look at the injured boy. Darius was at the perfect angle for her to give him a taste of the medicine he'd just given his younger brother. A hard slam to the kidneys immobilized him long enough for Tara to jump in midair, kicking him with enough force to send him staggering back four or five feet.

At that moment, Tara realized they had an audience.

Their grunts and accusations had attracted the attention of several guards who now stood alongside the house. One of them snickered and Darius turned to acknowledge their presence.

Tara laughed and jumped on him from behind, boxing his ears. She jumped off again before he could grab her, and as he turned, she belted him hard on his lower jaw. Adrenaline surged through her body now. All thoughts of aiding Torgo in a lesson were gone. The young boy had moved over to the side of the yard and was sitting on the ground, trying to breathe normally. Cycles of anger over his infidelity came to a head. Tara didn't worry about Torgo. All she wanted to do right now was kick Darius' ass.

She went after her claim as if he were a punching bag. She managed several shots at his face, one at his chest, and a swift kick so low in the groin, all those watching groaned loudly.

Tara didn't allow a second to pass when he bent over to regain composure from the blow that had been inches away from doing long-term damage. She flew through the air at him with a kick aimed directly at the side of his head.

Darius recuperated faster than she expected.

In midair, Tara realized he'd pulled a stunt she had used one too many times in his presence. Darius had been faking his lack of composure. He stood up quickly and intercepted her legs before they reached his face. His mighty arms wrapped around her body and tightened so quickly, all air rushed from her lungs with a howl.

Tara reached to attack his face.

He yanked her off him and threw her across the yard, sending her sprawling through the grass.

* * * * *

The guards roared.

One of the young Gothman servants came to the door, then turned, yelling for Hilda as she ran back into the house. Patha overheard the commotion and walked onto the balcony overlooking the yard. He looked down on his daughter and Darius.

"You two kids can play for fifteen more minutes, but then it's time to get back to work."

The humor in his voice was apparent, and the large group of guards looking on filled the yard with laughter.

* * * * *

Tara got to her feet quickly and flew at Darius again. He reached to grab her and she actually managed to flip the man twice her size and weight off his feet, causing him to land hard on the ground.

The guards completely lost it.

Tara stood over Darius, breathing hard. She studied the rippling muscles gleaming from sweat and saw how his shirt pressed to his chest. His curls stood in every direction, and the blond locks fell to his shoulders as well as sticking to the side of his face. Gray eyes swarming with emotion met her gaze, and Tara knew at that moment, Darius had the same thoughts she did.

She wanted him, but no longer as a sparring partner. And he felt the same. More than anything, Tara wanted him upstairs, in their bedroom. She wanted him naked, and she wanted him in her. The sensation of need that ripped through her took Tara's breath away, and almost made her knees buckle.

At a point much earlier in her life, Tara realized that often when she sparred, especially with a man, she found it sexually arousing. She'd never discussed this with anyone. She didn't have to. Many stories were told how the great warriors were conceived after their parents had spent an evening physically tearing at each other. In her teenage years, she'd been accused more than once of flirting with a boy as she sparred with him just to get him sexually aroused. Then she'd walk away.

Now memories poured into her mind as she recovered. The heat between her legs made moving difficult. She hadn't wanted Darius like this for quite a while. He looked incredibly seductive in his long brown leather pants with his shirt hanging sideways, just enough to show off the hair on his chest. She wiped sweat and drool from her face, a face she was sure was covered with lust.

But wait a minute! Reality hit Tara harder than a punch to the face. She was furious with him. He'd committed an unforgivable crime. How long should she make him suffer? How long must she suffer?

Darius rose slowly, smiling as if he'd been told a good joke. In fact, it was a grin of pure pleasure. And it was seductively wicked.

Tara braced herself as Darius took a moment to glance at his guards and at Patha, who was still looking down at them.

Referring to Patha's earlier comment, Darius called to him, "I don't know, kind sir. Fifteen minutes might not be enough time, I'm thinking." He turned to Tara and whispered, "So you want to play, do you?"

He threw himself at Tara and she met him with a hard punch to the stomach. He took the punch without a hint of reaction and threw her over his shoulder.

She flipped her body, but he managed to hold onto her as he ran toward the back door. The entire shift of guards on duty stood out in the backyard whooping and hollering as they cheered their lord on. Tara tried to grab the doorframe as Darius entered the kitchen, startling the two young girls standing there and sending them screaming and running for the pantry.

He made it as far as the bottom of the staircase before Tara managed to squirm loose and jump to the floor. Darius plopped down on the bottom tread of the wide, curving staircase and threw back his head laughing.

She kicked him hard in the shin.

"Ow!" He grabbed his leg and looked up at her with an evil leer. "That hurt."

"Good." She glared at him.

He leaned forward putting his head almost level with hers. "It's good to see my lady's got some play left in her."

"Then why'd you quit?" She still glared at him. But it was hard to keep her eyes from roaming over his body that was sprawled lazily across the bottom of the staircase.

"I haven't quit, no." Darius reached for her.

Tara jumped back and he grabbed air.

"Keep your hands off me," she said through clenched teeth.

"Ah, your eyes say something completely different, they do." He pulled himself up and hovered over her. Taking her chin firmly in his hand, he forced her to look at him. "I have the right to you whenever I please." He stroked her chin with his finger. "And, I will have you tonight."

"Darius, Tara, come here now!"

Patha's voice broke all the magic, all the possessiveness that had made Tara's knees feel weak. She could swear Darius jumped at the sound of her papa's voice. He turned and hurried up the stairs. But not before giving her a look sealing his words, his command.

Tara felt warmth travel through her as she held his gaze in that brief moment. And it dawned on her that her attack had driven him as wild as it had her.

Her punches might as well have been foreplay.

Talk about a plan backfiring!

Chapter Thirteen

"We did it, Tara-girl." Patha looked quite excited. "One of the flying motorcycles the Lunians use is on its way."

"Excellent!" Tara grinned with satisfaction as she moved to the screen displaying the message. "Who obtained it?"

"Frig, a young man with an excellent future as a warrior."

"The Runners of my generation shall be great warriors," Tara said, and gave Patha a hug.

Two other Runners sat in the room huddled together over the landlink at the other desk. One of them turned to give Tara his attention.

"What is it?" She still smiled. The thought of having an opportunity to drive a flying vehicle caused her adrenaline to pump almost as much as sparring with Darius.

"This last program ran successfully. All we need to do now is put it through a trial run," Pago spoke calmly.

Tara had known the Runner all his life, and had babysat him when they both were younger. Pago and Torgo spent time together occasionally, and Tara could see the two becoming good friends.

"Maybe we can communicate with Frig?" Tara still smiled as she looked over Pago's shoulder at the landlink.

Darius moved his comm to his ear. "Torgo, get up here."

Tara hadn't noticed the boy wasn't in the room. He was the one who'd written this new program. She mentally agreed that he should be the one to run it for the first time.

Torgo was there in minutes. Tara immediately noticed how bad he looked. Not from the roughing up his brother had given him. That hadn't left a mark. There were, however, deep-set dark circles under his eyes. His stare was blank, unconcerned. His blond curls seemed darker, more individualized, as if sweat from lack of showering had defined his hairstyle. Fortunately, he didn't smell. She could tell by his sad eyes that he missed Syra and was terrified at what might be happening to her this very minute.

"Your communications program is ready for a trial run, it is." Darius patted his younger brother on the back cheerfully as he entered the room.

Torgo looked at him in surprise.

"See if you can open a communication with Frig. He's the Runner bringing back one of those flying devices, he is."

"Really?" A glint of hope appeared in the form of a half-smile. "Okay." Torgo sat down and successfully opened a line with the warrior.

Tara joined Patha and Darius outside when Frig returned. The Lunian vehicle wasn't a bike at all, but more like a glider. And that is exactly the name it took. Tara could think of no other way to describe it. There was room for one person to sit in it. It had two wheels and the seat had been placed over the motor. Unidentifiable metal made up its body, and this particular one had been painted blue. A clear dome lifted to allow the driver to climb into the seat, then automatically lowered when the vehicle started. The wheels pulled up under the metal when the bike hit a certain speed and an overdrive button was pushed. Tara sulked a little too obviously when Patha suggested Darius be the first one to take it for a trial run.

She patiently waited — okay, impatiently — for her turn as Darius flew all over the meadow, taking the glider to incredible heights and diving like a daredevil. Patha did the same. She saw his face at one point as he did circles in the sky, taking the thing completely upside down.

Tara enjoyed her turn, however. The glider moved at a speed she hadn't dreamed possible. She cruised across Gothman countryside, hovering ten feet above the ground as she drove twice as fast as her bike could travel.

Suddenly a scene from her vision obstructed her view of the countryside. The ground below her dimmed, and she clenched the handlebars of the glider when suddenly she couldn't see.

Her vision cleared, but she no longer saw Gothman countryside. The glider no longer hummed underneath her.

She was climbing out of the Lunian underground cave after having seen Syra raped. The same awful feeling she'd had in her gut during the first vision flooded through her. Why was she reliving the moment?

Tara watched the Lunians walk around the campsite, and the sun blinded her as she moved out from under the canopy. Her hand automatically went to her eyes to shield them as she looked at the mountains and sky. She felt herself fall, as had happened when she'd had the vision the first time.

Tara's sight blurred. When it cleared, she looked at an open field. Turning her head to the left and right, she watched the rocky ground grew closer with each second. Tara screamed when she realized she would crash, and quickly veered to avoid the oncoming ground.

The glider maneuvered easily, avoiding large tree branches. Tara's heart pounded as she worked to regain knowledge of her surroundings.

Suddenly she had a revelation.

Tara turned the glider sharply and headed back to where Darius and Patha stood waiting for her. She'd enjoyed the contraption as much as they had, but now she needed to get back to the ground. She had to tell them what she'd just figured out.

As Tara climbed out of the glider, Patha and Darius stood several feet away grinning widely as if they'd just shared a good joke. The two of them glanced at each other, and Darius nodded slightly, patting the older man's back.

The bond between them kept her on the alert. She felt certain there was very little Darius didn't share with the old man. Patha had become like a father to Darius.

"It's quite a machine," Patha said to her as she walked toward them.

"I just had part of my vision come back to me."

"Is that why you almost hit that tree?" Darius teased.

She saw fire in his eyes again.

He and Patha chuckled, and Tara imagined they'd been joking behind her back about her driving abilities. She ignored them. "I know where the Lunian campsite is."

The two men looked at her and their smiles vanished.

"It's on the other side of the eastern mountain range."

* * * * *

The landlink room was crowded, but Tara didn't notice the confined space as she leaned over to look around Patha.

Hilda was speaking to the group and no one responded to her.

Tara noticed her frustration. "We'll be down in just a minute," she reassured the older woman, who was trying to let them know food sat waiting on the table.

"My servant girl told me you said those same words to her ten minutes ago, she did," Hilda mumbled as she surveyed the cluttered room.

Printouts covered both desks, and Patha and Darius hovered over a stack of papers.

"Runners have never been across the mountains, and we won't go about it blindly." Patha straightened and faced Darius.

"Gothman don't enter a battle blindly either, no." Darius cleared space on one of the desks and laid several pieces of paper next to each other.

"I daresay you'll be eating cold meat and potatoes." Hilda raised her arms in a frustrated gesture and left the group.

"And this is all the chartered area we show on the computer?" Tara had already turned her attention from the older woman and pushed her way between the two men to see what Darius had spread before them. "These maps go as far as the base of the mountains."

"We will need a lot of gliders to enable an army to fly over them without worrying about which parts of the mountains are passable." Patha stroked his chin with his fingers and studied his daughter's face.

"And we need to have those gliders immediately," Tara said, feeling she spoke aloud what her papa was thinking.

Darius placed his hands on Tara's shoulders and she turned to face him. "I'll organize men to learn about this glider and see how quickly we can make others like it." He looked over her shoulder at Patha.

"And I can prepare a route based on what we know to send our armies on ground over the mountains," Patha added.

"Okay, I'll contact the leaders and have them prepare for departure." Tara moved to the empty desk and sat in front of the landlink.

Two of the troops, one Runner and one Gothman, began the journey immediately. It would take several days for them to drive through the mountain range.

After two hours of driving at the highest speed they dared, communication was still intact. Tara prayed Torgo's new program would prove its worthiness throughout the entire range, as well as once they reached the other side.

* * * * *

In the meantime, Darius set about the task of organizing the best mechanics, electricians and scientists the two nations had to offer. They formed a team to discover how the glider worked and to see if they could duplicate it.

Darius honored their abilities. While he knew how his motorcycle worked and could maintain it when necessary, he couldn't presume to consider himself mechanically inclined. He was a warrior. He knew how to fight. He knew how to kill. He knew how to run a nation.

And he knew how to handle women.

Thoughts of how he would handle his claim later that evening sprang into his mind, sending blood rushing to certain parts of his body. Would she fight him? He imagined forcing her down, tearing her clothes from her body, and demanding her submission. Or would she still be as aroused as she'd been after they had sparred? Possibly once they were alone, she would pretend indifference, fight to maintain the charade, then aggressively take him on in lovemaking.

He wouldn't think about that, now. He couldn't think about that. Blood had quickly left his brain and his thoughts had clouded. He needed a clear head in order to give orders to the group working with the glider.

The assemblage proved to be an interesting mix of people. His best mechanics were not necessarily known for their manners, even for Gothman. The three he picked were crude, cut rough around the collar. And, they weren't accustomed to working with women. Of course, two of the top Runner scientists he wanted on the team were women. Good-looking women. They weren't impressed by his mechanics and talked down to them, which created tension among them. He'd also selected an inventor—a large older Runner—who'd created a motor found on many Runner bikes.

He found the insults tossed back and forth between the mechanics and the scientists amusing as they walked through the yard. None of them appeared willing to acknowledge the others' credentials, yet they all needed each other to complete the task.

Each of the five had test-driven the glider. Now, they stood in one of the garages at the side of the house, huddled around the contraption, arguing over possible explanations about how it worked.

"I want answers," Darius barked, and the group silenced and gave him their attention. "I don't want theories. You will make our motorcycles fly, and you will have results today."

He still had the picture of the five of them staring at him as he walked out of the garage. As if they'd just been condemned to death.

* * * * *

Upstairs in the house, Patha worked on a landlink next to Tara. They needed more information about the eastern mountain range. To this end, he'd contacted several clan leaders, but like most clans, they had not traveled east. While they seemed to know everything about the area west of the mountains, they had no idea what lay on the other side. Quite simply, the land east of the mountains remained unexplored.

As Patha continued to reach out to all those who could provide them information, he realized his connections with the cave people had been severed and wondered if the Lunians had destroyed them. He accessed Lunian transmissions, however, and gathered bits and pieces of information. Such as, the mountains were very rocky and snow lingered at higher altitudes year round. He was never able to find any indication that the cave people had bothered to map them. It made sense; they were more interested in the interior of the mountains than the exterior.

Patha also investigated several Neurian messages. This was tricky, since he understood Neurians to be paranoid people. Their communiqués contained traps. If an unauthorized user was discovered, a program infiltrated the trespasser's landlink and rendered it useless. Patha knew Torgo had devised a counter-program believed to prevent this detection and damage, but Patha still felt nervous whenever he opened one of their screens.

While the Neurians didn't have much information on land north of their continent, Patha did stumble upon something that interested him. "Look at this," he said, and Tara glanced over at his screen. "It appears to be the schematics of an engine. An engine belonging to a Lunian glider."

"Fascinating." Tara leaned forward and studied the screen. "It appears our southern friends have done a fair amount of research on the Lunians."

* * * * *

Patha rubbed his forehead, and Tara noticed his exhaustion. There was so much to do, and they had no idea if they were headed in the right direction. All they had to go on was a vision she'd had. "Patha, why don't you take a break and get yourself something to eat?"

"Not a bad idea, Tara-girl." Patha pushed his chair away from the desk and smiled at her. "You should come down, too."

"I'll be down shortly." She stood with her papa. "Let me poke around here a little bit and see what the Neurians can tell us about the Lunians."

"Be careful of their traps." Patha pointed to the landlink.

"I will." She remained standing until Patha left the room, then slumped back down in front of the landlink and printed the current screen.

Several hours later, Darius appeared in the doorway of the landlink room with a tray of food. He placed it next to her landlink on the desk.

"You'll need your energy." His voice was quiet and loving.

Tara noticed the look in his eyes didn't appear quiet and loving. It was hungry, animalistic, and possessive. She ignored it.

Torgo entered the room with one of the teenage Runners who assisted with transmissions from time to time. The two of them moved behind Darius, and Torgo pulled the chair from underneath the other desk and gestured for the Runner girl to sit.

"Torgo, I'm glad you are here," Tara said, popping a grape in her mouth and turned back to the landlink. "I have something to show you, all of you." She leaned forward to grab papers at the back of the desk.

Darius stood close, dangerously close.

She had to maintain her cool demeanor. He had to be thoroughly punished.

"I know you have something to show me," Darius whispered so only she could hear.

Warning bells went off in Tara's head. She realized at that moment that one way or another, he would not take "no" for an answer this evening. Tara turned to him. "Look, the Neurians have a schematic of the glider's engine."

Darius was so busy devouring her breasts with his eyes, it took him a minute to reorganize his thoughts and hear her words. He slowly shifted his gaze and looked at the papers.

"I also found this." She held up another printout from one of the Neurian screens. "It's the complete design for several different styles of gliders."

"The Neurians have been busy." Darius looked at the different sets of plans as well as the written directions on how to build the gliders. "How did you get these?"

"Well, I didn't ask for them, if that's what you're thinking." She crossed her arms across her chest and leaned against the desk. He still stood way too close to her. She could smell his body. He smelled clean, like soap, but there was that sensual odor about him, too, and it was doing strange things to her insides.

Finally, Darius moved away.

Tara looked over to watch Torgo as he leaned against the desk next to where the Runner girl sat. She had opened a program, and he appeared to watch her as she worked. Tara noticed Torgo seemed to stand very close to the girl as he pointed to her screen and spoke quietly.

"Torgo," Darius spoke with just the slightest sound of irritation.

Torgo met Darius' gaze.

"I want you to take these and your landlinks and relocate to the garage for the evening." He handed papers to the boy, who looked at them with interest.

"These are exactly what we were looking for." Torgo smiled at Tara, then looked at Darius and frowned. "Why do I have to relocate to the garage?"

"Don't question my orders," Darius barked.

The teenage girl turned to look at the two Gothman males. Darius kept his gaze on his younger brother.

"I am putting you in charge of assembling the gliders. There is already a team out there. You shall supervise. I want at least a handful of them ready to go by dawn."

Torgo's mouth fell open as if he were ready to object, but one look at his brother seemed to stifle whatever he was going to say. He turned to the Runner and told her to begin disassembling the landlinks.

Darius turned and spoke to Tara in a quiet authoritative tone. "I'm going out to the garage for a minute. Eat your supper. I'll be right back."

He left then, and Tara watched him walk out of the room. Instead of eating though, she turned and helped Torgo prepare the landlinks for their relocation.

"We'll be up all night preparing that many gliders," he grumbled to her as she helped stack the equipment into his arms.

"We have to do that sometimes." Tara smiled reassuringly. "We'll have Syra back here all the sooner once we have those gliders."

Tara glanced down at the Runner girl Torgo had been leaning over. She was on the ground unplugging equipment from the wall. He straightened, glancing toward her. Torgo didn't seem to notice the look of concern Tara had in her eyes. *Crator, please don't let him turn out like his brother.* He pulled one of the computers forward, then worked to free another. When she looked back up at Torgo's face, she knew she worried for nothing. He was intent on doing his task. He didn't give the Runner another look, but lifted the computer and stood.

"That's incentive right there not to get sleepy." He smiled back at her and headed for the door. Torgo made sure the Runner didn't have too much to carry, then watched as she left the room.

When he turned to face Tara, she saw worry in his eyes.

"Tara," he said quietly. "My brother will hurt you if you refuse him tonight." His voice sounded apologetic.

Tara looked at him surprised. Could he possibly have the entire house rigged with listening devices? Her expression turned to questioning.

Torgo responded to the look. "At supper, he arranged for Patha, Reena and the babies to stay out at the clan site for the evening, he did. Now he has us out of the house. You two are the only ones who will be here, you are." His voice faded with the last sentence.

Tara got his meaning. "You better get moving." She ruffled his hair. "Don't worry. I can take care of myself."

"I know." Torgo turned to leave but then looked back over his shoulder. "Just be careful. If he wanted to, he could really—"

"Torgo, don't worry." Tara put her hands on the boy's shoulders. "Nothing is going to happen to me. I plan on a good night's sleep and getting on one of those gliders in the morning."

Darius reached the top of the stairs and came down the hallway in time to hear Tara's words.

She ignored him, ruffled Torgo's hair once again, and sent him off down the hallway.

Darius stopped as Torgo approached him. "Everything is ready for you, it is."

Torgo nodded and continued toward the stairs.

"Torgo."

The boy looked up at his brother.

"Stay out of the house."

Torgo's eyes grew wider and he looked past his brother at Tara, but just for a second before he quickly descended the stairs.

Tara returned to her desk, sat down at the landlink, and began nibbling on a piece of cheese.

Darius was right behind her.

He turned her chair around quickly and straddled her legs, pinning her to her spot. "I owe you quite a beating for the one you gave me this afternoon, I do." His dark gray eyes looked hungry.

"You had your chance this afternoon." She responded with her mouth full, taking care not to appear amused or threatened, simply indifferent. Her heart started beating faster, however, and she felt a need to take larger breaths of air. Tara prayed she sounded calmer than she felt. "You're the one calling off the fight. I figured it was all you could take."

She shouldn't have made that last comment. The passion left his expression and an animal magnetism took over. He grabbed her under the arms and lifted her out of the chair. She had little time to resist before he tossed her onto the now empty desk where one of the landlinks had been.

"You can drop this little act any time now." He growled and placed a large hand over each of her thighs.

She placed her hands on his as if to remove them, but his grip tightened around her legs. So she sat there, facing him.

"At first, I thought you'd lost all interest. I thought you no longer loved me. You were cold and indifferent and, yes, I felt incredible pain, I did. I know now that was your goal, to be certain. You wished me to suffer as you have. Well, my lady, I have."

"Your crimes are unforgivable." She tried to keep her face like stone, not letting anything he said affect her. It would've worked too. But his hands on her upper thighs were driving her crazy. She was good at telling this man "no" as long as she had no physical contact with him. This afternoon, sparring in the backyard, had turned on juices that, so far, had not turned off. "I doubt very much you've experienced as much pain as I have."

"I know I hurt you, and I'm truly sorry. I thought my pain was because you no longer loved me." He leaned closer now, his thumbs pushing farther up her inner thighs. "Until this afternoon, that is."

Something in her eyes must have betrayed her at that moment and he used it against her.

"You're a true warrior, and you can't fight without passion. My lady, I think you fought too much this afternoon." And with that he kissed her. Gently, surprisingly so, a brush across the lips. He pulled away before she expected him to. "And you fought too well. Your actions and your eyes betrayed your little plan." He grinned now, reached up and pulled her head back, continually twining his hand through her hair. "I saw your love and your lust. You are still mine, yes."

She fought to control her senses and returned a cold gaze. "You do not control me." She struggled with her words.

He simply laughed. "Of course not, my lady." And with that he grabbed her. He pulled her off the desk and into his arms. One hand covered her rear end and slammed her against his groin. His hardness stabbed her as he pressed her into him. The other hand remained behind her head, so if she tried to turn her head in either direction, it pulled her hair. He shoved his tongue so far down her throat that she gagged.

Yet before she could stop herself, she'd taken his tongue and wrapped her mouth around it. She regained control after what seemed like hours and tried to pull away. But her ability to resist him had disappeared. She groaned as her attempts to free herself failed, and he pulled her even closer.

Darius wrapped her hair farther around his fingers and eventually pulled back her head so he could see her eyes. He held a fast grip on her body as he looked into her half-closed eyes and smiled. "I think it is bedtime for you."

Tara focused on his dark gray eyes, so close to hers, and knew he could see her inner soul. She no longer had the strength to fight him. "I hate you," she whispered, her eyes locked with his. She would have covered his mouth with hers, but he kept her head several inches away.

"Of course you do, I'm sure." He carried Tara into their bedroom and lowered her until her feet touched the floor. After wrapping his powerful arms around her, he kissed her, gently at first, then with a passion that would not be extinguished.

Tara slowly moved her hands up the rippling muscles of his back and allowed him to crush her body into his. When Darius pulled her head back so he could see her face, Tara's mouth felt raw and numb. The tug on her hair stung, adding to the many sensations assailing her body.

While holding her head in position with one hand, Darius unfastened the buttons of her pants with his other. Instead of pulling down the garment, his hand slipped inside and slid across her skin. He squeezed her rear end, pressing her against his hardness to the point of pain. Then his hands moved to her waist, and he yanked down the material to her thighs.

Moisture grew between Tara's legs, making her pants moist. She felt swollen, and a pressure she had managed to keep at bay for a long time now attacked her senses with such fury, she couldn't focus her thoughts beyond her need to have that ache satisfied.

"Step out of them," he ordered.

Tara couldn't respond fast enough. She lifted one leg, then the other, until her pants were a pile on the floor beneath her.

Darius released her hair.

Tara's head felt light with its sudden freedom. She licked her lips, which had gone dry from her heavy breathing, and stared in the darkness at smoldering gray eyes that looked more dangerous than a thunderhead.

The side of Darius' mouth moved slightly, as if acknowledging her needful pain and relishing it. He grabbed the bottom of her shirt and yanked it over her head, tossing it behind him without taking his eyes from her.

Darius lifted her naked body and dropped her on the bed. He stood over her, obviously enjoying the view, and she wondered for the first time since their foreplay began, if she was breaking too soon. All she wanted was his respect and undivided attention. He was a conqueror, and she'd given him reason to conquer her again. Was that all she'd accomplished?

* * * * *

Darius' blood boiled.

Tara lay there, spread out on the bed, more beautiful than she'd been in the many dreams he'd had since she'd refused to share his bed. She challenged him more than any other conquest he'd attempted. The look in her eyes suggested she wasn't submitting to him, but managing to get him to do as she wished.

Their fight this afternoon stirred feelings inside her that needed satisfying. He'd known that as soon as she'd thrown the first punch. He'd been so distracted by the sexual aura radiating from her while she'd attacked him, he'd been unable to concentrate enough to fight back.

He thought for sure he'd have control once he seduced her. Maybe he shouldn't have stated his intentions earlier that day, and instead, just carried out his plan to empty the house and attack her. Instead, he'd given her ample opportunity to prepare her defense.

Now, as he looked at her deliciously naked body, he realized how far he was from winning her devotion. The best thing he could do at the moment, with his thoughts so muddled by the ravenous power she had over him, was to satisfy her to the best of his abilities.

He prayed Tara would never truly be his enemy. He wouldn't stand a chance.

* * * * *

Their lovemaking was hot and passionate. He teased her with his fingers and tongue, ravishing every inch of her body. She surprised him by placing her hands on his chest and pushing him flat on the bed. She returned the favor with her fingers and tongue until he thought he would explode if he couldn't have her immediately.

He struggled to garner the strength necessary to force the upper hand. Still, he managed to lift her body atop him and penetrate until he was deep within her. She screamed in ecstasy and he lifted her slightly and thrust again. He wanted her complete, unadulterated submission. To gain it had become an obsession.

There was nothing submissive about her, though, as she took his hands in hers and locked fingers. Then she slowly began to rock back and forth bringing him to the inevitable climax. There was no way he would let go yet.

He forced himself into a sitting position and used brute force to turn her body and throw her onto the bed. The woman made him mad in the head with his lack of control over her. Now, he would dominate the situation.

Darius spread her legs, trying to be rough. But she willingly allowed it. Driving into her once again, he held on for dear life until he was blind with his need for release. All went black around him, and stars tormented him as they flew past in seething, white streams. He thrust one final time and filled her with his seed as her body spasmed under his.

* * * * *

They lay intertwined on their bed in the silent house. Not a sound broke the tranquility except for the occasional tree branch brushing the window, and faint noises coming from the garage as the team diligently worked on the gliders.

Tara had wrapped herself in Darius' arms, her body completely satisfied. He'd been right. Fighting him had aroused emotions demanding satisfaction. And he'd obliged. She knew he'd intended to do far more to her. In her opinion, he'd failed. Bottom line, he was crazy about her and she liked him feeling that way about her. One way or another she would have his undivided attention.

When she felt his muscles relax around her and heard his breathing deepen, she slowly slipped out of his arms, got up, and dressed.

As she entered the room containing the landlinks, she was shocked to see she'd left one of the devices turned on. Smiling, all too aware of the tingling rushing through her body from making love to Darius, she realized how easily he could distract her. It was still open to the Neurian screen. Under no circumstances would she normally leave a room with a program open. She walked over to shut it down when something on the screen caught her eye.

Small letters blinked across the top of the screen. She leaned over and stared at the question flashing in her face.

"Tara, is that you?"

Chapter Fourteen

ಐ

The flashing message emanating from the screen in the dark room created a surreal moment for Tara. Everything was visible in a dim blue light, then it wasn't, then it was again.

Tara rubbed her chin and stared dumbly at the message.

Who sent it?

When was it sent?

Her hand shook as she slowly reached for the control pad in the darkness, briefly lit, then again in darkness. She sat down in the chair and stared at the screen.

Okay, organize your thoughts. Someone had gone out on a limb to contact her. She was on a Neurian transmission. So that had to mean whoever sent it also transmitted from a Neurian source. Since the Gothman and Runners didn't have open communications with the Neurians, whoever sent the message had taken a huge risk.

Then again, she'd accessed the Neurian transmission and taken programs from it without Neurian consent. Had they discovered what she'd done and were now trying to reach her? Were they prepared to accuse her of theft?

Her thoughts reached beyond the immediate situation to the glider technology. How had the Neurians obtained it from the Lunians? Had they taken it, just as she had taken it from the Neurians?

The best thing to do was find out who sent the message before responding. Torgo had written a program to trace the source of transmissions. All she had to do was start it. She typed in the code name for the program, and the screen went dark.

She sat in complete darkness. The blue blinking light disappeared.

Wait a minute.

This wasn't what the program was supposed to do.

The Neurian traps!

The landlink was receiving a transmission. She could hear the dull hum as the chips inside accepted the information. If this were one of the Neurian traps, it would destroy all their programs. Without their landlink they would lose all communication abilities. She typed the abort code as quickly as she could. The box hummed louder.

Small letters appeared one after the other, from left to right, across the top of the screen.

"Tara, is that you?"

She took a deep breath, let it out, and typed, *"Who is this?"*

Every sound in the house exploded in her ears as she sat in the stillness waiting for a response. A branch rubbed against a window in one of the rooms down the hall. A rafter settled, groaning above her head. Muffled voices from the garage could be heard, and a dog barked in the distance. What usually were comforting sounds of home now caused her to jump, adding to her uneasiness.

She moved to the closest window and opened it. A soft, cool breeze chilled her sweaty body. She looked out on the grounds, illuminated by lights from the garage. Everything seemed calm and peaceful.

Except in her head.

An answer appeared. Tara stared at the one word blinking at her.

"Gowsky."

She'd figured Fleeders maybe, but not Gowsky.

She returned to her chair and leaned forward, struck by the magnitude of what was happening. The leader of the Neurian council was sending her a message in the middle of the night. Tara glanced around the room.

A new message appeared under the first. "*Tara?*"

She typed, "*What do you want?*"

As Tara sent the message, she thought about the bid request the Neurians had sent. In lieu of it, should she appear friendly or hostile? Let bygones be bygones. Could she do that?

And if she could for Gowsky, she would have to for Darius.

"*I was going to ask you the same question.*"

Tara frowned. He'd found her on their transmission and wanted to know what she was doing there. Should she lie? Could she think of a believable, harmless lie?

A cool breeze moved the handmade curtains hanging in the window, and again she felt a chill. She looked at the window, then back at the screen. She couldn't take too long to respond, or her answer wouldn't be believable. "*Doing research.*" That was the truth, answered quickly enough, and as little information as she could provide.

She reminded herself that she didn't rule a nation. Yet. And she had two leaders to answer to. What would they think of this communication? She answered her own question immediately. They would be suspicious. Tara felt certain Darius and Patha would not offer this man any information, and would be skeptical of anything Gowsky might say to them. After all, Gowsky had kidnapped her, then told both Darius and Patha she had been killed, causing upheaval among the Runners.

"*Tara, what research are you doing?*"

Tara knew he could find out what sites she'd covered on their transmission. He was testing her. Or maybe, he, too, was being cautious.

She suddenly looked at the door. Darius wouldn't be thrilled to see her talking to Gowsky in the middle of the night right after they'd made love. *Please let him sleep.*

Tara continued to stare at the shadowed doorway as she pondered her situation. During her escapades with Dorn Gowsky, she had learned of Crator. And Tara knew if she trusted Crator to see her through a matter, then all would be fine. History had proven that to be true. She decided to take a chance that this fellow believer in Crator could be trusted. *"Have you been contacted by the Lunians?"*

"Yes."

The answer was so quick, Tara could only stare at the tiny blinking word. *Had it been a positive contact*, she wanted to ask. After all, hadn't they contacted the Lunians a long time ago? Had they formed an alliance, or were the Lunians stealing people from them, too? How did she ask him that?

"We need help," Gowsky typed next.

So Tara had her answer. The Neurians appeared to be in the same predicament they were. She put her fingers to the keyboard and typed the question, *"Have they taken your people?"*

"Yes. We've searched for their campsite. I just awakened from a dream about you. I know you can help us."

What? He dreamed about her? What kind of dream? Had the dog-woman come to him in a dream? She tried to remember if he'd told her whether or not he'd seen the dog-woman before. She was guiding the Runners and Gothman based on a vision. She had faith in her vision. But did she have enough faith to guide another race that was far from an ally?

Okay, Crator, I could use some words of wisdom right about now.

She looked toward the window. Did she confide in this man who'd held her captive for six cycles?

"I don't suppose you could ever forgive me for what I did to you. Tara, I'm sorry. Like I told you before, I'm sorry we didn't meet under different circumstances. I was deceived about your nature. I see that now. Crator speaks to you."

Tara watched the words appear in front of her. He was asking to be forgiven. She thought about what Darius and Patha would say. Patha would forgive. She'd seen that trait in him as she'd grown up. She wasn't sure what Darius would do. She lifted her hands and held them above the keyboard for a second, hesitating, then she typed. "*I forgive you.*"

A floorboard creaked behind her. She turned to look but had no time to react before Darius grabbed her and yanked her out of the chair. He had both of his hands wrapped around her neck and lifted her straight into the air. "What exactly do you think you're doing?"

There was no way Tara could respond. She dug her fingers into his hands, desperately trying to release his grasp. He held her so her feet dangled several inches off the floor.

She kicked at him savagely as she gasped for breath. "Let me go!" She squeaked out the words as she tore at his fingers.

"You were in here plotting with the leader of a nation that we don't even have an alliance with, you were. In the middle of the night, almost as if it were behind your lord's back, I'd say. It looks like Tara the Great may not be so perfect after all." He shouted the words so loudly, several dogs started barking outside the open window. "I'm glad to see you have it in your heart to forgive him."

Then he threw her.

Violently.

Up against the wall next to the window.

She let out a scream in spite of herself and began gasping to fill her lungs with air. Her hands went to her throat where she could still feel his fingers. Coughing, she turned to confront him.

"You left our room every night for a half-cycle, refusing to share my bed. A punishment from my lady, it was." He was coming at her again. "Why haven't you forgiven me?"

"Darius, wait." She tried to block him but hadn't recovered enough from being choked.

He raised his hand and brought it down with incredible fury across the side of her face.

The impact sent her sprawling across the floor. She brought herself to all fours quickly, the coppery taste of blood filling her mouth.

"You were with him for six cycles, you were." He hovered over her. "I'm thinking you weren't his prisoner the entire time. And now you're caught red-handed, you are, having a conversation with him while I sleep in the next room."

She pulled herself up and wiped blood dripping down her chin. "You're wrong, Darius. The transmission was left open."

"Shut up!"

He took one large step and was on top of her, lifting her up in the air while she flung at him in self-defense. "I should have done this a long time ago, yes."

He lifted her above his head. Adrenaline brought on by jealousy and rage must have aided him, because he'd never been able to overpower her this easily before.

All of a sudden, an arm appeared in the darkness of the doorway. Someone pushed a laser into the back of Darius' neck.

"Put her down now, Darius." Torgo wasn't shaking and he didn't look afraid as he walked into the room. He was completely enraged.

Darius threw Tara and, once again, she slammed against the wall and slid to the floor. Her loud grunt was enough indication of the pain from the impact. She scrambled to her feet as Darius turned on his brother.

"I told you to stay out of the house, I did!" He moved toward his tall, but not yet as well-developed, younger brother.

Torgo leapt backwards to stay out of arms reach, but kept the laser pointed at Darius' face. "This is my house too, it is." He growled just as his brother often did.

And he sounded impressively confident. So much so, that not only did he stun Darius, but Tara looked at him with astonishment as she picked herself up.

"You lay one more hand on her, you do, and I swear I'll kill you."

"Torgo, this isn't your concern, no." Darius actually lowered his voice as he studied the laser. His gaze went from the laser to his brother's face. "Now turn around and go back outside. You've work to do, you do."

"My work is done, it is." Torgo sounded almost too calm. "Now I'm needed in here. Back down and leave her alone, I say."

"Torgo," Tara spoke with authority. "Put down the laser. You're very brave, but—"

"More like foolish." Darius glared at his brother.

"She wasn't doing anything wrong, no." Torgo held his brother's gaze.

"How do you know what I was doing?" Tara asked, alarmed.

For the first time, Torgo's confidence seemed to falter. He looked at Tara and began to lower the laser. Darius made a move toward him and Torgo backed up a bit, straightening his arm again. He glanced from Darius to Tara, but he didn't answer.

"I asked you a question." Now Tara spoke firmly. She walked up to Torgo and grabbed the laser without hesitation. "And put that damn thing down."

"I was monitoring your transmission," he said quickly.

Tara opened her mouth to say something.

Torgo hurried on. "I was bored, I was. There's nowhere comfortable to sleep out there, and you said to stay out of the house." Torgo tossed his head at his brother. "We've converted all the bikes you instructed us to use, we did. They've been tested and are ready to go, yes."

Torgo paused and saw that he had both of their undivided attention. He stood as tall as he could, spreading his legs slightly and puffing his chest. He spoke to Tara as he continued, although he kept giving his brother quick glances, feeling vulnerable now that he was unarmed.

"Tara, I knew he would try something like this when he emptied the house, I did. I daresay you embarrassed him out there this afternoon in front of his guards, yes." He swallowed, hoping neither of them would notice his growing uneasiness. He was defending Tara's honor, though. Certainly that amounted to something. "If he put a few bruises on you, broke a bone, something like that, he would save face in front of his soldiers. Tara, we're Gothman. We have to be lord over our claims, or we'll be thought as fools."

* * * * *

"And you?" She put her hands on her hips, still holding Torgo's laser. "Will you beat the woman you claim if she doesn't behave the way you want her to?" She moved a hand to her face and rubbed her jaw, sure she would be able to produce the wanted bruises.

"I'm thinking it would depend on the situation." Torgo now looked completely awkward stuck in the middle of Tara and Darius' argument.

"I see." Tara looked from Torgo to Darius. "I hope you're man enough to look over each situation very carefully."

Torgo turned red, and Darius looked like his anger would rekindle.

She challenged Darius with her eyes, then handed back the laser to Torgo. "Take some blankets and head back outside. Sleeping in the hay is pretty comfortable." She escorted him by the arm when he looked like he would protest. He still seemed worried that she was in danger with his brother.

"Maybe you should keep it, yes." Torgo tried to put the laser back into her hand.

"Don't worry about me." She turned and clobbered Darius in the stomach, causing him to clench his fists and tighten every muscle in his body. In spite of that intimidating gesture, Tara laughed. "He's not going to hurt me. I've sparred all my life. Do you think a Runner can't take care of herself? Go make sure my bike is converted as well."

Torgo's eyes widened at her request, and he looked at Darius.

Tara turned to her claim, as well, wondering if he'd given instructions for them not to convert her bike. If so, there would be somebody else getting hurt.

"Go take care of her bike," Darius grumbled.

Torgo headed toward the staircase, but he watched Tara until he began to descend.

"You forgive him but not me, I see." Darius followed Tara back into the computer room. It wasn't clear whether he was making a statement or asking a question.

"You haven't asked me to forgive you," Tara pointed out. She slumped into the chair, forcing a look of indifference at his deadly presence, when all she wanted was to hear those words from him. Nothing Gowsky did to her hurt as badly as knowing Darius was the papa of her sister's child.

But Darius was an incredibly proud man. He remained silent, studying her, his hands on his hips. Tara met his eyes, and he returned a scornful look.

For a second, he looked like he would strike her again and she braced herself. Instead, Darius dropped onto one knee before her. "Tara-girl, will you forgive me?"

She blinked, and in spite of herself, her mouth fell open. Was this her all-powerful, merciless Lord Darius? Was this the dark warrior who took what he wanted and offered no explanations in return? She stared into his dark, haunting gray eyes.

How could she refuse the most handsome, challenging man she'd ever known? Besides, hadn't he noticed she'd already forgiven him? Or at least, she'd decided to put it past them, and thought that had been apparent during their lovemaking. She smiled back and rubbed her jaw. "I was going to forgive you, but now I think you need to apologize for hitting me."

He took her face gently in his hands and leaned forward to kiss the green and purple marks that had appeared along her jawbone. She closed her eyes as his kisses began moving down her neck.

"Do you want to hear what else Gowsky said?"

"In a minute."

Chapter Fifteen

ಸಿ

Patha and Darius stood talking in the pasture behind the Bryton house the following morning.

Tara slowed and lowered her bike to the ground and parked not too far from them. She owned the only Runner bike converted the night before, and it ran like a charm. Torgo and one of the mechanics had made sure the bike had passed its test drive just that morning.

The sun barely shone above the horizon, but the activity of the household and surrounding yard would make one think everyone had been up for hours. In actuality, that wasn't too far from the truth.

A few hours before, Tara had noticed that Torgo, who had been making last minute adjustments on her bike, looked like he hadn't slept much at all.

"It's almost done," he said as she approached. He walked around the bike away from her and squatted to tighten a screw. To Tara, he appeared to be avoiding her interrogating look.

"I'm really proud of the way you acted last night," she said quietly.

Torgo stood and wiped a dirty hand across a dirty forehead. He was handsome and would be as captivating as his brother when he grew older. There was a different air about him. Something softer, smoother around the edges. He was the intellectual. His brother was the warrior.

"Tara, he was going to really hurt you, he was." He pulled a rag out of his back pocket and wiped some greasy fingerprints off the paint on her bike. "You really shouldn't have taken him on so seriously in front of his guards, no."

"I did kind of get carried away," she agreed. "I don't think that was the only reason he got upset, though. He wants to own me." She didn't finish. She almost said that would never happen, but didn't want to burden his young shoulders with so much worry.

His gray eyes studied her face before he returned his attention to her bike. "He might at that." He shrugged. "I daresay he was off to a pretty good start when I showed up. I couldn't, no, I *wouldn't* stand out here and listen to that."

"Thanks," she said, and he nodded.

She wanted to ask him why he'd been monitoring her transmission. Was he simply listening to other people's conversations because he could? Or had someone, like Darius, asked him to monitor her? Since several Gothman mechanics entered the garage, she kept her questions to herself.

"Any problems, my lady?" the Gothman mechanic standing next to Torgo asked her as he eyed the greenish bruise traveling along her jawbone. She remembered that Gothman men would approve if they saw a bruise or two on her. The mechanic gave no indication that it impressed him one way or the other.

"Seems to run just fine." She smiled at him. "Thank you."

Patha and Darius approached at that moment. She hadn't spoken to Patha yet this morning. The look on his face when he saw her bruised jawbone didn't resemble the look the mechanic had given her at all.

Patha balled his hands into fists as he stared at Tara. Suddenly, her gut swarmed with apprehension as she anticipated how he would react to her appearance. "Tell your team they did a good job." He nodded to Torgo. "Give them a break for a couple of hours, then have them reconvene in the garage. We'll need enough of these bikes converted for several armies."

"Yes, sir." Torgo took the cue that he was being dismissed. He stared at his brother, as if waiting to see if there were further instructions, but Darius' stare remained unreadable.

"I'll be in my room if you need anything, sir."

Patha focused on Tara after Torgo left. He didn't touch her, but his eyes studied the bruises.

Tara didn't move under the scrutiny as her gaze shifted from Patha to Darius and back again.

* * * * *

Patha had arrived at the house before the sun was up, requesting a servant girl in the kitchen to rouse Darius for him.

Darius opened his eyes to see the girl standing next to the bed, tapping him very gently with one finger on the shoulder. As she had leaned over him, the shoulder of her shirt had slipped down her arm, revealing a fair portion of overripe, young breasts that swelled with her breathing. She had made no effort to slide the shirt back to her shoulder and cover herself.

The girl whispered that Patha was downstairs to see him, hesitated for a moment, then backed up and left the room. He hadn't responded to her whispered request to come downstairs. His eyes simply settled on her and watched her until she'd left the room.

That was no way for a servant to wake her lord. Especially a servant who looked like she did, with her large breasts and full lips. She wore her sandy red hair pulled back in a ponytail, but several strands always seemed to fall around her face. And it to top it all off, she was very young, still possessing that untouched look, which made her contemptibly appealing.

Darius wasn't comfortable having a servant with her looks in his house. He saw the way she eyed him, too. With expressions of curiosity and a little fear. Not quite flirtatious, but definitely not unwilling. He knew he had a reputation. Most lords did. And young women had been giving him that look since he was younger than Torgo.

He had Tara, though. She wouldn't put up with him having sex with other women; that much she'd made clear. But if that girl kept coming around him like that...

Darius made a decision at that moment. It wasn't the most monumental decision he'd ever made in his life, no, not by a long shot. But he gave himself credit for being more of a man than most by coming to the conclusion. He would not lose Tara, no. And if altering his ways would keep his claim by his side, then he would do it.

This wasn't a decision he planned to announce publicly. That would not do. Gothman were proud, and he knew his Gothman blood ran thick. But Darius decided he would show Tara his loyalty. And he knew just how to do it.

When he'd left their bed, Tara had been curled up in a ball with her back to him. It had been easy to slip out of bed without bothering her. Now, he showered and dressed, then went straight to his mama's section of the house.

"Woman, I will speak with you." Darius found his mama in her room.

"Yes, Darius." Hilda smiled at her son as she straightened a few pieces of clothing in her hands she had just pulled from an overnight bag. "I daresay, I don't know how those Runners find peace sleeping in those trailers, no."

"They are accustomed to it, they are." Darius leaned against the doorway, filling the space with his massive frame. "I have made a decision which I need you to implement immediately."

"Of course, m'lord." Hilda placed the clothes in a wicker basket, then faced her son. "What should you like me to do?"

"You shall replace the young servant girls in the house with older women immediately." Darius added no explanation.

His mama seemed content with the instructions. "As you wish, Darius." She closed her now-empty bag and watched her son turn and disappear down the hallway. She didn't bother to mention that Tara had requested the same thing the day before.

* * * * *

"Have you heard that I talked to Gowsky last night?" Tara asked her papa. She let her gaze lazily fall onto Darius' unreadable face, then turned her attention back to Patha.

"I've heard a lot of things about last night," the old man said, frowning. "But I'd like you to tell me exactly what the two of you talked about."

"Of course." Tara nodded.

Patha held onto the two of them as they worked their way through the backyard and into the house.

"Patha, I have an idea," she said when they'd settled around the dining room table.

Hilda came in with a pot of tea and a large tray piled high with rolls and assorted jams. The dishes rattled slightly when Hilda set the tray heavily on the table. "I daresay I didn't realize it would be that heavy, no," Hilda mumbled, rubbing one wrist with her plump hand.

"Let me help you with that." Tara slid from her chair and reached for the plate of rolls, setting it on the table within reach of the two men. "We'll have new servants for you soon enough," Tara added quietly, knowing the woman had released the young girls from their service, and now had no help. Tara couldn't help but smile when Darius grinned at her as she handed him tea. Her jaw hurt but she had to admit, the rest of her felt pretty satisfied.

She proceeded to brief the men about the extent of her conversation with Gowsky the night before, brief as it was. Tara wondered what Gowsky thought when she'd simply stopped transmitting in the middle of their conversation.

"So what I had in mind," she said, as she chewed on a roll. "I think we should offer to work with the Neurians."

"What?" Darius slammed down his coffee mug and some of the liquid splashed onto the tablecloth.

"Why should we work with them?" Patha raised his hand to silence Darius.

Tara silently fumed at how well Darius obeyed her papa. She went on, "We agree to stop the Lunians and return any captured Neurians to their homeland. In return, they furnish us with the necessary oil to do the job. Runners and Gothman need the oil, and Neurians don't have the warrior skills to stop the Lunians. It's a fair trade." She sat back and smiled at the two men as they both stared at her, then added to support her argument, "They're not warriors and you know with these gliders, the Lunians will be no match for us."

"Another point of discussion," Patha spoke slowly and looked at no one in particular. "At what point do we assume we've stopped the Lunians?"

He now looked at both of them, first one, then the other. "You two have quite an ordeal on your hands with this one, I'm afraid. You may go in to their camp easily enough and get our people back, but I fear they're desperate enough to find ways to get what they want. How far are you willing to go to stop them?"

Tara didn't like the way her papa talked. He sounded so tired, almost defeated. This wasn't the way her Patha acted. At the first sign of battle, he'd be up pacing the floor barking orders right and left. Now he sounded as if it wasn't even his problem.

"Patha," Tara whispered his name soothingly as she laid her hands on top of his. "You're the leader of the Runners. I will fight until you say it is done."

Patha slapped her hands away.

She jumped back, falling against the back of her chair in bewilderment. What was wrong with him? They had a serious battle ahead of them. All indications were that it would be a war involving more than one continent. Why was he acting like this?

They shouldn't even be sitting here. They should be on their way to battle.

"Don't talk to me like I'm a child," he reprimanded her so loudly she jumped. "I'm not a senile old man. I know who I am!" He got up from his chair slowly, then slammed it under the table.

"Look at you two." He growled at both of them now.

She had no idea where he was going with this.

"You two are so busy fighting each other, you don't see what is going on around you. People with no passion for sex should scare you. They're desperate and will do whatever it takes to survive. The jealousy you feel over each other will prevent you from making clear choices. My god, woman, look at your face. When are the two of you going to figure out you can't control each other, and it's not your job to do so?" He broke down coughing, holding onto the edge of his chair.

Both Tara and Darius jumped to his side.

"Get away from him." Reena shoved open the door and pushed Tara from her papa. The older woman wrapped her arms around his wheezing chest and stroked his back until he'd caught his breath. "Sit down, old man."

"No." Patha put his arm around Reena and moved toward the door. "I'm done here."

"Patha," Darius began.

Patha stopped and turned back to them. "Here's how it is. I can't die peacefully in my sleep until I know you can rule the Runner clans as I've taught you, Tara-girl." He looked deeply into his daughter's eyes and continued, "This one is all yours."

"Patha, don't talk like this." Tara quickly moved to her papa, grabbing his arm. "You've taught me well, and I promise I won't let you down." She wrapped her arms into his and felt Reena's hand rub her arm.

But Patha took her hands and backed her into Darius. "You belong by his side now."

She felt her claim's body behind hers and his hesitation before he gently put his hand on her waist. She swallowed hard and looked at her papa, unable to comprehend what he said. She and Darius had already been bonded together by every treaty Patha had been able to think of.

Patha went on. "From now on, you are leader of the Runner clans. Show me you can do it, Tara-girl. Let me die a happy man."

She was the ruler now? Tara's heart skipped a beat. Then it did a double beat. *Breathe.*

A rush of thoughts tumbled through her brain at the same instant. She wanted to leap for joy. Scream at the top of her lungs. Sit on the floor and cry like a baby. Smack her papa across the face so he would come to his senses.

Her heart raced now, and her legs felt rubbery. The leader of the Runner clans?

"What are you saying, Patha?" It was all she could do to speak.

"Call it a trial run. Get yourselves out of this mess." He turned to Reena and brushed her cheek with his hand. "Take me home, old woman."

She smiled and led him toward the door.

He paused and looked back at them. "Oh, and quit hitting each other."

Then he was gone.

Chapter Sixteen

ଛ

Tara felt frozen in time as her papa's words rang in her head. Darius' hand was no longer on her waist. *When had he moved it?* She wasn't even sure he still stood behind her. Her feet might as well have been lodged in stone as she worked to turn around.

They were equals now. And Tara's heart pounded out an irregular beat as she wondered how Darius would react to that knowledge. The one thing he held over her had just been taken away. She should be elated, she told herself. Equality had been something she'd fought for since the beginning.

While Darius had grown up thinking of women as little more than property, she had to give the man credit that he didn't treat her as such. But to know *officially* they were equals…how would he handle it? It took all the effort she could muster to turn and stare at those dark gray eyes.

His gaze attacked her with incredible force.

She stood silently.

"We need to decide what to do." That was all he said as he stood as solid as a brick wall looking down at her.

"What we need to do is get those Gothman warriors on the road."

"Agreed."

Darius spoke into his comm and turned away. Walking toward the door, he opened it and stepped to the side to allow her to exit. His movements were mechanical.

He must be in shock, too. She wasn't sure why that thought startled her.

Tara followed Darius outside. Standing by the side of the garage, she watched him go into action.

He organized the Gothman he'd chosen to ride the gliders. Torgo drilled them on how to navigate. Test drives were taken. Directions were programmed into the gliders' landlinks.

Tara felt the shock wear off. Wait a minute! She'd just been given what she'd worked for all her life. Leadership of the Runners! Why was she just standing there? She knew what to do. All her ideas, all plans she'd made, all of it could be implemented now.

Darius spoke with his personal assistant on the other side of the yard. He knew what he was doing.

She had a job to do, as well. "Torgo," she said as the teenager hurried toward her with a landlink in his hands. "I'll be at the Blood Circle camp if anyone needs me."

"Okay." He smiled at her but kept walking, focusing on the small screen of the portable instrument.

They would all be busy for a while.

Tara dashed up to her room full of ideas and bursting with excitement. She plopped down in front of the landlink and sent a message to all the Runner clans announcing Patha's decision. At the same time, she spoke through her comm, contacting several Runners in the Blood Circle Clan whom she had in mind to become personal assistants.

Her children burst into the room screaming with delight at the sight of their mama.

"I'm sorry, Tara." Hilda followed the vivacious twins into her room. "I didn't realize you were up here, I didn't." She already looked frazzled from spending time with the twins even though it was still quite early in the morning.

"Look what I have, Mama," Andru said, showing perfect baby teeth as he grinned at Tara.

"What is it?" Tara went to her knees and smiled at her adorable children.

Andru pointed a laser at her.

Tara blinked, then instinctively reached to take the weapon from her son.

Andru moved before she could grab it and began making exploding noises with his mouth as he "shot" at items in the room.

"I want it," Ana cried and tried to take the laser from her brother.

"I told you already," Andru said, pushing his sister away from him. "I will protect you."

"Make him give it to me, Mama," Ana cried. "I want to protect me."

"One of the guards gave it to him, yes," Hilda offered when Tara finally managed to wrestle the weapon from her son. "I'm told it is broken, it is."

Tara inspected the laser until satisfied it couldn't shoot, then smiled at her children.

"The two of you will need to share this." Tara ruffled her son's blond curls. The boy would look just like his papa someday. "Has Ana had a turn with it, yet?"

"I will protect her," Andru insisted, and tried to grab the laser from his mama.

"No. It's my turn." Ana lunged at her brother, and the twins toppled to the floor in a mass of arms and legs.

"I'm sure I'm at my wit's end with those two, I am," Hilda said as Tara separated the twins.

"Neither of you will play with this if you are going to fight," Tara reprimanded. She looked up at Hilda. "Sorry, Hilda." Tara allowed both children to climb onto her lap, offering hugs as they both eyed the laser greedily. "I didn't know you were watching them this morning."

"Tara-girl, I declare. You've noticed those two servant girls are gone now, haven't you?" Hilda's hands went to her hips.

"Yes, I noticed. But please, don't worry about the kids. They can stay with me. We have quite a busy day ahead of us." Tara smiled down at her children.

The usual daily activities were underway when she arrived at the clan site with Andru and Ana. Most of the children were in school, but the young ones ran through the scattered evergreens playing with each other. The few people she passed raised their heads to acknowledge her, but continued with their business. Several girls, old enough to have finished their formal schooling, hung laundry on clotheslines. A handful of older Runners, men and women, stood around the cool fire pit in a lively discussion over something.

She was about to turn this clan site upside-down.

The three Runners who'd agreed to be her personal assistants were already at the location she'd chosen. The trailer she'd used to travel to the southern continent was being backed in among several large evergreens when she pulled up.

"I see one of my first duties will be finding you a nanny," a female voice said, and Tara turned to acknowledge the Runner.

A tall, stout, dark-haired girl jumped out of a parked jeep. She walked eagerly up to Tara and stuck out her hand in greeting.

"It's good to see you again, Jolee." Tara shook hands with the muscular woman, then turned to her children. "I would definitely say that would have to be done before we get any other work accomplished." She laughed as she grabbed Andru, who was ready to take off running, and restrained him while freeing Ana from her sidecar.

"I want to go play." Andru twisted in Tara's arms.

"Me too," Ana wailed as she tried to help her mama release the belts securing her to the sidecar.

"You two will stay put and be good." Tara's tone settled the twins, and they looked at each other, as if silently communicating their frustrations.

"I'll get her out, Mama." Andru smiled at Tara, and his gray eyes glowed in the sunshine.

Tara straightened and watched the twins as Andru helped his sister from her seat.

She squatted and began picking up contents of a bag Ana had accidentally kicked to the ground. She looked up to see Jolee already talking into her comm and smiled. She knew the young woman would be a good choice. She saw that things needed to be done, and she did them. It didn't matter if the job was pleasant or not. Jolee didn't mind getting her hands dirty.

Tara had grown up with Jolee, as she had with the other two assistants she'd recruited: Trev and Fartha. She'd hesitated on selecting Trev. He was handsome, but not her style. She knew Darius wouldn't be thrilled to see him among her trio. But he was good at strategic planning. His papa had advised Patha until he'd been killed during their war with the Sea People. Trev had learned his papa's trade, and she needed his skills.

Fartha had married Farn, the highest-ranking officer in Patha's army...her army. She'd actually decided on Fartha several winters ago because the woman had numerous connections among the army officers. Knowing personalities was as vital as knowing warrior capabilities.

"I have Cali on her way over." Jolee flipped off her comm but left it on her ear. Apparently, she was ready to work and excited to be involved in the heart of the action. "What next, boss?" The grin on her face was contagious.

Watching Cali take the twins stabbed at her heart. Andru and Ana should be with her; but this was war and she had a job to do.

Inside the trailer, Trev contacted all the clans for the second time that morning, and instructed them to journey toward the Blood Circle Clan site and remain on high alert. There were twelve clans on record, with the Blood Circle Clan having the most members. The clans ranged from as small as one hundred members, to the larger clans reporting almost a thousand in their ranks. There was power in numbers, and Tara's assistants agreed it was a good tactical move.

Fartha communicated with her husband, and he called in all armies. Some of their best warriors had left with the Gothman soldiers to cross the mountains the day before. Fartha now identified those fighters held in high esteem who remained on site. She continued to talk to her husband over her comm while connected through the landlink, compiling armies and preparing assignments.

"The Red Rock clan reports being the farthest away," Fartha said to him then stared at her landlink. She nodded to something said to her and punched keys as she spoke, "You're right. They have a little over a hundred members, but they are on their way."

"Haven't the Three Rings clan submitted some proposal for an improved version of the laser?" Jolee asked.

"Yes, that's right." Tara nodded and opened a nearby landlink, then pushed the button and watched as the screen lit up. "Make a note to see if any of the weapons are ready for battle."

Jolee sat at the large kitchen table with Tara and pulled up what maps could be found of the eastern part of their continent. She noticed Jolee's surprise when she accessed the Neurian transmissions and began searching their pages for maps.

"So now what are you doing?" Jolee seemed to have given herself to the position of first assistant. It fit her personality, Tara thought. She just automatically jumped into things.

"I learned a few things while in Southland." Tara smiled but didn't look up. "These people have some incredible landlink programs running." She stopped at the page containing the glider diagnostics and printed it for Fartha.

"Well, I'll be." Jolee kicked her long, thick legs up on the chair next to her. Her bright green eyes danced as she grinned at Tara. "You're good, Tara-girl."

"I want all bikes converted. Obviously, start with the warriors who will be our front line. Organize a team of mechanics and set up shifts to work around the clock. Tell them if they have any questions, to contact Torgo. A small team under his direction converted ten bikes last night."

In response to a small beeping sound, Tara reached across the table for her comm. At the same time, the screen on her landlink went black. After several images flashed in front of her, small letters appeared at the top of the landlink as they had the night before.

She watched the screen as she fixed the comm to her ear and heard Darius' voice. "Tara. We've company coming, we do."

"Tara!" Fartha sounded excited. "There's a large army approaching us from the east. I don't have a fix on them yet to give you a count. I'd say they're three or four hours away."

Tara looked at the landlink screen in front of her.

"Tara, I recognize your login number now. You've got a large army of Lunians approaching you. Estimated arrival time: 4 hours. I have an army equipped with 500 gliders that can reach your southern borders in approximately 5 hours. We don't claim to possess your warrior skills, but our technology is superior to yours. Do we have an alliance?"

Tara was being forced into a sudden decision about trade with the Neurians. If she took the wrong step, the Runners and Gothman could lose the chance at unlimited oil, something they desperately needed.

"Gowsky just contacted me," Tara relayed to Darius. She purposely cut short her message, knowing their comms could be tapped.

"I'll be right there." Darius cut the communication.

She stared at the screen and thought for a minute.

"I can speak for the Runners. We have an alliance. Our protection for your oil."

She exhaled and waited for a response. Her first command decision. Why did it have to be one concerning the Neurian government?

"We'll discuss that when I get there."

Gowsky was coming?

Darius entered the trailer without knocking less than ten minutes later.

She realized he hadn't asked her where she was, yet he'd come right to her. Oh, her stubborn pride. When would she admit she didn't yet possess the leadership skills he did?

He viewed the small group with an iron stare, then let his gaze fall upon Trev.

Tara introduced the three Runners as her personal assistants. No one batted an eye when she introduced Jolee as her first assistant.

Darius nodded and came around behind her to view her screen.

Jolee jumped up and pushed a chair to the back of his legs, and he sat.

She then moved into the kitchen and Tara realized she was making coffee. Jolee had been a good choice.

The brief conversation was still on the screen, and Darius showed no emotion as he read it. "Is the transmission still open?" he asked quietly, and with way too much control, Tara thought.

"I'm not sure. I haven't figured out how to tell if they're individually transmitting yet." Tara began to type.

"Gowsky?"

"Yes, Tara."

She looked up at Darius.

He reached in front of her and began typing.

"This is the Lord of Gothman. You may cross our nation's border in return for 100 flasks of oil. Other negotiations may be made upon delivery of the oil."

Tara looked up at Darius but he didn't return her look. His expression was cold and powerful. She hoped he wouldn't kill the Neurian upon his arrival.

"Lord Darius, I look forward to the opportunity of asking forgiveness for detaining your mate. Your terms are acceptable. Your reputation is well-noted, and I can only pray that Crator will allow you one day to consider me a friend."

Tara looked at Darius again. If anything, his expression appeared colder than before. His dark gray eyes finally turned and summed her up with a hard gaze. She met his gaze, hoping she didn't seem too curious about what was in his mind.

He turned back to the landlink and closed the transmission. "Come outside with me." He stood, causing her assistants to glance his way.

"Let me know as soon as we have details on this approaching army," Tara said to Fartha. "And I want to know as soon as other clans start to arrive."

Trev nodded.

Jolee looked at her questioningly, and Tara knew the woman wondered if she should accompany Tara or not.

"Get those mechanics in gear, Jolee." Tara followed Darius out of the trailer.

They walked toward an open area where mechanics already were working on the bikes. Darius led with his hand behind her elbow, barely touching her, yet steering her nonetheless.

"Since your clan site borders the Gothman nation, in the future, please don't agree to an alliance of any kind without consulting me first." He continued to look ahead, guiding them toward the bikes. He sounded nonchalant, as if they were talking about the weather.

"We need their oil." She felt a need to defend her decision. Tara wanted the alliance. Even if they'd discussed, or more like argued, over the matter, she would still want it. An alliance with the Neurians could only make them stronger. She'd bet on it.

"Which I negotiated, not you." He looked at her this time.

She felt the weight of his stare.

"I have the responsibility to protect Gothman, I do. If that means asking you this favor, then I ask."

Ask a favor? Did he actually sound humble? Not Darius. Yet, she thought he softened just a little.

No. He was working her, testing her leadership skills. That had to be it. Darius didn't ask favors; he issued commands.

She wasn't sure she liked this. He was easier to control if he didn't get under her skin too far. "I've called in all Runner clans. All the Runners on Nuworld wouldn't fit on that moon." She nodded her head toward the faded white crescent, still visible against the almost-white sky. "Your Gothman people will be protected."

"That, my lady, was a good military decision, it was." He reclaimed her elbow, and they continued to move toward the vast number of bikes parked in the field.

Tara reflected on the situation at hand as they walked. Whenever time needs to move quickly it's known to travel at a snail's pace. However, on the flip side, when there are many things to accomplish and only so much time to do it in, time is known to travel at lightning speed. Tara experienced the latter.

So many preparations were necessary for a successful battle. Of course, the art of surprise was a very effective strategy. And that was what the Lunians intended, she was sure. They had planned a quick, aggressive attack before the Gothman and Runners could organize all their troops. It was to their best advantage. She'd do the same thing in their shoes.

There was no way she would be in their shoes, though. Crator willing, the Runner and Gothman would never know how the Lunians had become so desperate to reproduce, they'd steal from others to do it. And to steal children, no less. The thought made her cringe.

The ten soldiers Darius had sent out first thing that morning reported in as the pair approached the head mechanic. The overweight Runner mechanic was soft-spoken, but knew how to work a crew. Hundreds of bikes were set in assembly-line fashion, with small crews each attaching the same piece to group after group of bikes.

Darius received a call on his comm.

Tara was more than curious about what was being said as she wandered down the rows of bikes and watched several Gothman mechanics skillfully detach and reattach exhaust pipes.

Darius didn't make her wait though. "Our men have spotted the Lunian army, they have." He walked up to her.

She noticed with interest how the Gothman mechanics suddenly began working twice as fast as they had minutes before. She also noticed Darius said *our*. Was he assuming they would rule both nations together, one law applying to two nations, one decision created by two rulers? Patha had known this would happen when he had them partake in the extra ceremonies during their claiming. She hoped for half of her papa's wisdom when she officially became leader of all Runner clans. "How many Lunians do they think there are?" She continued to watch the mechanics.

"Our landlinks detect five hundred gliders that should arrive on our eastern borders within the next few hours," Darius spoke quietly and kept his eyes fixed on his mechanics, as well. They must have assumed he wasn't satisfied with their work, because they now appeared to be working at quite an accelerated speed.

"I say we go out and meet them," Tara said after a minute of thought. "We don't want them getting close enough to steal more people."

Tara's comm beeped, and Fartha spoke into her ear. She verified what Darius had just said, since now she could access the landlinks of the ten soldiers. Tara switched over to Jolee, who told her she'd find every available body with any mechanical knowledge so they could convert the bikes faster.

Within the hour, the field swarmed with activity as young Runners helped bring in more parts so the bikes could be turned into gliders. Anyone not graced with mechanical knowledge was put to work providing necessary parts.

Darius ordered all Gothman women to cook meals for the workers. Hundreds and hundreds of people flooded the field, children and dogs ran underfoot, and the commotion was so loud it was hard to think.

"You've heard what they are saying now, haven't you?" a plain-looking, middle-aged Gothman woman said, as she stopped by a handful of ladies preparing sandwiches to be taken to the working men and women on the field.

Tara, who had stopped to help several teenage Gothman girls stack wrapped sandwiches in bags, couldn't help but overhear the women as they talked.

"I daresay I've heard the talk, but I don't believe a word of it." This came from a stout woman who walked with a limp. She dropped a sizeable amount of wild boar onto a table and began chopping it with a butcher knife.

"These people are going to invade us and steal our babies, they are." A gaunt young woman, with an infant secured to her back in a carrier, chopped cheese and looked at the other ladies with a terrified expression.

"Yes, it's true," another lady added as she wrapped sandwiches in thin paper. "My claim told me just the other night, he did. They come in during the night and steal them from the tit."

Tara listened as the gossip grew among the women. There would be no point in setting the women straight. No matter what accurate information she offered them, the ladies would distort it before the day was out. Besides, the point of the stories rang true. The Lunians would bring nightmares and anguish upon them if not stopped.

Tara's comm beeped in her ear, and she opened the link to acknowledge the call.

"Tara," a strange voice spoke.

"Yes." She frowned as she concentrated on the voice.

"It's Gowsky, Tara."

The singsong accent ran through her ear. She turned quickly to locate Darius, but didn't see him.

Tara was standing at the edge of the field, and quickly walked away from the crowd to better hear the voice that she found difficult to understand. Where was Darius? She scanned the crowd one more time. *Oh well, she could think for the two of them.* "Where are you?"

"About an hour from your southern border."

His accent was distracting.

"Someone was tapping your line," he continued. "I've secured it. We can talk freely."

"Who's tapping my line?" How she wanted his technology. *Imagine identifying a tapped line.* Tara could detect a simple bug easily, but knowing when someone else with different technology was listening would be an incredible advantage.

"The source is in Lord Darius' house."

Tara froze, not surprised that Darius would listen to her conversations. In fact, she felt sure the source would be Torgo. Whether or not he worked under Darius' instruction was another matter altogether. But Gowsky could conclude a lack of trust might exist between the two of them. Who was she fooling? Everyone knew there was a lack of trust between them. And everyone knew why. Even foolish teenage girls.

If Darius had given instruction for Torgo to monitor her comm, Torgo would report to Darius that the line had been secured. She turned again to watch the crowd, expecting Darius to come forward any moment.

"Tara, fifty more of our people were taken during the night." Gowsky paused.

She felt his pain and frustration.

"I come to you on faith. I need to know. Lord Darius, I mean, what I want to know is..." He hesitated.

She could imagine one of several questions Gowsky might want to ask about Darius.

"I know he has ill will toward me."

Ill will is putting it mildly.

"He has good reason. I want to talk to him. I know I won't be able to do it right away. This war will be in full force too soon."

Tara figured out where he was headed in his roundabout way. "You'll have your opportunity to beg forgiveness and clear your conscience, I assure you, Gowsky."

"Call me Dorn, please, Tara. You allow me to use your first name."

"Runners don't use two names. We have clans."

"Are you prepared for the Lunians?"

Were they? Tara looked at the number of completed gliders parked at the side of the field. Over one hundred were ready to go. While many of their warriors would fight on the ground, they would be able to annihilate Lunian gliders in the air. For those flying, Tara knew they would fight at a disadvantage since they had never used the machines before. But Runners had warrior blood running through them, as well as the ability to adapt to new culture because of their nomadic heritage. Tara relied on that, along with a prayer, to get them through this war.

"We're completely prepared." She watched Darius walk down one of the rows of bikes toward her. He moved quickly and had a concerned look on his face. She decided she wouldn't

Tara the Great

say anything about the secured line and see if he confessed to tapping her comm. "Crator is on our side, Dorn."

"Crator is with you, Tara. If we stay on your side, we'll all be safe."

No pressure with that comment.

"Who are you talking to?" Darius asked when he stood next to her.

She mouthed the word Gowsky.

Darius reached down and took her comm off her head and secured it around his ear. "Where are you?"

Tara followed Darius as he moved to a group of tables where landlinks had been set up. Runners sat before them. Jolee noticed Tara and Darius approach and stood.

Darius took her seat and began punching at the keyboard with his large fingers.

"Login to my signal and pull up the screen I have in front of me," Darius instructed.

So he did have an idea of the level of technology the Neurians possessed. What was Gowsky saying to him?

"I want you at these coordinates, I do." He tapped the screen with his fingers as if Gowsky could see it.

Tara marveled once again at the technology the Neurians possessed as Darius talked. Apparently, Gowsky had been able to pull up the same screen Darius viewed.

"One of our armies will meet you there, yes."

Tara watched her claim as he gave orders into her comm. He looked so powerful with his long muscular legs, broad chest, blond hair hanging in curls, bordering his profile. His jaw was set, his lips closed. He stared at the ground. She guessed he focused on the strong accent, working to understand the head of the Neurian council.

"That hasn't been decided yet, no."

What hadn't been decided yet? Tara frowned and wished she could hear the other half of the conversation.

Darius flipped off the comm, pulling it out of his ear. He looked at her, somewhat distracted, and shoved the comm into his pocket.

"Darius?" Tara wondered if he realized what he had just done. Did he want control over her communication that much? She placed her hand in front of him, palm up. "That's my comm."

"Of course." His distraction disappeared and he focused on her.

She could tell he was processing something in his mind. He had the look of a conqueror, an intense passion for control accenting the lines under his eyes and on either side of his mouth. His dark gray eyes were almost black.

He handed her the device and pointed to the parked converted bikes. "Are those gliders ready to go?"

"They haven't been tested, but they're as ready as they're going to be," Jolee spoke up.

Tara half expected Darius to give her a reprimand for speaking out of turn. Instead, he turned and acknowledged her statement with a nod.

Feeling rather satisfied that he appeared to approve of her choice in a first assistant, Tara flipped on her comm as she wrapped it around her ear. "Fartha, organize one hundred soldiers. We're heading out."

Darius took Tara's arm and walked toward her trailer. He spoke into his comm, replaced around his ear.

She wasn't sure, but she thought she saw him also signal Jolee with his eyes to follow.

Either way, Jolee looked at Tara for confirmation.

Good. Jolee respected Darius as a leader, but her loyalties were to Tara. Tara gestured with her head for Jolee to follow, and the stout woman fell in behind them.

"Torgo," Darius spoke as they walked. "Link with Fartha and line up an army of one hundred warriors. The gliders are ready, they are. Have them report to the Runner site immediately."

"Are we sending out half Gothman and half Runners?" Tara asked as they approached her trailer.

"Is that all right with you?" Darius asked.

"I think so." She couldn't think of any reason why it mattered. All their warriors would be used before this war was over, she feared. "And us?"

"We go."

Patha surprised her by greeting them as they entered the trailer. She hadn't noticed his bike parked outside. He leaned over Tara's landlink at her kitchen table and straightened as they entered. His face showed his concern, but Tara noticed something else. Was it the smell of battle?

Patha had looked almost defeated back at the house. Tara was nervous enough to know that she now had rank, but seeing her papa look beaten had terrified her. Now she saw the fire back in his eyes, but Patha still looked tired.

"So it's time for battle." He reached out to them, and they each pressed a hand into his. "May Crator guide both of you. We'll be triumphant today."

"The Neurians have arrived, they have." Darius offered the information to the older man.

"I see that. It looks like a fairly large Lunian army as well." The thrill of battle increased on Patha's face. "You can outdo their numbers with the Neurians, but don't have faith in their warrior skills. Rely solely on our warriors, and you shall be triumphant in battle."

"They'll be able to help us in other ways. With their technological skills," Tara pointed out.

"True," Patha said. "Use their abilities well. They'll be an asset."

He'd come to give them moral support and to see them off, Tara realized as her Papa squeezed her hand. Tara suddenly felt very proud of him. Everything she had in life, Patha had given her. She was in his arms before she realized it, and the rest of the room stood silently as she embraced and hugged the old man.

Patha walked alongside Tara and Darius, and she noted his proud gait, one of a seasoned warrior who had earned the respect of every warrior in the field.

"Your troops are ready," Geeves said to Darius when the trio approached.

"Landlinks have been tested on all gliders." Farn wore the insignia showing his rank on his Runner jacket.

Tara acknowledged that she outranked him only due to being Patha's heir.

"You realize we haven't had time to test the gliders."

"Yes." Tara nodded and surveyed the field, where row after row of warriors sat on gliders waiting for their orders. "The reports show they are as ready as they will ever be."

"We have fought under worse circumstances and been triumphant," Farn said.

Tara returned her attention to him. "And we will be triumphant today." Tara smiled at the older man.

Farn nodded.

Darius lowered the mouthpiece of his comm, adjusting it in front of his lips. "Prepare troops for departure," he commanded.

Tara adjusted her comm and issued the same order. She mounted her glider, quickly noting the new instruments added to her panel. Darius' glider stood next to hers, and she met his gaze after watching him finger his new controls.

"Ready, Tara-girl?" he asked quietly, and the corner of his mouth turned up in a roguish grin that caused her gut to tighten.

"Damn straight, I'm ready." She grinned at him and felt the rush of adrenaline swoop through her as she started her glider.

They'd meet the Neurians and destroy the Lunian soldiers before the Lunians reached Gothman.

Chapter Seventeen

※

The Lunians looked like a dark swarm of flies hovering just above the ground when Tara first noticed them. Tingles ran throughout her body as she realized what she was seeing. A mixture of excitement, nervousness, and anxiety coursed through her at the thought of battle. She'd fought in many engagements, usually for lower stakes, and had experienced similar sensations.

The fight awaiting her now was for a cause like none other. The fight was for the right to choose when life would occur and how. It was for the basic right to which all people of Nuworld were entitled, and she would see they continued to have it.

Tara glanced at her new control panel once again to familiarize herself with it.

Torgo had decided, after reviewing glider schematics they'd obtained from the Neurian transmission, that Runner and Gothman vehicles should be slightly different.

Schematics didn't show any weaponry. Torgo had welded an Eliminator under the front headlight. An additional screen indicated when the deadly weapon locked onto its target. He'd also had the domes coated with the same basic substance used in Runner clothing to make them bulletproof.

Although several of Patha's advisors argued that it would make the gliders slower, two shields had been installed on either side of the bike, underneath the dome, to protect the warriors' legs as they flew. Torgo insisted the gliders were for attack purposes, and therefore needed to provide defense for their warriors to do the job.

Tara remembered seeing something close to pride cross Darius' face as he explained to her the features Torgo had added.

She felt comfortable riding the glider and was impressed by how smoothly it maneuvered. The translucent dome surrounding her upper body minimized noise. She could see around her easily since she didn't need to wear eye protection. Neither did the wind deter her. She could turn and talk to Darius on her comm and see him plainly flying next to her.

These gliders were an incredible invention, and as long as they didn't fly into each other during combat, Tara knew her warriors would eliminate their enemy easily.

* * * * *

The Neurians appeared to the south shortly after the Lunians became visible.

Tara's stomach flip-flopped as she watched the two races hover like dark clouds, moving toward inevitable collision. The Neurians approached at a greater speed. When they had first been spotted, they seemed to be a hovering cloud, but they quickly materialized into individual gliders flying in unison.

She reflected that while Gothman and Runners had improved the glider by making it a deadly weapon, the Neurians had turned it into a faster, more technologically advanced machine.

"Your Neurians have arrived, I'd say." Darius' baritone tickled her ear.

She glanced sideways at him, then looked beyond him toward the dark cloud. "*My* Neurians?"

"You invited them, didn't you?" His face was close enough to see his disapproving scowl, but she thought she also saw a glint in his eyes. Pride might have prevented him from asking help from a man who had done him wrong by taking his claim, but he'd wanted the Neurians there, too.

She smiled. "They're probably listening to you."

Within less than five minutes, the dark cloud to the south started to take shape. Individual gliders became distinguishable. All of them were painted midnight blue. Each glider displayed a silver-painted symbol on its side from an alphabet she didn't know, but recognized as Neurian. Within minutes she saw they also had larger consoles. And, instead of handlebars, a small wheel extended from a column in the middle of the console. No wonder...the Neurians drove automobiles, not motorcycles, Tara thought.

Darius slowed their army and they hovered above ground for the first time.

Looking down, Tara could see the tops of the tree branches and rejoiced she didn't fear heights. As the Neurians continued to approach and the dark cloud to the east grew increasingly larger, Tara gasped. Gowsky was flying toward them.

Try as she could, she wasn't able to move her eyes away from him. In her peripheral vision, she saw Darius watching Gowsky — or Dorn, as he'd asked her to call him.

She worked to suppress her confused emotions before they enveloped her. But they raced through her body with minds of their own. She felt recognizable fear. Racing toward her was the man who had succeeded in imprisoning her for six cycles. Due to his actions, the Test of Wills came to pass. She was also fearful because Gowsky, due to his race's technology, knew more about the Runners than they knew about him. No other race, let alone one man, had ever accomplished such feats.

Tara experienced awe, too. Awe for all the same reasons she felt fear. And awe because his race had brought the knowledge of Crator to her. She'd seen the dog-woman for the first time while in Semore.

There was another emotion twirling around inside her, less identifiable. Was it curiosity? Disgust? Did she loathe him? No, none of those things. But more like interest, casual interest in the mind and body of a very attractive man.

She wondered if Darius had detected that in her before she could mask her expression.

Darius had nothing to worry about. There was a big difference between noticing how attractive a man was and actually wanting him. Did Darius know about that difference? Or maybe the better question was, would he ever know the difference?

"Greetings, my lord." Speaking through his comm, Dorn Gowsky lowered his head respectfully as he moved his glider to hover next to them. "It's an honor to meet you in person, although I regret we have to meet under such militaristic conditions."

Tara silently thanked Torgo for her ability to listen to the men's conversation. He had converted their comms from a duplex system to multiplex.

"Are your troops armed?" Darius didn't acknowledge the greeting but turned to the heart of the conversation.

"Of course." Dorn smiled and looked at Tara. "I see you've altered the schematics you found for these gliders."

She smiled graciously, but remained guarded. "They were very helpful."

Jolee spoke into Tara's ear at that moment. "I anticipate fifteen minutes before our Eliminators can hit the target."

"Darius," Tara said and noticed Gowsky's smile disappear as he watched them. "Let's get ready."

Darius instructed the troops to prepare for combat. "Gowsky, instruct your troops to fall in with Gothman, yes."

Where the earlier part of the day had gone by way too quickly, the final fifteen minutes crawled so slowly as to induce madness. Tara watched the still-dark cloud now spread across the horizon. This was an army of only five hundred?

If some of the Lunians approaching them didn't have landlinks installed on their gliders, the Runners and Gothman wouldn't be able to detect them. They had based their count on how many Lunian landlinks registered. This army was twice the size they had assumed, half of them apparently traveling without communication. Her stomach dropped.

"Crator," she whispered out loud. "Please allow us to stop the Lunians from trying to reproduce by stealing from us. I know this is something You frown upon."

"Have faith," The whispered response was the dog-woman's voice.

Tara turned her head quickly, but all she noticed were Darius and Dorn suddenly looking at her with raised eyebrows.

"Are you all right?" Darius asked.

"Yes." She felt slightly unnerved. "Everything is perfect."

Tara looked at the approaching army, then around at their surrounding army. Glancing down at her screen, she noticed the target was moving slowly into the circle designed by the program, which indicated their wait was about to end.

"I have faith," She spoke out loud, and again Darius and Dorn turned to look at her.

Darius ignored her comment, or didn't feel a need to respond. He held up his hand, indicating they should prepare themselves. "All troops, ready weapons."

Rows of gliders pushed the necessary buttons on their consoles. Hundreds of Eliminators lifted their long noses from underneath headlights.

"Fire!" Darius yelled the command like a war cry. He turned his attention to Tara. "Now!"

The two of them dived out of formation and flew to the ground, launching a plan she'd developed that morning. They'd been so excited about these gliders and fighting in the sky, they'd overlooked a large factor. The ground.

Not much effort was needed to organize another army. Now over one hundred Runners took off on motorcycles as they would for any battle, while the other Runners and Gothman took off in the air.

When Tara first considered the strategy, she'd thought about leading it alone, but decided it might take more than one person to pull it off well. At the last minute, she'd made Darius aware of this line of scrimmage. And after minimal discussion, they'd agreed to move to the ground the second the fighting began—to make sure no one sneaked past them toward the border.

Their world appeared surreal as they landed. The sky full of warriors from three different races made the early afternoon appear to be the middle of the night. Occasionally, the sun would peek through a gap in the troops and flood the area with quick sunlight. Their movements were slowed by the need for their eyes to continually adjust to the rapid shifts between light and dark.

The ground troops hadn't arrived yet. The gliders only took thirty minutes to reach this destination, but their land army would not arrive for another hour. In the meantime, she and Darius would have to handle any survivors from the sky with their own ingenuity.

Explosion after explosion occurred above their heads and in the distance. While Eliminators were clearly reducing Lunian ranks, they were handicapped in one respect. They were designed to attack straight ahead only. To compensate, Tara and Darius had armed themselves with additional Eliminators strapped to their backs in leather cases. Preparing them only took seconds, and the first Lunians proved easy targets for the pair as the enemy flew above their heads.

At such close range, the Eliminator functioned true to its name. The Lunian gliders exploded in midair turning into raging balls of fire. As burning contraptions plummeted to the ground, they bounced, sending pieces of equipment and body parts flying in all directions, littering the terrain, and providing an obstacle course for the pair to maneuver through.

Tara choked on the stench from smoking body parts and flaming metal as she maneuvered around the debris, then focused on the sky, targeting Lunians on her landlink.

"Tara!" The tone of Darius' voice through her comm alerted her, and she lowered her head, realizing she'd had her neck strained backwards for quite some time now, staring upward.

"Darius?" She looked around quickly for movement of his glider, but was forced to focus on her own driving as more rubble fell from the sky into her path. She dodged what was left of a glider and realized it was one of their own. Her throat tightened, unable to tell who had just crashed to the ground. *Please let our deaths be minimal, Crator.*

"Look ahead of you, to the east," he said through the comm.

Tara did so and sucked in her breath. Approaching from the distance were more gliders riding along the ground. How many Lunians could there be? Was the moon larger than it appeared?

"Our ground troops have us in sight but are still a good fifteen minutes away. I daresay those Lunians will reach us sooner than that. Retreat toward our troops, yes."

"Darius, we can't—"

"Do as you're told!" Darius appeared out of the smoke forcing her to a stop. Rubble continued to fall around them. "Two people can't fight an army, they can't."

Tara eyed the approaching army. Retreat of any kind went against her grain, and she knew it went against Darius' as well.

"They don't have anything that matches our Eliminators, Darius." She challenged him and knew this time they were equals. "I'm pulling down some of our warriors. With the Eliminators, we'll slow down that ground army. When our ground troops arrive, it will be simple to stop them completely."

Darius looked ready to respond when suddenly another glider pulled next to them.

It was Dorn Gowsky. He held up an Eliminator for them to see, then lowered his dome.

Two other Neurians landed behind him.

"Couldn't help overhearing," he smiled and looked at the two of them. "I'm surprised at you, Darius. Your records don't suggest you're the type to retreat."

Darius scowled and moved quickly toward Dorn.

Tara jumped forward with her glider and intervened by pulling between the two. "We don't have time for this, gentlemen." She looked from one to the other, and gestured toward the oncoming army. "They're getting closer."

Darius gave Dorn a look that assured Tara he'd have it out with the man later.

"Spread out!" Darius ordered. "You'll stay by my side, you will."

Tara looked at him. "Have faith, Darius. We won't die today."

"I know we won't, I do. They want us alive, remember?" He gave her a hard look, then adjusted the controls on his panel to rotate the Eliminator toward the army.

Tara froze at his words. So that's why he was willing to retreat. An army that size could capture them easily. She glared at the oncoming gliders. Well, she would just have to see that they didn't get close. Still, they were within a proximity enabling her to identify outlines of their bodies inside the domes.

She fired first. Having the most experience with the weapon, she didn't hesitate. Her aim was true and the front gliders exploded, sending surrounding gliders skidding into each other.

Dorn and Darius started firing, and Tara was impressed by the accuracy of Dorn's aim. She wondered if it was her encounter with him that resulted in the improvement of his performance. Had he realized that a good leader needed the skills of a warrior in order to protect his people? If he hadn't figured that out before, certainly he would learn the lesson today.

The Eliminators, backed by the skills of those using them, successfully held off the Lunian army until Gothman and

Runner ground troops appeared. The Lunians still succeeded in close confrontation, though. Tara found herself in continual one-on-one combat.

The field was soon filled with warriors from the three nations battling for the victory each believed imminent. Above them, fighting continued in the sky. Tara no longer had time to focus on that.

Lunians began to surround Tara, and she resorted to her laser to prevent them from capsizing her glider. Fire as she would, soon four gliders forced her to a stop. A glider pulled in front of her, and she swerved to the left. But another glider skidded into her path and she slid the bike to a one hundred-eighty-degree turn. She bumped into a third glider and another one pulled up behind that one.

The faces of the Lunians showed their determination. She noted the pale eyes of the rider she slammed into. Eyes that looked desperate. Challenged. Focused. Guided by madness. They watched her and her glider carefully, trying to immobilize her and not hurt her. She could easily guess the Lunian orders and it chilled her blood. *Bring her back alive!*

Tara slowly came to the realization she was trapped. Captured.

She wouldn't go down without a fight. And with the knowledge they wanted her unharmed, she viewed herself at an advantage. Even if she were outnumbered, she had no problem harming them.

"Darius, I need help!" She spoke into her comm and, at the same time, gunned her glider into the one blocking her way.

The man fell to the side, capsizing his glider.

While accelerating, albeit not to any great distance, she lifted the dome of her glider and jumped free. Two of the Lunians collided, and she rolled to safety. Pulling out her Eliminator with one hand and holding the laser in the other, she fired first at the two collided Lunians with the larger weapon.

The explosion caused the other oncoming gliders to dart to either side. Jumping to her feet, she used her laser to eliminate another Lunian approaching her. Much to her delight, she discovered their domes were not bulletproof. The dome shattered and she heard the screams of the woman inside as the laser beam penetrated her chest.

Turning quickly, Tara aimed at the next glider coming toward her. There were too many of them. She needed help. "Darius, where are you?" she shouted into the still-open line of her comm.

"I see you. I'll be right there, I will."

How did he keep his voice so calm?

A strong arm wrapped around her chest. She elbowed her would-be assailant in the face and fell, tumbling to the ground. Scrambling, she just avoided another Lunian bike, which likewise, struggled to not run over her.

As she got to her feet, a little slower this time, three gliders pulled around her. One of the domes was down, and a long, thin black weapon pointed straight at her head.

"It is done," she heard the woman speak into her large microphone which wrapped completely around her head.

The woman obviously received instructions through the headgear she wore because her facial expression changed. She looked worried, nervous as she lowered her weapon, now aiming at Tara's chest. She bit her lip and Tara guessed she'd never shot another person before.

One woman's disadvantage was another woman's advantage.

As the Lunian female hesitated, Tara didn't bat an eye. She swung her arm and knocked the weapon out of the woman's hand. At that same moment, she felt something pierce her back.

Tara collapsed to the ground.

Chapter Eighteen

Darius heard Tara cry through his comm. He redirected twenty Gothman to attack and kill Tara's Lunian aggressors. His heart raced in his throat as he struggled to move with any speed across the littered field. Glider after glider obstructed his path. His lasers shot through their unprotected domes like a knife cuts butter. He left a bloody trail behind him and had no desire to keep track of the dead.

Now they seemed to be coming out of the ground, from the air, appearing everywhere at once. Without hesitation, he pulled out his Eliminator and attacked. Tara, as well as Patha, had advised not to use the weapon on targets at close range. He needed a large explosion, however, for a quick escape. The speed of the glider would save him.

Darius fired. Body parts blinded him, staining his dome with red and black mini-bombs. He accelerated, driving through the path he'd created. Fire and smoke obscured the field ahead. Still he rode the machine underneath him as fast as it could move.

Just as quickly as he'd accelerated, he forced his glider to a stop, unable to see. He raised his dome and slapped off the slippery droppings that fell on him as the clear cover slid away.

"Tara?" He'd lost sight of her and tried to get a response from the comm.

No answer.

"Tara?!" He yelled into his mouthpiece.

Nothing.

Not twenty yards in front of him, Darius caught sight of a handful of Lunian gliders riding east, away from the battle site, at an incredibly high speed. One of the Lunians had a black-clothed body thrown over the front of their glider. The rider flew with his dome down, and Darius noticed long legs with black boots bouncing up and down to the vibration of the glider as it raced away from the battle scene. Off the other side hung the head of the person, long, light brown hair blowing wildly in the wind.

"Tara!" Darius screamed.

The kidnappers vanished from his view.

Darius wouldn't tolerate the thought of Tara taken from him again. The woman was his, and he would kill to keep her with him. He couldn't survive without her.

He panicked. Although only briefly, it was long enough to make him realize the Gothman and Runners believed in and followed her visions. They needed her in order to win this battle. He couldn't let her get out of sight.

Darius yelled orders with more harshness than most of his warriors had ever heard from him. Immediately, a handful of Gothman and Runners broke free from the fighting and flew across the field in hot pursuit of Tara. He contacted Torgo, Jolee, then reluctantly, Patha.

Once in flight, he left the battle behind and headed toward the mountain range. His troops ahead informed him the Lunian kidnappers were firing on them. They returned fire and eliminated two but hesitated in aiming at the other three for fear of hitting Tara.

Darius realized that the Lunians probably anticipated he would follow Tara. He'd risk that, though. He was no prisoner, at least not at the moment, and he would do everything in his power to remain free.

From behind, Darius noticed gliders approaching him, gaining speed.

Now what!

Darius lowered his dome, making a mental note that he'd have rear weapons installed on these things, and shot at the pursuing gliders with his laser.

"I know you want me dead, Darius," came the familiar singsong accent through his comm device. "I always figured you'd make more of a show out of it than idly taking me out with your laser."

Darius turned his head to catch a glance at Gowsky grinning at him, his white teeth shining in his dark-skinned face. The man might be infuriating, but he was not Darius' enemy. At least, not at the moment. Darius stood down, more annoyed with Gowsky's good guy role than if the man were acting like a prick. *Probably doing it intentionally.*

He closed his dome and pushed his glider even harder to catch up with his warriors. The sun grazed the horizon, and the eastern mountains receded behind them. Darius finally managed to catch up with his group, and they all proceeded across a forested terrain.

"I daresay they disappeared just minutes ago," said one of Darius' men, who flew alongside him. "We tracked them as they flew down among the trees, we did, but then they just vanished off our landlinks."

"We're going down," he announced. "They couldn't disappear into thin air." He was beyond annoyed with this spontaneous mission.

Darius and the small group flew to the end of the forest, then backtracked. No luck. It was as if the Lunians simply no longer existed.

On top of losing Tara and her captors, Darius realized they would have to land and set up camp. Whether Gowsky and his Neurian troops liked it or not, they would be hunting for their supper this evening. Darius didn't know how much experience the Neurians had at *roughing it* during war, but at the moment he didn't care.

"What are your plans?" Gowsky walked over to Darius after they'd landed in a clearing among the woods.

Darius had no clue what their plans were. He wanted to say, *to find Tara, I'd be thinking*! But, instead, he pulled the flat Runner-style console from his glider and took a good look around them.

"Find out who among these men is best at hunting and send them out for supper, you will." He didn't look up as he spoke. The last thing he'd accept right now was Dorn Gowsky telling him he wouldn't take his orders. No one asked the man to come along. Darius didn't want the man anywhere around him. But he was here, and he *would* follow orders like everybody else.

Gowsky seemed to be aware of Darius' feelings because he walked over to the soldiers, apparently doing as Darius had asked.

Darius was glad of that, and he turned his attention to establishing a link with Gothman. It was to no avail. Even though Torgo had boosted communications, apparently the result of his efforts couldn't reach this far east of the mountain range. They were out of range.

A couple of Runners, one man and one woman, started a fire, and several Neurians created torches to keep any curious animals, as well as insects, away from the campsite. The Gothman used axes to chop a fallen tree, and one of them rolled a thick log over toward Darius and offered it as a chair.

"Best there is to offer, m'lord." The Gothman grinned a toothless smile. "I daresay those Neurians had to go and cut a log for that pretty-boy Gowsky," he continued, under his breath.

Hopefully they left a few splinters. Darius snorted, and the Gothman apparently interpreted that as approval to the comment just made.

Darius sat on his makeshift chair and pounded his keyboard until he could no longer stand Gowsky's curious stare. The men and women around him readied the camp for the evening, but the *pretty boy*, as his warrior had called Gowsky, seemed content to sit next to Darius and seemingly occupy himself doing nothing.

"We've lost communications with Gothman, we have. I daresay our resources are limited, but somehow we need to find a camp that is underground, yes."

Gowsky turned and spoke to one of his soldiers, a woman a little too pretty to be lodging with his Gothman, Darius feared.

Darius watched her walk across their camp and noticed several of his men watched her as well. "Keep her well guarded when she sleeps tonight, you should," he said under his breath.

"It's already crossed my mind."

Darius noticed Gowsky didn't smile for the first time since he'd arrived. "Good." He dropped the subject. "Tara told me what the Lunian campsite looked like, she did."

"What? She's already been there once?" Gowsky looked toward him and his brow narrowed. He was smiling less and less.

If he kept this up, Darius feared he might start to like the guy. "She saw it in a vision, yes."

The Neurian woman who'd been working on the landlink joined them and heard Darius' comment. She immediately brought her index finger, middle finger and thumb to her mouth, kissing them.

Gowsky did the same.

Darius looked at them in bewilderment.

"Crator has chosen her as His prophetess. Not many are privileged to have the visions," Gowsky explained.

"I don't know if Tara would agree that it's a privilege, no. She told me the Lunians are underground and that a canopy covers the entrance, it does. She wasn't sure of the timeframe of the vision, no, but was under the impression that she had time to prevent the things she saw from happening."

"What did she see?" Gowsky's curiosity seemed piqued.

Instead of answering, Darius looked up at the young Neurian woman who stood next to Gowsky. He didn't want to share this information in front of her. She was a delicate-looking woman, hardly someone he'd want to bring into battle. Maybe she was Gowsky's woman.

Her silky, long black hair disappeared over her shoulders and her dark skin was flawless. She almost appeared to blush at his gaze. She'd be an easy conquest if that were something he had on his mind at the moment.

Gowsky looked up at the woman. "Were you able to establish communication?"

"Yes, sir."

Her singsong accent added to her beauty. This race had its appeal. Darius wondered for the hundredth time if Gowsky had seduced Tara.

The woman offered her landlink to Gowsky. "I've opened transmission with Patha of the Runners."

Gowsky gestured with his hand that Darius should take the landlink, and he did.

The woman's hand shook as she handed it to him, and he wondered if she feared the Gothman reputation with women. If she didn't, she should.

After updating their condition to Patha, Darius typed in the question concerning the safety of their boundaries. To his surprise, Patha informed him that the Lunians retreated shortly after Darius left the battlefield.

Was all that bloodshed simply to obtain Tara and him? He couldn't fathom it. But why would they retreat as soon as he'd left? Was it coincidence? He had no answers.

"I take it your homeland is safe," Gowsky said, after Darius closed the transmission.

"At the moment," he said, still pondering the reason for the Lunian's retreat. Maybe Darius' troops had been winning. In the middle of battle, it was always so hard to tell.

"You're distracted," Gowsky noted. "You're worried about Tara."

Darius scowled. Of course he was worried about her. Knowledge of her vision didn't help his thoughts, either. "She's my claim. I'll kill to protect her, I will." He looked at Gowsky, deciding the Neurian had the kind of face and body women would like. "And I guess I haven't said yet how considerate it is of you to offer your assistance in rescuing her." He let the sarcasm drip. Why was Gowsky here anyway?

He watched the Neurian's face grow guarded. The repulsive smile returned. "We're here to help and do Crator's will."

Help yourself to what? Darius found comfort in his dislike for the man. "I can't help but wonder at your true intentions, no." He leaned forward and stared into Gowsky's dark eyes. "After all, you held her captive for six cycles, you did. She's an incredibly beautiful woman."

"Yes, she is." Gowsky matched his stare. "You're a very lucky man."

Darius watched Gowsky's muscles tighten and laughed inwardly at the notion that the Neurian might challenge him.

"I tell you this, Lord Darius," Gowsky continued. "She lay in my home, unconscious for six cycles, under false pretenses created by a Runner you later killed."

He obviously spoke of Kuro. The Runner had fed the Neurians lies about the Blood Circle Clan. And the man would have won the Test of Wills if Tara hadn't returned from the Neurian nation when she did. But how did Gowsky know he'd killed him?

"Tara's loved ones and clan were lied to under those same pretenses when her family was returned to them." Gowsky didn't bat an eye and continued to stare him straight in the eye. "Those conditions make it difficult for you to trust us. I regret that and have begged your forgiveness."

Was Gowsky actually raising his voice to him? He'd humiliate him in front of his own soldiers, the pretty-faced scoundrel!

"I tell you this, lord." Gowsky's eyes burned like hot coals. "I am not an adulterer! And I am not a rapist!"

What? Darius stared at him. Was that an accusation? It most certainly was, even though there was no law against adultery in Gothman, and rape was not an issue unless the woman was claimed.

He thought about his own actions. He could justify his adultery, given the circumstances, even if Tara had fumed over the injustice she felt she'd experienced. Silly girl. Like some tramp could ever replace *her*. But why had Gowsky mentioned rape? Unless…

Darius knew that no document existed charging him of rape. Indeed, no woman had ever come forth and accused him of such. Yet Gowsky had just implied that rape existed among Darius' crimes.

Still, one instance rolled through Darius' thoughts like a bad headache. His time with Tasha. What had happened to Tara's sister after she left the clan site? She'd never reported her whereabouts. Darius hadn't given thought to where the woman and her bastard son had gone. Until now. But Gowsky was implying Darius had committed rape, and Darius guessed he referred to Tasha.

Suddenly Darius knew where Tasha had fled when she'd left the clan.

"Our laws are very different," he said, still lost in thought. He felt the need to make his position with this foreigner very clear. "If I ever find out you laid a hand on Tara, you will not see the end of that day, no."

"Your threats aren't necessary." Gowsky's smile appeared forced. "The Neurian council sees the advantage in an alliance with your people, and so, I am here."

Movement behind Gowsky caught Darius' eye. He looked at his troops settled around the campfire, some of the soldiers turning a shaft over a large fire. Several wild birds were skewed and cooking slowly. Beyond that activity, however, he noticed one of his men had the pretty young Neurian woman by the arm. She obviously protested, but seemed stifled with fear.

Provoked by his conversation with Gowsky, he stood quickly and with several long strides, crossed the campsite, knocking a small stack of firewood over as he went.

"Arien, you'll leave the Neurian soldier alone, you will!" His command was spoken so loudly, several birds in a nearby tree complained and took to flight.

"Of course, my lord." The powerful Gothman warrior looked somewhat startled but backed away quickly and disappeared to the other side of the campfire where he sat without a word. The man was known for his pleasure in raping unclaimed women. Although he had a pretty claim, a woman like the Neurian wasn't safe in his presence.

Darius looked at the young woman, who seemed to be trying to figure out what she possibly could have done to deserve such treatment. Her eyes met his, then she looked down quickly.

Darius figured if she'd heard any rumors of the Gothman men, she'd certainly heard rumors about him. He hadn't asked her to be here. Maybe deep down inside, she was curious about his race. "I'm going to do a little exploring, yes." Darius turned to face the camp.

"My lord, you shouldn't go alone," one of his soldiers spoke from the campfire.

"I'll go with you, I will." Another jumped to his feet.

He raised his hand for silence. "No, none of you are any good to me if you don't eat, I say. I know what I'm looking for, and one man makes less noise in a forest than an army."

"Lord, if you'll let me put a monitoring device on you, then we'll know exactly where you are if you need us." One of the

Runner females stood authoritatively and moved to a bag from which she pulled a small box. Opening it, she selected a small, flat disc and held it on her finger as she walked over to Darius.

"It works best on your skin. It's seldom found when placed on the back of the neck." She held out her finger and he took the small disc, placing it as she instructed.

"I want continued monitoring of the area and an immediate report if any human life is detected," he said, moving across the camp toward the woods.

Behind him, he heard Gowsky say, "Tealah, you're with me."

Turning, Darius saw Gowsky gather a few items into a tote bag and gesture to the young Neurian woman. He caught Gowsky's look as the Neurian stood and placed the tote over his shoulder. At the moment, he really wanted to be alone, but decided not to argue the point in front of the camp. Grunting, Darius turned and headed off quickly through the trees, vaguely hearing Gowsky leave instructions with his troops.

Darius felt the need to see the sky, to leave the closeness of so many trees. He knew they camped within walking distance of the edge of the woods, since they'd flown over the area several times earlier that day. That's where he headed.

Night covered the trees with blackness, and he was forced to slow down long enough to attach a light to his laser. Footsteps behind him announced Gowsky and the way too pretty Tealah were gaining. Every crunched leaf or broken twig indicated their presence and added to his aggravation.

"Why are you following me, I'm wondering?" Darius finally confronted them.

"It must be frustrating being lord of a land and not being allowed any time to yourself," Gowsky said, as he and Tealah stopped next to him.

Tealah had a monitoring device in her hands, and she pushed buttons and scanned the area.

"The only frustration occurs when my orders aren't followed."

"Oh, did you give us an order?" There was that disgusting smile again. "Too bad we don't fall under your jurisdiction."

Darius growled and Tealah seemed to focus even more on the equipment in her hands. He started walking again.

"Why don't you tell us about Tara's vision?" Gowsky suggested and fell into line next to him, leaving Tealah hurrying behind to keep up.

"She would be better at telling you what she saw, I'm thinking."

"She's not here."

Darius stopped and glared at Gowsky. *Of course, she's not here. That's why we're here.*

Gowsky's smile disappeared, and he seemed to read Darius' thoughts. His dark chocolate eyes were searching and Darius didn't like it.

"The vision showed her what their campsite looked like. She was also told there was time to change everything she saw, but she didn't know how much time, she didn't."

"Told?" Tealah looked up from her equipment.

"The dog-woman speaks to her, she does." Darius stared down into the almond-shaped dark eyes surrounded by perfect, golden-brown skin. "She tells Tara what to do."

Tealah gasped and covered her mouth. He watched her kiss her fingers again. She had to be Gowsky's mistress. No man could work next to such a beautiful creature and not take her.

"There's time to change everything she saw?" Gowsky asked, and Darius turned his attention from the girl, to stare at Gowsky. The Neurian leader met his gaze. "What else did she see?"

"The Lunians are collecting fresh breeding stock, they are." He stared Gowsky straight in the eye and let his words have their impact.

"Breeding stock for what?" Gowsky asked.

"For themselves."

Silence.

Tealah whimpered.

Darius noticed her complexion had assumed a green hue as she covered her mouth and looked up at him wide-eyed. Dried leaves and small twigs cracked under their boots as they neared the forest's edge. "From what I overheard with my own ears, they can't have children, or they find the act of lovemaking so repulsive they've forgotten its pleasures, they have," he said this to the young woman, softening his tone as he did.

Tealah seemed unable to pull her eyes away from his face and her dark cheeks went crimson. Gowsky, on the other hand, showed no offense that Darius spoke to the woman in such a manner.

"So all the people kidnapped from our cities are to be used to help the Lunians reproduce?" Gowsky looked outraged. "I can't imagine a greater crime," he whispered.

"There are cures for impotency," Tealah spoke to Gowsky now, avoiding Darius' eyes.

Darius reached forward to lift a low hanging branch and held it until Gowsky took it. Looking ahead, he realized they'd entered the clearing. His light spread across trampled field grass. As he scanned the area, he saw a yellow tapestry pulled tightly over four slender silver poles. The poles elevated the cloth high enough that Darius was able to walk under it without stooping over.

He stopped under the tapestry. At his feet was a round hole with a ladder descending into darkness.

Chapter Nineteen

Tara studied the room from a large cage. She'd awakened some time ago to find herself locked within the confining space, and now was trying to get her bearings. From the strong dirt smell surrounding her, she guessed her cage sat inside a manmade underground cave. The walls and ceilings were probably dirt, painted with a white substance that seemed to be a clay mixture. It lightened the room a little, but other than that, Tara wasn't sure what purpose it served.

Wooden planks less than an inch apart provided flooring. She guessed this was also a cosmetic addition. More than likely, they planned on using these facilities for a while and wanted something easier to clean than dirt floors. Footsteps and voices in the hallway told her the room wasn't soundproof.

Tara wondered if this place would be the location the Lunians planned to inhabit on Nuworld. Creating underground rooms like this one, with finished walls and wooden floors, had taken time. The Lunians had been here longer than she realized. She pondered how many Lunians were in this underground campsite. And where were the other prisoners?

As for her personal cell, Tara could lie down on the cold metal floor with her feet against one wall, and stretch her hands above her head without touching the other wall. Long metal bars, about as thick as two of her fingers, stretched from floor to ceiling, creating the sides. They'd been welded into the cage's ceiling as well as the floor, eliminating the ability to turn them. The bars were far apart enough that she could stick out her arm to her shoulder, but no farther. Her leg could extend outside only as far as her knee. A laser would slice through the bars easily enough, but she wasn't surprised to see her weapons were missing.

Tara hated being unarmed. She hated the feeling almost as much as she hated feeling confined. Aggravation set in when she realized she couldn't escape, and had to simply wait until her captors decided to pay her a visit.

Tara guessed an hour had passed since she first awakened. She'd finally settled on the cage floor, leaning against one of the walls as she listened to people roaming the hallway outside.

"Well, I see you're awake now." A tall thin, pale man opened the doors and smiled a yellow-toothed smile. "I brought you some company. Your kind don't seem to take to her too well."

"This one is so damned timid; she probably won't make it through the night." The shorter Lunian, who had followed the guard into the room, scanned the exterior of the cage as he spoke. "Maybe she will be a distraction for you, so you don't try to damage our cage." The man laughed and gripped one of the bars.

"You ask me, she's too pathetic to be good for much anyway," the guard said. "Even if she didn't fight the take, she probably doesn't have the life in her to carry a fetus."

He pushed forward a small-framed beautiful Neurian woman. Tara thought she looked vaguely familiar and assumed she was one of those who had accompanied Gowsky. *Please tell me this doesn't mean Gowsky's been captured.*

The two Lunians carried a long thin pole she recognized from her vision. They both watched Tara like a hawk as one guard gripped the Neurian's arm in one hand, while struggling to open the lock with the other.

"No tricks now, okay?" He pulled back the woman and released the lock. "You know what these sticks can do?" He held the stick toward the woman's chest, and her brown eyes opened wide. She cowered from fear.

Tara's blood boiled. "I know what that stick is," she said as her muscles tightened. "I assure you the only way I will move is if you use it."

The Lunian holding the woman tightened his grip on her arm and slowly pulled the lock off the bars while watching Tara. "Don't you move now, hear?" Then he paused. "How do you know about these sticks?"

"I saw them used in my vision," Tara muttered, hoping to distract the men.

The tall man stared at her, then broke out laughing. "Your vision, huh? Oh, that's right boys, their god speaks through her. Remember hearing about that?"

The pair laughed, their sticks coming dangerously close to touching the Neurian woman.

Tara's body jerked and they stopped laughing.

"Down, girl." The one who'd been speaking pointed his stick at Tara. "Unless you really do want to find out what they're capable of doing."

"I saw them used in a room full of naked women," Tara said. "They were used again after several women were washed with hoses before they were taken upstairs to be bred." She looked at the men with revulsion before glancing at the girl. The poor thing was literally shaking, not a warrior at all, probably some type of scientist. "Touch her with that thing, and I'll find out for myself if your sticks are capable of killing."

The tall guard opened the cage quickly and threw the Neurian inside.

Tara caught her in her arms. She held her tightly as the woman started crying. "Tell Polva I want to talk to her." Tara watched as the man locked the cage.

"Polva?" The man turned at the door. "What makes you think she's here?"

"Just tell her I have a right to know the woman who wants to raise my baby."

The man snorted and slammed the door.

"I'm sorry, my lady." The young woman pulled away from Tara and wiped her face. "I'm sure I seem pathetic crying like this."

"Call me Tara," she said. "And it's understandable."

"I'm pretty sure Lord Darius and Dorn got away," the woman offered.

"Got away from where?"

The young woman didn't answer, but instead reached inside her shirt and slid free a flat piece of equipment. After glancing at the door, she used it to scan Tara.

"There," she said, pointing to Tara's arm. "A monitoring device of some kind is under your skin."

Tara felt her arm and, sure enough, on her right forearm, directly under the skin, was a small circular device. She rubbed across it, realizing the only way she could remove it was to dig it out.

Tara studied the interior of the cage, then sat and braced her legs against the bars alongside her. The Neurian watched.

"You may not want to look," Tara said.

"I have a medical degree," the woman said and squatted next to her. "Here." She pulled a small tool from her pants pocket and flipped it, producing a small sharp blade.

Tara smiled. "Wow, they really didn't search you, did they?"

"At times, it's an advantage to not appear a threat."

Tara noticed an odd expression on the Neurian's face but dismissed it so she could focus on removing the disc. She pushed against the bars of the cage with all her strength, bracing herself for the pain. Placing the tip of the blade next to the disc, Tara closed her eye, and slid the sharp edge into her skin.

Tara opened her eyes and pulled the minute disc from the bloody flesh. Pain shot through her arm, and she took deep gulps of air to prevent herself from crying out.

The woman grabbed Tara's arm to stop the bleeding while Tara gritted her teeth. "Rip my sleeve off and we can use it for a bandage," she said through her gasps.

The Neurian obliged.

Tara remained motionless until she could control the pain, then relaxed her body. She stared at the disc even as blood spread through the black material wrapped around her arm. The Lunians would control all of them this way, if they weren't stopped. She felt anger overcome her pain, then shifted her focus back to her cellmate. "What's your name?"

"I'm Tealah."

"And you're a doctor?"

"No, not exactly. I'm, well, I guess my title is personal advisor. I write a lot of our programs and came along to ensure the gliders' programs ran properly."

"Why aren't you a doctor?" Tara slowed her breathing, working to focus on this Neurian who still squatted in front of her.

"I practiced medicine for a while." Tealah smiled.

Tara studied the pretty face, wondering what made the woman stop practicing. "A woman of many talents." Tara noticed the expression she'd detected before. The look was guarded. "Why don't you tell me what happened right before you came here? I'm sure we'll have company as soon as they realize this device is no longer in working order."

Tealah briefed her, pausing when she reached the point where Darius, Gowsky and she had found the canopy and been ambushed by Lunians. Taking a deep breath, she went on, describing how Gowsky had turned tail and run, not fighting to save her.

Tara noticed resentment in Tealah's tone.

The Neurian also said that Darius appeared to have killed most of the Lunians, but she'd been pulled down the hole before he could save her. She admitted not knowing where he'd gone after she'd been taken.

"I see." Tara took in what Tealah said as she studied the room for the hundredth time and listened to the noises beyond the door.

"I wonder why these people can't reproduce anymore," Tealah was almost whispering.

"I've wondered the same thing. Then again, you can't have a baby if you don't try." Tara looked at the young woman. "This nightmare scenario they've created seems to be an extreme answer to a simple problem."

"I agree. Many ways exist to cure impotency, if that is the problem."

"Is this a matter you could discuss with some familiarity?" Tara focused her attention on Tealah.

The woman's eyes were loaded with emotion, but Tealah didn't respond right away.

Tara studied her face until she noticed Tealah's cheeks begin to crimson. Tara narrowed her eyes, and Tealah began to look uncomfortable. "You want to say something to me, and you're holding back." Tara frowned, but held her gaze.

"There are a lot of unwanted babies we could offer the Lunians," Tealah whispered. "And I heard Lord Darius say something earlier about these people really wanting you two."

Tara stared hard at Tealah. What was she getting at? Adoption? That made sense if the Lunians were willing to listen. But why would she present an obvious alternative in such an evasive manner? And what did she mean about overhearing Darius talking? Did she think they should put one of their children up for adoption? That was absurd.

Tara's eyes opened wider, and she stared at Tealah almost in shock. "Wait a minute." Her stomach tightened as an incredible thought entered her mind. "What are you suggesting?"

Tealah's face reddened as she looked at Tara, then dropped her eyes as she ran a finger along the seamless floor as if suddenly finding it interesting. "I just thought..." She didn't continue.

"You thought what?"

"What if I knew about a baby?" After another pause, she glanced at Tara. "I mean there are babies out there that shouldn't have been born, that could cause trouble." Now she did look at Tara. "That could cause *you* trouble."

Tara simply stared. The young woman sitting in front of her no longer looked like the helpless female thrown into her arms. A transformation had occurred before her eyes.

Tealah's jaw clenched and her features hardened. There was a vendetta behind her dark eyes as they focused on Tara without blinking. It came across loud and clear. Revenge. Spite. Jealousy. Tara saw it all in her face. Tealah looked like a woman with a purpose and a plan. Something, or someone, had harmed this woman, and she had a look about her as if she had just figured out how to even the odds. The ugliness of Tealah's expression lessened the woman's beauty.

Tara stood and walked to the other side of the cage.

Tealah didn't move.

Suddenly, Tara knew exactly what Tealah was saying, and she pivoted to face her.

The beautiful young woman sat cross-legged on the floor looking up at her. She cocked her head and looked far from helpless.

"How do you know about a baby who could cause me trouble?" Tara worried she might not be able to stomach the answer.

"I have seen Runner transmissions. You have a handsome family, Tara," Tealah spoke with a tone of authority.

Tara raised an eyebrow at the assuredness in this woman's voice.

"A visitor arrived before we made the trip to your land, and she brought a baby with her. I could be convinced the child is yours."

The door to the room opened and Tara turned, startled. She'd been so disturbed by Tealah's words she felt jumpy, and fought to remain calm as she turned to see who approached the cage.

Polva entered the room with four guards behind her. The woman looked nervous, but there was a sense of curiosity about her. Polva didn't speak right away. She stood and studied Tara, her gaze traveling from Tara's face, to her feet, and back up again.

Tara took the time to do the same to her. Runners lived their lives learning about new people and their cultures. But Tara couldn't remember ever meeting another person who came across in such a unique manner as the woman standing before her. She guessed that Polva might think the same of her.

Suddenly Tara had a plan.

Polva was a woman with a mission. She couldn't have children, for whatever reason, and she wanted them enough to commit horrendous crimes. Tara was about to appeal to that desire. If Polva wanted a child badly enough, Tara guessed the woman would listen to what she had to say.

Tara met Polva's gaze, and the woman looked at her suspiciously.

"You wanted to talk to me?" Polva's voice cracked ever so slightly, revealing her nervousness.

"I'm glad you got my message." Tara smiled, trying to ease the woman's nerves. "I have some concerns I wanted to share with you."

Polva laughed, somewhat forcedly. "Concerns? I don't care about any of your concerns."

"You will. But I really don't feel like sharing them with you with those brutes behind you."

"Oh, I bet you don't." Her laugh wasn't forced this time. "I'm no fool. You'd break my neck just to stretch your fingers if I gave you half a chance. You're barbaric, Tara. You belong in a cage."

"Forcing people to have sex and stealing their unborn child seems rather barbaric to me."

"It's necessary," she said with enough indifference to bring acid to Tara's throat.

"Hmm." Tara nodded. She turned toward Tealah who sat looking at her. The scared, unprotected look was back on her face. Tara wondered if she actually could fight. She covered her true nature so well.

Tara walked over to Tealah, reached down, and took the small knife from her hand. She then moved slowly back to the bars and leaned against the door to the cage.

"I've a very busy schedule," Polva hissed. "What do you want?"

"I want you to know I have no plans to hurt you." Tara glanced at Polva, then the guards behind her.

"I know you won't hurt me," Polva said.

With a move so slight it was hardly detectable, Tara used the knife to pick the cumbersome lock. She'd watched the guards lock and unlock it twice now, and had seen the simplicity of the device.

"No!" Polva screamed. "She'll kill us!"

Two guards jumped in front of Polva before the lock could fall to the floor.

But Polva tripped over them as she tried to race toward the door.

Tara shoved open the cage door, forcing them to stop rather than be hit by its swinging impact. Jumping out of the cage, she kicked one of the guards in the face so hard, she heard his cracking bones. She grabbed his electrical stick, punched the other guard in the stomach causing him to double over, and disarmed him just as easily.

Polva had stumbled and straightened to find herself staring at the end of the stick.

"Tell your guards to leave. If they tell anyone what they just saw, I'll kill you." Tara found the button on the stick and placed her thumb over it as she pointed the weapon at Polva's neck.

Polva backed against the wall of the room, looking like a trapped animal. The two guards still standing, blocked her ability to run. Polva also blocked the guards' path to Tara. She returned her wild stare to Tara and studied her for a minute. Then she glanced at Tealah, still sitting on the cage floor with an equally uncertain look on her face.

"I don't want them to leave." Polva sounded like a child, almost begging. "I'm scared."

"Step to the side, ma'am, and we'll put the bitch back in her cage," the larger of the two guards said, although when Tara looked over Polva's shoulder and smiled at him, the look of confidence faded from his face.

One of the guards on the floor moaned and attempted to stand.

Tara grabbed Polva by the shirt and pulled her away from the four men as she pressed the stick against Polva's chin.

Polva yelped.

"Stay where you are," Tara ordered, and the guard froze.

Tara realized these people weren't accustomed to dealing with resistance among their breeding stock—something else to use to her advantage. She softened her face, trying for a motherly look. The woman looked terrified and desperate. Putty in her hands. She let go of Polva's shirt and put both electrical sticks in one hand as she concealed the knife in the other.

Tara offered the two sticks to Polva with her injured arm. "I would like to speak to you."

Polva's mouth opening slightly. Her eyes riveted to the black material tied around Tara's arm and her complexion paled.

Tara imagined the woman had just thought of the pain she had endured to remove the disc from her arm.

Polva's hands shook as she grabbed the weapons, pulling them from Tara as if she feared a fatal disease. She held them upright in her hand, appearing to detest them as much as she did Tara.

"I won't hurt you," Tara said again, smiling gently and adjusting the small knife in her hand until its cool blade pressed against her wrist.

"You don't need weapons to hurt me." Polva's voice cracked several times. "Why are you doing this?"

"Polva, I want to help you." Tara stood back now, crossing her arms, looking as casual as she could. The last thing she wanted was the woman to become hysterical. "But this," she said, pointing to the cage, "isn't the way. I have an idea, a proposition so to speak. I just wanted to tell you first without others hearing."

Tara leaned forward as if to tell a good secret. She'd watched the old Gothman women assume this position so many times she knew it by heart. "I know how quickly gossip can travel through servants and guards."

Polva raised an eyebrow and pursed her lips as she studied Tara. Understanding seemed to flutter across her face. Tara had appealed to her female curiosity, and it worked.

Polva waved a hand to dismiss the guards. They looked at her, hesitating, then at Tara.

"Stand outside the door," Polva ordered. "I'll call if I need you."

"Good." Tara smiled and turned her back on Polva as she walked to the cage. She sat at its entrance, then crossed her legs and leaned forward to study Polva. "The first step in establishing a relationship between two races is trust."

"I have no desire to establish any kind of relationship, as you call it, with your people." Polva curled her lip in disgust. "And I certainly don't trust you."

"Well, I'll work on softening your heart, if I can." Tara maintained the gentle smile she'd plastered to her face. The woman was despicable, and it would be so easy to kill her and get out of this hellhole. Syra and the others needed to be rescued, though. Patience. She needed patience. Her plan would work if she could force herself to see it through.

"There is a problem I don't think you've taken into consideration," Tara began. "I can't speak for Neurians, but Runner women use birth control. You've stolen a lot of our women, and they won't be able to conceive for at least six cycles, depending on when they took their last dosage. Now Gothman women aren't that way, they have strong beliefs about such things. They breed again and again. Still, it probably wouldn't take too long for you to run into the same problems with them that you're having with your current breeding stock. They will die from overuse before they really matured. Gothman and Runner men, however, assuming you don't care about mixing the races, will be hard for you to keep in captivity. If you do manage to keep them confined in a cage like this, I'm afraid you'll break them. If you do that, you'll run into impotency. Don't let any of them know I said that to you, though." She paused and grinned, allowing a small giggle at the thought, then turned to Tealah, encouraging her to smile and thus support the statement's accuracy.

Tealah grinned and her eyes danced as if she'd just heard a good joke.

She was a master, Tara thought to herself. This woman could convince anyone of her sincerity to obtain what she wanted. It was a gift, or possibly a curse, depending on how a person looked at it.

"I suppose you have a solution to this problem you've created," Polva said, trying to sound bored, but obviously interested.

"There are many cures for impotency. Our doctors—"

"We've already researched that, and our medical knowledge is far superior to yours. The only problem you have described to me in your pretty, little fairy tale is that your men can't perform if held captive. I am guessing you wish to talk to me in order to explain how to solve this."

Tara wanted to smack her. "Neither one of us has time for me to attempt to explain the nature of men to you, Polva."

Polva gestured in frustration. "Then why are we having this conversation?"

"Our cultures are very different, you'll get no argument from me there, but I don't think you're that much more advanced than we are." Tara fought not to sound annoyed. "Besides, Polva, you'll not get a child from me and Darius. I won't allow it."

"And what makes you think I would want your child?" Polva rolled her eyes. "I suppose you're going to tell me you know that because of some vision, some omnipotent being provided for you."

Tara imagined wrapping her fingers around this pompous woman's neck. "Actually, Polva, when we first met you during our visit to your president, and the explosion occurred, we overheard you tell Brev why you so desperately wanted Darius and myself. It was no vision. You were on the other side of a capsized wall, and I heard you clearly list the qualities you now act like I don't have." Tara closed her mouth and grinned, haunting Polva with her own words.

"And if we explored your options and had your doctors offer their solutions, in return I expect you'd want us to release your people."

"Not exactly," Tara said.

Polva's eyebrow shot up.

"I want you to allow Darius and Dorn Gowsky of the council from Semore, to rescue them." Tara cocked her head to see the reaction.

"What?" Polva's eyes opened wide. "Let those two rescue them?" She laughed. "They haven't done a very good job so far."

Tara allowed herself to laugh, too. *Oh, it was hard to humor this monster of a woman.* "Two reasons why I want you to do this. First of all, it will help feed those male egos of theirs. They get difficult to live with if they don't keep their ego blown way out of proportion. And second, it will keep them busy."

"Keep them busy?"

"Yes, so they won't realize what I'm doing."

"And what are you going to be doing?"

"I'm going to get you a baby."

Both Polva and Tealah gasped. Now Tara had Polva hook, line and sinker. The bitch of a woman almost started drooling. Polva checked herself and narrowed her eyes, trying to look skeptical.

Tara leaned against the bars and smiled. She waved her hand in front of her as if to dismiss any ideas Polva might have that it wasn't a legitimate offer. "You can't have a child from me and Darius. I understand why you want one but, for those same reasons, you can't have one. But I can offer you the next best thing."

Tara paused and Polva listened without batting an eye.

"He's about five or six cycles old right now and in perfect health. He's a beautiful child, looks just like his papa." *Oh, it was hard to speak this way about a baby she detested.*

"And who are the parents?"

Tara licked her lips and forced the calmness to remain intact. "Darius is his papa," She exhaled in spite of herself.

"Who is the mama?"

Again, Tara licked her lips. This was harder than she thought. She couldn't even talk about it without rage churning in her stomach. She blew out a breath involuntarily. "My sister."

Polva laughed out loud.

Tara almost jumped.

The woman smiled harshly and walked across the room, away from the door, then back so she was standing directly in front of Tara.

Tara had just given Polva the upper hand, or at least she hoped that's what the woman thought.

The hatred Polva felt for Tara rose to a head in the look she gave her. The woman grinned and her eyes sparkled, showing cruelty in their glint. It was all Tara could do not to shove the look down the woman's throat.

"Well, the reputation of your claim is accurate," Polva snorted. "How terribly painful that must be for you."

Tara just stared. She wouldn't be able to take this much longer.

"Did you allow your sister to live?" Polva asked between evil giggles.

"She's in Southland."

"So there is something in this for you too, isn't there? I'd bet you'd do anything to hurt your sister for the way she's hurt you. I bet you live with pain from the knowledge of this child every day."

"Do you want the child or not?" Tara would allow the plan to bite the dust if this woman didn't shut up.

"Well, let me think." Polva rubbed her chin and walked back and forth in front of Tara, throwing glances every now and then. "You get yourself out of here and have that child back to me by tomorrow—before midnight—and your people will manage to escape."

"Shake on it?" Tara held out her hand.

Polva reached out her hand and shook Tara's, seemingly forgetting the repulsion she'd had for her minutes ago. "You've got a deal. Just see if you can get yourself out of here." Polva smiled smugly and pulled her hand back.

"That won't be a problem." Tara stood up and punched Polva in the face, knocking her out cold.

Chapter Twenty

"I can't believe you waited this long to do that." Tealah jumped up and stepped out of the cage.

Neither can I. Tara stared at Polva lying unconscious on the floor. She moved to the door and put her ear to it. The two guards talked quietly to each other, but Tara couldn't make out what they said.

"Are you sure you can get us out of here?" Tealah followed her to the door.

"Getting out of here isn't what I'm worried about," Tara said, almost to herself.

"Oh," Tealah understood. "Lord Darius and Dorn, huh."

Polva moaned on the floor and Tara looked at her, then Tealah. "If you don't know how to fight, I suggest you learn quickly."

Tealah opened her mouth to respond, but Tara pulled open the door and jumped into the hallway. Tealah was definitely no warrior. She did her best though, and managed a punch here and a kick there. Tara held the weight for both of them and, although she acknowledged Tealah slowed her down considerably, the two of them found the surface with little difficulty. Lunians had no warrior blood in them.

It was daytime, midmorning by the location of the sun, and as Tara lifted her head and upper shoulders through the hole in the ground covered by the canopy, she was dismayed to see a handful of Lunians setting up tents.

Just like in her vision.

Were the scenes she'd witnessed about to take place? Was her time running out? She blew a breath from her mouth, studied the landscape and its occupants, and prepared her strategy.

She hoped she'd made the right decision to flee the area in order to steal her sister's son. Maybe she should simply organize a rescue mission. But she'd shaken hands on a deal with Polva, and if there ever was to be any type of mutuality between the two people, she had to hold up her end of the bargain. If Darius knew where the prisoners were, which he did, he was more than capable of freeing them, with or without the Neurians' help.

"There's a large group of Gothman and Runners in the woods," Tealah whispered.

Tara turned to see Tealah holding her black pad and scanning the area.

"There are two gliders parked over there." Tara pointed with her finger, as she read what her findings told her on the thin instrument in her hand. "We'll have to make a break to take them. Let's hope Darius provides us with a good distraction."

"The group in the woods are getting closer," Tealah said. The two women stood on the wooden ladder, made with boards so thick, they almost resembled narrow stairs. Looking out the hole, the women's heads were barely visible through the prairie grass covering the surrounding ground.

"Let me know when they're—"

"Now!"

The two women exited the hole quickly and ran in the opposite direction from the Lunians working on the campsite.

"Hey!" A voice yelled causing both of them to run faster.

"Stop them!"

In the next moment, a loud explosion sounded, and Tara knew the Gothman and Runners were attacking. She desperately wanted to turn her head and confirm her suspicions, but the gliders were right in front of them. Tara straddled the glider nearest her, and Tealah climbed on the other one. Obviously, Tealah had studied the schematics on the Lunian gliders as well, because they both started the machines with ease. The two women left the scene as the attack began.

Neither one had a communications device of any kind with them or on their gliders. They were forced to fly close enough to each other to use hand signals. Tara discovered that the landlink panel attached to the dash of the glider pulled off easily. She threw hers to the ground and gestured for Tealah to do the same. She didn't want to leave any trails, and without landlinks, no one would know where the two women were going. No telling how many people would disapprove of the mission she was about to undertake.

For the second time in her life, Tara traveled over uncharted land without a landlink.

The sky grew dark as they entered Southland. Semore was under tight security and the two had no weapons, shy a tiny pocketknife. They landed in the desert, to the southeast of the town, not too far from where Tara had first met the dog-woman.

"You can't enter town looking like that," Tealah said, sitting on her glider next to Tara.

"I didn't bring any other clothes." Tara didn't turn to address the Neurian woman, but studied the town lights, trying to remember the layout.

"The first poor sap who sees you will recognize your attire as a Runner," Tealah pointed out.

"We don't have a lot of time." Tara looked at Tealah. "How long would it take you to get some clothes and bring them to me?"

"I'll have to go on foot." Tealah hopped off the glider. "These things aren't exactly commonplace in town."

"How long?" Tara didn't want to miss their deadline, and she wanted this mission completed.

"I'll be back within the hour." Tealah didn't wait for consent and began jogging across the sandy terrain toward town.

Alone in the desert, Tara watched the stars as they became more pronounced in the dimming sky. The cycle was new and the darkness from lack of a moon accentuated their brilliance. She studied them, making note of the lights that flickered and those that radiated continuously. She wondered what these little flecks of light would look like if she could get closer.

Pulling her thoughts together, she studied the dark desert and wondered if the dog-woman would approach her while she was alone. The desert was the first place she'd ever met the old lady and also where she'd buried her. *Any advice or words of wisdom would be really helpful right about now, dog-woman.*

Not quite an hour passed when she noticed a figure approaching. It was Tealah and she had a bundle under her arm.

"Here, these should fit you," she said and handed a pair of khaki pants and pullover tunic to Tara. Tealah also produced two Neurian guns and a small landlink. She held a small black bag under her other arm

"What's in the bag?" Tara asked as Tealah set it down.

"Medical supplies. I can take a look at your arm and clean it better, if you like."

Tara glanced at the twisted bandage barely covering the dark spot of dried blood on her arm. She'd grown accustomed to the pulsing pain from the cut, but agreed cleaning it would be a good idea. "The last thing I need right now is an infection."

Tara donned the Neurian outfit Tealah offered her, then watched the lights from the town while Tealah cleaned and redressed the wound.

They left the gliders and began the short walk across the desert toward Semore. When they reached town, Tealah suggested they enter through a yard as opposed to simply walking down the street. "Neurians don't go into the desert at night," she explained. "We don't want to arouse any suspicions. There are police everywhere."

Tara remembered Fleeder's reaction when she suggested they take a ride into the desert to find the dog-woman. He had shown the suspicion common to a people filled with myth and superstition. What they didn't understand, they feared. She'd seen the look of terror and disbelief in his face at her suggestion.

She nodded to Tealah and they quietly entered the town after passing between two houses, appearing like they'd simply left one of the houses after a visit.

"Tasha moved into a place just a few streets over from here," Tealah said quietly as they walked. "She must have approached Dorn the day she arrived. I think he's helping her pay for it."

Being a tramp has its advantages, Tara thought to herself, remembering her not-so-friendly welcome by the town.

"We don't have many fair-skinned people around here," Tealah went on to say. "I doubt most of the guards have a good idea of what Tasha looks like. They will probably think you're her, if any of them stop to talk to us." She shot Tara a quick glance before continuing. "No offense, but you do kind of all look the same."

Tara didn't respond, but thought she could say the same thing about the Neurians.

They traveled down a red paved road until they reached a small plain flat-roofed stucco house set in the middle of a neglected dirt yard. *Definitely not Tasha's style.* Tasha liked her things to be nice, and liked taking advantage of men to gain frivolous items that otherwise would have been difficult for her to obtain.

Tara placed her hand on the gun in her pocket as they quietly moved to the back door.

The house was dark inside. Not a good sign, considering it wasn't that late in the evening. She hadn't considered that her sister might have someone watching the child. Tasha enjoyed the nightlife. It might take most of the night to locate the baby.

She was relieved to find the back door unlocked. At least, they wouldn't cause a commotion by breaking into the house. They entered a dark room, obviously the kitchen. A small counter ran along one wall with cabinets above it. A kitchen table was pushed against an open window. Directly in front of them, a doorway led into a larger room. The bedrooms were more than likely on the other side of the living room, since the house wasn't that big.

With mounting frustration, Tara noticed that the house was empty. Two of the cabinet doors stood open revealing empty shelves. As they moved through the house, they saw only a chair in the middle of the large room and an empty bag lying on a bedroom floor. She kicked the bag with aggravation. "She's not here."

"I bet I know where she is, the bitch. I wouldn't have guessed she would pull a stunt like this." Tealah sounded angry, although in the darkness of the room, Tara couldn't see the expression on her face.

The Neurian stood quiet for a moment.

Tara waited to be enlightened.

"She's at Dorn's house." Tealah hissed the words, sounding extremely jealous.

Tara didn't have time to listen to how her sister had stolen another woman's man…again. "Is there still a force field around the house? When Gowsky held me captive, I remember he had a force field surrounding his property."

"Yes," Tealah sounded distracted but quickly pulled herself together. "But it only goes up twenty feet."

"Okay." Tara thought for a moment. "I'll go in by myself. There's no reason for you to burn bridges."

"I have no intention of giving up my home." Tealah showed the stubbornness that obviously aided in getting her where she was today. "I plan on walking in through the front door."

The two women discussed a course of action. Tara would walk back to the gliders. She'd allow a half-hour to pass before flying over the force field directly to Dorn Gowsky's house.

Tealah would allow the same amount of time to pass, then approach the front entrance.

She assured Tara the guards would allow her to enter; after all, it was her home and when they'd left, she'd been in good standing with Dorn. She was sure Tasha manipulated her way into the house, and Dorn would kick her out when he returned. Tara didn't bother to mention how manipulative her sister could be, and that Tealah might have a fight on her hands.

They agreed Tealah would say she'd escaped from the Lunians, and with the Neurians aiding in battle, she'd been unable to find her people and had returned home. She would make a big deal out of the battle and how the Neurians were fighting desperately to help save the planet from these invaders. Both women hoped such a story would provide ample distraction to allow Tara to find and take the baby, Tigo.

"One last thing," Tealah said as they stood in the dark of the vacant house. "When you take Tigo, would you please kill your sister?"

The question came as a shock to Tara, and for the first time she was glad for the darkness. She guessed eliminating Tasha would make life much easier for Tealah, who obviously didn't want to lose her place at Dorn's side or in his bed.

"Tasha won't stop me from taking the child," Tara said, hoping Crator didn't have a problem with the feelings that ran through her at Tealah's request. Tara wanted to assure Tealah that Tasha would be killed, and she had to admit she'd imagined different ways of eliminating her half-sister. A Runner didn't attack unless attacked first, and certainly Tasha had started the battle when she birthed Darius' bastard child. But for some reason, voicing premeditated consent rubbed wrong with Tara. She couldn't place her finger on the reason why.

As the two women returned to the gliders, Tealah briefed Tara on what she'd see approaching Dorn Gowsky's house. The front doors opened to the north. Tara would land on the southwest side, where there were fewer windows. The garage and barn were on the opposite side of the house. Other than the trees planted along the edge of the property, there was no foliage near the house. This meant Tara's glider couldn't be parked there long before it would be detected. Explaining why Tara was there if she were caught would be difficult. Her presence would be viewed as hostile. She'd have to be quick.

Tara sat on her glider in the long shadows at the edge of the yard and studied Gowsky's house. Fortunately, the structure stood only one-story high and was rather large. Tara could see to the end of the back of the house, but no farther. If someone walked around the corner, Tara would see them immediately. Plenty of time to be airborne before they could get to her.

The second window from the southwest corner was where Tealah suspected Tigo would be. Tealah had given Tara an overview of the layout inside, and this window was next to a small bedroom, which, in turn, was next to the master bedroom.

Tara had very little time. The longer she sat there, the more she risked being discovered. Time to implement her plan. Tara needed to move her glider into the open long enough to park next to the window, confirm the child was in that room, and take him. Tara took a deep breath, assured herself Crator stood beside her in this matter, and put her plan into action.

The window opened outward and two curtains moved gently with the breeze. Tara stared inside the window, taking in what she saw. A small lamp shed light across the room, and in a crib along the opposite wall slept a baby. Tara saw blond curls and a small body dressed in a long white shirt. All she had to do was crawl through the window, grab the child, and leave. This would be simple.

As long as no one saw her.

Tara looked along both sides of the house, saw no one, then stuck her head into the window. The door to the hallway was open, and she heard voices coming from somewhere in the house. Another doorway led into what she assumed was the master bedroom, from Tealah's description. The door opened toward her, however, and she couldn't see beyond it.

Climbing through the window proved no problem. She could hear the child breathing—a congested snore. She'd never thought the baby might not be healthy. Hopefully, it was just a cold, and not a bad one.

She made no sound as she moved across the room. Halfway to the crib, she could see past the open door. Tara froze at the sight in the master bedroom. Tasha was in there with another man. They were both half-naked, their shirts on the floor.

The woman had nerve.

Tara felt a sudden urge to pull her laser and kill her sister. Never before had she experienced such intense animosity toward another person. Tasha continued to rub salt in the open wounds she had created in Tara's emotions. Not only that, but the woman could offer Gowsky incredible knowledge of the Runners. The fact she had her bastard child with her was a reminder to all knowledgeable Neurians that a potential threat to the heir of Gothman resided in the Neurian leader's home.

It would be so simple to raise her laser and kill both of them. Tara's fingers itched to grab her weapon, and she hesitated as she approached the crib.

No, she wouldn't kill her sister tonight. The baby needed to be turned over to the Lunians, and a war needed to be stopped. Tara forced herself to focus on the mission.

She kept walking, leaned over, and raised the sleeping child to her breast, wrapping the blanket that had covered him around his pudgy body. He groaned and coughed, then nuzzled up to her and went back to sleep.

She had him.

Crawling out of the window, trying not to wake the somewhat heavy bundle in her arms, wasn't as easy as getting in had been. Although just brief minutes had passed, it felt like hours before she jumped onto the glider and lowered the dome. Tara hadn't seen, or heard any sign of Tealah, but couldn't worry about the Neurian woman right now. She had the baby. Now all she had to do was escape without confrontation.

Tara adjusted the baby in her arms and started the glider.

Something caught her eye as she drove quickly away from the house. She turned in time to see Tasha standing at the open window, screaming into the night.

"No! No! My baby. Someone's taking my baby!"

That was the last Tara heard as she accelerated with haste in order to gain enough speed to go airborne and clear the force field.

An hour at high speed passed before Tara believed she'd pulled it off. No one appeared to be following, although she knew she'd been seen. Maybe they'd tried, but didn't know what direction she'd taken. Maybe she'd gained enough distance on them that they weren't able to find her. Maybe she'd make it back and turn over the child before they could find her. Maybe.

Tasha might assume her sister stole her child. But what could she do about it? Her sister had no clout. If she got the child to Polva, it would be her word against her sister's. Tasha wasn't even allowed in clan territory—especially now that Tara was clan leader.

Would Darius prevent Tasha from entering Gothman as well? Tara could only hope. She maintained her speed but relaxed her body and her grip on the sleeping baby.

His breathing seemed to come easier now. He stretched his long pudgy legs and his feet stuck out from underneath the blanket wrapped around him. The infant's small hand found her hand stretched across his hip and leg, and his fingers wrapped around one of her fingers.

She looked down at his relaxed expression. Blond curls fell loosely across his forehead. She stared at his innocent face. He hadn't asked for any of this—all the hatred that stemmed from his very existence. He'd been conceived from a malicious, hateful act. But it wasn't his fault. She prayed Polva would be a good mama to him.

He looked just like Andru.

He looked just like his papa.

A lump formed in Tara's throat. He was beautiful.

Tara fought to calm her agitated emotions. But when she did, she felt a pang of guilt for what she planned for this child. Tara didn't like Polva; the woman was spoiled and self-focused. What kind of mama would she be to this boy? Not to mention the fact that the Runners and Gothman planned to attack the Lunians until they changed their way, or retreated from Nuworld. Then what would happen to this boy?

Tara looked away from the child. Her duty lay with the Runners and with Gothman.

She forced herself to believe she was doing the right thing. This child threatened her children by his mere existence. According to the law, if something happened to Andru, this boy would be heir to Gothman.

Tara refused to allow her sister's bastard that right.

She stared into the darkness and ignored the twisting discomfort growing inside her. "You'll make up for your birthright, little guy," she spoke quietly to the sleeping infant. "Tomorrow, you'll help save a planet."

Chapter Twenty-One

ೞ

Darius and Dorn Gowsky stood at the edge of the forest. After discovering the location of the Lunian campsite, they'd made arrangements for every available troop to meet them. Over a thousand warriors waited for orders to attack.

Torgo contacted his older brother. "I'm on my way."

"No." Darius shook his head as he spoke. "You serve me best where you are, you do."

"You can whip me within an inch of my life, Darius. But you've kept me out of battle long enough, you have. I daresay my functions can be better performed if I'm on site."

Darius knew his brother anxiously waited for news of Syra. And maybe the boy was right. Torgo might be ready for battle. Either way, Torgo would show up whether he approved or not.

Temporary hospitals were set up to take the injured once they were released. Reena insisted on being part of this.

Patha contacted Darius and told him there was no keeping back the old woman. "She won't be happy if she isn't making sure everyone rescued is treated properly." The old man laughed as he said this. "I'll keep an eye on her, Darius. She wants to make sure Tara is okay."

Darius had plenty on his mind, keeping the attack and backup teams in order. Therefore, when he signaled for the first regiment to move out against the exterior Lunians, he wasn't sure, but he thought he saw two individuals escape from the tunnel. The first round of explosions wiped out the unprepared Lunians, and as the smoke cleared, the two individuals—if they'd ever really been there—were gone.

"It's amazing their landlink technology isn't more advanced," Gowsky commented. "They didn't even see us coming."

"I noticed that," Darius answered, as he stood by his glider, consulting a landlink. With his comm hooked around his ear, he seemed to be constantly in conversation.

He'd decided not to enter the battle, but instead monitored activity from the side. Three nations were a lot of people to lead in battle. He wished Tara were here. He was doing her job as well as his, providing information to her advisors and his. Answering questions and delegating responsibilities. Directing troops and preparing strategies. The best way to accomplish this successfully was to allow his troops to fight and keep himself out of the confusion of battle.

As desperately as he wanted Tara by his side so she could do her job, he also worried for her safety. True, she'd be harder than any other woman the Lunians captured to get to cooperate with their atrocious scheme. But if they drugged her…

The smoke thinned around the aboveground campsite, and the troops—which had actually done very little work—assumed formation. Lunians corpses were scattered about.

Darius remained still, watching the ground, the canopy, and the hole, his eyes burning from smoke. No one appeared. He didn't like this, no. Lunians should be crawling from that hole, begging mercy, and pleading for their lives.

"I'm not convinced their technology is that inferior." Darius studied his surroundings. "This was way too easy, but not because they didn't know we were here."

"What are you saying?" Gowsky almost whispered.

"I'm not sure yet. My instincts tell me something's not right here, they do."

"You're an outstanding warrior. I trust your skills," Gowsky said confidently. "Make the call."

Darius looked at Gowsky quickly. He wondered if the Neurian knew the compliment he'd just paid him. Neurians weren't warriors though. Darius decided that the man simply made a statement, an accurate statement.

"We need to go down that tunnel, we do. I just wish I knew whether we were walking into an ambush or not." Darius rubbed his forehead, thinking. "It would help to get a count of how many Lunians are down there, it would."

Darius' comm beeped in his ear.

"Ask Gowsky to use their radar sensor, you should." It was Torgo's voice.

Darius quickly felt his temper rise at the fact that his brother, once again, was eavesdropping.

"If one person can get down there and have two or three minutes to do a scan, we should be able to get a count and a layout of their tunnels, I'm thinking."

Darius didn't respond to his brother. It was a good idea, but one of these days Torgo would get into more trouble than he knew with his listening habits.

Instead of reprimanding his brother, he turned to Gowsky. "Do you have a radar sensor here?"

"I'm pretty sure." Gowsky didn't look surprised that Darius was aware of their technology. "That was Tealah's department. I'll have to check."

Gowsky spoke into his comm, a slightly smaller version of the Runner device. "One's on its way," he said to Darius. "It won't read through the ground, though. Someone will have to take it under."

"Pick your man," Darius ordered.

Within minutes, a Neurian woman, slightly stocky and with streaks of gray running through her inky black hair, approached them. She carried a shoulder bag made of leather.

"Will this thing tell us how many people are underground and the formation of their tunnels?" Darius asked.

"I told you it would, I did," Torgo spoke in his ear.

"Yes, lord," the woman answered, looking a little nervous as she threw a side-glance to Gowsky.

He smiled reassuringly.

Darius thought the Neurian would make a better diplomat than leader. "Come with me." He moved toward the open field, gesturing for the woman to follow.

She did so, Gowsky with her.

Darius instructed several of his men to escort her down the tunnel. They were to ensure she had time to take her readings and get back out. His men understood. They moved proudly. It was a potential suicide mission, and they knew it. A Gothman would die in battle without hesitation. Better that, than old age.

Obviously Neurians didn't share the same belief. The woman looked at Darius, then at Gowsky with pleading in her eyes.

Gowsky placed his hand on her shoulder. "These men will see to your safety. They're outstanding warriors and would take laser fire for you without hesitating," he said quietly.

The surrounding Gothman probably heard him but none, including Darius, acknowledged his comment.

"Tell them to transmit their readings directly to my landlink." Torgo's voice was beyond irritating Darius. "I can translate it faster for you, I can."

"Where are you?" Darius let his frustration come forth.

"At the med unit where you told me to be, I am." He sounded defiant. "Where else would I be?"

"Get over here; it'll be easier for you to listen, yes."

"On my way."

Moving with caution, the Gothman soldiers headed toward the hole under the canopy. About three feet in diameter, it was large enough for an adult to climb down. The grass growing in the field stood tall enough that it provided a natural camouflage for the entrance. Two men approached on all fours, two others walked behind them offering backup. The Neurian woman followed. She studied her equipment as if she'd never seen it before, appearing to be psyching herself up for the mission she'd been ordered to undertake.

Darius positioned his men so they'd be ready to enter quickly, as soon as they ruled out a possible ambush. The two guards looked down the hole, then one of them threw a small Gothman-designed hand bomb down the tunnel. This particular explosive, with its quick detonation, worked best for maneuvers exactly like this one — to flush out the enemy.

Immediately after the Gothman soldier threw it into the tunnel, frantic voices were heard. Their suspicions were correct. An ambush laid waiting for them. The bomb rolled down the hallway and out of their line of vision, while the two soldiers cast light with their beams, trying to see farther into the underground complex.

Darius felt the ground shake as the muffled explosion went off.

"Now move," he ordered.

The two warriors leapt down the hole, not bothering with the large wooden ladder resting against the entrance.

"Move, woman!" Darius put a hand on her back and pushed.

She obliged, but took the ladder.

"Get your readings and get out of there."

Gunfire could be heard and smoke drifted up from the entrance. The two other Gothman warriors jumped down the hole and immediately started firing. Darius signaled several other soldiers who immediately ran for the hole, also, jumping and firing almost simultaneously.

Minutes seemed like hours before the Neurian woman crawled out of the hole. She was covered with dirt. Even her skin looked ashen, instead of the glistening black it had been when she climbed down.

She looked up at him and smiled. Her teeth glistened white in her soot and dirt-covered face. "I got it!" She held the instrument above her head as she climbed the last few ladder rungs. "I did it."

Torgo surprised Darius as he reached around him and grabbed the instrument. Torgo quickly attached it to the flat landlink he held, and the woman moved to his side to watch the results.

Darius saw Gowsky look at Torgo with interest, obviously noticing the strong family resemblance. Their eyes quickly returned to the hole as voices cried out.

"My lord," one of the Gothman soldiers yelled from below. "We've secured the entrance, we have."

"How long is the hallway?" He moved to the hole and bent down to be heard better.

"I daresay about fifteen feet, yes m'lord," the Gothman spoke with a thick local accent. "I wouldn't be for sure on that though, to be certain. The hallway splits, it does, and goes in two different directions after that, yes."

"Good job men," Darius yelled, and some of the troops behind him hooted in support. "Try to maintain the entrance, I say. We'll send down reinforcements as soon as we get these results, yes."

The Neurian woman worked with Torgo to plug a printer into the landlink, and printed copies of what they had discovered for Darius and Gowsky.

As the two men studied the information, Torgo explained, "We've successfully obtained a map of the Lunian underground camp. I believe these large rooms might house the prisoners, I do."

Darius noted the authority in his younger brother's voice. He looked up approvingly and noticed Torgo looking directly at him. Darius saw a small smile appear, then disappear. The boy thrived on his praise, he thought, and he certainly hadn't given him much over the winters. But approval acknowledged a job well done. Torgo knew what he was doing, and he knew what he was talking about. That merited commendation as far as Darius was concerned.

Now if he could only get the boy to show respect and learn how to follow orders. Darius realized it would be worth his effort to spend more time with Torgo and fine-tune him into a great warrior.

"This place is huge," Gowsky said, as he stared at the sheet. "There are several ways to get to each large room. How do you suggest we proceed?"

"We have enough troops, we do," Darius said. "We'll send a squadron through each tunnel. It will guarantee quicker annihilation of these people, I'm thinking."

"We plan to annihilate them?" Gowsky seemed surprised by the suggestion.

"Do you want to give them land to settle on your continent?" Darius cocked his head, trying to relate to a man who wasn't a warrior.

"No." Gowsky drew out the word, as if hesitating. "At least, not the way they are acting today. If they accept a different approach, show a willingness to change…"

Oh, he was definitely a diplomat. Darius contacted his squadron leaders and had Torgo prepare a map for each one showing the tunnels they would access. The squadrons descended one after another and headed in their assigned directions.

Each large room was positioned at a considerable depth underground. It crossed Darius' mind that the Lunians had to have been on Nuworld for quite a while to create such a maze of tunnels and rooms, thereby forming a small underground city.

At Gowsky's suggestion, a team of Neurians organized to expand the entrance to the city. This would make it easier to help out the prisoners, especially those injured.

It struck Darius as odd that the Lunians had only one exit to their camp. He stood studying the printout his brother gave him, wondering if it was completely accurate. Any good military camp would provide more than one method of escape.

As several hours passed and darkness set in, the Neurians constructed a ditch of sorts, more than eight feet long. It exposed the entryway and provided illumination for the rest of the hall, making it easy to see where the split began. Each passage led to different levels in the subterranean city.

Darius used the time to study the maps showing the patterns of tunnels. Soon he felt familiar enough with the layout that he knew he could casually stroll through the maze and know where he was going.

His thoughts drifted to Tara. Was she all right? Had any of his soldiers reached her yet? Was she being rescued at this very minute? His mind swarmed to distraction.

Darius rubbed dirt from his eyes as he thought of his claim.

Tara couldn't stand confinement, and he could only imagine how she felt being imprisoned underground. The woman would fight the Lunians at every move. If it weren't for the fact that the Lunian leaders wanted Tara and Darius alive, he would have worried they might have killed her.

No, his claim lived, he felt certain of that. But Crator help any man who dared lay a hand on her. His temper soared as he allowed thoughts of her being sexually abused to enter his mind. Darius searched the field, looking for nothing in particular, other than a means to clear the unpleasant thoughts that consumed him. More than anything, at that moment, he wanted to jump into that hole, and search those tunnels until he found Tara.

He imagined many of the people in his camp, Gothman, Runner and Neurian, worried about their family and friends as well. And Darius shouldered the responsibility of seeing that everyone was returned safely. He had to remain in place and let his men do their jobs.

"Darius?" Torgo's voice came from a distance.

He snapped away from his thoughts and turned to look at his brother standing next to him.

"I was saying, there are people approaching through the tunnels, I was. Man, you were a million miles away, weren't you?"

"How long until they get here?"

"Less than an hour, I'd say."

They both studied the entrance. In the dark, it looked like a long grave, freshly dug. The grass, once providing a natural shield for the hole, now lay flattened and matted into the dirt, having been packed down by many boots.

"Do you miss Syra?" Darius asked quietly.

Their backs were to the rest of the camp, and no one stood near enough to hear their conversation.

Torgo looked up at his brother quickly, seemingly shocked that he was asked to reveal his emotions on a subject. "If I think about what she might be going through, it makes me want to throw up, it does. At least she can't come back pregnant."

A sudden sound caused both of them to turn quickly and look at the ditch.

Lights flickered, and voices rose from deep within the tunnel. Darius quickly alerted the medic teams to prepare themselves and for guards to stand at the ready. The noise from the group of people coming down one of the still hidden tunnels increased as they grew nearer.

Prisoners began to appear as they climbed the ladder, dirty and smelly, sweaty clothes hanging to their bodies. They reached out with eager hands to be helped to the surface. Gothman men and Runner women, jumped joyfully out of the ditch on their own. Neurians yelled praise to Crator as their feet touched the ground. Some of the Runners and Gothman screamed their delight at breathing the fresh night air. A thick aroma of wet dirt and body odor filled the night air.

Darius ordered additional lights, which both Neurian and Gothman quickly provided. He stood alongside his guards, helping men, women, boys, and girls to the surface.

In the end, almost fifty people were rescued that hour. Darius stood back as medics began walking among the dirty group, inspecting each person. Most seemed unharmed. A few had minor scratches and bruises.

Slowly, the newly freed began moving toward the forest, anxious to reunite with family and loved ones. Tara and Syra were not among them.

"That was everyone found in the room, it was," the soldier in charge reported, after the activity settled. He went on to tell Darius that his men had met minimal resistance. They'd suffered few deaths while Lunian deaths had grown in number.

"Good work." Darius slapped the large Gothman on the back. "Take your men back for some food."

Several more hours passed with no sign of the other two squadrons still underground. Darius felt the edge from waiting. He wondered in what condition the other captives would be. The men and women just freed had reported being stolen from their families or jobs within the very recent past. But Darius knew many still underground had been missing much longer.

How many would be dead? How would these families seek their revenge?

He also wondered about what state of mind the remaining captives would be in once freed. Many would have endured incredible torture if Tara's vision had been accurate — and Darius believed in her vision. Thus, he feared the mental state of the people who would next surface, especially the women. A strong man could take extreme conditions, but what of the females?

Darius didn't understand Gowsky's obvious distress at the notion of killing the Lunians. Any people capable of doing this to another race, needed to be destroyed. Darius didn't want to know of any Lunian living anywhere on Nuworld by the time all of this was said and done. And he wanted this Lunian matter cleaned up quickly.

Just when he'd decided the best approach was to send down more men, Torgo ran forward with a message. "The second squadron is approaching, they are. They have many injured and have been forced to move slowly. They request assistance, yes."

Darius had thirty men down in the hole within seconds.

Medics appeared with stretchers and more came running through the forest. Was Tara among the injured in this party? How had they been injured? Was it just through escape attempts? Or did the second room hold prisoners that had already been *used*?

The smaller group of prisoners appeared before long. None of these people leapt to the surface with joy. Their faces were gaunt and filthy. Some of them attempted smiles but most looked terrified, as if they'd just lived through a nightmare. Each one needed to be lifted from the ditch, and most were carried away on stretchers. More than one of the women shook uncontrollably and balled up into a fetal position on the stretcher.

"Syra!"

Darius watched his brother run to the ladder. Syra had climbed up stubbornly, then fallen face-first onto the ground. She looked at least twenty pounds thinner, and Darius wondered if she'd eaten at all during her captivity. Her skin was pasty-white and smeared with mud and dirt. Her light brown hair hung in strings to her shoulders and strands stuck to the side of her face.

Torgo had an arm around her immediately and a stretcher arrived within seconds.

"Give it to someone else." Her voice was a raspy whisper.

Darius cringed when he remembered Tara describing her screams. He moved next to Torgo and the Gothman medics who were failing to convince the bullheaded Runner to allow them to help her.

"Get on the stretcher," Torgo said. She blinked, staring up at him with dark, distrusting eyes. She didn't remove her gaze for a moment.

"Get your hands off me," her rough whisper broke as she looked toward one of the medics trying to assist.

The medic let go of her arm and glanced up at Darius.

"Let her be," Darius instructed and raised a hand to still the people surrounding the hole.

Syra climbed onto the stretcher without assistance, and the medics quickly carried her away.

"I'm going with her."

"Go." Darius waved his hand. "Don't neglect your duties though."

"Don't worry, no." Torgo ran to catch up with the small party carrying his girlfriend to the makeshift hospital.

Still no Tara.

Another hour passed at a snail's pace.

The injured prisoners were receiving treatment. Dr. Digo reported that no one seemed near death. He sadly added that most women from the second group reported being raped.

So they hadn't moved fast enough to prevent Tara's vision from happening.

But where was *she*?

Suddenly, Darius realized the Lunians probably hadn't kept her with the others.

There was still one other room full of prisoners. The leader of that rescue mission, Arien—one of his best warriors—had contacted him shortly after the last group of captives had been escorted to the makeshift hospital. He and his men were under severe attack, but holding their own. He said the Lunians were worse than ants in an anthill. They kept appearing in one tunnel after another.

Darius also learned the maps they had of the Lunian underground camp weren't completely accurate. While he'd only accounted for small deviations, they were enough to make him wonder if there might not be another way out of the camp.

He couldn't accept the fact that the Lunians would set up camp in enemy territory with one access point.

A vibration under his feet caught his attention. The table next to him rattled as the ground moved. The soldier working at a landlink grabbed the contents on the table to keep them from falling to the ground. Everyone braced themselves until the minor quake stopped.

Questions and explanations drifted across the field.

"What was that?"

"My, now, that was quite odd."

Another tremor hit, this one more severe. A large explosion filled the air with dust. The soldiers took cover instinctively.

Darius stood his ground and searched the dark sky, but saw no indication of an air attack. "Light!" he yelled to no one in particular. "Give me more light, I say."

He aimed powerful beams across the field in front of him. Awestruck, he watched a billow of smoke fill the air. The ground imploded. Obviously, they'd experienced an underground explosion.

He wanted to explore the large mass of collapsed ground, but didn't trust the safety of it, especially in the dark.

Had everyone still underground been destroyed?

Who ignited the explosions?

Where was Tara?

The last thought sent a panic racing through his bloodstream. She had to be alive.

Gowsky appeared. "How many do you still have down there?" he asked, squinting at the billowing dark cloud that spread across the field in front of them. He also used a powerful handheld beam to cut through the darkness with its bright light.

"I don't have a count yet," Darius answered. "The third squadron hasn't returned, no."

Another explosion rocked them.

More light appeared and one of Darius' warriors trained the beam on the other side of the field. They all witnessed a large expanse of ground sink, followed by a brown cloud filling the air.

Darius stripped off his shirt and quickly tied it around his nose and mouth as the dirt-filled cloud spread across the campground, surrounding them, and reducing visibility to a few feet.

Darius turned his head and covered his eyes to avoid the inevitable burning. Gothman, Runner, and Neurian coughed and waved their hands in front of their faces until the cloud lifted.

"There can't possibly be anything left down there," Darius said, turning to where Gowsky stood.

The Neurian didn't hear him. He stood over by a tree, leaning over, his hand to his ear, listening to something on his comm.

"Darius." Torgo appeared next to his older brother.

Darius turned and pointed toward the Lunian camp. "Can you reach anyone?"

"I'll check." Torgo put his hand on his brother's shoulder. "But first, something's going on, it is." Torgo had his comm hooked up to his landlink and pressed his hand to his ear. He looked to his brother, and an expression Darius couldn't read covered his face.

"Who are you listening to now?" Darius wrinkled his brow.

"Shh." Torgo waved his hand at his brother.

"You don't tell me to—"

"Please." Torgo's eyes looked desperate now, or maybe worried. "It's Tasha. She's talking to Gowsky."

He whispered the words, and Darius looked over in the direction of the Neurian. The man had his back to them, with his head down and hand smashed to his ear.

"Tasha?" Darius whispered back, wondering why in the hell that woman would be talking to Gowsky.

Darius grabbed Torgo's arm and moved the two of them over to the seclusion of some trees. His mind raced at the significance of what he'd just learned. "What's she saying?"

Torgo handed the comm to his brother so he could listen. "Something about her baby. It's missing."

Something grabbed Darius' stomach and twisted it in a death grip. An emotion he couldn't name seized him as he stared at his younger brother. He put the comm to his ear and heard Gowsky tell Tasha to calm down. Her voice was close to inaudible. The connection was bad, and she was hysterical as he listened to Gowsky telling her he would look into it. The connection was severed. He could only assume Gowsky had turned off his comm.

Turning slowly, Darius looked at Gowsky, who turned at the same time and stared at him. Their eyes locked for a moment through the darkness, then Gowsky entered the forest and disappeared. "What did you hear before you handed the comm to me?"

"I, uh, heard her say someone took her baby."

Darius saw his brother swallow and squirm under his stare.

"She said whoever took it, I mean, um, the baby, they didn't have a landlink, and they were on a glider." Torgo paused and looked at his brother.

Darius tightened his brow even more. "What else?"

"Well, she thinks it was Tara, she does." Torgo dropped his head and began to mumble. "She said Tara always managed to ruin her life, and that Tara would be the only one who had reason to do it."

Torgo looked back up at Darius and hesitated before asking. "So what do you want me to do?"

"Keep an eye on Gowsky. I want to know his every move." Darius felt too many emotions ripple through him. Tara should be here with her people, fighting to be rid of the Lunians. This news of a kidnapped baby was nothing to worry about, he told himself. But Tara hadn't surfaced from the underground city, and Darius feared everyone still down there was dead. Would Tara have left for Southland without letting him know? "Tell me if any activity stirs to the south, you will."

He turned from Torgo, dismissing him silently. Had Tara somehow learned that Tasha now resided in Southland? And if so, how would she have gathered that information after being captured by the Lunians?

Darius remembered seeing the two figures run from the hole right before the Gothman and Neurians had attacked the Lunians. He had dismissed what he had seen at the time, deciding it had been irrelevant. But had one of them been Tara? Had she escaped prior to their attack?

Another thought hit him, and even in the midst of the confusion of explosions and rescue, he wondered why he hadn't thought of it before. The young Neurian woman, Tealah, had not surfaced in their rescue attempts, either.

Staring at the uprooted ground through the darkness, the worry and panic he'd experienced through the evening now changed to unleashed fury and outrage. *So that's where you are, my lady. What a fool I was to worry about you.*

Chapter Twenty-Two

৪১

Tara hadn't taken one thing into consideration. As her glider began making funny, jerking motions, and she looked at the panel in front of her, she realized what it was. Fuel.

"Looks like we'll have to land," she said to the sleeping child.

The front beam on the glider provided the necessary light to land, and the open rolling ground south of Gothman offered few obstacles to block her path. There wasn't much she could do other than desert the glider and start walking. About all she knew was that she headed north.

Her eyes burned from lack of sleep. Lack of food—she hadn't eaten since the day before—hindered her perception. The child seemed to gain weight in her arms, and she felt clammy and cold, even though the night air was almost muggy.

You should stop. You have until midnight tonight. Or, was it tomorrow night already? Now she wasn't thinking clearly, either.

"Come on, Crator," she cried out loud. "Talk to me. Where are you, dog-woman? Help me stay awake."

There was no answer.

She was on her own.

"Don't you approve of what I'm doing?" She kept talking out loud, deciding a conversation, even with herself, might help keep her awake. "You said I needed to get rid of the evil. That's what I'm doing."

She looked at the bundle in her arms. "He doesn't look evil."

Did Crator not speak to her because He didn't approve of her actions? Panic surged through Tara at the thought that she could be making a grave mistake. The dog-woman not appearing could be a sign. Tara almost stumbled over protruding rocks in the ground.

Tigo stirred in her arms and his small hands reached out.

Tara regained her footing and snuggled the child until he relaxed and continued his slumber.

This had to be the right thing to do.

Tara focused on her children, and the future each of them had as great leaders. No one would endanger Andru's right to rule if Tara could prevent it. And just the thought of a bastard child of Darius' interacting in their lives made Tara sick. She didn't want a continuous reminder that he had been unfaithful.

She wasn't sure how long she walked, but she saw no indication of sunrise. It was so dark she began to feel the night would last forever.

"Just put one foot in front of the other," she ordered herself.

The next thing Tara knew, she lay on the ground. She didn't remember stopping. And she certainly had no recollection of falling asleep. Maybe she fell asleep while walking.

Had she fallen in her footsteps and simply passed out? She couldn't have. Tigo would have started crying and that would have awakened her. Instead, the child lay cuddled next to her.

Tara puzzled over the situation until consciousness drifted away again.

Dreams filled her sleep.

She couldn't move her legs, and when she tried, a pressure around them tightened, holding her fast. Tara struggled with this sensation as her inner thoughts told her to just sleep and not worry about it. She inhaled, but then found she couldn't. She gasped for breath. *Breathe. Move your legs. A nightmare.*

Get up. Go to sleep. Can't breathe.

Her thoughts bordered on waking up. The child could be in danger, and she had to protect him. Did little Tigo still lie next to her? Her arms didn't want to cooperate. She tried moving them, wrapping them around the warm bundle that she felt sure was Tigo still asleep next to her.

But something was on top of her. Try as she would, Tara felt hot steel imprison her limbs, immobilizing her on the ground. Warmth crept through her wherever the steel-like pressure touched her.

She told herself she should fight to be free, but a familiar scent confused her. How could she smell a dream? Tara focused on the scent, musky and close. She tried to raise a hand to find the source of this smell, but her hand met resistance.

Panic.

Tara woke up.

There *was* something on top of her.

Opening her eyes, a dark figure loomed over her. She opened her eyes wider, struggling to focus.

Someone straddled her body. Legs trapped hers. A hand covered her mouth.

"Don't make a sound," a voice said quietly into the night air.

A familiar voice. *I know that voice.*

Focus. Tara strained her eyes.

"Wake up," the voice said, "but stay quiet. They're looking for you."

The dark sky outlined the figure, even though the person was dressed in black.

She struggled again and the legs tightened around her. Panicking, she thrust her body upward, trying to knock the person off her.

"Tara. Be still."

Darius held his hand over her mouth. He leaned closer. "What are you trying to do?" he whispered in her face.

Tara relaxed and closed her eyes again briefly. Her arm had fallen asleep. The other arm was free and she grabbed the hand that covered her mouth.

Darius let her move it. He then reached for the sleeping child, which nestled next to Tara, using her arm as a pillow.

"No," she whispered the word.

He picked up the baby and pulled him to his chest. "He's my son, he is. Don't tell me I can't hold him."

Darius still sat on top of her, and she watched him warily as he looked at the sleeping baby in his arms. Her gut clenched. *Don't love that child. Don't look at him. Don't want him.* Tara felt her insides burn with agony as she studied Darius. His expression offered no indication of his thoughts.

He freed a hand from the baby and reached up to his comm, flipping it on. "Torgo," he spoke quietly.

His voice sounded so gentle. Were fatherly instincts kicking in just by looking at the baby?

Just because he looks just like you, just like your other son, your real son, don't love him. Please, don't love him. Tara's thoughts racked her soul as she feared Darius would want the child. She felt nauseous with his weight on top of her.

"I've got her." He listened. "Tell Gowsky you've intercepted the message from Tasha. Let him know that Darius has claimed his son, as is his right, it is. Make sure you emphasize that Tara had nothing to do with this."

Darius flipped off the comm and stood, releasing her.

The tingling sensation began in her arm and legs, which had been numb from lack of circulation.

"Get up." He walked over to an unmarked glider that stood not ten feet from them with its dome lifted.

Tara stood slowly, everything around her spinning. Her stomach growled loud enough to violate the peace of the night air, and she realized how much energy she had burned without eating.

"What do you think you're doing?" she asked. "You can't claim him."

"I'm saving your ass."

Tara straightened, and glared at Darius. "Saving my—"

"Yes," he interrupted and handed the baby to her.

Tigo stiffened, then stretched tightly clenched fists toward Tara's face. Arching his back, he pulled his knees toward his chest before going limp in her arms once again. He pulled one of his hands to his mouth and began sucking.

The child was cute. Adorable, in fact. And Tara felt a knot of bitter resentment twist in her gut. The child bore the strong resemblance to his papa, and more than likely would look just like Darius as he grew into a man. His existence would prove to be a burden to her and her children if he remained in Gothman.

Darius climbed on the glider. "Let's go."

Tara wanted answers. But her head felt like mush, and her gut ached. Darius' sudden presence here in the middle of nowhere confused her. She didn't understand how he had found her, and why he would tell Torgo to announce that he had claimed the infant.

She wanted to demand explanations, but her mind felt so tired she couldn't form the questions. Instead, she climbed onto the glider and decided there would be time to demand answers after she had rested.

"Where are we going?" she asked, once they were airborne. Tara noticed the glider didn't have a computer.

He didn't answer, but instead reached for his comm. "Torgo. Do you read me?" After a brief pause, he said, "Is there anyone around me?"

Tara waited while he remained silent.

"Good," Darius finally stated. "They won't find us, no. What did Gowsky say?"

Tara listened as Darius cursed. Gowsky must not have had nice things to say about him being responsible for the child's kidnapping.

"I need you to scan the ground east of the Lunian site and tell me if you find any survivors."

"Survivors?" Tara grew concerned as she imagined what happened between her people and the Lunian's in her absence.

"Do it quickly. I don't want to get shot down in the air, I don't." He ignored her question. "I know you will, yes."

What was that? A nice word spoken to his brother? Tara inhaled and pulled her lips over her teeth. It wasn't possible that those two had actually bonded, was it? "What did you mean, survivors?" she asked after he'd turned off his comm.

"The Lunian underground camp is destroyed, it is."

"Did we get all the prisoners out?"

"No," he answered simply, but there was ice in his tone.

Are they dead? She didn't ask the question on the tip of her tongue. And, she couldn't yet ask the other question coming to mind. How did they die? But she had to know one thing. "Is Syra…"

"She'll be fine," he said it with such finality Tara wondered what condition Syra was in *now*. Had Polva not held up her end of the bargain? It didn't sound like it. Well, Tara would honor her part of the deal. She had no idea what plan Darius had spawned, but she would see to it that this child was in that woman's hands by the deadline. If Polva still lived.

Tara wanted to know if any of the Lunians were captured or still alive. What would she do with the child if Polva had died?

The sun began to rise and Darius landed the glider in an area Tara didn't recognize. She looked at the surrounding countryside. Trees grew higher than she'd ever seen before. Their trunks were wide, too wide to wrap her arms around them. From the air, she'd seen a fast-moving wide creek, with protruding rocks, weaving through the thick foliage. She wondered how far east they were from the mountains. She couldn't see them. Low clouds covered the western horizon. She guessed the mountains might be visible if it weren't for them.

"Torgo?" Darius spoke into his comm. "Have there been more explosions? I could see the smoke when we were still airborne, I could."

Smoke? From explosions? Had they blown up the underground camp? Tara wondered at the amount of people killed, and anger toward the Lunians pumped through her like adrenaline.

"How far? Quarter mile? Good," Darius said as he lifted the dome.

Tara climbed off and shifted her hold on Tigo, looking around at the dense forest.

"I don't have all day to deal with this, I don't," Darius continued to speak into his comm, as he sat on the glider.

"No one asked you to..." She let the sentence die on her lips. Tigo had awakened and began squirming, then broke into a full-fledged cry. The infant nuzzled his face against her breasts, his mouth open and searching. Tara had nothing to offer the baby and bent her index finger for him to suckle.

Darius tossed her a bag with food in it, and Tara decided not to chastise the man. He was taking care of her; she could have run into problems if he hadn't shown. Especially if the Neurians were looking for her. Stealing a child would not be a good thing for a leader of a nation to be charged with.

Tara sat on the ground with the crying baby wiggling in her lap, and searched through the contents of the bag.

"Are you armed?" Darius asked, and she suddenly realized he hadn't gotten off the glider.

"Yes, why? Where are you going?" Tara glanced up at Darius, then focused on squeezing part of a banana into mouth-sized pieces for Tigo. The banana quieted the infant, much to her relief, and she exhaled to relax her nerves. "You're not leaving me here."

He tossed a comm to her. "It answers to Shalee."

She stood up as Tigo reached for the banana. "Who's Shalee?"

"Mikel's claim," he said simply, referring to his younger brother whom he'd killed right before Tara had gone into labor with the twins.

If the Neurians or the Lunians managed to track Tara or Darius' comms, and detected them here, the signal from the comm would identify Darius and some woman named Shalee—if, in fact, Darius had his comm programmed under his own name.

"I have no intention of altering the course of my plans, Darius. If you are here to assist, then I am appreciative. But I am doing what must be done."

Darius didn't respond at first. He stared at her, with eyes darker than storm clouds, and not one muscle moving in his face. His expression appeared so blank, Tara couldn't tell if her words annoyed him or not.

She glanced at Tigo, who lay on a blanket that had been in the bag, then back to Darius. "Don't try to stop me from doing what we both know must be done," she said in a tone barely more audible than a whisper.

Darius reached to start the glider.

She was there in a second and grabbed his hand, before he could flip the switch to raise the dome.

Darius' look grew almost hostile. "Your plan is faulty, Tara. You have erred in running out of fuel, and you have no food. I am not stopping you, but I will guide you to make sure you make no further mistakes."

Tara shook her head. "I'm the one who will talk to the Lunians. You don't need to be involved."

"I don't want to be involved, woman." His eyes flashed fire. "This was your idea, not mine. I don't know what possessed you, I don't. Tasha took the kid to the Southern continent. Why wasn't that good enough for you?"

"I made a deal with Polva," she began, but immediately regretted it, when Darius looked stunned.

"You did what?" Now he grabbed her hand. His grip was like steel.

"I told her I'd get her a child. She wanted a child from you and me, but I convinced her that wouldn't happen. So she agreed to take a child that was your bastard. In return, she'd allow you to rescue the prisoners," she blurted out the words, looking at her throbbing hand.

Darius stared at her.

She couldn't tell if he was speechless or too mad to speak, so she continued, "You think it's good enough that Tasha took that kid out of Gothman country? You think I don't know that Tigo was your grandpapa's name? She has every intention of making sure this kid knows he's the son of a lord — with a title to claim."

"Allowed us to..." He either ignored what she'd just said or hadn't paid attention. "I guess they underestimated what we were capable of, they did." He smiled now and pulled her to him. "My lady, we destroyed them, we did," he whispered in her face, then pulled her closer and brushed a kiss across her lips. He settled her on his lap and made love to her mouth with his tongue.

When he finally let her go, Tara fought for a second to regain her balance. He sat straddled across the glider, his long muscular arms once again gripping the handlebars with gloved hands that had just ravished her body. She stared at his chest, at the blond curls tangling around his face, and finally into those dark, possessive gray eyes. In spite of the seriousness of her mission, she wanted the man, but she knew that would have to wait, and her body cried in retaliation.

"Okay, Tara." He revved the motor on the glider. "You win, you do. This child will disappear. I'll be right back, yes." Then he was gone.

She glanced at Tigo, then began looking for something she could use to clean off the banana he'd smeared all over his face, including his right ear.

By the time she and the baby had eaten their fill and she'd cleaned up the area, Darius had returned. She looked over her shoulder when the sound of another glider caught her attention, and she realized he had company. A second vehicle rode alongside him through the trees.

As they grew nearer, she saw Brev driving the second glider with Polva sitting behind him. Polva strained to see past Brev, and Tara watched as the woman pointed at her.

Tara picked up the child and stood as they pulled near her.

The domes opened and Polva jumped out. She literally ran to Tara and grabbed the baby from her arms.

Tara felt disgusted by the woman's lack of manners and respect. The urge to yank Tigo back from her consumed Tara for a moment, but she doused the feeling as quickly as it surfaced. The time had arrived for the baby to disappear from their lives, and this bitch played a necessary role in that happening.

"Brev, he's perfect." Polva turned to go to her husband

But Darius intercepted, taking the child from her.

Polva reached for the child. "He's mine."

Only Polva had the nerve to speak to Darius like that. How spoiled she sounded. Tara found it hard to hide her disgust.

With one look, Darius had Polva cowering toward Brev. Tara watched Darius pull several folded papers from inside his jacket and hand them to Brev. "Sign these, then you can have the child, yes."

"What?" Polva looked at Tara. "We had a deal. You didn't say anything about signing anything."

"The child isn't hers to give away, no," Darius spoke before Tara could say that Polva hadn't held up her end of the bargain, either. "If you want him, sign these, I say."

Brev looked over the papers. He looked up at Darius and nodded. "I see what you're doing. We sign these and this child has no past, no bloodline, and no ties to the Gothman throne. He takes on our bloodline and can never know otherwise."

"Who cares about any of that?" Polva rolled her eyes as if the whole thing were stupid. "Sign the damn things and let's get out of here."

"What's this?" Brev had reached the bottom of the agreement and again looked at Darius. This time he looked guarded. "This says we can't settle any land on the western side of the mountains. Any Lunian found west of the mountains will be shot on sight. Is that necessary?"

"Yes," Darius said.

"Whatever." Polva tapped the papers with her finger. "Sign them." She eyed Tigo and licked her lips, then bit her lower one.

Tara felt conflicting emotions tear through her. Polva didn't deserve to be a mama to any child. She wanted to grab Tigo and run, get him away from the likes of that woman. But Tara knew this to be a means to an end. Tigo would disappear from their lives, never to know his heritage, and never to be allowed to cross the mountains.

She wanted Brev to sign the papers so she and Darius could get out of there. *Be done with it.*

Brev signed the papers.

Chapter Twenty-Three

Tara read a copy of the contract that Brev and Polva signed as she and Darius flew toward the mountain range that now separated Gothman and Runners from the Lunians. Darius had put some work into the contract, or someone had. Had Torgo written it? Maybe Darius told him what he wanted it to say. Tara wondered when the time had been taken to create it.

The contract stated that Brev and Polva agreed they'd adopted a child with no known family history. Any resemblance the child had to anyone on Nuworld was completely coincidental. Both the baby's mama and papa were deceased. There were no known relatives.

Tara finished reading and couldn't help but smile as she saw how well Darius had severed all connections with the child.

She thought back to the last few hours. Darius hadn't seemed surprised to see her, and he knew exactly what she was doing. When and how had Darius discovered her plans? Tara knew if she asked him about it, he'd tell her a good leader always knew what was going on in his kingdom.

Darius had offered her that standard response too many times in the past, when he didn't feel a need to enlighten her of his methods. So had he created this contract when he found out her intentions? She doubted she'd ever know the truth. Tara conceded that her curiosity was piqued in the matter, but she wouldn't press Darius for answers. She wished to simply put closure on all of this. Now little Tigo couldn't threaten her children, and that was all that mattered.

"And what is this?" Tara sat behind Darius on the glider and propped the contract against his back. She tapped the contract with her finger.

"Is there a discrepancy, my lady?" Darius stroked her thigh with one hand, while maneuvering the glider with his other hand.

"It says, *Those who sign below acknowledge the law and power of Gothman. All Gothman borders will be acknowledged without exception, and crossing to the west side of the mountain range shall be deemed as entering Gothman territory, with consequences resulting as stated above.*" Tara read the contract out loud.

Darius nodded. "As it shall be."

"Gothman just got a little bit larger." She handed back the contract.

"Our people have been through a lot, they have. Recovery will be slow. They deserve a little something to show them we triumphed in the end, they do."

"You always see to it that Gothman thinks it's a little better than everyone else, don't you?" Tara wrapped her hands around Darius waist and hugged him.

He squeezed her hands and rubbed her forefinger with his thumb. "That's the true secret to being a great leader, my lady."

She rested her head against his shoulder blade and relaxed her body. As she fell asleep, she felt complete forgiveness and undaunted love for him. He'd shown her how little that child meant to him. And, rescuing her when his people were in jeopardy showed her where she rated on his list.

A slight jolt raised Tara from a dreamless slumber. She felt groggy and incoherent for a moment. When Darius lifted her off his bike and into his arms, she woke up completely. The masculine smell of him, a mixture of leather and sweat, consumed Tara. Without thought, her body reacted and moisture spread between her legs. And although Tara didn't doubt her love for Darius was as strong as her physical desire for him, she felt a pang of regret at the realization that she still didn't completely trust him.

Tara straightened to free herself from his hold, but Darius' arms tightened around her. "Relax," he whispered in her ear.

"Remember, I'm supposed to have just rescued you from the Lunians."

Tara laid her head on his shoulder and allowed her eyes to take on a blank stare, though she paid attention to everything she saw as they approached a makeshift hospital tent. Darius had brought Tara to where all the other rescued Gothman and Runners were being cared for. Around them, a field buzzed with activity, and two other large tents sat nearby.

"Here. Bring her over here." It was Torgo's voice.

"How is she?" Dr. Digo appeared at Darius' side and looked at her face. "Is she in shock?"

"She'll be fine," Darius said in his quiet baritone.

"Tara!" Reena ran to the side of the cot Darius laid her on. "My lands, girl, I've been worried about you, I have. Let me take a look at you."

Tara tried to sit up, but was immediately guided back to a reclining position by Reena's hand. She noticed Syra sleeping in a cot next to hers. A thin sheet was pulled around the two cots. Dr. Digo, Torgo, and Darius stood gazing down at her.

"I'm fine," she said, looking from one face to another. "Really, I am."

"I'll be the judge of that, I will." Reena put her hands on her hips. She turned to look up at the three men towering over her in the small space provided. "Out of here. Don't you all have other things to keep you busy? Go on now, be gone with you." She waved her hands.

The three men disappeared to the other side of the curtain.

"Did they touch you, Tara-girl?" Reena leaned down and grabbed a bowl of warm water from the floor, setting it on the stand next to her daughter's cot. She took a cloth out of the water and wiped Tara's face.

The warmth soothed Tara more than she would have imagined possible. "I woke up in a cage, Reena. When the guards came to get me, I managed to escape." She smiled and arched her neck slightly as Reena wiped the back of it. "That place was one huge maze underground. I couldn't figure my way out. I finally located a hall that opened into a cave, but I wasn't anywhere near Gothman. I can't believe Darius found me."

"He loves you so much, Tara, he does." Reena smiled.

Tara reflected that Darius probably did love her as much as he could.

Reena kept talking as she dipped the cloth in the water and wrung it with her hands. "When you didn't come out with the other prisoners, I knew he'd look for you and wouldn't stop until he found you."

Tara turned her head on her pillow and studied Syra's sleeping face. "What about her? How's she doing?"

"I daresay she didn't fare as well as you, no."

Tara's stomach lurched.

"She's been beaten and raped, and she won't talk to anyone, she won't. I was able to examine her only after the doctor sedated her." Reena shook her head. "I'll never approve of those doses of anti-conception medication you gave her, no. But I don't think she would have been able to handle it if she'd gotten a baby out of this deal. Some of the other girls here won't be as lucky, I'm thinking."

Reena didn't raise her voice, but looked toward the hanging sheet. "My lord, you can come in now, you can."

Tara smiled as Darius pulled back the sheet and entered the small room. He gave her a small smile and it warmed her soul.

"What she needs is sleep, a lot of it." Reena patted Tara's hip with her bony hand. "The best place for her is her bed, I'm thinking. She should be taken to the house, yes."

Arrangements were made to move Tara and Syra from the makeshift hospital tents to the Bryton house where they'd be more comfortable. Some of the other patients in relatively good enough condition were also transported from the base of the eastern side of the mountain range. Hundreds of gliders lifted into the air simultaneously, each one carrying two people. It would take time to transport every one home, but the process had begun.

Tara watched the hospital tents grow smaller and smaller as they flew higher and farther away. She had no desire to come to this part of their world again any time soon.

* * * * *

Darius made no ceremony about parting ways with his men and taking Tara home. He left the lot of them and flew around Bryton, landing in their backyard minutes later.

Tara's bedroom looked more delightful than she expected it would. The double doors leading to the upstairs balcony were opened. A soothing breeze caressed the room. The smell of fresh linen, mixed with the aroma from an arrangement of cut flowers on her dresser, filled the room. Tara noticed the room had been scrubbed and furniture polished to a shine. She smiled, knowing Hilda had put effort into making their homecoming a nice one.

Tara insisted on seeing her children before anything else, and pulled Darius by the hand into the nursery before he could insist she climb into bed. Andru dropped his toys and ran into Darius' arms as soon as his parents entered the room.

"Papa, I wuv oo." The little boy wrapped his thin arms around his papa's muscular neck.

Ana stood on the floor, jumping up and down with her arms outstretched, and grinned at Tara. "Me too. Me too. I want up."

Tara reached down and grabbed Ana, covering her face with kisses before she picked her up and buried her face in the child's hair. Kissing her neck, Tara murmured, "My precious, I love you."

Tara stood next to Darius, who had lifted his son into his arms, and she reached for Andru's golden curls. "And I love you, too, sweet boy."

"Play with me," Andru reached out his hand and leaned toward Tara.

"Mama has been working, she has," Darius whispered into Andru's ear, tickling the boy's cheek with his unshaven face.

"I work someday." Ana's expression grew serious.

"When I'm bigger," Andru finished.

"Yes, you will." Tara smiled and placed Ana on the floor.

Darius stood Andru next to his sister and squatted in front of them. "The two of you will lead nations."

The children studied their papa with solemn gray eyes, although Tara knew they had no idea what he was talking about.

"We be great!" Andru jumped up and down with his hand held high in a fist, as if showing his parents what his interpretation of *great* meant to him.

Ana joined in with the gestures, and the two of them jumped over toys as they chanted, "We be great! We be great!"

Tara spent precious minutes with the children, then left them in the care of a Gothman servant. She joined Darius for an update from Torgo, who had returned home as well.

Once again, the young man had set up camp in his comfortable little landlink room—the same room where Darius had attacked her before they had left for the other side of the mountains. It all seemed so long ago to Tara, so much had happened.

Torgo stood in front of the two landlinks, his back to them, as Tara and Darius entered the room. People continued to be transported to their homes, and Torgo was supervising the process. Hundreds of Gothman and Runners still remained on the other side of the mountain range.

Apparently, Gowsky had returned to Southland. *Probably to soothe Tasha.* Tara wondered about the fate of Tealah at the same time. She didn't dare ask about the Neurian woman, though.

"What reports do you have in?" Tara moved to stand next to Torgo, but Darius placed his hands on her shoulders and pulled her back into him.

"No, my lady." Darius leaned down until his unshaven face rubbed against her cheek. "Now is not the time for you to look at reports. All of this can wait for you, yes."

"But there is work to do," Tara protested. "I want to know what Runners have arrived at the clan. How many are still being transported?"

Tara began firing questions at Torgo, who never got a chance to respond because Darius lifted her and hauled her out of the room.

"I'll have a report ready for you, I will," Torgo called after them.

Darius carried Tara to their bedroom and closed the door behind them with his foot. "Put me down." Tara slapped at his chest, but Darius simply smiled as he let her slide down his body until her feet hit the ground. She felt her breasts smash against his chest, and her nipples hardened with need.

Darius reached to tweak one of them, and Tara slapped at him again, even though his masculine presence caused a swelling ache between her legs. The man hadn't showered since their journey across the mountains. He had a thick shadow of whiskers covering his chin, and she guessed a good night's sleep would do him good as well. But damn, she wanted him. Her body reacted to him in spite of her mind saying she should not let him see her need.

"Get out of your clothes, woman." Darius ignored her slapping at him and pulled his shirt over his head.

Tara watched the action without moving, and crossed her arms to prevent herself from running fingers through the thick golden hair that spread across his chest. "I'd like some time alone, I think." She turned from him and walked toward her dresser. "A hot bath sounds nice."

"Some time alone?" Darius asked.

He stopped her in her steps by grabbing her hair.

"Ouch," she protested. "Yes. Some time alone. You just told Torgo that I needed some rest."

Darius released her hair and let his hand slip around her neck, not to restrain her, even though she had stopped moving. Instead his long fingers caressed her.

Tara felt every inch of the man as he pressed his body against her backside. His erection felt like steel against her lower back, and she reacted by growing moist as the swelling in her crotch grew to distraction.

"There is something else you need," he whispered into her hair, his free hand reaching for the bottom of her shirt. Darius moved both hands and yanked up her shirt so the material against her breasts scratched her nipples. Her inner thighs were soaked.

"You're right. I need to go over reports, and I need to find out the status of my people." Tara wanted to remain stubborn and not give in to this man, but she feared he knew as well as she did, that her body needed him as much as he needed her.

"Our nations will always require our attention, yes." Darius turned her around and removed her shirt.

Tara couldn't fight him, due to exhaustion, she told herself. Her body screamed for relief and he wanted to give it to her. Tara couldn't stop herself from placing her fingers on his chest and feeling the powerful heat of his body. She looked up at him and saw that passion had darkened Darius' gray eyes. "And you and me?" she asked.

"I will always need you, my lady," Darius whispered. And he kissed her.

Tara knew she always wanted Darius to need her, and to be with her, but she couldn't say what she thought as Darius stroked her mouth with his tongue. The fluids released between her legs, and Tara leaned into him, stretching her body against his as she went up on tiptoe.

Darius wrapped his arms around her, squeezing her breasts against his hard chest, smashing her hardened nipples into the roughness of his coarse chest hair.

"Damn it, Darius," Tara managed to say when he ended the kiss and released her to reach for her pants' buttons. "I need you now."

"Don't make it sound like such a curse." Instead of removing her pants, Darius grabbed onto them and pulled Tara to the bed.

"I can't live with you going to other women." Tara allowed him to seat her on the edge of the bed and looked into his eyes as he took off his pants.

"Well, I wish for you to live," he said as he met her gaze and dropped to his knees. He pressed her to the bed, then slid her pants down her legs. "I wish for you to live by my side for the rest of our days, my lady." He freed her legs, then spread her open. The fresh air in the room hardened her sex, and fresh moisture sprang from her.

"Oh Crator," she yelped when his mouth covered her, and she felt his tongue stroke her opening.

Darius made love to her with his mouth, and Tara wrapped her fingers in his hair, pinning his head between her legs. She pressed her feet to the bed and lifted her rear end off the blankets, making it easier for him to soothe the ache that consumed her.

Tara exploded and pulled on his hair, smashing his face between her legs. "Darius now!" she screamed. "Make love to me now!"

He rose over her, grinning as his face shimmered from her moisture. He brought her legs up with him as he knelt over her. Tara could feel the hardened throb of his penis at her entrance and bit her lip as she waited for his thrust.

Darius slid into her slowly, closing his eyes, and arching his neck so that she could see the stretch of his Adam's apple. She watched him as she felt the length of him fill her, and stretch her. Her insides gripped around him, and she focused on the contractions as she exploded again around his sex.

Tara felt every orgasm ripple through her body with a heightened awareness she didn't remember experiencing with Darius before. He felt so good inside her, satisfying every need her body had, as he managed the pace of their lovemaking for maximum effect. He whispered his love for her repeatedly as he quenched her desires.

Tara couldn't help herself in the moment, and confessed how much she loved him, too. Everything he did felt so perfect, and Tara wondered if they could carry the strength of this love throughout the rest of their lives.

"You've got me, woman," Darius howled when he exploded inside her.

Tara felt the pulsating as he came deep within her womb, and she ran her hands down his sweat-covered, muscular back when he collapsed on top of her. She prayed to Crator that she could keep this man, and keep this love for always.

Sleep came quickly and easily after their lovemaking, and Tara didn't dream. But sometime later, a noise awakened her and she raised her head from her pillow. Was that gunfire?

Tara sat up.

There it was again.

Shouts.

Screaming.

She stared at the dark bedroom, then at the empty space next to her. She sat in her bed, alone, and allowed herself a moment to wake up. But the slamming of the back door downstairs, then muffled voices outside, had her tossing off blankets. Tara ran to her dresser, and pulled clean clothes out and dressed in the darkness.

What was happening?

What time was it?

She glanced outside and noted how dark it was…how very dark.

Tara tucked her shirt into her pants and recounted in her head what she had just heard. Someone had fired a Gothman gun. The realization that she had heard gunfire twisted her stomach into knots. She pulled on her boots, feeling sick at the thought that someone in the house might have been shot.

But who?

And where was Darius?

Another gunshot made her jump.

Tara searched for the pants she'd worn the day before and found them crumpled on the floor. She pulled her laser from the pocket, taking another minute to find her shirt so that she could get her comm. Tara hurried out of the room, stuffing her comm into her pocket.

"Torgo, what's going on?" She stopped at the open door of the landlink room, from which light flooded the hallway. "I heard gunshots."

Torgo turned and stared at her, looking for a minute like he'd forgotten how to talk.

"Torgo!"

He licked his lips and that's when she saw the panic in his eyes.

"What is it? Where's Darius?"

"He's outside." He glanced at his monitor, as if it would tell him what to say, then turned and looked up again at Tara. "Andru's gone, he is."

Tara felt panic rising from her gut, forming a nasty-tasting bile in her throat. She gripped the doorway and stared at the teenager. "What do you mean, he's gone?"

"Someone took him."

Tara tightened her grip on the doorway as she felt the sensation of the room turning sideways. It took her a second to organize her thoughts. "Someone took Andru?" she asked, as she tried to organize her thoughts. "From his room?"

Of course, from his room. Oh, Crator, no! Her thoughts raced into gear, and her heart pounded, making it hard to breathe. She couldn't fathom the thought that her own son could be stolen from his bed during the night. Even though she had managed a similar act not so long ago, Tara had to work to accept the fact that the safe haven of their home could be violated in a similar sense. "Someone was able to sneak into this house and take my son?"

"Yes."

"Did anyone see who it was?"

"Tasha." His voice was quiet, like he'd done something wrong.

Tara blinked. Her head began to clear as anger replaced panic. *The bitch!* "Have they caught her?"

He turned to look at the computer. "Not yet, no."

Tara turned and ran down the stairs, three at a time. Outside, she grabbed the nearest glider and focused on the landlink between the handlebars. The lights on the small monitor blinked on as she started the machine, and Tara took off as the dome closed silently over her. She left the ground with more speed than she had ever managed before. "I'll kill you, you little bitch," she muttered, punching keys on the landlink with one hand, steering with the other.

The landlink let her know that a glider flew ahead of her, and Tara accelerated until she recognized the Gothman insignia on the side of the machine. Within seconds she had the machine in better view from the light of her glider and recognized Darius inside the dome.

Tara cursed out loud that she hadn't insisted on knowing the status of the guards before falling asleep. They should have expected that Tasha would retaliate in some way. Still, Tara never would have guessed her sister possessed the skill to maneuver her way into the Lord of Gothman's house. But Tasha was a Runner, and had been trained over the winters just as Tara had.

The battle against the Lunians had stolen their attention from their home and focused it across the mountains. She and Darius should have briefed the attending guards who had remained at home, but their thoughts had been on their homecoming, and the many tortured and abused people needing attention.

Tasha had found a weakness in the line, and she had made her move.

A glider appeared ahead of them. Tara punched buttons on her landlink, identified the glider as Neurian, but found no other vehicles in the area. It had to be Tasha.

Tara pushed her glider as fast as it would go. If Tasha said or did anything to Andru...

"Sweet sister," A voice came through Tara's comm.

"Land that thing, now," Tara hissed into her comm through gritted teeth.

"Yeah, right, so you can blow my head off." Tasha laughed. "Not today."

"You won't get away with this. We're not going to just give up. Land the thing and end the inevitable."

No response.

Tara glanced at Darius. He focused on the glider ahead of them. She tasted blood, and realized she'd bitten her lip in fury.

Tasha would die for this. *Crator, you can't possibly argue with me on this one.*

Darius veered away from Tara's side and flew toward Tasha at an angle.

Tara took his lead and leaned on her glider as she slanted through the air, then turned to head toward Tasha's glider from the opposite side.

Tasha dove her glider toward the ground to avoid them, and Darius dove after her. Tara followed.

"Did he ever tell you what he did to me?" Fear could be heard in Tasha's voice as she tried to navigate the glider and talk at the same time.

"Hurt one hair on my son's head..." Tara growled in response.

"He laughed through the whole thing, did he tell you that?"

Darius soared around and came up alongside Tasha's glider. Tasha dodged to avoid him again.

"Land!" Tara yelled.

"I still hear that laugh in my nightmares." Now Tasha whispered. "He tortured me, you know. Tied me down and broke bones and laughed. Always that laugh."

Tara cringed when she saw Tasha's glider decelerate, then accelerate, as the woman looked about her wildly. The whole time, she held Andru around his waist.

"I have scars. I'll show them to you sometime." Tasha laughed, but her expression was frantic, Tara noted when her light hit her sister's face. "He's a monster, dear sister. A monster. He raped me, he's raped others. They told me he did. He lies and he rapes. Women, always women. I wasn't the first...has he raped you, yet? He will, you know...he will..."

Darius cut her off from the front, forcing her to slow down. Tara caught occasional glimpses of him through the glider's beam. He appeared focused and determined. Darius could hear what Tasha said to Tara, if he chose, but the hard look on his face gave no indication whether he was listening to the words, and if he was, if they fazed him.

Tara watched her sister turn from side to side in the seat of her glider. Strands of hair covered her face. The woman wore her Runner clothes, although not the headgear. Tasha controlled the glider with only one hand and held Andru with the other. When she altered course, the glider jerked, making the two of them bounce within the confines of the dome.

When Andru saw Tara, his arms reached toward her. Tara saw his mouth move as he called out to her. His blond curls stuck to the side of his face, and Tara guessed he had been crying hard enough to soak his cheeks. Her heart tore in two at the pain she knew her son was suffering.

Tasha would die for this.

Tara pulled up alongside her sister to force her down.

Darius blocked the other side, keeping his eyes locked on Tasha's glider.

"The way I see it, you're two up on me." Tasha looked straight at Tara. She saw the crazed look in Tasha's eyes. Her desperation. Her pain. "He raped me. You stole Tigo. I owe you this."

Tasha dove toward the ground.

A suicide dive. *Crator, no!*

Tara screamed.

Darius dove faster. He was almost underneath Tasha.

Tara saw her sister's face. She looked confused.

Tasha pulled up to avoid hitting him, probably instinct. Her glider hit the ground, bouncing but not losing control.

Darius raced his glider next to her, swerving in front of her, again forcing Tasha to slow down.

Tara remained behind Tasha, on her tail, ready to dart to either side if Tasha tried to take off over the rocky ground.

Darius slowed his bike further, and Tasha slowed as well. Tara matched their deceleration from the rear. Finally, the three gliders stopped.

Tasha's dome opened first, and she pulled out Andru.

His screams were hysterical, mixed with hiccups, and he twisted and thrashed his body violently in his aunt's arms.

Tara pushed herself free of her glider as soon as her dome rose. "Put him down, Tasha." Tara aimed her laser at her sister's head, knowing without doubt she could kill Tasha without harming Andru. But in the darkness, after being kidnapped and subjected to a high-speed chase, Andru had been through enough in the past hour. Tara wouldn't force him to see bloodshed if she could avoid it.

Tasha tightened her grip around Andru and shook him until he stopped kicking.

Darius climbed off his glider and moved quickly to Tara's side. He continued on, passing her as he headed toward Tasha.

Tasha backed up and tried to grab her laser, although Tara could see it was almost impossible for her sister to restrain Andru with only one arm. "Get away from me," she screamed.

Andru jumped from the loudness next to his ear and reached for Darius.

Tasha didn't focus on Darius, but looked around him to see Tara. "The Runners mock him, you know that, don't you? They know he lies. A hypocrite and a liar. Some ruler!"

"Papa, I want you!" Andru reached his hands out toward Darius.

"You don't want him, Andru," Tasha spoke loudly with her face pushed into the boy's hair. "He'll raise you to be just like him, raping women, lying to his people, his family, his claim."

Darius aimed his laser, fired, and hit Tasha broad in the shoulder.

She screamed and staggered backward a couple steps, then released Andru.

The little boy fell to the ground. Tara ran past Darius and scooped the boy into her arms.

"Mama, I will be like Papa. I will, I really will." The little boy shook uncontrollably.

Tara wrapped her arms around him, as if she could block out the atrocities. "It's okay, baby. Don't worry. You'll be just like your Papa. He just saved your life." Tara shushed her son as she knelt on the ground rocking him.

The little boy continued to shake and cry, burying his head into her chest.

She wished she had more arms to wrap around him. Anything, so she could soothe her baby. Tara tried to calm herself so she could better reassure her son. But her anger still flared.

Darius stood over Tasha, a death grip still on his laser.

Tara could see his arm, every muscle flexed.

Tasha lay in her own pool of blood at his feet. Burnt flesh and fresh blood filled the air with their vile smells. The laser, at close range, had dismembered her arm from the shoulder.

Tara walked toward Darius, Andru embraced to her chest. He pulled both of them into his arms. He felt good, holding them, and Tara leaned into him with her son, not moving for a minute.

She'd heard about two soldiers, once they'd bonded, being able to act as one person, without thought, without words. And that's what she and Darius had just done. Letting out a sigh, she knew, in her heart, that even though neither one of them were perfect, they were bonded…for life.

"Take him. I'll be with you in a moment," Tara whispered.

Andru willingly crawled into his papa's arms. "Be careful, mama. She's bad."

Tara didn't speak but rubbed her hand along her son's cheek and smiled.

Darius carried their son to the gliders.

Tara stood over Tasha. She would have to tell Patha about the whole terrible episode. He wouldn't be happy until he knew everything. And then he still wouldn't be pleased. She knew her papa well. He would know if parts of the story were missing. She'd have to tell him she'd taken Tigo, even though she hadn't planned to.

She breathed deeply and covered her mouth with her hand, staring at her almost-dead sister.

The gurgling coming from Tasha's mouth was sporadic. Blood poured from her mouth, nose, and ears. It also gushed from her shoulder where the arm had been severed. Her eyes opened and she looked up at Tara, moving her mouth.

Tara squatted next to her sister and studied her face, knowing her own expression was blank as a sudden calm soaked through her.

"I'll tell you," Tasha's voice came in spurts between choking fits. She spit blood with each movement of her lips. "He said no. He told me to go away. I wouldn't..." she coughed again.

"Nothing you've said has changed my opinion of him," Tara said to her dying sister.

"But I tried to make you believe, I wanted you to believe..." She grimaced in pain.

"It's done," Tara said simply.

"*I* allowed evil to be born, no one else." Tasha squeezed her eyes shut and coughed. "He didn't know. No one knew."

Tara watched the blood soak the ground until it came within inches of her boots. The smell of the blood and Tasha's burnt flesh nauseated her, but she didn't move away.

"I wanted revenge," Tasha continued. "You're right. It's done." She tried to keep speaking, but choked. Her one hand, now covered with thick, red blood, reached toward Tara, but fell back to her chest. She whispered, "Not in my hands any more, not in yours. It knows where he is. I can't change it."

She didn't make any sense, and Tara didn't ask her to explain.

Tasha coughed again. "Tara." She made an effort to move her still attached arm, but failed. "Tara?"

"What?"

"End it."

Tara remained squatting, adjusted her laser for close range, and shot her sister.

Tasha lay still.

Tara looked at the mutilated woman for a moment, then sighed as she dropped back to sit on the ground. All her life, Tasha had been a thorn in Tara's side, taking every opportunity to point out Tara's mistakes, or a job not well done. The two of them had fought over attention from Patha, how a task should be handled, even who had more right to pursue a boy.

Tara had reminded herself again and again that Tasha despised her presence because Tara had been brought into the family, and not born into it. Tasha had been jealous and resentful of Tara's accomplishments, when Tasha hadn't been able to measure up. But over the winters, Tara had learned that the two women chose their own paths.

Tasha still remained Tara's sister, however, and a sense of loss Tara hadn't anticipated crept through her. Maybe it was a result of all that had happened in the recent past, but grief swarmed through her, and she felt her throat tighten. Her sister lay mangled, bloody and dead on the ground in front of her, and she stared at Tasha until her vision blurred.

Tara finally allowed her head to sag. She laid her head on her knees and cried.

"Tara." Darius' voice was gentle, but it seemed to travel over thousands of miles. "Andru and I are going home."

She looked over at papa and son, thankful for the darkness so Andru couldn't see the atrocity at her feet or the tears on her face. He'd been through enough. His face seemed calm now, but the night and blurred vision from tears could be fooling her. His tiny arms wrapped around his papa's neck. He looked so small next to Darius, so innocent. How long would that innocence last?

"Papa, look." Andru pointed at Tara. No, he was pointing to something else. Tara turned her head to see what he looked at.

The dog-woman stood on the opposite side of Tasha. She waved a deformed finger at Andru and smiled her toothless smile. A cold breeze rippled through the grass. A chill went through Tara, and she shook in spite of herself.

"Now is the Waiting," the dog-woman said and looked down at Tasha. "Bury her according to your customs and pray for her soul. She made her decisions and now she stands before Crator."

"Waiting for what?" Tara asked. She glanced at Darius and Andru.

Andru looked completely relaxed, no fear at all on his gentle face.

Darius watched her, and did not look in the direction of the old woman. He still couldn't see the dog-woman.

"I told you the evil was done. His tools are scattered, but not destroyed. He won't let go." The old woman looked into Tara's eyes. "Crator knows your heart, Tara-girl. He knows your intentions and motives."

"I didn't know what the evil was. What was I supposed to destroy? If He knows my thoughts, then He knows I didn't know where the evil was." Tara paused, then said quieter, "I saw it in several places."

"You saw the tools. Evil uses, destroys, and moves along."

Tara didn't say anything for a minute. She sniffed and wiped her eyes. "Is Crator mad at Darius or me?"

The dog-woman laughed. It was a gentle, loving laugh. She looked at Tara, then over at Darius, who held Andru in his arms. When she turned back to Tara she clasped her hands together and smiled, a motherly smile, full of wisdom. "Darius is a product of his culture. He feels no remorse for his actions and acts only upon what he believes to be true and right. He would not be a good tool for Evil." She chuckled. "Crator gives all his creatures free will. You are His tool. He instructs and you carry out. If you falter, He will guide you, if you let Him. Crator loves his people."

Tara decided the answer was no.

"Your work is laid out before you. Build a strong army and be prepared." The dog-woman raised her hand and disappeared.

Chapter Twenty-Four

The morning smells of coffee brewing and bacon frying awakened Tara. Sore muscles racked her body and made movement slow. She'd flown back with Darius to put Andru to bed, then had returned immediately to bury her sister.

Tasha had been easy to find again. The birds of prey led Tara to the corpse. She'd gathered branches, working through the night in order to give her sister a proper Runner's cremation, saying the entire ceremony herself. The sun wasn't quite up when she'd returned to the house, showered and climbed into bed next to Darius.

She entered the kitchen, greeting Darius, then stopped dead in her tracks at his gentle teasing words.

"Two days I've been sleeping?" she asked, staring at Darius' smiling face. She couldn't possibly have slept that long. "Is that what you said?"

"You needed the sleep, you did. You slept yesterday away. And, my lady, you look fabulous, I'd say." He reached and pulled her to him. She submitted to his powerful kiss. "You taste good, too."

"I love you," she whispered and wrapped her arms around his neck.

The grin that crossed his face was better than anything he could have said in response. It was charming, boyish. All domination and control vanished from his face with that one smile. That was when it dawned on her that love was new for them.

Their relationship hadn't been about love. It had been about control. When had all that changed? All she knew right now, was she felt more at peace with him than she'd ever felt before. Felt more like they were a team, one part of a whole.

"I love you, too."

Breakfast was excellent. The four of them sat as a family while Fulga, the new house servant Hilda hired, brought bacon, boiled eggs, pastries, and fresh fruit to them.

Andru told his sister about his adventure one more time, how he'd ridden on the glider with his bad aunt, then returned with his papa. His animated version had Ana listening to him wide-eyed, though she'd heard the story before. When he finished, she demanded her turn on the glider.

Darius told Tara that the entire day she'd slept, all he heard from his daughter was that she wanted her ride on a glider.

Tara giggled. "That's my daughter." She told Ana she'd take her for a ride after breakfast.

And she did. Andru rode with his papa. They flew low, over the rolling hills to the east. They didn't go close to the mountain range, turning around long before the children could see them and wonder what they were. The unpleasantness of what their people had endured while over there made that direction unappealing for Tara, and she guessed Darius had sensed her feelings. Several hours later, they pulled into their yard.

"My lady?" Fulga stood at the back door. Her large figure nearly filled the doorway.

She wasn't old, but she had five grown children. She'd work well as a nanny, too. Tara liked her.

Tara looked up after placing Ana on the ground.

"Reena's here to see you. I have her waiting in the living room, I do." Fulga disappeared back into the house quickly.

"Hi, Mama." Tara entered the living room all smiles and extended her arms to hug the old woman.

Reena's swollen eyes and shaking hands brought Tara to a halt. "What's wrong?"

"Oh, Tara-girl." Reena choked on tears and ran to her daughter's arms.

Tara held her mama as she cried. After several minutes, she gently pulled the woman to arm's reach and looked down into her face.

"Patha is dead." Reena could barely utter the words.

The words hit Tara like a steel beam in the gut. She blinked twice, the burning already starting in her eyes. Her mouth fell, but words didn't come. She looked into Reena's eyes, searching. For what, she didn't know. "What? How?" Tara couldn't understand how her papa could be dead.

"He passed in his sleep, he did. We, um, had a wonderful night last night. I fell asleep in his arms, I did." Reena whispered the words.

Tara rubbed her arm to let her know she shared her pain.

"He died happy, Tara-girl."

The two women collapsed into each other's arms and cried.

Tara had never discussed death with her papa, well not a natural death. More than once, while sitting around a campfire, they had mulled over dying in battle. Tara always remembered Patha being the one to reassure the other warriors that a death in combat would be a proud way to pass on. But Patha didn't die in such a manner, and he had never shared his feelings on a Runner dying under other circumstances.

She hadn't had the chance to tell him about Tasha. *Oh, Crator.* Her heart was breaking. After so much happiness from the morning, she couldn't handle the pain. When had she last spoken to him? Why hadn't she gone to him the second she'd buried Tasha?

She'd been afraid, that's why.

Reena said he died happy. Would she have said that if he'd known one of his daughters had killed his other daughter?

Patha forgive me.

She didn't hear Darius enter. He approached from behind and his strong arms provided the strength she couldn't find at that moment. He held both women, remaining silent while they cried.

Tara finally pulled away. Without speaking, she went upstairs to her room. She should be doing something right now—organizing, delegating, preparing, something—she just couldn't figure out what.

Walking aimlessly around the room, she stopped to stare at the pictures of her children Darius had hung so long ago when he thought her dead. Time was an odd thing, she thought. Sometimes there wasn't enough of it, and other times there was too much. Over the span of a lifetime, so much could be accomplished, but when all was said and done, there was always more to do.

Had Patha died satisfied? Had he been pleased with his life's work? Was there anything he felt he hadn't accomplished? Oh, if only she'd made an effort to see him.

But she'd been exhausted. She'd been so wrapped up in dealing with the Lunians, then her sister.

Why couldn't she keep a bigger perspective on things?

She always focused on the task at hand and ignored the circumstances going on around her in the bigger picture. She hadn't gone to see her papa, and now he was dead.

Another thought struck her. Her stomach tightened as she turned from the pictures and walked to the double glass doors. The balcony offered none of its usual hospitality. Her thoughts plagued her as the new realization sunk in.

She was the leader of all the Runner clans. The entire Runner nation was her responsibility.

Her thoughts took her back to the age of twelve. She remembered Patha complaining to Tasha's mama that he felt he had no real heir. It was right after Tasha had been caught stealing a motorcycle from one of the adults in the clan. She'd been caught red-handed and simply laughed it off. Patha said she had no scruples. But Tara did.

Now, Tara realized she'd work hard to earn the right to be Patha's heir. She'd learned all the laws, the history, and the heritage of the Runners. They were a people to be proud of. She was their leader.

I'm their leader, she said to herself. Or she thought she said it to herself.

"Yes, you are." The voice came from behind her, quiet and calm, in Darius' usual manner.

"Oh, Darius." Tara moved quickly and found comfort in his strong embrace.

"Contact Jolee," he whispered into her hair. "She'll come straight here when she hears the news about Patha, she will. Have her send soldiers to prepare him for burial. Do it."

"Yes, of course." She pushed herself away and tugged her shirt.

She walked back into her bedroom and stopped. *Oh Patha, you can't be dead. I'm not ready.*

Tara watched Darius walk past her. He picked up her comm from her dresser.

I was going to tell somebody to do something. Patha, come back. I'm not ready to be in charge. You didn't give me any warning. I'm not sure I'm ready.

"Tell Jolee that your papa has died. Have her send soldiers to prepare him for burial." Darius smiled gently as his eyes met hers.

He handed her the comm. Could he see her fear? No. She wouldn't let him.

"Jolee," Tara said.

"I was beginning to think you'd forgotten about me." Jolee sounded cheerful. "How are you doing?"

"Jolee." *Oh Crator, can I do this?* "Jolee, Patha is dead."

Silence on the other end.

She thought she heard Jolee clear her throat.

Darius studied her and she wanted to collapse into his arms again.

"I'm so sorry." Jolee spoke quietly. "Where is he? I'll send someone to him. The ceremony should be held day after tomorrow. Is that good for you?"

"Yes, that sounds good." *Oh, Jolee, what would I do without you?* She managed a smile for Darius. Stay in control. "An announcement will need to be made."

"I'll make the initial announcement, if you like. The family needs the *Time of Sadness*. You can make your speech at the burial ceremony." Jolee paused, then repeated, "Is that good for you?"

"Yes," Tara said. "Jolee, thanks."

"Don't say another word."

Tara could hear Jolee typing.

"I understand. My grandpapa passed away last winter."

That's right. She'd forgotten.

"Is there anything I can do for you?" Jolee sounded concerned.

Had Jolee noticed her fear? "I'm fine. Darius is here." Tara turned off the comm and looked up at him.

He stroked the side of her face, and with his other arm, pulled her gently into his grasp once again.

She wanted to stay there all day.

* * * * *

Darius read her thoughts. In fact, he'd seen right away that Tara wasn't handling the tragic loss well. He'd anticipated her falling apart when the time came. She idolized her papa. It might be the only time during their relationship, but for now, he was in charge. Something inside her had shut down the second she'd heard the tragic news. He would take care of her, willingly.

Darius suggested she rest while he instructed the servants. She looked so beautiful lying on the bed. The usual lustful feelings didn't enter his thoughts when he studied her body. He felt compassion. He'd never loved anyone the way he loved her right now. She needed him, and she wanted him to care for her. He'd longed for this moment.

Fulga accepted his instructions with a nod of her head. She'd take Tara's meals to her. No one was to speak to her unless cleared through him first.

Darius knew Tara wasn't fit to rule at the moment, and he wouldn't let anyone see that. He'd keep her confined until the shock wore off. Tara was numb, and no one would confront her with anything he didn't know about first.

Hilda apparently had taken Reena under her wing. She confronted Darius on Reena's behalf after he'd finished briefing Fulga. "She's Gothman, Darius, she is." His mama reminded him of the Gothman burial traditions. "Of course, she respects the Runner traditions, she does, and understands Runners burn their own according to their rituals. But she'll be needing to have the traditional dinner here. She has a right to mourn according to our customs, yes. I'll organize everything."

"That'll be fine," Darius agreed. It would keep his mama busy as well. Everyone would be affected by this death.

Quick footsteps along the hallway upstairs alerted him that someone had approached Tara's bedroom. He hurried back up the stairs to investigate.

Tara still rested on the bed, but Syra was now draped across her. Their arms intertwined and Syra was sobbing hysterically.

"You need me, and I want to be strong," Syra choked out through hiccups, and more tears.

"I want to be strong too." Tara stroked her niece's hair and pulled the blanket over the two of them. "But right now, all I really want is Patha to tell me how to be strong."

Darius stood silently in the doorway, remaining unnoticed, as the two women cried together. He could see Tara's swollen eyes and tearstained cheeks, and watched as she brushed Syra's hair to the side and stared up to the ceiling, crying the whole time.

Torgo stood beside the bed. He turned when Darius entered the room. His eyes looked watery, but only for a moment.

Darius saw his brother tighten his upper lip and toughen up.

Tara and Syra didn't seem to notice either one of them.

He took Torgo by the arm and led him out of the bedroom. "Let them be women for a change," Darius whispered as he slowly shut the door.

"The way Syra's acted for the past couple of days, I'll be glad to have my warrior back, I will." Torgo shook his head. "But I guess I never had a chance to get to know what a docile woman is like before." He grinned.

Darius understood that Torgo wasn't in mourning like the women were. Sure, he had known Patha, but not as well as the women. Darius reflected that it would be good to have someone levelheaded and able to follow instructions by his side over the next few days.

"There are advantages to both, yes." Darius allowed a small laugh and slapped his younger brother on the back. He then sobered quickly and added, "Runners have a *Time of Sadness*, they do. The family is isolated and the friends prepare the burning ceremony. No one will disturb them in our bedroom, under my orders. Let them mourn, I say. Meanwhile, I want you to keep close eyes on any incoming traffic. Word will travel through Nuworld quickly, it will. I want our defenses up, yes.

Send the orders through to the Runners, as well. Contact Jolee. Tell her the orders come from Tara."

Torgo raised an eyebrow at Darius' last comment.

He saw the questioning expression and narrowed his eyes. "Do as you're told," Darius ordered. "If any messages come in for Tara, bring them to me, you will."

Now Torgo did question him. "You can't—"

Darius grabbed his brother by the arm and led him forcibly down the hallway to the computer room. "Now look," Darius hissed when the two of them were alone in the room. His voice wasn't quite harsh, but very controlled. "Tara isn't thinking clearly. She went numb, she did. If the wrong person realized the leader of the Runner nation wasn't thinking clearly, they might decide to take advantage of the situation. She'll snap out of it soon enough, she will. We'll all know it when she does, and she'll start giving her own orders, yes."

"That's for sure." Torgo chuckled, but it sounded forced as he eyed the grip Darius had on his arm.

"In the meantime, do as I say."

"Yes, my lord." Torgo still smiled as he gave his brother a foolish salute. Darius swatted at his head, but Torgo ducked causing Darius to send blond curls flying.

* * * * *

Tara and Syra remained in the bed together for the rest of the day. Several Runners visited the Bryton home, but were escorted to Darius instead of the women. He wouldn't allow them to be disturbed. Flower arrangements and baked goods arrived with solemn condolences. By evening, the living room was full of flowers, their fragrances filling the house. This wasn't the smell of death, Darius thought to himself as he wondered at the Runner tradition of flowers at funerals; this was the smell of mourning. Mourning was for the living. So maybe they viewed flowers as a way to remind themselves that they still had their lives ahead of them.

Darius awakened the next morning to Tara pounding the keys on the computer in their bedroom. He rolled to his side and rested his head on his hand as he watched her. Tara's hair lay damp and silky past her shoulders. Her elbows moved in and out slightly as she hit the keys with her fingers. She sat straight, proud, and never hesitated as she worked. Her white undershirt hung on her, revealing the outline of ribs and the inward curve at her waist.

"How are you feeling?" He broke the silence.

She jumped. "Did I wake you?" She turned in her chair to glance at him, then turned back to the computer. "I woke with a start this morning, realizing everything I have to do. I guess I lost it a little bit yesterday, huh."

He got out of bed to stand behind her, massaging her shoulders. "What are you doing?"

"Writing my speech."

"Of course, for the burning ceremony." Her muscles were so tight.

"You're familiar with it?"

He almost said Patha explained it, but caught himself. He remembered the vague details. It was an all-day event, a celebration of a life now over. A description of the person's life was given, their accomplishments. Usually the oldest child did this, in this case, Tara. Runners didn't believe in an afterlife. He wondered if Tara would incorporate her new belief in Crator into her speech.

"I know it will create a stir, but I think Patha would like it." She pulled a piece of paper off the printer. "What do you think?"

Darius glanced at the first few paragraphs Tara had typed. The speech was an introductory lesson to Crator.

"Patha believed in Crator." She justified as he read. "I'm in a position where I can introduce His ways to many people at the ceremony. I know it's just the beginning, but Runners will learn of His power. Patha would approve, don't you think?"

He saw the look in her eyes. She wanted Darius' approval. She needed his approval. Her mourning wasn't over, but she was in control once again.

"Yes," he said.

* * * * *

A mini-tower stood in the field by the Blood Circle Clan for the ceremony. It was made of large white bricks and shaped like a triangle. The bottom was square and over twenty feet in diameter. It narrowed as it rose to the sky. The top was flat, and Patha's body lay on its surface under a glass coffin. His body was dressed in full Runner uniform, and all badges of honor he'd received through his lifetime adorned his chest. After the ceremony, his body with all his dearest possessions would be incinerated, forever removing him from Nuworld.

His memory would live through stories told by the fires.

Wooden benches created rows in front of the burial tower. A wide middle aisle separated the benches into two groups. At least thirty Runners could sit in each row and there were over one hundred rows. Twelve large wooden torches, standing over twenty feet high, lined either side of the burial tower. Each torch represented a clan. As the clan leaders arrived for the ceremony, they assisted in lighting a torch using a long narrow rod.

It was an incredible sight.

Tara lit the torch for the Blood Circle Clan last, and thousands upon thousands of Runners cheered their new leader.

Each leader spoke briefly of their knowledge of Patha.

When Tara gave her speech late in the afternoon, it was so quiet, wind could be heard blowing gently through the pine trees.

"Patha and I discussed a new way of looking at the world, not too long ago." She stood in front of the burial tower, using a handheld voice projector in order to be heard. "And today I will share that new way with you."

"I have been shown the way of Crator, my fellow Runners, and today I stand before you, to make you aware of Him as well." She wore her Runner outfit except for the head covering. And, according to tradition, she wore the long black cape used at the initiation of a new leader. "Crator guided me back when I was captured by the Neurians. And He stood by my side as I triumphed in The Test of Wills. He gave me a vision that led our armies across the mountains to defeat the Lunians, and He will guide me as leader of the Runners to make our nation the strongest in all of Nuworld."

Tara stood proud, confident, and encouraging as she spoke of the time ahead for all of them. "With Crator by our side, we will know prosperity, and respect. His ways are simple, and as each of you learn of Him, you shall see how your families and clans shall grow and strengthen. We shall learn about Crator together, my fellow Runners, and together, as His people, we will be undefeatable."

Tara paused and smiled as the crowd broke into applause.

Soon they started a repetitive chant as they paid tribute to their new leader. "Tara the Great, Tara the Great!" the crowd shouted.

She lowered her head in a slight nod, and silently asked Crator to help her not let them down.

Later that evening, everyone attending the funeral sat down to the celebration dinner. From an aerial view, it was a magnificent show. Hundreds of tables spread across the clan site. The Gothman women took to the challenge of feeding such a crowd with enthusiasm.

Tara had approved the Gothman menu early that morning, and the women had spent the entire day preparing hundreds of dishes to serve the multitudes. They were proud to show off part of their culture.

"Runners enjoy dishes from many different cultures," Tara commented to Reena. "But Patha always did especially like Gothman food."

She sat back in her chair at the head of her table, content with a full stomach, when a guard approached her. It was Arien, one of Darius' best warriors. He stepped between Tara and Darius and looked from one to the other, hesitating.

Finally, Darius looked up. "What is it?" he asked, as he wiped the few crumbs from an apple pie off his face.

"A small group of Neurians sit at the southern border of Gothman, they do, requesting permission to enter our land." Arien straightened as he spoke.

Tara looked up at the handsome guard, who in turn gave her the once-over. She knew Darius was probably pleased that one of his best men made it back from the Lunian underground city, but Tara thought the man had a rather high opinion of himself, and knew he had a bad reputation for abusing women.

"Who are they?" Tara asked before Darius could.

"They claim to be a group of Crator's priests, my lady, but there's a woman with them, there is. She's a pretty young lass, and I daresay doesn't look like a priest to me." Arien winked at Tara.

"Well, who is she?" Darius asked when the guard didn't offer the information.

"It's Tealah, the woman who was with Gowsky."

Darius gave consent for the group to enter his land. He ordered they be taken to a boarding house in Bryton and be kept under close guard. If they desired to see the Lord of Gothman or the Leader of the Runner clans, they could have an audience the following day. The guard left with his instructions.

Tara watched Darius' face as the guard left. She could tell he was as curious as she was about why the group was there. He stared across the field with a frown on his face, and she wondered if he anticipated problems from the visitors.

Chapter Twenty-Five

୫୬

Andru and Ana awakened them the following morning. The four of them romped in bed until Fulga politely knocked on the door, asking if she should keep breakfast warm.

"I'm hungee."

"Me too. I want bwekfast," the twins yelled amidst giggles.

"We'll be down shortly," Darius said.

Darius carried Ana down the stairs on his back, and Andru ran in front of them to reach the dining room table first.

"I have the daily reports ready for you, my lord." Geeves approached from the front room where he'd been awaiting Darius.

Tara took Ana from Darius' back and placed her in the chair next to her brother.

"You will sit and eat with us, won't you?" Tara asked, as Darius studied the landlink Geeves had handed him.

"Duty calls, my man," Darius told Geeves and swatted Tara on the rear as he moved next to her at the table. "I'll contact you within the hour."

"Of course, my lord." Geeves nodded and accepted the landlink from Darius, then left them.

"I want more bacon," Andru said with his mouth full.

"I can get it." Ana went up on her knees and reached for the plate.

Tara slid the plate within reach of the twins just as her comm beeped.

"Several of the clans will be leaving within the hour," she told Darius after talking briefly into her comm.

It beeped a second time. It was Jolee saying, "We have a large number of gifts down here, all left by clan leaders."

"Why don't you bring them up in one of the jeeps, and we'll go through everything together?" Tara spoke between bites of Danish.

"Sounds good. We need to plan your initiation ceremony as well."

Tara ended the call and reached for a napkin to wipe her daughter's face.

"I want to fly with you today on your glider, Mama." Ana had a beautiful smile, and her long golden hair glistened from the morning sun streaming through the windows.

"The Neurians are asking to see us," Darius said as he put his comm down on the table.

Tara could tell he wasn't overly enthusiastic about the interruptions, just as she wasn't. "Mama has to work, sweet child." Tara lifted her daughter to her lap, but turned her attention to Darius. "I'll call the nanny for the children."

* * * * *

Four Neurian priests entered the living room later that morning. Two large Gothman guards escorted them, and Tara noticed the presence of the guards seemed to unsettle the small group as they kept looking behind them at the two muscular Gothman.

Darius nodded his head and the guards retreated from the room, closing the glass doors behind them.

Immediately, the small group appeared more at ease. She wondered at their earlier nervousness, but decided she would know their thoughts soon enough, and took a moment to study the men standing in front of them. The priests wore long, cream-colored robes. They each had small circular hats of the same color that came down over each ear to a point. Roped sandals were visible under their robes. They were quite tall, and Tealah was hardly visible as she stood quietly behind them in a modest Neurian khaki outfit.

"What can we do for you?" Darius asked.

He and Tara sat in large, matching wooden chairs in front of the fireplace. The chairs had been brought to the room just before the meeting. Darius had them made for the time when they would rule together, and they'd been stored in the garage until now. The old living room furniture had been removed and the servants had hurried to clean the room, preparing it for their rulers' first audience. Tara and Darius knew that over the winters, they would spend plenty of time in this room, in these chairs, hearing the requests and complaints of their people.

Darius reclined in his large chair, enjoying the comfort of the soft cushions beneath him and against his back. He took a second to watch Tara as the small procession entered the room, and saw how she straightened, giving him a wonderful profile of her ample breasts and long neck. Her hair fell past her shoulders; her expression appeared grave.

He didn't care about these people. More than likely, they wished to offer their blessing. But Tara took these matters seriously, and for her, he would give the group his full attention.

One of the tall priests moved forward and bowed. "Lord Darius, Lady Tara, thank you for seeing us."

Darius nodded and Tara smiled.

"Lady Tara, we've heard great stories of how Crator speaks to you." When she didn't say anything, he continued, "If permissible, we would like to set up a small place of worship. A place to…ah…spread His laws, discuss the teachings, learn from each other the ways of Crator."

* * * * *

Tara felt Darius' eyes upon her and she turned to study the expression on his face. The man had less knowledge of Crator than she did, and since he didn't respond to the request, she felt he'd given her the floor. She turned her attention back to the small group and leaned forward, quite interested. "What do you mean by His laws and teachings?" she asked.

The priest took a step toward her and spoke in a more relaxed tone as he explained, "On one of our retreats into the desert of our continent, we discovered the ruins of an ancient Crator temple. The priests found some writings. Of course, they're still being translated. We brought some of them with us. We would be honored if you'd look at them." The priest was enthusiastic.

"I'd like that," Tara said thoughtfully. "To find written documentation on Crator would help so much in understanding Him." She paused and the room grew quiet. Tara knew all eyes were on her, but she felt as excited as a child who had just received a surprise gift. She couldn't wait to see these writings the priest referred to, but her priority at the moment was to secure these foreigners among her people. "I'm sure we could find a trailer for you to stay in. I don't know how the Runners will accept you. It will be a challenge for you."

"And a challenge we are anxious to accept." The priest grinned, and the other men around him nodded.

"I don't want Crator force-fed to anyone, is that understood?"

"Yes, my lady." The priest bowed his head, then looked up. "Walk with Crator."

The group bowed their heads and brought their fingers to their foreheads, then to their mouths, in the gesture Tara had seen before. The priests stepped to the side.

Tealah lifted her head, shifting her glance from Tara to Darius.

Tara decided she didn't want Darius to lead the conversation with the beautiful woman standing in front of them, no matter her modest attire. She guessed that the young lady was looking for a place to live, and she had high standards when it came to finding that place. After all, the Neurian woman had lived with a leader in her own nation. Tara didn't want the woman getting any ideas that Darius could be used in similar fashion.

"So what brings you to our humble home?" Tara asked, cocking her head. *This should be good.*

"I agreed to bring the priests here," she said calmly.

Her face looked incredibly humble. Too humble. Tara remembered the woman's ability to present a non-threatening attitude, and didn't trust her.

"Now you will help prepare their temple?" Darius asked. He leaned back in his chair, studying the Neurian woman. His face looked hard.

Tara wondered if he, also, did not trust her. Or was he preoccupied with self-control?

She looked back at Tealah for the answer.

"I guess so, for as long as they need me," Tealah answered. She looked as if she wanted to add something, but didn't.

"We'll try to visit you, we will. Let us know if you need anything." Darius' face showed no expression.

Tealah raised an eyebrow. He'd just dismissed her and she seemed surprised.

For her part, Tara hoped the Neurian would not say anything that might incriminate her as an accomplice in kidnapping Tigo. Tara didn't want the woman held for questioning or detained for any reason.

Tealah lowered her head, giving a very slight bow. Not too humble. Then she turned and left with the priests.

Tara flipped her legs over the side of her chair and dangled her feet next to Darius' arm. "We did it." She smiled and leaned her head back on the opposite arm. The woman was out of her house, and with her staying on the Runner clan site with the priests, Tara knew she could keep a close eye on her.

"The first of many such events," Darius agreed.

"Does her presence here bother you?" Tara leaned forward and pulled her legs down off the side of the chair.

He looked at her sideways—a slow, long look—as if he was trying to decipher the meaning behind her question. Finally, he sighed and ran his fingers through his thick curls. "Yes, she bothers me." He glanced out a large window overlooking the front porch. "I know her kind all too well, as you know. She'll use whatever she can to get what she wants, she will. And she knows what she's got, I'm thinking."

Tara wasn't sure, but she thought he groaned at that comment. Tealah had tempted him. Tara knew it. She ground her teeth and decided she'd put a few soldiers around that new temple and give them specific instructions to keep their eye on Tealah.

Darius pulled his comm from his pocket and wrapped it around his ear. "Geeves," he said, without ceremony, and within the minute, the glass doors opened and Darius' first assistant entered the room.

"You have compiled a list of people imprisoned by the Lunians?" Darius asked.

"Yes, m'lord." Geeves didn't look at Tara, but approached and handed a landlink to Darius. "Several of the women have turned up pregnant, they have." Geeves stood next to Darius now and tapped a stocky finger on the screen that Darius held. "I made a list of them here, like you asked."

"Have two guards escort us and prepare our gliders. We are ready to visit each of them."

Tara and Darius flew into town, with the two guards following, and went from house to house, checking on the condition of the recently impregnated women.

"Odd how chilly the air is considering the bright sun," Tara commented after the two left the last house on their list.

"It seems rather warm to me, it does." Darius wrinkled his brow at her. "Are you sure you feel okay?"

"I feel fine." Tara crossed her arms across her waist as a chilled breeze brushed through her hair.

She notified Jolee they were on their way to the clan site, and the two left on their gliders, deciding to drive the distance, instead of fly. Tara wanted to see how the Runners progressed cleaning up after the ceremony for Patha; her view would be better from the ground.

Twenty or so Runners and Gothman worked at tearing down wooden tables and chairs from the burial ceremony. Children and dogs in the open field looked for anything left on the ground.

Tara and Darius parked amidst the activity. As Tara climbed off her glider, another cold breeze wrapped itself around her.

"Hello there," Jolee said as she trudged through trampled grass. "I hear we're going to have a Crator temple." Jolee handed a disc to Tara.

"Yes, four priests from Southland. How's that going?"

"Well, we're working on the trailer, so right now I have them in one of the storage tents." Jolee added quickly, "It was empty." She pointed to the disc as the three walked toward the rows of trailers. "You'll find current lists of all Runners still convalescing from the Lunian ordeal. We don't have any confirmed pregnancies, but you'll note I've also identified those still suffering from shock."

Tara glanced down at her screen. Syra was included in the latter group, along with five others. "Is this everyone?"

"Yes. Everyone else reported for duty this morning."

That was a Runner for you. Tara smiled to herself. *We're a race not to be conquered.* She handed the flat landlink to Darius. "We'll see Syra last."

When they arrived at Balbo's trailer, no one answered the door. Tara opened it slowly and said, "Hello."

No answer.

"She must be asleep," Tara said quietly as she opened the door and the two of them entered into the vacant living room. "Good grief, it's cold in here."

"It's not cold." Darius frowned at her. "You really are cold, aren't you?" He took off his leather jacket to wrap around her shoulders. "Go see how she's doing. I'll wait out here, I will."

Tara nodded and walked down the dark hallway. Syra's bedroom was even darker, and all Tara could see was a figure wrapped in blankets on the bed.

She knew what her cousin had been through. The memories of her vision haunted her as she sat on the bed next to Syra and stroked her hair. "I wish I could take all the pain and ugly memories away," Tara whispered.

Syra groaned and rolled over. "Tara," she whispered and lifted her hand out from under the blanket.

Tara held Syra's hand and noticed her bruised wrist and another long bruise going up her forearm. Tara shuddered, and even Darius' jacket didn't keep out the cold. Then she noticed red, purple and green marks around her niece's neck. Her vision flooded back into her thoughts, and she remembered Syra being yanked by the chain secured around her neck every time she fought off her rapist. Tara's stomach doubled over. *Oh Syra, I'm so sorry you went through this.* "Go back to sleep," she whispered out loud. "I'm here, and you're going to be just fine."

Syra squeezed Tara's hand and didn't let go. Even as her breathing settled back into sleep, her grasp didn't lessen.

Tara sat in the dark and studied Syra's room.

Something like laughter caused her to look down at Syra. Her niece breathed deeply and her face looked relaxed.

"Tara," a voice whispered.

Tara looked around the room quickly, working at the same time to free her hand from Syra's. The room was so cold she could see her breath through the darkness.

"We want to thank you, Tara." The whispered sound came again.

It almost sounded like several voices speaking at the same time. Tara squinted her eyes and moved to the door. Opening it, she allowed some light into the room. After glancing around her, Tara confirmed that she and Syra were alone in the space.

"You have given us the tool we need, Tara," the voices whispered. "We'll grow strong and multiply, just as it's written. No one will be able to resist us. All will join." There was laughter, high-pitched and eerie. "Doesn't that scare you, Tara?"

"How can I be scared of something I can't see?" Tara answered softly. "Who are you?"

"We're here because of you. Our strength is because of you. We will let you name us. Then all credit will be yours, Tara the Great." The laughter became hysterical.

Tara quickly turned on a lamp sitting on the dresser.

Syra slept soundly with blankets cocooned around her. The laughter continued, but Syra didn't seem to hear it, or else she simply slept through it.

Was this another vision? But how could one have a vision, if there was nothing to see?

"You're evil. Go away," Tara ordered.

"Then you've named evil." Now the voices chuckled impishly. "Certainly you can name us better than that."

"Where are you?"

"We'll be there soon. But for now, we will wait. It will only make us stronger," the voices hissed.

"Only a coward hides like this." Tara studied the room. The windows were closed and the curtains drawn. There was no closet. Certainly, this was a spirit, like the dog-woman. She doubted Crator sent this spirit, though. She lifted the landlink from the inside pocket of Darius' jacket, just to eliminate any other options, and set it to scan the area. Nothing unusual was detected.

"Is cowardice a trait of evil?" the voices cooed.

"Leave now. There's no room for you here."

"Oh, there is plenty of room for us here." The chuckle that followed curdled her blood. "When the Waiting is over, you'll see, Tara the Great."

The Waiting? What did she wait for? How long was she supposed to wait, and how would she know when it was over?

She stood in the middle of the room, her back to the open door, staring at the empty room. Minutes passed and there were no more voices. She felt rather warm in Darius' jacket and pulled it off. Footsteps behind her caused her to turn as Darius came down the hallway.

"How's it going?" Darius squinted, then gently took her arm and led her down the hallway into the well-lit living room. "What's wrong?"

"I heard something," she spoke cautiously, still listening to the sounds in the trailer. Whoever, or whatever, it was...was gone. The chill she had felt a moment before was gone, also.

Darius studied her face. As he brushed her cheek with the outside of his hand, she saw concern on his face, although she had to search deep into his eyes for it. He was controlled, always under control. He did nothing and felt nothing unless he commanded it. The dog-woman was right. Darius would not be swayed by a belief unless he felt an advantage in having it. And as far as Tara could tell, this man felt very confident that he had everything he needed to be in control. Evil would not be able to manipulate him. No one would.

"Someone, or something, spoke to me in Syra's bedroom. It's gone now." An uncontrollable chill went through her body.

Darius leaned against the back of the small couch so he could look her straight in the eyes.

She felt his gaze dig deep into her thoughts, searching for what she hadn't told him yet.

"Another vision?" His voice was calm, quiet.

"I didn't see anything. I heard them talk," and after a pause, "and I felt them."

An eyebrow shot up. "Felt them?"

"It was cold." She looked down at his jacket, then handed it to him.

"What did they say?"

She could tell Darius wouldn't leave the trailer until she'd told him everything. His calm eyes demanded enlightenment. "They thanked me for giving them the tool they needed to grow in power. They said I would name them, because I helped make them. I don't know what they were talking about, but they said they had to wait right now. They called it the *Waiting*." She paused.

He cocked his head although his expression didn't change. "What are they waiting for?"

"I think to become more powerful. I don't know." She looked at her hands, then back into his eyes. "What tool could I have given to someone?"

Tara immediately had her answer; she had given someone a child. And as she studied Darius' face, she felt he had drawn the same conclusion. But how could giving the bastard to the Lunians be considered some type of tool?

"Could the Lunians have made the voices?" Darius took the landlink and began scanning the room.

"I considered that, but my landlink didn't show anything unusual. I don't believe they could have done this." She thought about the time in the cave when the Lunians made the dog-woman appear. She hadn't experienced any emotional reaction to that sight because it had been a hoax. The event she'd just endured was far different. It was real.

"Let's go." She shrugged. "I don't have time to let evil preoccupy my thoughts."

She walked out of the trailer, and Darius followed. Tara decided that the only way evil could grow would be if she allowed it to. The best thing to do would be to forget about the eerie vision, and force it to die, instead of take root.

"Let's give the Neurians time to set up their temple before visiting." Tara slid her hand around Darius' arm. "I think I would like to head home and spend time with the twins."

Tara and Darius did manage to get some time in with the children later that afternoon. They flew the children to the cliff where Tara and Darius had first made love, and where Tara had found Darius with his mistress. Tara wanted to clear ugly memories from the beautiful, well-hidden spot. There, the children enjoyed an afternoon snack of cookies and plums.

Tara looked up from a flower necklace she had been making. Andru had yelled for her attention from his spot next to Darius, who leaned against one of the large rocks in the grassy area.

"Look mama, she's back."

Tara immediately saw the dog-woman and watched as the elderly lady picked up a flat shiny rock and offered it to Andru.

He smiled and eagerly walked over to accept it.

"I want one," Ana said, and dropped the flowers she'd been gathering for Tara. She didn't walk over to the dog-woman, though. Instead, she went over to Andru and tried to take the rock from him.

"Here, Andru," the dog-woman said and picked up another flat shiny rock. "Give her this."

"Okay." He took the rock and gave it to his sister. He looked at Tara quickly, as if remembering something, then looked back at the old woman. "Thank you. Why can't my sister see you?"

"Maybe she's like your papa," the dog-woman said.

Andru turned to study his papa.

"And what is this look for?" Darius frowned at his son.

"She said Ana is like you," Tara said, and wondered what the dog-woman meant when she compared the daughter to the papa.

"I like you, Papa." Ana laughed and ran to Darius' arms.

"What else has she said?" Darius allowed his daughter to cuddle on his lap, but focused on Tara.

"Nothing yet," Tara said.

Tara knew Darius didn't enjoy the fact that he couldn't see the dog-woman, and understood that he probably felt left out. She watched the old lady cup Andru's face in her hand and study the boy. Andru seemed relaxed in her presence.

"Do you like our sankoo, um," Andru wrinkled his brow and stepped backward out of the dog-woman's grasp to look at Tara.

"Sanctuary," she said the word he was trying to pronounce.

"Sankoowardy," he said proudly, smiling at the dog-woman.

"I do," the dog-woman answered, then settled on the ground with more ease than Tara would have guessed a woman of her age would possess. The dog-woman sat cross-legged and reached into a bag that lay on her lap. She pulled out two peppermint sticks and handed them to Andru. "One for you and one for your sister."

"Look Ana!" Andru held out his hand to show the hard candy to his sister, who immediately jumped up from her papa's lap.

The children shrieked with delight and immediately sat down facing each other to eat their candy.

Tara laughed at their antics.

"The dog-woman gave them candy?" Darius sounded a bit grouchy.

"Yes." Tara stopped laughing and offered her claim the details he couldn't see. "The dog-woman sits here on the ground." She pointed. "And she pulled candy from a bag that she has on her lap."

"I see." Darius studied the area Tara had indicated, and Tara wished he *could* see the woman.

"Some of the sacred writings are here." The dog-woman looked seriously at Tara now.

"The books the Neurian priests brought?" Tara confirmed, partially so Darius would know what they were talking about.

"Pay attention to them. There's much to learn. Teach your children. You must take advantage of the *Waiting*."

"What are we waiting for?"

"*You* aren't waiting for anything," the dog-woman said. "Educate your children. Teach them the sacred writings so they'll know Crator. When the *Waiting* is over, they must be ready."

Then she was gone.

Chapter Twenty-Six

The following week, Tara visited the new temple at the clan site. She pulled up to see that no trailer had been provided. Instead, two large white tents stood alongside each other.

"My lady, what a surprise." The tall Neurian priest, who had presented himself in her living room, turned when she approached. He was on his hands and knees by one of the tents, planting seeds in the ground. Standing, he wiped off his hands on his robe. "This is quite an honor. We haven't had many visitors."

"Give it time." She smiled and looked at the two tents, then the exposed ground where the priest had been working. "I never asked your name."

"My name is Seth." He bowed in front of her.

"Do you have a title?"

"We are servants of Crator, my lady. Titles are reserved for those who tell others what to do. We do as we're instructed."

"I see." Tara was quiet for a minute. "I'm interested in knowing what you've done so far. And I want to look at the sacred writings."

Seth nodded and gathered his robe in one hand as he moved toward a tent. "I would be honored to show you."

Tara followed behind, feeling a peaceful presence surrounding the place. She decided it had been a good idea to make time to see the temple; it was a practice she needed to add to her schedule.

The opening to the tent had been pulled back and tied, and Tara followed the priest inside. A small table stood along the opposite wall, and a large, straw-woven mat covered the ground. Several brightly dyed, square pillows rested on the ground and the priest gestured for Tara to sit.

"This you must see first," he said. "Are you comfortable?"

"Yes, very." Tara nodded, and watched as the priest turned his back to her and lifted a large brown book out of a square glass case.

"You should scan this to disc," Tara said as she accepted it from him and gingerly handled the dilapidated bound papers.

"We have. I thought you might want to see the original. We don't wish to make it available to just anyone. There are several discs available to view, if anyone is interested."

"Have many people visited?" She cautiously turned the yellowed papers, looking at the foreign print. On some of the pages were pictures, so faded she could hardly make them out.

"A handful has come out of curiosity." Seth shrugged.

"Maybe you could announce an educational class that will meet at the same time each week. See who shows up."

Seth nodded in consent.

"Keep me posted. I will come to as many sessions as I can." She handed the ancient book back to the priest and started to leave, then paused and turned back to him. "Have you heard of a period of time called the *Waiting*?"

"The *Waiting*?" Seth looked confused. "No, my lady. What is it?"

"I've been told we've entered the *Waiting*," Tara said as she remembered the dog-woman's words. "How far along are you with your translation?" She nodded her head toward the book that Seth had returned to the glass case.

He moved to the small table and lifted a flat animal skin bag that she hadn't noticed until that moment. As he handed it to Tara, he said, "This disc contains what we've done so far. Myro is working on one of the pages right now. Would you like to talk with him?"

"No, don't bother him." Tara accepted the disc from Seth. "I'll return this soon."

"Please, we'd be honored if you kept it as your personal copy. As Myro translates further, we will bring more discs to you."

"Thank you. I'd appreciate that." Tara slipped it into her pocket and thought how best to probe for some information. "Seth, do you know how the Neurians are doing after returning from fighting the Lunians?"

The priest folded his hands in front of him. The long sleeves of his robe covered them. "Our people are recovering as are yours. The young girl that brought us here, Tealah?"

Tara nodded. *Go on*, she thought anxiously.

"She lived in Dorn Gowsky's house prior to traveling here with us. She might be able to answer more specific questions on the political side of things. We try not to get too involved in government issues. It can cause distraction in prayer."

"I don't know if I agree with that," she smiled politely as she added, "I need Crator to help me with every political decision I make."

"Of course," Seth said. "You rule a nation, we don't."

* * * * *

Darius wasn't at the house when she returned, and one of Fulga's granddaughters watched the twins play in the backyard.

Tara watched them toss a ball to each other from the balcony before she returned to her chair at the landlink in their room. She inserted the disc into the slot and began scanning its contents.

She read about places and people she had never heard of. The calendar described in the material was unfamiliar, so she had no idea when the events had taken place. But she found that the adventures of the people ran parallel to her own life.

Tara found herself lost in a story about a man leading his clan across barren land to a place proclaimed to be fruitful. The dog-woman wasn't mentioned in the story, nor was Crator. The man heard voices, though, and saw visions that the others in his clan didn't see. Tara understood how the man felt when some of his clansmen questioned him, and she paid close attention to his response.

"He helped them to have faith by telling them that his Crator was more powerful than anything they had ever known," she muttered and kept reading.

She decided the temple at the clan site would be helpful to her people. Seth had told her that he was careful who he allowed to see the old writings, but Tara considered the possibility that if she encouraged Runners to read the old book, it would help them to believe in Crator.

Much later, she heard Darius outside their door. He opened it and fell into the room. She looked at him, stunned, until she realized he was drunk. Very drunk.

"Where have you been?" She looked at his tousled clothing.

"Celebrating." He reached down and, before she could stop him, he lifted her into his arms. "It's my gift to you, you beautiful wench."

She struggled to be released and realized he wasn't as drunk as she originally thought.

He grinned wickedly at her and tossed her onto the bed. He literally jumped on top of her and she rolled quickly to avoid being squashed. Grabbing her with one arm, he leaned his head against his other hand.

"Seriously, my lady, it has been a great day and I feel like celebrating." He pulled her toward him.

"Celebrating, huh?" She fought a smile, but his hands found their way under her shirt and she smiled at his touch. "Why are we celebrating?"

He began kissing her neck and she felt the temperature rise between her legs. "Well, my lady, the River People have approached Gothman and requested protection."

"They've what?"

His lips found her mouth.

"They've acquired some of the Freeland north of them in return for unpaid debts, they have. The land touches the southern Gothman border, and spreads south to the Neurian border. They feel they are large enough to be under the control of a government, but have been unsuccessful in establishing one of their own. They accept our rule, and we protect their land, yes." He smiled as her mouth fell open in surprise. "That means the Gothman nation now extends south all the way to Southland, it does."

Tara managed to sit up, staring at him with disbelief. "All the way to Southland?" she whispered and her grin widened.

He wrapped his hand around the back of her neck, pulling her down on him.

"Yes, my lady. We've just doubled the size of our nation. Tomorrow, we'll make the announcement to all of Gothman and the Runners, we will. An invitation will be extended for some of our people to form a colony south of here. I'm thinking we'll create a new town. I thought we'd call it Taratown." He pulled her closer and stole a kiss. "What do you think?"

This time, she kissed him and he wrapped his arms around her quickly in a death grip. Within seconds, he'd rolled them over and was on top of her, sliding her shirt up. She managed to pull away one more time and adjusted her clothing, covering her breasts as Darius watched, pouting.

"We're truly the greatest nation on Nuworld." She smiled and stroked his cheek, then allowed him to kiss her fingers.

"This is just the beginning, it is. I'm working on a proposal for the Cave People. They need to rebuild and could probably use the help." He tugged at her shirt.

"We'll rule our entire continent. We could probably take over the Sea People without too much resistance." She smiled at his mischievous face as he massaged one of her breasts. "Crator may call this the *Waiting*, but we'll hardly be sitting around doing nothing."

"Hardly," he groaned.

She'd teased him long enough, and this time he simply overpowered her and forced her to lie down by rolling on top of her and pinning her hands with his. His kisses were affectionate but powerful, and they didn't come up for air until he permitted them to.

"There's one more thing," he said as she struggled to breathe and clear the sexual fog from her brain. "I saw Tealah while we were at the tavern with some of the River People."

There went the fog. She noticed he enjoyed the instant jealousy he'd created in her. He licked his lips and allowed a pause almost too long for her to bear, before continuing.

"My men aren't too accustomed to women joining them for a drink, I'd say." He paused again and she fumed at his enjoyment of drawing out the point of this topic. "Quite a few of them bought her drinks. She got rather drunk, I'd say."

Now she was angry. It was one thing for him to walk through a contract without even mentioning it to her, but to be drinking ale…with that woman…

Darius began laughing as she turned her expression from passion to outrage. "You are so beautiful, you are." He kissed her, but she didn't respond to him. It didn't seem to bother him as he pulled his face away several inches to look at her stone cold expression. "One of my men took quite a liking to her. He demanded the claim, and she accepted."

She watched his smile widen, and she knew her face reflected the triumph and relief coursing through her. "Tealah's been claimed?" Her voice had laughter in it. "I think she might have beaten my record for entering this nation and being claimed."

"No, my lady, you were claimed the second I saw you." He lowered himself slowly and kissed her again. Slowly, passionately, aggressively.

This time, she didn't pull away.

Now Available from Cerriowen Press

Nuworld - All For One
By Lorie O'Clare
Book 3 in the NUWORLD series.

Secrets never stay buried.

Lord Darius and Lady Tara have a secret they've kept for over thirteen winters. And if it comes out it could destroy the powerful Gothman nation.

Time is running out for Darius and Tara. With the arrival of the Tree People—a unique race with piercing green eyes and an unknown agenda who hail from an unexplored region of Nuworld—life as Darius and Tara know it will change forever.

A chain of events is unleashed that will thrust twins Andru and Ana into a maelstrom of confusion, lust and intrigue that will forge an unlikely bond between all.

Old grudges must be forgotten, hearts must be softened, and the secret that has closed Tara's heart to Crator must be exposed. If this doesn't happen, it will be the end of the reign of the two largest nations on Nuworld.

Why an electronic book?

We live in the Information Age—an exciting time in the history of human civilization, in which technology rules supreme and continues to progress in leaps and bounds every minute of every day. For a multitude of reasons, more and more avid literary fans are opting to purchase e-books instead of paper books. The question from those not yet initiated into the world of electronic reading is simply: *Why?*

1. *Price.* An electronic title at Ellora's Cave Publishing and Cerridwen Press runs anywhere from 40% to 75% less than the cover price of the exact same title in paperback format. Why? Basic mathematics and cost. It is less expensive to publish an e-book (no paper and printing, no warehousing and shipping) than it is to publish a paperback, so the savings are passed along to the consumer.

2. *Space.* Running out of room in your house for your books? That is one worry you will never have with electronic books. For a low one-time cost, you can purchase a handheld device specifically designed for e-reading. Many e-readers have large, convenient screens for viewing. Better yet, hundreds of titles can be stored within your new library—on a single microchip. There are a variety of e-readers from different manufacturers. You can also read e-books on your PC or laptop computer. (Please note that Ellora's

Cave does not endorse any specific brands. You can check our websites at www.ellorascave.com or www.cerridwenpress.com for information we make available to new consumers.)

3. *Mobility.* Because your new e-library consists of only a microchip within a small, easily transportable e-reader, your entire cache of books can be taken with you wherever you go.

4. *Personal Viewing Preferences.* Are the words you are currently reading too small? Too large? Too… ANNOYING? Paperback books cannot be modified according to personal preferences, but e-books can.

5. *Instant Gratification.* Is it the middle of the night and all the bookstores near you are closed? Are you tired of waiting days, sometimes weeks, for bookstores to ship the novels you bought? Ellora's Cave Publishing sells instantaneous downloads twenty-four hours a day, seven days a week, every day of the year. Our webstore is never closed. Our e-book delivery system is 100% automated, meaning your order is filled as soon as you pay for it.

Those are a few of the top reasons why electronic books are replacing paperbacks for many avid readers.

As always, Ellora's Cave and Cerridwen Press welcome your questions and comments. We invite you to email us at Comments@ellorascave.com or write to us directly at Ellora's Cave Publishing Inc., 1056 Home Avenue, Akron, OH 44310-3502.

THE
✢ ELLORA'S CAVE ✢
LIBRARY

Stay up to date with Ellora's Cave Titles in
Print with our Quarterly Catalog.

To recieve a catalog,
send an email with your name
and mailing address to:

CATALOG@ELLORASCAVE.COM

or send a letter or postcard
with your mailing address to:

Catalog Request
c/o Ellora's Cave Publishing, Inc.
1056 Home Avenue
Akron, Ohio 44310-3502

Please be advised, Ellora's Cave Books and Website contain explicit sexual material and you must be 18.

Make each day more *EXCITING* with our

Ellora's Cavemen
Calendar

www.EllorasCave.com

Cerridwen, the Celtic goddess of wisdom, was the muse who brought inspiration to storytellers and those in the creative arts.

Cerridwen Press encompasses the best and most innovative stories in all genres of today's fiction.

Visit our website and discover the newest titles by talented authors who still get inspired—much like the ancient storytellers did…

once upon a time.

www.cerridwenpress.com